A. D. HOOK

What You Wish For

A D Hook

First edition self-published July 2017

ISBN 9781521953600
Imprint: Independently Published

Copyright © 2017 by A. D. Hook

The right of A.D. Hook to be identified as the author of this work has been asserted by him in accordance with the Copyright, Designs and Patents Act 1988

All rights reserved. No part of this publication may be reproduced, stored in a retrieval system, or transmitted, in any form, or by any means (electronic, mechanical, photocopying, recording or otherwise) without the prior permission of the author.

A. D. Hook does not have any control over, or any responsibility for, any author or third party websites referred to in or on this book other than for his own website and social media accounts, as they appear below.

Printed and sold through Amazon.com

This book is sold subject to the condition that it shall not, by way of trade or otherwise, be lent, hired out, or otherwise circulated without the author's prior consent in any form of binding or cover other than that in which it is published and without a similar condition including this condition being imposed on the subsequent purchaser.

What You Wish For

Acknowledgements

To Alexia

For allowing me the time, giving me your love and support, and occasionally cracking the whip in order for me to realise my dream. I couldn't ask for more. Je t'aime.

To Kerry and Nan

For all of your support both before and during the writing of this book. Home truly is where the heart is. Thank you both for taking the time to proofread for me.

To Alex

For the consistent friendship and support you've given me over just short of two decades. You're an inspiration.

To Simon

Without your help this book would be without a cover and I'd still have one hell of a headache.

To My Readers

I cannot thank you enough for choosing this book. Since childhood I have dreamt of one day knowing that someone can pick up, read and enjoy a realisation of my imagination. With this novel, I can now proudly do that. I write for you, in the hope you find it entertaining.

Here's to getting "Hook'd" once more very soon.

What You Wish For

For Sam

Bright, caring, and conscientious.

My urge to leave a legacy is driven by you and the pride you've instilled in me.

I can only dream that I am able to make you just as proud.

Just leave it ten years or so before you read this book… you're a little young right now!

What You Wish For

Chapter One

With a deft swoop of her slender finger the page turned.

Her lower lip throbbed under her vice-like teeth and she exhaled heavily through her nose; the tumultuous pounding of her heart moving her chest rhythmically as her eyes dashed from left to right, hurriedly scanning each paragraph in the desperate need to reach her characters climax.

In her mind she imagined herself as the submissive, consumed in a rapture at the prospect of being at the Masters will. And Master was being *very* dominant. Once again, and very much to her liking, he was seducing her with pure aggression. His left hand was locked tightly within her hair, holding her head firmly in place, with his lips perilously close to her own. The heat she felt emanating from him was unbearable as she fought the urge to pull away from his grip, to touch her face to his; to simply reach out with her tongue to taste his warmth of his skin. Master would disapprove, she knew that well enough, and it was this knowledge which would save her from an unwanted, most certain punishment.

His right hand cupped her heaving breast as he spoke in his strong, gravelly tone, relaying to her his dark desires which she felt only too willing to obey. Randomly he would take her by surprise, moving his tender hand away from the mass of her breast before swiftly whipping the tips of his outstretched fingers down over her erect nipple. With each merciless strike she was overcome with delightfully mixed emotions of pain and pleasure, arching her back against the wall and letting out slow, excited whimpers.

Consumed by the absorbing fantasy unravelling across the pages, she reached out blindly for the nightstand, to the open tub of ice cream. Obliviously she moved it through the air towards her, resting it on her flat, pulsating stomach. Its bitter condensation formed a wet ring around the base, sending two opposing streams of excess skimming down either side of her torso and onto the bedsheet beside her. Levering the spoon from its sunken position she braced herself, then placed the concave scoop down onto her erect nipple, letting out a heightened gasp as the ice cold sensation bit into the hardening button and drew the surrounding flesh to tighten. She closed her eyes and was taken there; within the fantasy. The sudden sting was from the stern whip of *His* fingertips. She had felt it; her Master's will. She soaked in the moment, shuddering, and felt an intense surge explode deep within her chest, passing through the length of her body all the way to her feet, where the fireworks exploded in a crescendo that made her toes curl. The book slipped from her fingers onto the bed beside her shoulder. Her eyes gripped shut and she released a long, low hum from deep within her throat, listening to it as it meandered effortlessly out from between her lips. She craved that loss of control, the sense of feral abandon only *He* could craft from her.

Opening her hazy eyes, she shakily raised the spoon to her mouth and licked its surface clean, slowly, as if *He* were watching. Then, in an effort to obey his next imaginary command, she tenderly cupped her hand under her breast, lifted it to her mouth, and sucked her areola until every remnant of ice cream was taken from sight, leaving only a glistening, sticky sheen across her goose pimpled flesh.

Almost as if stepping out of a trance, she felt the bed

beneath her again. She grasped awkwardly at the book lying to her side while, with her other hand, she guided the moist tub back to the nightstand. Just then, a couple of inches short of the table top, she paused, and pondered. Considering the tub with a devious intrigue she ran her tongue slowly over her swollen bottom lip, manipulating the sore, puffy cushion over the jagged tops of her lower teeth, and bit down with her upper set. A few seconds of intense pain passed, after which she let the now lightly punctured lip flick back out to its normal position. It had been thinking-time for her, and she'd used it. She was now committed to follow her compulsion, although she doubted if she would have ever said no to begin with. Of course Master would demand it, and she refused to disappoint *Him*.

The tub was placed upright on the bed, propped tightly between her inner thighs, its cardboard packaging now soaked with condensation. She took the book in her right hand, held it above her head, and firmly wedged her thumb into the lowest inch of its fold. Within a few seconds she had fully re-engaged with the intense sexual encounter unravelling before her. Her body heat was instantly turned up, high enough she felt her skin might melt. As she read through each tantalising paragraph with increasing eagerness her left hand began to stroke the far side of the tub, edging it slowly into the narrowing cleft between her legs and closer to the centre of her body. In the book, her character was experiencing the intense pleasure of Master's rough fingers entering her for the first time, a sensation which she made coincide expertly with the moment the tub made contact with her outer labia; an icy sharp touch which made her hips jolt upwards from the bed. She let out a high pitched whine as a cool trickle of condensation ran down her, until her body succumbed and she felt herself ease back into the familiarity of the mattress. Folding the page over impatiently with one hand she saw the story intensify, her Master's masturbatory thrusts growing in increasing aggression within her, and she couldn't help but let her body respond. Her hips were now lifting off the bed and dropping repetitively, each jolt grinding herself against the tub. Beads of sweat were formed within her brows, her once blonde hair now stained a slick brown from the exertion and laying fanned out around her head like a mane. Lower down her body she could feel herself opening up as the cold wet cardboard stroked her intimately and with vigour. The contrast between the warmth she felt growing just inside of her and the cold brushing against her exterior sent forks of electricity dancing across her hips and pelvis, up into her stomach, and down through her thigh muscles, into her legs.

The page was being scanned more and more rapidly now, her eyes transfixed and wincing as she grew ever closer to reaching her orgasm. Without moving her eyes from the heady description of lust in front of her, she grabbed blindly for the spoon with her quivering hand. It came, with just the lightest of pulls, and she closed her eyes again in anticipation. A heavy yet steadying breath exited her pursed lips. In the absorbing darkness she could see His face clearly. He was watching her every move. Hearing her every thought. Staring deeply into his penetrating gaze, she lowered the spoon between her legs and smothered it over her clitoris.

"*Ohhhhh FUCK!*" she let free, her voice instantly reaching a screaming crescendo. Her body reacted violently, convulsing and jerking into the air, her thighs vibrating uncontrollably as she reached for a pillow to smother her escaping squeals of pleasure.

Desperately she wished she could cry out His name. To cry out and have Him hear her.

With a series of short, rapid breaths, her body eased from its arched position and unmajestically crumpled to the beds surface. She was deep in a post orgasmic euphoria, her heart pounding in both her chest and ears, so much so that at first her cell phone struggled to break through the numbing cotton wool whistle. When her ears finally let the sound through, she hit reality with a bump. With the muscles in her arms still enduring the latter stages of spasm she clumsily reached out for it, scooping the phone from its cradle and peering at the flashing screen through her weakened eyes. A brief, shallow sigh escaped her before she swiped the screen to life and placed it to her ear.

"Hello Shanna", she said labouringly, unashamedly conveying her exhaustion.

"Hi Kelly. Did I catch you at an awkward time?"

"You know how it is. Just making the most of the time to myself. What can I do for you, Shanna?"

"I was just checking we were still good for lunch tomorrow. I just saw La Tartaruga Scattare has a special on, and I have a voucher that's good for tomorrow. Plus I know how much you love their chili calamari linguine, so it'll be my treat!"

"That sounds great, Shan. Yeah, I'll be there. Meet you at the usual parking spot, same time as always?"

"Be there or be hungry!" Shanna laughed.

Kelly feigned amusement with a lacklustre chuckle.

"How's work?"

"Oh, same old story, Kel. Fuckin' printers on my floor are down again, so I'm spending half my time fetching papers from down in the factory. I saw Matt when I was down there earlier, he seemed good. You two still having your barbeque the weekend after next?"

"Yeah, we're still going ahead, so long as the weather holds out, and assuming I haven't killed him by then!" Kelly joked

"Hush, Kelly, you don't mean that! He's one of the good guys, and you know his chicken skewers are to die for!" Shanna paused, waiting for a response. After a few seconds she broke the awkwardly dragging silence, "Plus it'll probably be your last chance before autumn arrives, right?"

"Yeah, that's true. We wouldn't want to waste the last opportunity." Kelly said with a dry, sarcastic tone.

"Anyway; lunchbreak's just starting and I better get some food before the factory hits the cafeteria. I'll let you get on with…err…whatever it was that had you so preoccupied!"

"Thanks, Shan", Kelly smiled, her relief at being let go of so soon drifting audibly down the phone-line, "I'll see you tomorrow!"

"You will indeed!" Shanna retorted, "Bye for now." The phone line made a click, instantly falling silent.

Kelly slid the phone onto the nightstand, lay her head back onto the pillows, and let out a sigh from deep within her chest. After a minutes thought about whether she actually felt like getting out of bed, she dropped her unenthusiastic legs over its side and lazily stood herself up. Scooping the book up en route, she made her way to the bathroom, studying her reflection in the square mahogany-framed mirror above the wash basin once there. She swept her hair, still matted with sweat, away from her face and gazed aggressively into her post orgasmic eyes. Maintaining a fixed stare, she raised the palm of her right hand and slapped it across her cheek. It stung acutely, prickles of pain like pins and needles surged through her skin, immediately summoning a well-defined hand-shaped print of rushed blood to her skins ordinarily porcelain surface.

Kelly turned her face to the side, admiring the mark

as if it were a freshly made piece of art. A wry smile crept out from the corner of her mouth as she spoke confidently towards the doppelganger beside her

"Kelly Buchanon…..you were made for this shit."

Chapter Two

The First Aid room was cold. Sounds echoed around its sparse interior; the potent aroma of surgical spirit burning Matt's nose as he looked up from the examination beds uncomfortable pillow, watching the attentive nurse pressing white gauze against his wound. Blood seeped through the padded webbing within a matter of seconds, the time it took for his brunette Samaritan to turn away and reach for the rolls of bandages and surgical tape laying on the counter behind her.

"It's a nasty split, Matt" she grimaced.

"Tell me about it, Jo!" he replied, frowning at the growing red patch in the centre of his palm.

"How did it happened?"

"The new kid; Danny. I was overseeing him as he was pulling a piece of scuffed metal trim away from the edge of a glazing unit he was refurbishing and whole thing slipped off the workbench. Instinct told me to grab it, and the damn thing cut straight through."

"Why didn't you just leave it?" the nurse asked, dismayed as she expertly spun the bandage around his hand, "It's not like you don't know how lethal they can be! This has to be the fifth time I've had you in here with a glass slice since I started last year!"

"The shits like razor wire, I know that!" Matt glumly chuckled, "But we're low on glazing stock, and orders from up top are that we can't waste a single unit or we'll miss our orders. It's tight enough that we're having to recycle old units, if they'll fit, so if that one had broken we'd have really be in trouble. And poor Danny, he'd be the one getting the worst of it, which wouldn't be fair. He's only eighteen, and he's trying his best to learn."

"Still….you're the one paying for it now, aren't you? Look; don't get me wrong Matt, you're a nice guy and I appreciate your compassion for the kid but, next time, do yourself a favour and let the damn thing go. If there'd been any more of an edge to it, that piece of glass would have taken your fingers with it. You're lucky I don't have to send you to hospital as it is! Any problems with it between now and tomorrow morning and you have to promise me you'll get yourself to A and E."

"I will, definitely", Matt agreed, wincing as he flexed his hand as best he could around its tight binding. Using his forearm to prop up his twisted torso, he shuffled to the edge of the treatment table and reached for his navy blue fleece jacket. "Thanks Joanne".

"Hold up a second, *Speedy*. This might help." Joanne slipped a length of uncoiled bandage under Matt's armpit and looped it over his opposite shoulder, tying its ends to form a simple sling. "Pop your hand in there as often as you can, for as long as possible. Keep your hand near your shoulder and the height should stem the flow of blood and give the wound a chance to heal a little quicker."

Matt nodded gratefully.

"You look tired, Matt." Joanne commented as she loosened her tabard and passed the neck opening over her head. "Are you sleeping well?"

"I've been putting in the extra hours lately, but yeah, I'm sleeping OK. I think it's probably just the overtime grinding me down a little."

"How much overtime are you doing at the moment?"

"With my ordinary shift and the overtime on top, I'm hitting around thirteen hours per day"

"Thirteen? You can't be serious?"

Matt appeared unfazed. "Yep. If I average it out over the full week, thirteen per day is about right"

"Jesus Matt. How long has that been for?"

"Roughly the last four or five months, I guess. I'm not gonna lie, it's bloody hard sometimes, but some days are better than others…. and needs must, you know?"

"What needs, Matt? There are few reasons I can think of for why you should put yourself under such a heavy workload so consistently. Are you and Kelly saving for something?"

"No, it's not that. It may sound ridiculous, but I made a promise to myself on our wedding day that I would keep my new wife in the manner to which she'd become accustomed, so that's what I'm striving to do."

Joanne gave Matt a questioning stare.

"Well that's noble, and romantic, but carry on like this and it'll be the death of you. There's more important things in life, and a healthy work-life balance should be more appreciated by your wife than whatever you can afford to provide for her."

Matt spoke tentatively, almost intimidated by the nurse's forthright attitude. "I'm doing fine, Jo. I appreciate the concern though, but seriously; you don't need to worry. If it felt like it was getting too much I'd be the first to do something about it."

"I'm glad to hear that although, having looked at the state of that hand, I can't say you're convincing me just yet."

"I've applied for a promotion in my team. Robbie's leaving us soon, and we need a new team coordinator. If I can get that, then I won't have to worry about needing so much overtime to get by anymore."

Joanne nodded as she simultaneously scribed into the medical records log. "Well it's done now, isn't it?" I just don't want you being exhausted and to have to see you in here so often. You're a good man, Matt. Danny owes you one. If I were you I'd be sure to make that clear to him."

He'll pay it back when he's good and ready." Matt said, convinced. "He seems like the type of kid who'd do the same for someone else given similar circumstances, and that's good enough for me."

Nurse Joanne conceded to him begrudgingly. "OK, if you say so. Now, will you take the rest of the day off? I'd highly recommend it."

"No, I think I'll try to carry on. The Kurtzman order's due for shipping first thing tomorrow and there's still six end panels to finish, plus packing. I promised Kelly a West End show this weekend too, so the extra money will come in handy."

"Well, that's your decision to make honey, just don't say I didn't try" Joanne said, disappointed.

"Thanks Jo; I owe you one too" he said, smiling and gesturing with a nod towards his sling as he rested his thickly padded hand into it. "Well… I actually owe you quite a few!" He opened the door and stepped out, into the factory walkway.

"Bye" Joanne said as he walked away.

Closing the door shut behind him, she thought briefly of him standing in the doorway, hovering in the space like a residual fantasy caught somewhere between her eyes and heart.

"You don't owe me anything, honey," she muttered to his memory, a heavy sigh escaping into the safety of the quiet, now lonely feeling room. "I wish I could give you so much more. A hell of a lot more than that *Queen Bitch* of yours gives you; that's for sure."

Chapter Three

Matt walked into the cafeteria just as Shanna was moving across the room to place her used food tray into the metal trolley along its side wall. Spotting her recognisable flash of red dyed hair atop her well rounded, curvy figure, he stealthily crept behind her, casually dropping his head over her left shoulder.

"BOO!" he blurted right next to her ear, making her jump. Her hands jolted, sending the contents of her tray into the air, before it all came back down with a loud, shrill clash of porcelain and metal.

"Jesus Christ; don't do that to me!" Shanna screamed. She was physically shaken, but smiling nervously.

"Sorry Shanna. I'd say I didn't mean to intentionally scare you, but that would still be a half-lie!"

Shanna placed a quivering hand on Matt's shoulder, leaning into him to steady herself. "It's a good thing we're friends, or else I'd be kicking you in the balls right now, fucker!" she joked. Matt laughed, somewhat nervously.

"Uhh….so what's good today?" he asked, looking over his shoulder, through the curved glass panel of the food counter.

"Well the homemade kebabs look anaemic, and I didn't think much to their avocado salad, so I went with fish pie. It wasn't bad, maybe just borderline mediocre" Shanna giggled.

"Well; with a glowing report like that, you can guess what I'll be having!" Matt smiled.

Shanna moved her hand down to Matt's side,

cradling his elbow. "What's happened to your hand?" she asked, her tone resounding with concern.

"Just an accident with a chisel, Shan." Matt lamented, bluffing convincingly. "Nothing to worry yourself too much about."

"I hope not." Shanna said, glancing at his raised, padded fist one more time and catching sight of the glaring time on his wristwatch. "Listen, I gotta go. I'm due to take minutes at the directors meeting. I spoke to Kelly a little earlier though, she said the barbecue's still going ahead? I'm meeting her for lunch tomorrow, so have a word with her tonight and decide what you need me to bring. I'm sure she won't mind passing the message on."

"I tell you every time, but you just can't seem to take no for an answer, can you? You don't need to bring anything Shan!"

"You know me well enough by now, Matt. I never come to a party empty handed."

Matt could sense he wasn't going to win. "I'll have a think. That's all I'm going to promise."

"Good enough for me. Anyway, I'll catch you later. Take care of that hand."

Shanna gave Matt a warm smile and a wave, the tips of her fingers wiggling in the air as she backed away, before turning on her heels and swiftly leaving through the cafeteria archway. At that same moment Matt watched as Connor, walking in the opposite direction, glided past her so closely, he thought, that it was a miracle they had not collided. He saw Connors eyes flash wide with excitement as they persistently followed Shanna's voluptuous form around the corner. His familiar charming smile had spread rapidly across his face as he turned to face the centre of the room.

"Matthew!" he boomed, careless to their being no

more than six feet apart. He strode up to Matt; his height, broad physique and raucous energy combining to seemingly swamp Matt's shorter stature in a dusky shadow, with just the promise of daylight sneaking over the broad shoulders of his black suit.

"Jeee-zus Christ! That woman has the hottest combination of tits and arse! You say she's a friend of your other half?"

"I've actually known her longer than my wife has, but yeah, they're pretty close friends."

"Well any time you feel like introducing her to your new best work buddy, you go right ahead!" Connor laughed, rattling Matt's ears with the deep sound. His broad grip came down over Matt's shoulder blade, squeezing it firmly whilst steering him around to face the food counter. Briefly noticing Matt's wadded fist, he pointed to it. "What happened to the other guy?" he asked, bursting into another fit of rich laughter before instantly changing the subject. "So what are we having today?"

"Shanna was saying that the uh-"

"Shanna huh?" Connor interjected. "I like it! Trust a stunning body like that to have a sexy name to go with it."

"Yep, that's Shanna. She's the part-time PA to the Operations Director. It's not often you'll see her down here, just lunchtimes mainly. She's rarely in the main office either. She's got her own office next to the Directors."

"So?" Connor smirked, leaving the question hanging in the air.

"So, what?" Matt looked confused.

"So….you know! In the past, have you and her, like… Well, has Shanna met Matthew's ba-na-na?!" He gestured with his eyes down to Matt's waist, before breaking into another riotous all-out laugh and slapping his hand down onto Matt's shoulder a second time.

Matt felt instantly foolish. "Oh I see," he admitted, "But no is the answer to that question."

"Oh - okay. It was just....when you said you'd known her longer than the wife had, I just assumed maybe you'd...."

"No, it's nothing like that." Matt's face visibly tightened and his expression turned sombre. "She was married to my best friend back in the day."

"So what's the story there? They split now?" Connor pushed, ignorant to the change in Matt's demeanour.

"That's really not for me to go into, Connor; Sorry.

"Oh go on; you can tell me! It sounds juicy!"

"I'm sorry, Connor. It was an incredibly hard time, and extremely personal for Shanna. I wouldn't want to go into any detail without her full knowledge.

"Okay, but... would you say, given the curious circumstances, that she's a free agent now?"

Matt took a moment to compose himself, and shook his head. "You'd have to ask Shanna that, Connor. In terms of whether she feels ready for something new; I can't answer that"

"But your wife might be able to?" Connor said cheekily, forcing the issue with a subtle wink.

"Kelly might know more, yes" Matt had to agree, a knot of frustration tightening in his chest, "I guess that means you want me to ask her?"

"I'd say you should at the very least give it a go!" Connor almost demanded, squeezing hard enough to feel shoulder-bone under his hand and making Matt feel helplessly put upon.

"For a worthy friend. What d'ya say?"

"I'll ask, Connor. Anyway," Matt awkwardly changed the subject, "what about food?"

Matt couldn't help staring across the table at his lunch companion. Connor was in full conversation, as he had been for at least five or six minutes, and Matt hadn't heard much more than a few words of it. His head was a jumble of self-demeaning questions, each one unsettling him in his seat that little bit more.

'How did one guy deserve to be so fucking good looking? He told me he doesn't even work out! How come I got to be so short? And why the fuck has my stomach always stuck out with a bulge, no matter whether I work out or not? Chiselled, clear complexion, charming....where are his faults? Everyone must have one, at least! Perhaps it's his arrogance, or his ignorance....after all, I've known him for a couple of weeks and he's been nothing but blatantly consistent with them. Would Shanna fall for that, if he tried? God I hope not, she's way more sensible than that, surely.

DUMPH! The table rattled under his arms.

Surely she couldn't go from someone like Ray to someone like....him!

DUMPH! DUMPH! Two more bone shaking thuds reverberated through him.

He was brought back suddenly by the heavy rapping of Connors knuckles on the table in front of him.

"Hey! *Space Cadet!*" Connor laughed, clicking his fingers in front of Matt's eyes. "You with me?"

"Yeah, sorry. I just got swept up in a thought, I didn't mean to be rude."

"I'll forgive ya. Anything interesting?"

Matt stumbled for words, looking for a way to avoid explaining further.

"No, no. Just…umm…home stuff."

"Christ; is the trouble and strife really that bad?"

"No; she's good." Matt searched for a new direction.

"Anyway, sorry. What were you saying?"

"I asked about this barbeque! Are you definitely doing one or what? I've heard a few people around here saying that you throw a pretty decent party since you mentioned it a few days back."

"Oh. Yeah, that'll be going ahead. It's the Saturday after next, if you still want to come along?"

"I wouldn't ask if I didn't" Connor stated, combining an almost indistinguishable mix of humour and sarcasm throughout both his tone and facial expression.

Chapter Four

The first sight to greet Matt following his turn of the key in the front door was Kelly, distantly sprawled across the brown leather sofa, her head resting on its nearest arm and with her book raised in the air above her. She did not look up, or say hello, despite hearing the familiar heavy lurch of the door as it sprang away from its frame and into the hallway.

"Hey sweetheart" Matt called to her."

"Uh-huh." Kelly's eyes remained transfixed on her page as she slowly guided it over to its other side.

"I'm so glad today's over. My hand hurts like hell! How's your day been?"

"Uh-huh" Kelly said again, autonomously.

"Baby?"

Kelly tore her face away from the book, turning to Matt with a look of irritation.

"Huh?"

"I asked how your day's been."

"Oh…yeah. Not bad I guess. Had a call from Shanna earlier, around lunchtime. Did some washing; had a bath. Read a bit of my book, that's about it." She immediately turned her head back to resume reading.

Matt craned his neck around the kitchen door, looking through the open utility room door, and saw the washing machine full of damp clothes. Looking back into the lounge and being met with the back of Kelly's head he realised that particular conversation was over. He slid his jacket from his arms, hung it on a coat hook, and made his way through to begin unloading the wet washing from the machine, awkwardly moving each piece of clothing into the dryer with his good hand. A few minutes later, after switching on the machine, he stepped back out, closed the door, and was met by Kelly now sat up and glaring at him. She was clearly unimpressed.

"You ok, babe?" he asked, unsure.

"I will be later, when I can carry on with my book in peace and quiet!" Kelly swung her arm roughly in the direction of the utility room, to the faint noise of the machine and its damp, heavy load shifting inside its turning drum.

"I can't concentrate now, with that racket going on."

"I'm sorry, honey. I didn't realise you could hear it that loudly in here. Not enough to disturb your concentration at least."

"Well you should try it; it's impossible!"

"I pulled both doors shut?"

"You shouldn't have bothered; it's made fuck all difference. What's happened to your hand?"

"Oh, it's nothing, baby. A silly accident at work, nothing major", Matt assured her, shrugging it off. "There's a cut across the width of my palm, but Jo says if I keep it in the sling as much as I can it should heal pretty quickly."

"Jo again, huh?" Kelly snapped. Matt threw her a questioning look. "Just make sure your hand's the only thing she'd like you to *keep up*".

"Jo's our staff nurse, Kelly. I don't know what you're suggesting, but there's nothing funny going on if that's what you mean!"

"Well I get to hear her fuckin' name often enough, seeing how you can't seem to stop yourself from getting cut in accidents! Glass again, was it?" Kelly fumed, launching herself from the sofa and lunging at him with accusing eyes.

"Yes, it was." Matt said, anxiously. "But I work

predominantly with glass, sweetheart. I'm surrounded by it all day! It's natural, whenever there's an accident, that it's highly likely it'll be glass related. Seriously!"

"Don't you fuckin' '*Seriously*' me!" Kelly roared furiously, before consciously stepping back inside herself and exhaling a few deep breaths.

"OK, I'm sorry", she mumbled, "I appreciate your point, and I'm sure Jo is very good at what she does. I'm just sick of hearing her name, can you understand that?"

"It's not as if I bring her name up that often!" Matt said innocently, but instantly regretting doing so. '*Why didn't I just leave it alone?*' he asked himself. Kelly handled his comment with unexpected leniency.

"Just… don't bring her up again… that's all I'm asking", she calmly demanded. Matt nodded his understanding.

"Thank you! So…" she started, "what are we having for dinner tonight? I think maybe you should treat us to a takeout; to make it up to me. Besides…you're not gonna feel like cooking with your hand fixed up like that and, quite frankly, I'm exhausted, so I won't be wasting any of my time at the sink later this evening."

Matt glanced over to the open plan kitchen. Through the now dimming, dusky light flooding in through the front window, he could see a pile of dirty dishes, exactly where Kelly had instructed him to stack them the night before. He sighed, inaudibly. "Takeout it is. Have a think about what you want Kel, I'll get rid of these dishes".

"You're a sweetheart" Kelly chimed, laying a peck on his cheek before watching him walk back into the kitchen, past the centre island to the sink, and reach for the hot tap.

"Love you baby", she called after him.

"Love you too" he called back, a thinly veiled tone of contentment masking his growing frustration. He looked at his hand as the sink filled with steaming water. *'This is gonna be awkward'*, he muttered to himself.

"Chicken fajitas", Kelly scoffed through a churning mouthful of spring roll. "Shanna's fajitas are the business."

Matt looked at her, uncomfortably. "It's our barbeque sweetheart," he said, concerned. "We're supposed to supply the cooked food. Not our guests!"

"Matt," she looked at him sarcastically, "If anything's gonna spoil our own barbeque, it's going to be your burnt burgers in dry friggin' buns. I'd take Shanna's fajitas over anything you can burn and then claim to serve as edible."

"Fine, Kelly; but I'd feel a lot more comfortable asking her to bring a dessert, or drinks. I tell her every time that she doesn't have to bring anything, and she always refuses. The least we can do is suggest she brings something that isn't a lot of work."

"She's offered us anything, Matt. And I say we're taking her up on her offer."

"Well you're gonna be the one to ask her so, when you see her tomorrow, you can break the news to her."

"She'll be fine, stop worrying."

"I know she'll be fine, Kelly. She'll be too polite to say no. Oh; there'll be a guy from work coming this time by the way. Connor. You've not met him yet."

"Who's he?" she asked, intrigued.

"Just a new guy from the main office. He's been there for a month or so, seems harmless enough. We got chatting and now I can't seem to shake him at lunchbreaks." Matt laughed. "I think he's got a thing for Shanna too."

"Doesn't everybody?" Kelly chuckled. "Although I'm not entirely sure why. She's a chunky thing nowadays."

Matt ignored Kelly's obvious spite. "He wants me to introduce them properly. He actually asked me to ask you whether she felt ready for a new relationship."

"Why would he think I have a clue about that?!"

"I told him you two were close, when he first started asking about Shanna."

"Well not that's it's any of his fuckin' business, but she hasn't said anything to me to suggest she's over Ray yet. Personally I think she should be by now. She's so damn pretty, and guys seem to be falling over themselves to get a date. Time moves on; know what I mean?"

Matt watched Kelly's open mouth grind as her words made their way around the mess of shredded cabbage and beansprouts.

"Ray was one of the good guys, Kelly" he muttered. "If Shanna doesn't feel ready to move on from what she had with him yet, then that's her choice. She's entitled to feel that way for as long as it takes."

"It's been nearly four years, Matt. There comes a point when she'll just have to bite the bullet and take a chance. If Ray wanted Shanna's future to consist of her dwelling on the memory of him, then he's a selfish son of a bitch."

Matt slid his half-finished tray of food onto the coffee table. His appetite was lost.

Chapter Five

The sun shone majestically onto Archer's Plaza as Kelly speedily approached it. Pulling her car to a sudden halt at the traffic lights she eased back into her seat, crossed her arms, and watched the bustle of Friday lunchtime business people as they determinedly surged around each other. The blatant ignorance displayed in their single-minded dance had always made her smile.

Across the plaza she noticed Shanna's blue Honda, parked within a neat row of cars outside the furthest of the shopfronts. It was Kelly's usual place too but, this time, she could see there were no available spaces. Kelly was instantly incensed, the thoughts going through her mind littered with insults, each one aimed towards the absent owners of the other parked cars.

It was this distraction which caused her to not see that the lights had changed to green, and made the waiting driver in the car directly behind her toot their horn. Jumping from her seat at its sound, Kelly glared vindictively in her rear view mirror as her heart pumped furiously against the grip of her seatbelt. The driver made a pushing gesture with his hands, mouthing the words *"Come on!"* Kelly turned to look back through the gap between the seats, furrowing her brow at the man, while placing her car into gear angrily. As she accelerated onto the junction she raised her bunched fist into the air, extending her middle finger and mouthing *"Fuck you"* into the mirror. The man stared perplexed into her reflected eyes, unimpressed and shaking his head. Kelly smiled to herself as she turned her eyes back onto the road ahead of her. "Arrogant piece of shit" she muttered self-righteously.

Having driven the entire length of the plaza, Kelly was furious to find there were no ordinary spaces within the main square. She gripped the steering wheel, tightly twisting the rubber under her fingers, cussing to herself.

"For fuck's sake! I'm not parking all the way out on Graves, they can fuck that! I'm not walking five minutes each way just to have some fucking lunch. URGH!" she grunted at the windscreen, "I *hate* this piss-take of a town!"

Yanking the steering wheel violently, Kelly turned the car sharply in the road, sending the car behind into a swerve to avoid her pivoting back end. She began driving in the opposite direction, sound-tracked to a hail of horn blasts.

"Oh piss off" she screamed through her window as she drove alongside the long line of enraged motorists, each shouting through their own windows and flailing their arms at her in dismay.

From the terrace of La Tartaruga Scattare Shanna sipped the froth from her cappuccino and watched as Kelly brought the Prius to a screech in front of the one remaining disabled parking bay. Glimpsing to her side, briefly contemplating her lack of options, it was only a matter of seconds before Kelly manoeuvred her car around the street and slotted into the space.

"Oh my God, what's happened? You weren't disabled when we last spoke!" Shanna called sarcastically as she watched Kelly exit the car.

Smiling through her gritted teeth, Kelly stepped up the kerb onto the pavement, faking a limp and clutching at the rear of her thigh, moaning

"*Oooh*" she let out ironically with every other step. It took a few of these utterances before she broke into a fit of hysterics, stumbling onto the restaurants terrace and tumbling forward into Shanna's outstretched arms. Shanna took Kelly by the elbow, helping her straighten up.

"You okay?" she asked.

"Yeah I'm fine, Shan. Parking here is a fuckin' shambles today though, don't you think?"

"It's a shame you weren't here a few minutes earlier; there were plenty of bays free. You're not seriously gonna leave it parked there, are you?"

"Don't sweat it." Kelly shrugged. "We'll only be sat here, and if I'm unlucky enough to have a warden pass by then I'm sure I can find a way to distract him from his duties."

She threw a suggestive wink at Shanna, hooking the loose neckline of her purple blouse down with her finger to show three inches of plump cleavage.

"Unless you'd rather do it for me, Ms F cup?"

"What kind of girl do you take me for?!" Shanna giggled, a tinge of mocking shock in her voice.

"You know the boys all want a piece of you! Speaking of which, I do have something I have to ask you, but it can wait 'til later."

Kelly lengthened her neck and peered over Shanna's shoulder, squinting to see through the front window to the chalkboard hanging over the bar. Sporting a wry smile, she turned her head back.

"Right now I need a drink. What are you buying?"

Shanna smiled automatically in return, knowing full well that, despite Kelly's comical tone, the question was a genuine one.

Kelly's arms were stretched flat out on the table in front of her. Cradling the restaurant menu in the gap between them, her eyes scouring its contents as she ducked her head and sipped at her Mojito through its straw. Shanna was watching her intently from the opposite side of the square glass table, tracking her eyes as they darted over the double sided card, and noticed them repeatedly pausing as they fell to the same spot.

"Well, I think you know what I'll be having" Kelly finally declared, looking up and smiling inanely.

"Chili calamari linguine?" Shanna joked.

"Chili calamari linguine it is!" Jesus, I must be so predictable.

"I'll go and order," Shanna said, rising from her seat, "You stay here and keep an eye out for any traffic wardens. I'm sure I saw one snooping around here earlier, before you arrived. He could still be lurking somewhere."

"Got it!" Kelly assured her, sticking her thumb in the air. She rose up, moving around the table to take Shanna's seat

Shanna had stepped away, entering the restaurant doorway, when Kelly called after her.

"Oh, could you grab me another Mojito while you're in there? This one's not got long left."

Shanna gave her a prolonged stare, the majority of which hit the back of Kelly's head as she turned to face the busy street again.

"Sure thing", she succumbed, irritated.

Kelly put her straw to her lips and slumped back into the canvas seat of her wooden framed, movie-director style seat. She looked across the large square, to the people buzzing in and out of the shop doorways, and the numerous near collisions as commuters rushed to find the quickest way around each other. Her smile crept back, with her periphery seeming to blur as she found herself mesmerised by the chaos of life on display. Absorbed in the moment, at first she failed to notice the brown haired man as he stepped into her side-view. It took him to raise his hand and wave it in front of her before the glaze across her eyes receded and her view returned to the full panorama. Looking towards him, she was immediately taken by how charmingly he presented himself. His hair was well groomed, swept up at the front in a pompadour style, its tips rolled to the right across its top. His eyes were an appealing shade of blue, and Kelly couldn't help feeling drawn into gazing over his face. Pulling her eyes away, she scanned the length of him, silently admiring his well-tailored suit, and picturing his body underneath it in her mind's eye.

"Hey" he breathed gruffly towards her.

"Hello" she smiled.

"You're not here alone, are you? I'd hate to see someone so beautiful with no one for company on such a gorgeous day."

"I have to say, I'm disappointed to have to say no!" she blinked rapidly at him.

She leant forward, placing her forearms on the glass table-top and interlocking her fingers, creating a triangle with her arms pointed directly towards the stranger. The neckline of her blouse fell forward, revealing the soft inner curves of her cleavage; exactly as she had intended.

"I'm here with a friend, unfortunately. *Very* unfortunately. She's in there, ordering our food." Her eyes sparkled at the stranger, fixing him with a stare he found hard to look away from.

"That is a shame," he stammered, absorbed. "We would've had a wonderful time, I'm sure."

"I can guarantee that", Kelly gazed into him, melting.

The suit all of a sudden became rigid, straightened himself and looked at her, disappointed.

"I think that must be your friend returning" he said, gesturing to Kelly's rear.

She turned her head, seeing Shanna exiting the

doorway with a pair of fresh drinks in hand, and turned back to the man, nodding.

"Yes, that's her."

"Maybe another time, hey?" he suggested. He fished around in the inside pocket of his suit jacket, bringing out a business card which he leant forward and dropped onto the table in front of Kelly.

"Whenever I come here I keep an eye out for the best looking guy in a suit. Today it's definitely been you."

She put her fingers to her lips, kissing them tenderly, before lowering her flattened palm to her chin and blowing the sentiment seductively towards him. He winked casually, and started to walk away.

"Who was that?" Shanna asked, placing the fresh Mojito in front of Kelly and returning to her seat. Kelly moved around the table to retake her own.

"Just some charmer, no one I know" she replied, scooping up the business card from the table-top and swiftly dropping it into her handbag at her feet.

"Well, whoever he was, he must have been quite the distraction!"

"Well he was pretty cute, wasn't he? But…" she looked at Shanna, puzzled, "wait, what d'ya mean?"

"I mean…he was obviously so cute that you didn't see whoever it was that gave you that damn parking ticket!"

Shanna scoffed, gesturing over Kelly's shoulder with her outstretched forefinger, whilst shaking her head in bemusement.

Kelly turned to her right, placed her hands on the arms of the chair, and lifted her body from the seat. Across the sea of multi-coloured car bonnets she rested her eyes on the bright red sheen of her own. At the bottom of the windscreen, tucked under the rubber fin of a wiper blade, sat a bright yellow plastic envelope glaring at her.

"Oh, for fuck sake!" she seethed.

"Looks like lunch today is gonna be more expensive than you were expecting!" Shanna lightly joked, somehow managing to make her sarcasm sound consoling.

Kelly puffed out her cheeks. "Yeah, I guess it is" she said, lowly.

"So what was that, with that guy? You say you don't know him?"

"Not at all! He just walked up and started speaking to me. Hot guy though;" Kelly looked thrilled with herself "I think he wanted a date out of it too, in a 'might-happen-one-day' kinda way!"

"You're a married woman, Kel! He was okay. I mean; he wasn't what I would call hot as such, but he looked smart, if that's what you mean."

"Don't you just die for a guy in a suit though, Shan?"

"Not really, Kel. To be honest guys in suits have a tendency to come across as quite arrogant to me!"

"I know what you mean, but at the same time I kinda like that about them. You know I'm hooked on Curtis Sharp at the moment, don't you?"

"At the moment, Kel? Who are you kidding, it's been nearly a year, and yeah I know you are! I haven't been able to get you to shut up about the damn guy! What are you up to by now…the third book?"

"Yep, and I've gotta get through it soon. I want to read through them all again before the fourth book comes out, and that's next month! Jesus, I seriously can't get enough of him. It's like his character has something over me; something I can fantasise about in my darkest dreams, you know?"

Shanna chuckled. "I think our dreams may be slightly different from one another's!"

"Seriously, Shanna. You're missing out. The books are so descriptive, and Master is so dangerous and yet so… so magnetic, I can almost clo-"

"The Master?" Shanna stared at her, open-mouthed, "Kelly, are you hearing yourself?"

"Read the damn books, Shan. Then you'd know exactly what I mean."

She looked at Shanna's wide eyed expression with a sense of utter dismay.

"Seriously, I'm glad to be so addicted. You would be too if you gave them a try."

"Maybe one day…but I'm not promising. And even if I did I certainly would not sit around introducing Curtis Sharp as *Master*!"

Kelly scowled, taking her fresh Mojito in hand and sucking a good third of it up through the straw. Placing it back down heavily onto the glass table-top, she ran her tongue between her lips and looked at Shanna intensely, as if analysing her.

"Tell me something;" she asked, "If I told you that I knew someone who was so into you that I could get you a guaranteed date, would you take it?"

Shanna looked back at her curiously. "Who's the guy?"

"Fucked if I know, honey!" she joked. "I've never met him!"

"I'm not sure I understand. So… you're telling me you know a guy who likes me, but you've never met him?"

"He's a friend of Matt's from work. Seems to have taken a fancy to you, albeit from a distance so far. I think you may already know him."

"Don't tell me, his names Connor isn't it?" Shanna

looked at Kelly distastefully.

"Umm…Yes? Jesus Shanna, put that sour face away! What's so wrong with a guy showing some interest?"

"Firstly, he's the definition of arrogance in a suit. Secondly, he's a fucking letch! Yesterday he rushes past me, brushes his hand across my tits, and doesn't even say sorry to suggest it might have been accidental! All I got was a creepy smile and one of his theatrical winks."

Kelly winced, smiling awkwardly through her teeth. "Oh, really? Matt didn't tell me about that side of him, sorry honey."

"Matt hasn't seen him for what he is yet. At least I don't think he has. I honestly don't know why he gives the guy the time of day."

"Matt told me that at first he felt sorry for him being the new guy, and from then on this Connor just kinda latched onto him."

"Matt's too compassionate sometimes."

"Well, with all that being as it is and out in the open now, I'm afraid I've got a bit of news for you that you might not appreciate."

Shanna frowned. "He's not-"

"Coming to the barbeque," Kelly finished for her, "Unfortunately, yeah."

Shanna swallowed her mouthful of cappuccino with a gulp. Puffing out her cheeks she looked Kelly hard in the eyes, perturbed, before taking in a heavy drag of air.

"It is what it is, I guess," she conceded, "But I'm not backing out of the barbeque; no way. I've been looking forward to it for months, and *I'm* not missing out just because I'd prefer to avoid *him*! Matt will just have to keep him occupied, the poor thing!"

"I'll make sure he understands the situation, Shan" Kelly reassured her. "But, it does raise a bigger question."

"What question?" Shanna enquired.

"Whether you're ready to get back on the horse; so to speak." Kelly smiled at Shanna inanely again.

"You can say it with a devious twinkle in your eye, but it doesn't make the prospect any easier to get my head around, Kel" Shanna said, stubbornly. "And the very least appealing option for me right now would be to settle for a guy like Connor!"

"I'm not talking about Connor anymore. Just men in general! There's a lot of single guys out there who'd love to get to know you, honey. I hate to see you wasting great opportunities over a broken heart." Shanna frowned intensely upon hearing the words, but Kelly continued, "One of these days, someone could come along and fix it for you, you never know!"

"Ray may not exist in a physical sense anymore, Kel, but he's with me. I still feel him, and I love him as much as I ever did. I simply don't feel in need of anything from anyone else! I know it's probably hard to grasp, but give it time with Matt and I'm sure you'll appreciate where I'm coming from. You two are only a couple of years into life together, just wait until it's been ten, or fifteen!"

"Hmm…" Kelly pondered audibly, "I'm not so sure."

"What do you mean, Kelly? Matt's a great guy! And he's been a wonderful husband so far, hasn't he? Last thing I'd heard, he's treating you to the theatre this weekend, isn't he?"

"It's not so easily explained as that, Shanna. Yes he's been devoted… and romantic… and he's very thoughtful and generous."

"So where's the issue?"

"Don't get me wrong," she implored, "they're nice to have in their own sense, but there's more I need now. I don't honestly think he's the type of person I'd get it from."

Shanna stared at Kelly with her mouth agape.

"What are you getting at, Kelly? How exactly is he falling short? And I hope it's not what I think you're gonna say!"

"So what if it is?" she snapped defensively, before taking a measured pause, and returning to her imploring tone. "I want to feel controlled, Shan. That can't be impossible to understand, can it?"

Shanna could sense the passionate frustration in Kelly's words, but the prospect of her acting upon those urges sickened her.

"You're basically saying you want a Curtis Sharp, Kelly. That's a fantasy! It's not a healthy relationship by any stretch of the imagination."

"I'm not saying that it needs to be permanently like that. Just that… at the right times… I'd like to be made to feel dominated; to have my urges fulfilled, you know?"

"I wish I did, Kel; but no! I don't see that Matt's failing you in any way. Now if you'd said Matt was being horrible, or abusive towards you, then I might understand. But if it's simply because you want a bit of, what… aggression in your sex life… then make that clear to him! If he knew you're one hundred percent willing then I'm sure he'd be prepared to give it a go."

"He's just not *that* type of guy, Shanna" Kelly rebuked.

Shanna leant forward on her elbows, confronting her. "You don't know that. Given the chance, maybe he could be *exactly* that guy. But you don't know until you give him that chance."

"If you'd read the books, Shan, you'd know exactly what I mean. You don't understand the character needed in a man to be a dominant. There's a magnetic charm needed, that…that you can't help but let drive you crazy. It's almost more than lust, I can't explain the feeling. A higher sensory level somehow. All it takes is the perfect guy to show up, and the whole world can change. Jesus Christ; the more I talk about it, the more I realise it really is just a dream."

Kelly's face turned sour, the corners of her mouth dropping as she turned silent, reflecting inwardly.

Shanna felt it best to not speak. She felt extremely pleased with herself in having broken Kelly enough to allow her to see sense, but she was not going to break her any more than was required. Instead she filled the silent spell by starting on her own Mojito, sucking on her straw and watching Kelly carefully over the rim of her glass. It was the waiter who eventually knocked Kelly back to full consciousness, arriving at her side with a load tapping of his polished black shoes on the pavement.

"Chili Calamari Linguine?" he asked, flitting his eyes between the ladies.

Kelly looked up to him. It was his beard she noticed first, cut short, neat and elegantly styled. And, below that, his pressed white shirt, elegantly matched with a smart black silken tie. All topped by a wide, pearly white smile. Enticed, she fixed him with a stare, slowly widening her mouth to reveal her own brilliant smile.

"I'll take it", she stated directly, batting her eyelashes.

Chapter Six

"What the fuck do you mean we *aren't* staying the night?"

Kelly's eruption echoed around the barren, dimly lit car park. She stepped moodily into the cars open passenger door, gracelessly slumping down onto its leather coated seat. Grabbing for the inner handle, the metal door frame was snatched from Matt's hands with a sharp jerk, stinging his palms as they scored across it. Scowling up at him through the narrowed gap, she screamed loudly.

"You've gotta be fuckin' kiddin' me!" Her head teetered on her shoulders, dizzy with the alcohol still coursing through her bloodstream.

Nervously, Matt began to walk around the cars exterior. Kelly slammed the door so hard he saw the car lurch to its side, before rocking back steadily. He stopped, helplessly mesmerised, watching its rocking motion gradually slow until it had come to rest. He let out a sigh, realising he was simply stalling for time.

Looking in through the rear window he saw Kelly, her body thrashing around in her seat as if trying to break loose from the imaginary straightjacket she felt he had placed her in. Another, slightly lighter, sigh escaped him.

"It's only a couple of hours until home" he reassured himself. "The drive will be over sooner than you think."

The motorway was empty; almost eerily so. The late night temperature had recently dropped significantly, lending itself to the spooky feeling. Matt stared intently through the frost-framed windscreen, eager to keep his focus on the road ahead, while his ears were being pulled in another direction.

"Never ever... have I *ever*... been to the *fuckin'* West End and not stayed the night in *fuckin'* London!" she screeched, aggressively slurring.

"Do you understand, Matt? Matt! Don't fucking ignore me; I'm telling you this is stupid! You could've arranged a cheap room somewhere, surely to God?"

Reticently, Matt broke his determined concentration, all the while keeping his eyes forward.

"I tried to book somewhere baby", he spoke calmly from the side of his face, "but nothing's cheap here anymore. Originally I'd intended to make this more of a weekend break, but I couldn't afford both the theatre tickets *and* a hotel this time, and the show was more important to you, after all. I'd promised you a trip to the theatre, so that's what I made sure you got."

"Oh, promises schmomises." Kelly ridiculed him. "This is a *half* a promise. You could've at least warned me so I didn't get my hopes up."

Matt spoke dryly, while studiously maintaining a cautious control over his words.

"I'm sorry, honey; I didn't realise a hotel stay was a pre-requisite of a trip to the theatre, but I'll know for next time. Just try not to be so pissed with me if it's a slightly longer wait between tonight and the next show we have a chance to go to."

"Who's pissed?" Kelly riled up, incensed. "I'm not pissed, and I'm allowed to have an opinion! Jesus; why do you always have to be *such* an arsehole?"

"I'm not being an arse-"

"Excuse me! I was asking Jesus, Matt. Or did you not you hear me as per usual?" She watched Matt's face for a few seconds, sullen and reactionless, before bursting into a fit of laughter which rolled on for the better part of a minute. Matt felt increasingly humiliated.

"I'm sorry," Kelly said eventually, sobering, "It would appear I've got the giggles, wouldn't it! But fuck it; yes! You're being a *total* asshole about this!"

Kelly flailed her arm around towards him, uncoordinatedly waggling her index finger in his general direction.

"We saw a great show, and I was having a really nice time at that bar afterwards, until *you* started bleating on about us having to go."

"It was twelve-thirty in the morning sweetheart, and I still had to get us home!"

"My point exakly," Kelly slurred, smugly. "You could've fuckin' relaxed if we'd stayed somewhere; but NO!"

"Well, what with having to pay off your surprise parking ticket this week, a hotel stay became even less of an option!" Matt blurted in a momentary lapse of self-control. He gripped the steering wheel tightly, anxious of the backlash to follow.

"Well excuse *me*! Obviously this is *my* damn fault! It's not as if I did it intentionally you know? Do you think I wasn't just as fucked off about getting the damn thing in the first place?"

Matt shuffled in his seat, raising his shoulders and gritting his teeth.

"It would just be nice", he began tentatively, "if you could keep some of your money for things like that, rather than it always falling on my shoulders."

"I told you already, *Matthew*; I've had an expensive month. I had to buy my outfit for Doug and Carolyn's wedding; that's only a few weeks away; and you know exactly how frustrated I was with my phone acting up like it was. New phones aren't cheap you know! I had just enough money left for my hair and that was it! I even had to do my *own* nails this month cos I couldn't afford the salon!"

"Don't you think it's a bit unhelpful that you haven't put *any* of the allowance you've had in the past two years into savings?" Matt questioned, braving slightly. "I don't begrudge giving you a sizeable chunk of my wages each month but, whenever something expensive happens, it's all on me because you don't have any money left. This time nearly broke the bank, babe, and you're griping at me right now over my not being able to afford to book a hotel room?"

"You should be asking for more money; I've said that over and over again, but you're too much of a pussy so you won't. That's your problem! I keep telling you but you never listen," Kelly subverted, "That place has you round their little finger, working all the overtime they ask, doing all the shitty jobs so they don't have to dirty their own hands, and then they pay you pennies by the hour? It's about time you grew some balls and fuckin' used 'em!"

Matt looked up to the rear view mirror, staring weakly into his tired eyes. With Kelly's self-righteous words circling his brain, he thought to himself '*Tell me about it*'.

"My wages aren't going up any time soon, Kelly;" he started, turning his eye to her, "I'm paid as best as I can be for the job I do, and I'm taking the overtime because I literally have to. I just can't afford to keep-"

A sudden flash took Matt by surprise, interrupting his surge of bravery and making him sit bolt upright in his seat. He frantically swept his gaze over every mirror. As he looking deeply into his rear view again, he sank inside as he watched the slowly reddening of the speed camera bulb receding into the black shroud of night behind them. "Shit!" he cried out, hurriedly looking down at the speedometer. Its needle sat quivering between two of its line-marked dividers, eighty-two miles per hour being the closest Matt could judge it to read. He smacked his flat palm against the top of the steering wheel, cursing through the windscreen repeatedly under his breath.

"That one was *all you,* baby!" Kelly mocked at him, sniggering to herself and turning away to face out of her side window. With her arms tightly crossed, she stared defiantly into the blackness; fully aware that she was partly to blame, yet excited to have gotten the last word, and tickled by the irony. If she turned back now, she pondered, he might find words to challenge her with. That simply wouldn't do. In Kelly's drunken mind, if the night were to end this way; emotionally cold, awkwardly silent, and with the satisfaction of owning the last winning hand; then it was satirical perfection.

Matt obliged her, seething inside but unwilling to weaken himself by initiating any further argument. Arguing would be senseless, he thought to himself, cursing his prior lapse in judgement.

His eyes stayed fixed on the road ahead of them for the remainder of the journey. His mouth remained firmly closed.

Matt was surprised to wake up to the rich aroma of fresh coffee circulating around him.

Opening his bleary eyes toward the bedside table, he watched wisps of steam swirling up from a hot mug, with Kelly's blurred hand nearby, cautiously retracting after having seemingly just placed it there. He curled the warm duvet away from his face, tilting his head forward to see Kelly better. Squeezing his eyelids open and shut repeatedly, trying with each attempt to pierce their misty veil, he failed to see Kelly descending over him until she was within a few inches of his face.

"Good morning baby," she cooed delicately down to

him, "I didn't mean to wake you. I was hoping the smell of the coffee would do that nice and slowly."

Matt could now see that she was fully dressed, with tight leggings and a loose, brightly coloured exercise vest.

"Don't worry honey, it was the smell that woke me. I didn't realise you were there until afterwards", he comforted her in his sleepy euphoria. "Thank you for my coffee sweetheart. Is… is everything okay?"

"Everything's fine sweetness," Kelly beamed at him, leaning in to lay a soft kiss on his dry lips. "I just wanted to treat my man for a change. I, uh… I thought I should apologise for last night as well. I don't remember a great deal of it to be honest, but I do remember saying a few mean things, and I wanted you to know I'm sorry. I loved the show, and I shouldn't be so expectant just because of how we've done things in the past. I'm not as ungrateful as I must've sounded; honestly."

"I wish I could've made it the night you were expecting, I really do." Matt's pained expression emphasised his own sense of failure. "But this time it was past what we could afford. I know you would've liked to stay, and I should've told you before we went there; I guess. You were just blowing off steam in the car, that's all. Plus you being drunk didn't help the matter!"

"Let's not dwell on it, hey" Kelly offered, cynically.

Matt's mention of her inebriation stung her sensibilities, and she didn't appreciate the suggestion that her mood could be so easily affected, even though she knew better. Controlling her urge to give a more usual retort she leant forward again, placing a second kiss, eager to scupper Matt from making further conversation.

Relishing the tender moment, Matt rested a hand on the curve of Kelly's hip, smoothly caressing it in his palm. He moved it steadily downwards, taking the rounded cheek of her backside in hand, and pulled her onto the bed. The top half of her body fell against his, the side of her face coming to rest on the pillow next to his. Losing himself in Kelly's bright blue eyes he took his open fingers, intertwining the loose hairs which had fallen across her face within them, and combed them aside. As his hand encircled her face, her cheek fell into his palm naturally, and he began lovingly stroking her temple with his thumb.

"I've missed these times" he lamented, staring penetratingly into her eyes.

"Me too. We don't get enough time with each other anymore," Kelly agreed, mirroring his expression and snuggling her head against his cradling hand.

"What do you say you get back under these covers and we spend a lazy Sunday together, hmm?" he asked eagerly.

"I... I can't; sorry baby," Kelly spurned his attempt, reaching behind her back to take a grip of his hand, prying it away from her rump and resting it down onto the bed beside him as she lifted herself from the bed covers. "I wish we could, but I already made commitments while I was making coffee."

"What commitments?"

"I'm meeting up with Tara. We're gonna go for a run around the reservoir. She'd text me while I was making your coffee, and I wasn't expecting you to wake up so quickly, so I said yes."

"Oh. Well, what's the time now?"

"It's eight-twenty sweetheart."

"Do you think you'll be back by eleven-ish?" Matt asked with renewed hope.

"Uh... well... I doubt it to be honest." Kelly shook her head, feigning regret. "Tara said we'd go back to her house for coffee, and then we'd maybe find lunch somewhere afterwards. I'm sorry sweetheart; I was going to leave you a note."

Matt's smile sank from view as he gave Kelly a disappointed, yet accepting nod of his head.

"It's fine, these things happen. Go and enjoy your morning, and tell Tara I said 'Hi'. I'll be here whenever you get back."

"I will, thank you baby," Kelly smiled gratefully, forcing a tinge of remorse from behind her eyes. She leant forward a final time, kissing Matt slowly, lingeringly. Matt felt her mouth open slightly, the merest touch of her tongue on his making his heart race. He reached for the back of her head, aiming to place his hands in her hair again and hold her closer in an embrace, but Kelly broke the clinch, pushing herself away before he could lock in his manoeuvre. She stroked his jaw with the edge of her finger as she stood upright, then walked away to the far wall of the room where she slid her feet into her running shoes.

"Don't let your coffee get cold," she called over her shoulder as she quickly exited the bedroom.

Chapter Seven

Matt gulped from the still steaming mug, his back slouched against the headboard, listening to the recognisable sounds from the floor below as Kelly zipped up her jacket, grabbed her keys, and made her way out of the house. The moment he heard the door latch click and Kelly's steps become distant outside the bedroom window, he pushed the duvet aside and climbed out of the bed. He locked his hands together, raising them above his head to stretch his arms and back until their burning muscles convulsed, shuddering him from the inside out. After lowering them, energetically shaking his limbs loose, he opened the wardrobe and took a baggy grey hooded top from the rack, along with a pair of black jogging bottoms. If he was to have the house to himself, he decided, then he fully intended to do nothing more than remain comfortable until Kelly returned. He could hear the sound of her car accelerating into the distance as he slipped the loose clothing over his body.

It felt, to Matt, like an incredibly long time since Kelly had first urged him to buy her the first of the Curtis Sharp novels as a birthday present. Now, walking past the book cabinet at the base of the stairs and seeing all three novels in a neat line, he felt a twinge of curiosity. He had brought every one of them at her request and yet, to this day, had only once gone so far as to try to read one of their back-page synopses, let alone ever considered sampling their contents or flicking through the initial chapters. He had noticed a marked change in Kelly's behaviour within that time though, with her devoting so many of her days to reading and then re-reading them, while their sex life had become increasingly stagnant. The frequency with which she spurned Matt's advances had begun to concern him and it was partly due to this concern, spurred on by his own increased inquisitiveness and the unexpected sense of freedom he now surged with in Kelly's absence, that he found himself sliding the first of the series from their shelf.

Minutes later, with a fresh coffee on the table in front of him, he took up a comfortable position on the sofa and turned his full attention to the books first chapter.

It was just after five in the afternoon when Kelly returned home. The sound of her cars throaty engine pushing through the gravel driveway signalled just enough time for Matt to replace the book, now two thirds read, back on the shelf. He knew Kelly would not appreciate him reading it. He could almost picture her outrage if she were to discover it. Her reaction when she had found him simply scanning its back cover, his interest having peaked at the time after seeing her so absorbed and distant from merely her first week of reading it, had been impassioned enough to discourage him from returning to them for well over a year. To Kelly, the books were somehow her exclusive domain; a private escape. And, now that Matt had properly introduced himself to their new and exciting world, he could almost appreciate the consuming feeling she had seemingly felt towards them for so long. So much so that, as he slid the book neatly into its designated space on the bookshelf, he resigned himself to finish it. If it meant him waking up early to read more before he left for work, he would. Kelly simply didn't need to know; he assured himself it would be better for the both of them that way.

Kelly breezed in through the front door, throwing

her training bag carelessly against the hallway wall with a loud thud, and kicked off her shoes in a heap. Matt called over to her from the lounge, having just resumed his position on the couch. He could not deny to himself; he liked how fast his heart was racing at the thought of such clandestine behaviour.

"Hey baby. Did you have a nice time?"

"I'm tired, Matt" she mumbled, irritated. "I need a hot bath and a nap."

"Oh; okay."

"You can make me a coffee too."

Kelly moved through the room in front of him, heading for the stairs. Matt rose from his seat and dutifully followed her to the bottom step.

"I'll bring it up sweetheart. Instant, or one of your speciality ones?"

"I *really* don't care to be honest."

"Mm-hmm. How about a kiss before you go up then?"

"Sure" she conceded with effort, pursing her lips for him to lean forward and kiss. Their lips had merely touched, nothing more than a peck shared, before Kelly pulled away and looked around the room, her eyebrow raised.

"Have you done *anything* today?"

"I have to admit, I've been quite lazy. But it is Sunday after all, so I made the most of the time to myself."

"Nice. So I guess the laundry basket is still full and there are no fresh towels then. Epic."

"Well, I-"

"Thanks, Matt. Don't worry though; I'll use the towel that's been in the bathroom for the last three days, and I'll just have to get the washing done in the week, won't I?"

"I'm sorry, Kel. I didn-"

"What's for dinner? Or have you not thought about that either?"

"I did but, to be honest, I didn't want to decide without you, since you would've eaten already. What do you fancy?"

"I wasn't expecting to have to come home and decide - *to be honest!* Just do whatever Matt, and call me when it's ready. Not before eight though. I'm fuckin' knackered and you're not making it any easier."

Kelly trudged heavily up the stairs, muttering to herself incoherently. Matt watched her ascending, feeling anxious and guilt-ridden.

"And don't forget my coffee" Kelly shouted from the bathroom doorway.

Chapter Eight

Shanna stepped out through the door of the accounting office and into the hallway. At the top of the stairs leading down to the entrance lobby she halted, allowing Connor to continue his walk up the flight. Reaching the top he paused, leaning casually towards Shanna.

"Thanks beautiful", he whispered, so closely that she could feel the warmth of his pungent breath wafting into her face. She instinctively pulled away from him, squeezing between the bannister and his encroaching body to descend the first step, when he wrapped a hand around her upper arm and stopped her.

"Listen, Shanna; I wanted to ask if you fancied going out one night."

"Umm… No thanks, Connor; Sorry."

"Don't be so damned hasty woman! We don't know each other so well, and I just thought it would be a good chance for us to get a bit more… well acquainted!"

"Look, Connor; I know you've made pretty good friends with Matt since you started here, and I'm obviously a common link between the three of us, but I can tell you're just not my type. It's nothing personal, just…well, you know what I mean."

"I know you're making a mistake! A damn big one, if *you* know what I mean!"

"That's not the way to win me over, Connor. You couldn't if you tried anyway, but if you think size is what impresses me then you're sadly mistaken."

"That's fine, Shanna, but you should know; I rarely take no for an answer."

"Well then you'd be wise to prepare yourself for routine rejection, Connor. I'm attracted to a certain type of guy and, I'm sorry, but you're miles away from what that is."

Connor lowered his head intimidatingly close to Shanna's, speaking deep and gravelly into her ear.

"Time will tell sweetheart. You know, I quite like it when a girl has a bit of fight in her, but I always train it out of them in the end. I could have you begging soon enough."

Shanna pushed him away by the shoulder, horrified.

"Ease up, Connor" she warned him, "However much you may think you're God's gift, you're in danger of seriously offending me."

She stepped firmly away from him, breaking his grip on her arm, and rapidly descended the stairs.

"I'll see you at the barbeque, Shanna" Connor called down to her. Shanna turned at the last step, looking up to him as he confidently winked at her, smiling charismatically.

"Do me a favour Connor."

"What's that, honey?"

"Two favours actually. Firstly; don't talk to me like I'm some floozy. I don't need to be called any of your creepy nicknames. And secondly..."

She paused as two female colleagues walked through the factory door and into the corridor. As they turned the foot of the stairs and began to ascend, Connor impatiently asked "Secondly, what?" Shanna, angered that her obvious aims at sensitivity were being rushed, continued.

"Fine! Secondly, if you thinking of talking more of your arrogant bullshit to me at the barbeque, either do it from a distance or remember to bring some breath mints."

The by-passers looked up at Connor as his face contorted in abject humiliation, frowning strenuously.

Bursting into laughter as they came alongside him on the top step, Connor thumped the banister and barged inconsiderately between the women as he stormed, red-faced with embarrassment, back towards the main office door.

Matt was seated at the farthest table in the canteen, engrossed in an open book cradled in his left palm, with the fingers of his right hand placed flatly over the bottom of its separated pages, splaying them apart. His untouched lunch, a jacket potato filled with a pool of melted butter, had long since gone cold in its sweated bowl.

As he read the last couple of lines; sliding his hand to the right in preparation for the next turn of the page; his attention was drawn to a figure approaching his table with definite intent. Looking up he saw a troubled Shanna; her lacklustre smile atop a body fraught with obvious tension. Matt told himself to quit thinking about the last time he had seen Shanna with that same face. She slid onto the bench seat opposite him.

"Hey" she said quietly, attempting a wider smile.

"Hey! What's up?"

"Oh, nothing. Nothing I can't keep a handle on anyway. Although I'm starting to think Connor might be a little... unstable; if you know what I mean?"

"Unstable?" Matt scoffed. "In what way?"

Shanna shook her head delicately. Matt's heart was eased to see a more natural smile emerge.

"Don't worry; it's nothing you need to be concerned about. Anyway; how are you? All set for the barbeque?"

"Yeah, everything's on order. It's being delivered late in the week. All that's left is the actual cooking on the day!"

Shanna reached across the table and flicked the books front cover with the pink painted nail of her forefinger. "What's all this about?"

"Well I thought it was about time I gave them a go, but Kelly's overly precious about them being *her* books, so I left home early yesterday morning and brought my own copy. Saves any arguments in the long run."

Shanna peered over the top of the book, noting how far Matt had seemingly worked through it.

"What page are you on?"

"Uh, three-ninety-three."

"Jesus, you're a fast reader!"

"Huh? Oh! No; not really. I read a lot of Kelly's copy on Sunday, and it was compelling enough to make me want to finish it, but I couldn't have brought her copy in today or she'd have noticed the gap on the shelf. I've only read a chapter or three today. It's surprisingly not bad!"

"Ah; well that explains not seeing you with her on Sunday then!"

"You saw Kelly?"

"Oh only very briefly. She was just walking into the cinema complex as I was walking out. I called over to her but I don't think she noticed me. Her friends were being quite loud if I remember well."

"What time was that?"

"Umm… My movie finished around eleven-thirty, so maybe five minutes later I guess. Why?"

"Nothing, I guess. She'd told me her plans were to go out running and then have lunch or something with Tara."

"Hmm. I don't remember seeing Tara there, but I may have missed her. Carolyn was there, with her fella, and a couple of other guys. I assumed they were all mates."

"Ok. Thanks Shanna."

"Sorry, Matt. It feels like I might have just set the cat

amongst the pigeons."

"It's not your fault, Shan. I often wonder whether I'm getting the true story from her. She just acts so distant lately. Sorry to ask so many questions, but I don't suppose you caught which movie they were there to see?"

"Something not dissimilar to that, to be honest!" she pointed to the book. "They were being all giggly around a poster, so I think it must've been that. Can't remember the name, mind, but I caught the trailer before my film started. Some bizarre tosh about a rich, generous guy. Charming, yet with a ridiculous need to punish the woman he loves…blah, blah, blah."

"You don't buy into it? The whole dominant – submissive thing?"

"It's all I've heard from Kelly for the past year! Curtis Sharp this, Curtis Sharp that…It gets a bit tedious if you ask me. I mean; it's hardly an acceptable lifestyle. Sure, for the guy it must be bloody lovely! Some swooning weak femme polishing your shoes for fear of upsetting your delicate sensibilities and getting a spanking. But why on God's green earth would a woman strive to live a servant's life?"

"You think some women actually do this stuff for real? I just took it to be a romance, of sorts! It's just a book after all. A bit of fiction."

Shanna stared Matt hard in the face. Words were coming into her mind, words which she knew she couldn't speak. They would destroy him if he knew. She breathed a heavy sigh.

"Well, that's what I've been led to believe, anyway."

"No. Surely that can't be true. I mean, some of this is brutal. Drawing blood and allsorts!"

"Everything has been done at some point in time by someone, Matt. It would be incredibly naïve to assume this is beyond the limits of every single woman out there."

Matt slid the book onto the table and closed it shut.

"That's enough for today I think."

"Look, try not to dwell on it. And, on the other subject; Kelly's entitled to do whatever she likes when she's off with her friends. I mean; I get why you'd be pissed that she didn't tell you the full story, but the same applies to you when you're out with friends. Speaking honestly as your friend, you live your life in her shadow somewhat. Read the damn book, and enjoy it! Kelly doesn't have the right to tell you that you can't."

Matt, feeling mildly consoled, nodded timidly. He picked up the fork beside his bowl and began to scoop large chunks of the potato and butter into his mouth, gulping them down uncomfortably, determined not to waste the meal.

"Listen, I gotta go" Shanna's arm stretched across the table, reassuringly patting Matt's bunched hand. "I actually came down to run off some printing… until Connor came along and broke my stride."

"I'm sorry Shanna, we never got onto that. Do you want to get it off your chest?"

"No; it's fine. Like I said, I can keep a handle on it. If anything more develops I might come and find you for a whinge, if that's ok?"

"I'm here any time you need to."

"Thanks, Matt. Keep your chin up, hey?" Shanna lifted her body from the table, winking to Matt as she turned away.

Matt couldn't help but smile. Shanna seemed to possess a very natural way of raising his spirits. He gulped down the remaining forkfuls of cold beans, washed them down with the dregs of cold coffee from his cardboard cup, and stood up from the table. Looking at the book below him, he considered leaving it where it lay.

Someone else can read it, he thought. Over the last few minutes he felt his eyes had been opened, in more ways than one, and he had lost a degree of interest in it. He took two steps from the table and paused, questioning whether he really could end it there, and how much he might hate himself for not getting to its end. After a few more seconds of pontificating he turned around, scooping it from the table-top. He knew the intrigue would get the better of him in the end. He would have to finish it.

Chapter Nine

The factory held a depressingly gloomy haze, its dirt-speckled skylight windows limited to offering the greyest of daylight from a heavily overcast sky. Leaving the dining hall, Matt made his way around the yellow-marked walkway bordering the first row of refrigeration units. Halfway across the factory he came alongside the exit door to the hallway, behind which the building's front entrance was located and, so too, the staircase leading up to the offices. As he passed it, his attention was caught by two figures seeming to manoeuvre aggressively around each other, just outside the building's wide glazed entrance doors. Intrigued, he halted his walk and took a step back; peering through the small window at the tense scene. It was some distance away but Matt quickly determined that the taller of the men appeared to be Connor. He also seemed the angrier of the two; gesticulating wildly with his hands in the face of his company. But who was the other man, Matt pondered. Tall, suited, and with a neat crop of brown hair above a well weathered face, the man looked as if he had only recently taken to keeping good care of himself after some time, possibly decades, of neglect. There was clearly tension between the two; in fact Connor's face portrayed a man ready to explode. His fists were tightly clenched, balled up as though he were preparing to swing one of them.

Matt's inquisitive side took control and, before giving himself time to contemplate it properly, he impulsively pushed through the heavy door and stood halfway down the hallway, his body tucked stealthily beside the staircase. From his new position he could see much better, but was still unable to fully make out the words they traded. Their mouths moved clearly enough for Matt to know that Connor felt aggrieved by the stranger's presence. He crept forward through the hall, until he was stood at the start of the stairway. Their words were now drifting quietly through the thin gap between the doors, delicately touching Matt's straining ears.

"You have no right, Doug!" Connor hurled at the man. "I'm trying to get on with my life; you can't keep hounding me over something I had no part in!"

"You and I both know that's bullshit; but fine… keep up your act, you vile little shit. We'll see how far that gets you."

"I don't have to put up with this. It's fucking harassment. You're gonna regret-"

You just trust me, fucker; I'll keep watching. And boy; you best hope you don't put one of those big feet out of line, 'cos I promise you I'll be all over you like a rash."

"Jesus! You must really be bored. You should try finding something better to do with your time?" Connor challenged sarcastically.

"I can't think of one damn thing better to do with it."

"Then I really do pity you, Doug. You know, it wasn't so long ago I considered us good friends."

"Oh, you're gonna start playing that violin again are you? It didn't wash with me back then son, and nothing's changed to make me think any differently since. Friends? Well maybe so, but you burnt that bridge yourself when you-"

A delivery lorry drove between the two men and Matt's line of sight, rumbling slowly past them, its engine complaining in its low gear. Even after it had moved out of sight, the throaty grumble continued drowning out the conversation. Matt followed Doug's lips intently, trying in vain to make out his words. Normal sound resumed just in time for him to see Connor push Doug harshly by the shoulder and begin walking towards the entrance doors, shouting back over his shoulder.

"This is the last time I listen to your *fucking* paranoid crap; d'ya hear me? Stay away, Doug."

Connor grabbed at the slim metal bar running vertically down the right-side door, noisily launching yanking it outwards while he continued shouting over his shoulder.

"Just stay the fuck away from me."

As the door swung closed, Doug curled a final warning around its edge.

"I'll be waiting, kiddo. One foot, that's all it'll take."

Matt, having crept back to his hiding place near the underside of the stairway, stepped out and moved forward just before Connor turned from the now closed doorway, heading towards the stairs.

"Oh! Hey Connor!"

"Matt! Umm... Hey. Listen; now's really not a good time." Matt could see he looked shaken.

"Everything okay?" he asked, brazenly.

"Could be better, Matt. I just... Look; I'll pop down a bit later, okay?"

"Yeah, no problem. I wasn't looking for you anyway to be honest. I just wanted a breath of fresh air before the afternoon shift starts."

Connor looked over his shoulder, through the glass double doors, at Doug as he slowly walked across the car park towards a black Audi saloon.

"Little chance of finding fresh air out there", he murmured.

"Excuse me?"

"Oh... nothing. I'll... uh... I'll see you later, Matt."

Chapter Ten

Matt shook a second layer of charcoal briquettes into the smouldering barbeque pit as Kelly moved slowly; unenthusiastically around him. She placed her precariously overstretched handful of utensils down onto the ornate glass topped garden table, before loading its surface with every bottle of alcohol she could carry from the house, which she held in two awkward lines wedged between her inner arms and her waist.

Her second trip outside; to place a range of glasses onto the table in front of the bottles; she made her last, after which she broke the cap off of the fresh brandy bottle and measured herself a healthy double. As she downed it greedily next to him, Matt glimpsed at his watch.

"They'll start arriving in the next half hour or so, sweetheart," he informed her. Kelly took her time to refill her glass and then raised it to him, smiling sarcastically.

"Well I've got just enough time to start feeling the effects of this then!" she replied, opening her mouth and knocking the second double down with ease, gulping the mouthful and ending it with an over-emphasised *'Aaahhh'*. She glared at him over the top of the empty glass as she held its cold crystal to her chin.

"Just remember that this is *your* thing, Matt," she hissed, moving her index finger out from the glass to wiggle at him. "If you want to do this all by yourself then you just carry on the talking to me like that."

"I wasn't getting at you, honey! I was just letting you know that-"

"Shut up, Matt; its punishment enough that I have to

get through another one of your bloody barbeques, so why don't you do what you do, and I'll do whatever I have to do to get through it. And, just so you know, that will definitely include a few drinks, starting with these! Is that okay with you?"

Matt looked back at her, baffled.

"I want you to enjoy yourself Kelly, I'm not telling you *not* to do anything, and that includes enjoying a drink! I just honestly don't understand what the problem is every time we have a barbeque. It's a great excuse to get friends together and catch up; don't you think?"

"Yeah…your friends, Matt. Not mine."

"They're *our* friends, Kel. Not just mine! What about Shanna?"

"Shanna is the one and only exception… but she always ends up talking more with you anyway."

"Why don't you ever invite your friends? They've always been welcome."

"You and I operate in very different social circles, Matt. You've never seemed to grasp that fact, have you?"

"I have, and I appreciate that, but-"

"My point being, Matt; my friends would never get on with yours! They're *totally* different types of people. Hence I save them the discomfort by not inviting them. I just haven't yet found a way to un-invite myself."

"Well it's your choice whether they're invited, although personally I think you'd be surprised if one day you did. They're not so different; from what I know of them."

Kelly scoffed indignantly, slamming the brandy glass down onto the glass table top and walking away from him towards the house.

"Shows how much you know, doesn't it!"

"And you know everyone else who'll be here today well enough by now," Matt called after her, "Just get into a few conversations. Mingle! They're all coming here to see you as well as me!"

"Oh look..." Kelly pointed with both index fingers towards her face and its unimpressed expression as she backed into the patio doorway, "can't you tell how grateful I am?"

Matt frowned at first, but clamped his lips closed and remained silent, cautious of giving further inspiration to Kelly's escalating mood.

"Didn't think so."

Shanna could hear vibrant party music drifting over the top of the house from the rear garden. Noticing Matt scurrying frantically through the kitchen, she rapped her knuckles on the window. Matt span around at the sound, the heavy tapping disrupting the frantic mind-set he was caught up in. He was panicking, trapped in the feeling that he still had so much to do. For the first time in at least an hour though he found an excuse to pause, and took a much needed, stabilising breath. Shanna smiled widely at him through the glass, tilting her head rapidly to his right a few times, gesturing with her eyes for him to move towards the front door. Matt obliged, taking to a slow jog across the room, reaching the door a few seconds later. As he pulled it open towards him, a steaming Pyrex dish was thrust to his chest, its base and lid held firmly together by two patterned tea cloths. He instinctively took a hold of it and stepped back from the doorway. Shanna walked in through the hovering wisps of steam, dispersing them around her as she moved, sending their broken sections spiralling out of the door behind her.

"Put that dish down, quick as you can. It's fucking hot!" Shanna warned as she pushed the door closed with the heel of her brown leather boot. Matt, having been up to that point oblivious to the heat within his hands, suddenly came to the same urgent conclusion and made a dash to his left, through the kitchen doorway to the nearest worktop, where he slid the dish from his hands like a bartender in a Wild West saloon. Shaking his stinging hands as he stepped back out into the entrance hall, he found himself greeted by Shanna's open arms, thrown tightly around him. A welcome hug ensued, albeit as much of a hug as Matt could return, given that his arms were tightly trapped at his sides.

"How in the hell did you manage to hold that for so long? My hands are screaming!" Matt asked.

"Hands of asbestos, these" she replied, stepping back from him and vigorously rubbing them together. "Right; I'm a woman of action, and for today I'm all yours. Where do you want me?"

"I *want* you to be going outside and getting a drink! There's a few of the others out there already. Kelly's upstairs re-doing her clothes and makeup, and I've got everything else in hand."

Shanna raised her left eyebrow to him, silently questioning his claim.

"Seriously, Go!" Matt urged. "You are hereby banished from being within the four walls of this house, until either the time comes for you to ask for your coat, a bathroom break – obviously, or-", he paused.

"Or what?" Shanna asked.

"Why, my dear girl; 'tis the thing we don't dare speak of on barbecue day!" He spoke in a hushed tone. "Young children cry at the sound of its name, it's not uncommon for the trees to wet themselves at its presence, and even fully grown men are known to run like girls for shelter at the feel of it falling upon them!"

"What in the actual fuck are you talking about, Matt?"

"The rain of course!" Matt exclaimed.

"Oh, for fuck sake!"

"Seriously, you call yourself one of the more educated among us. Shameful!" he giggled.

Shanna couldn't help but smile.

"You're such a dick!" she laughed, pushing jokingly at his shoulder with her bunched fist. "Seriously; you must have had to go to some special school or something to learn how to be so gloriously random!"

Matt blushed, before walking her to the patio door and shooing her from the interior.

It was just under an hour later and the garden bustled with mingling friends, echoing from all corners with hearty bouts of laughter and exuberant chatter. Matt stood behind his billowing barbecue, proudly relishing the lively scene from the patio while routinely turning his attention back to flipping the array of sizzling meats laid charring at his waist. To his side, Shanna enthusiastically filled the empty glasses of the other guests; placing the first of the cooked burgers and sausages into their bread buns and rolls whenever the time allowed, in preparation for their first shows of hungry interest.

Kelly's lithe figure was draped across a sun-lounger six feet away, just after the point where the patio's stone slabs broke away and the lush green lawn began. Her left arm lay curled dramatically over the top of her head; a near-empty, thick-cut crystal bourbon glass cradled in her right hand near the ground, brushing languidly at the longest blades of grass. Her final choice of outfit had been a white bikini, eager to make the most of the hot streak while also aiming to outshine everyone else there. To moderate the ensemble she had thoughtfully clad her shoulders in a tiny white cotton shrug; her waist bound with a pearly, silken sarong. Now though, spreading herself indulgently over the sun-lounger, both of these lay open offering no real modesty. In a different context; a lavish poolside at the rear of a Hollywood mansion perhaps; she would have certainly not looked out of place. In the much more normal setting of the suburban garden, however, she looked alien amongst the sea of crop tops, polo shirts, and shorts. The party atmosphere appeared to happen all around her, and yet she remained abstract in her own air of superiority. Disturbed, she looked up as a shade was cast over her, and saw Shanna step into view at her shoulder with a bottle of sour mash.

"Can I top you up, Kel?"

"You can go right ahead, my lovely!" She smiled, holding the wavering glass out to her side.

Shanna poured steadily, fighting a constant battle against Kelly's random swaying of the glass as it moved on the end of her now uncoordinated arm. At one point she miscalculated, flooding the glass with whiskey and filling it three quarters full. Kelly winked at her as if receiving a favour.

"You know; you're a guest here, Shan. You shouldn't have to run around doing the job of your host. Come and have a drink with me."

Shanna looked Kelly in the eyes, hoping to see some recognition of the blatant irony in her face. *She must be joking*, she asked herself. *Anyone else would have classed themselves as 'hosts'; plural; and got involved, rather than keeping the term singular, surely.* After more than five seconds of silence between the two of them, Shanna realised that there was no recognition to be achieved. No ironic joke to laugh along with.

"I like to help, Kel; It's ok. Matt's doing the important stuff; I'm just helping out where I can."

Kelly raised her glass to her eye line, pointing her finger out from it towards Shanna. She paused for a moment, puffing her cheeks as she searched for her words, before realising she had nothing witty to say in return.

"Suit yourself" she shrugged, placed the thick glass rim to her open mouth, and then swallowed a third of the glass down with one swift tip of her hand.

Shanna, shaking her head in disbelief, returned to the patio table, placed the bourbon bottle onto its surface, and approached Matt with a full glass of red wine in hand.

"Refreshment for the chef?" she smiled, offering it to him.

"You're a star; thanks Shanna."

"You're welcome. Barbecue's always look like thirsty work to me."

"This one sure is! Can you believe this weather?"

"It's beautiful, isn't it?"

"We couldn't have hoped for a better day. Well... I say 'we' but-"

Matt's beaming grin all of a sudden turned to a look of concern, and he reached out to lay his hand on Shanna's arm.

"Listen; I really do appreciate your generosity, but I wish you didn't feel you had to spend your time helping out like my glorified waitress. I heard what Kelly said to you and, in all honesty, in some respects she's perfectly right. You *are* our guest, and it seems wrong that you should do so much. It's my problem to deal with if Kelly and I don't share the same sense of hospitality."

"Well, it seems just as wrong to me that-"

Shanna started, halting herself as she looked at Matt's guilt-ridden face.

"Don't worry," she patted Matt's hand with her own, "Like I said to Kelly, I just like to help out."

Through the open patio door, Matt and Shanna heard the doorbell ring, followed by a quick succession of taps on the front doors metal knocker. Shanna surveyed the garden, ticking off her mental list of attendees. She turned to Matt, troubled.

"That's can only be Connor, can't it?"

"I would imagine so. Everyone else is here."

"Look; I'd offer to get the door but, honestly; I'm not overly thrilled he's coming today, let alone eager to be the person that welcomes him. Would you mind?"

Matt shook his head sincerely.

"Of course not!" he told Shanna reassuringly. He looked over to Kelly, still laid across her lounger; the last of the bourbon disappearing into her mouth. He turned back to Shanna, holding out the handle of his tongs towards her.

"We'll have to do a trade. Would you mind watching the barbecue for a minute or two while I get the door?"

Shanna eagerly took the tongs from his fingers, smiling gratefully.

"Thank you, Matt. I'll try my best not to burn it all, I promise!" she joked.

Chapter Eleven

Matt snatched open the front door and thrust his hand towards Connor's. After giving it an enthusiastic shake he welcomed him, with arms wide, into the entrance hall. The smile on his face was so unreservedly honest with warmth that Connor could not help but feel compelled to respond; taking himself by surprise as a broad beaming grin spread between wide his ears.

"Thanks for coming, Connor," Matt said appreciatively, "It's great to see you".

"Thank you for the invite!" Connor laughed. "I haven't kept you waiting, have I?"

"Not at all. Everyone else is here, but the last of the food is a little way off from perfection. Should be enough time for you to grab a drink and get through a few introductions."

"Well; a drink sounds like a great idea to me!"

Matt took a step back, casting an appreciative eye over Connor's attire. A pristinely pressed dark-blue two-piece suit framed an equally dazzlingly white shirt and slim black tie, the ensemble completed smartly at the ground by a pair of elegant, square-toed, immaculately polished black shoes.

"Do you ever go anywhere without a suit?" Matt joked.

"I hope I've not come over-dressed? I just feel comfortable in this sort of thing, I guess."

"Well there's a modicum of smartness out there; but mostly casual like me. As the afternoon wears on it's bound to get shabbier, trust me; but they're all good people and they don't judge. If you're comfortable, we're comfortable."

Matt led Connor through the lounge, snaking skilfully around the furniture until they reached the patio door, and then turned to him.

"Bathroom is at the top of the stairs. As you can see, it's a little bit tight through here, so try not to trip whenever you come back through. Kelly prefers the room arranged this way, which is fine, but it isn't the most functional when there's more than just the two of us around the house."

"Oh, I don't know; I quite like the feel of it in here. It's very... cosy."

"Yeah; it is nice, don't get me wrong. I'm just conscious of what tends to happen in a few hours' time, when everyone's had a few more lemonade's than could be deemed sensible and they start coming back through the house! You tend to find Feng Shui and all its harmonious benefits quickly go out of the window when someone calls our coffee table a *'fucking piece of shit'* after breaking their toe on it!"

Connor laughed heartily. He patted Matt's shoulder, squeezing it as though his best friend.

"I can believe that, but don't worry," he paused to cockily shine his knuckles on his lapel, "When it comes to alcohol, I'm more than a little experienced. A few bits of troublesome furniture won't faze me, no matter what my final intake may be."

Kelly looked up as the two men emerged through the doorway. Lowering her sunglasses down the bridge of her nose, she eyed Connor up and down with heightening intrigue. His pressed suit enthralled her, hugging at his broad, athletic figure as he made his way closer beside Matt's diminutive frame.

Shanna arrived at her side with a fresh drink,

lowered it to her and then leaned in to whisper in her ear.

"Prepare yourself. The stench of arrogance is on its way."

Kelly laughed along but, turning back to the approaching pair, felt a wave of anticipation wash over her. Matt presented Connor towards Kelly with a lowered palm.

"Connor, this is my wife, Kelly. Kelly; Connor!"

Kelly swooned as Connor's wide hand came down for her to shake, dwarfing her own, and he leaned in to place a kiss on her cheek.

"It's a pleasure", he greeted her throatily, sending a shiver down her spine which she found difficult to conceal.

"Welcome!" she replied, a little lost for words.

"And here's Shanna; you know Shanna, obviously!"

"Hello, Shanna", Connor smiled somewhat awkwardly.

"Hi Connor" she responded, forcing a smile.

"How's that meat going, Shan?" Matt asked.

"Take a look. I think it's done, but you're the expert."

"That's debateable!" Kelly chuckled lowly.

Matt strolled over to the mildly smoking barbecue, turning the meat left steadily charring on its grill-rack.

"Good job, Shanna! Looks pretty damn good to me! I think it's high time we put a plate in everyone's hands and let them go wild."

The large group chatted excitedly ahead of the heaving table as Matt and Shanna moved busily around it, removing plastic-wrap from the numerous buffet bowls. Kelly opted to keep Connor's company; standing to his right and smiling uncontrollably each time his gaze fell onto hers. Matt suddenly appeared in the small gap between them, aggravating Kelly somewhat, and began to speak loudly.

"Well... what a day for it! As always; it's great to see you all again, and thank you all so much for gracing both Kelly and myself with your persistently wonderful company."

Kelly peered around Matt's back, catching Connor's attention and raising her eyebrows as if to say *'here we go again'*.

Matt continued, "Today we're joined by our newest guest. Everyone; this is Connor. Please do show him a great time, introduce yourselves – although not all at once, of course – and get to know him. He's one of the good guys, just like the rest of us."

Shanna turned her face towards the house for fear of the party seeing her emphatic disagreement.

"Now I'm sure you're all hungry, but before we tuck in I'd just like us all to recognise the hard work from both Kelly and Shanna in getting all of this together today. I couldn't have done it without them."

He raised his glass of wine first to Kelly on his right, and then to Shanna on his left.

"To the women in my life; Cheers!" he said vibrantly, echoed by the resounding cry from the sea of guests across the table.

"Now if you'd all like to form an order-"

Kelly had already begun reaching for the top plate off of the pile, when Shanna interrupted Matt mid-sentence and caused her to pause, arm outstretched.

"Hold your horses, cowboy. I actually think we owe our greatest appreciation to the chef of the day! I'm sure everyone will agree with me; Matt, you've done it again. Today wouldn't be anything without you and your wonderful food. A show of appreciation for the chef, please!"

The crowd cheered and whooped joyously. Connor patted Matt's shoulder encouragingly as he stood blushing from the attention.

"Thank you", he murmured, gesturing to the table in the hope of its distraction. "Please; help yourself."

Chapter Twelve

The party guests had loaded their plates and were settled around the garden in small groups to eat. The sound of energised chatter still circulated in the air, but had grown much lower in volume, with sporadic pauses as mouths were filled and mounded plates were eagerly emptied.

Shanna was perched on the end of Kelly's sun-lounger, her plate resting on her knees. Matt, positioned at her feet, sat cross-legged on a tartan picnic blanket. He was looking up to the pair and talking elatedly about how well the day was going when Connor approached. Kelly was stunned to see a mountainous plate of food thrust in front of her. Looking up to Connor, she raised a hostile eyebrow.

"Would you mind holding this for a moment? Just so I can sit down" he requested defiantly.

Kelly instantly felt strange. Matt had long since learned to be responsive to her intimidating looks and, given the same circumstance, would have taken the glare as a clear answer. Looking up, Connor seemed nonchalant, maintaining a persistent look of superiority. He was sporting an expectant glare, tilting his plate from side to side as though growing impatient. She found herself looking for support from Matt and Shanna but found they had continued to talk, oblivious of the tensing exchange. Though incensed, Kelly reached out and took the heavy plate in her hands.

"Thank you" Connor said plainly, crossing his legs and lowering himself down onto the blanket beside Matt. He folded his legs tightly in front of him and then reached up, beckoning for the plate, smiling ironically to Kelly as it slid from her hands into his.

"So, Shanna?" he interjected, disregarding the duo's ongoing conversation, "How did all you guys come to meet?"

Shanna threw an insulted scowl at Connor. "Sorry, Connor; Matt was actually just saying ab..."

"Its fine, Shan." Matt calmed her. "I don't mind explaining, so long as you don't mind?"

"You've worked so hard at making today as great as it is, Matt. It wouldn't be fair on you if the mood was brought down."

Kelly lowered her half-finished plate onto the grass at her feet and turned to Shanna, her voice stern and insistent.

"No-one's trying to bring the mood down, but seriously, enough time has passed that you should be able to talk about everything openly by now! Jesus, Shanna! Do you think Ray would've wanted you to live your bloody life so trapped by the past?"

"Ray?" Connor asked.

Matt watched Shanna's face turn angered. He caught her by the knee before she could turn to Kelly, soothing the rounded bone with his palm.

"Kelly's not exactly putting it in the most sensitive of ways. She just means that she – we all – want you to heal. It took me a long time. Hell! I don't expect that I'll ever *truly* get over it, so I can totally understand if it can't be as quick for you as others might think it should be. No one's suggesting Ray should be forgotten in any way though. Talking about him is the best way we have to remember him. That way he's never forgotten."

"Sorry to have to repeat myself, but who's Ray?" Connor asked again, this time much louder. Shanna snapped back at him, angrily.

"Ray was my husband, Connor."

"Ah, I see. I take it then, from the excessive past-tensing, that Ray's not with us anymore?"

"That's correct, Connor." Matt said morosely. "Ray and I were best friends since childhood. We grew up a few houses down from each other. Went to the same school... had the same hobbies. Kinda followed each other all the way through 'til our mid-twenties. Back then I'd just got my job at the factory, and Ray had been studying marine biology since the end of school. Anyway; he got a placement on a research expedition with one of the local college's, which turned into another, then another. He was away for a few years before I saw him again. When he did came back it was like nothing had changed, except for this pretty little brunette he'd discovered somewhere along the way; huh Shan?"

Shanna's face spread with the type of smile only the fondest of memories could summon. Her eyes had welled up, and she swallowed with difficulty on the lump in her throat. It was visible to everyone that she felt joyed to be taken back to that place in time.

"And so that was how I first came to know Shanna. Ray and I still hung around like we did in our younger days; fishing and stuff. Shanna hardly ever came along at the time. I don't think fishing was ever your thing, was it?" he laughed. "But she was always ready with a nice meal and a beer when we got him back."

Matt squeezed Shanna's knee a little harder, rubbing it supportively as if to soothe her from what inevitably came next.

"Our birthdays were close to each other's. Mine came first, so we'd had a party to celebrate. With it being our joint thirtieth we naturally wanted to make a big deal of it. We'd planned another party for Ray a few days later, and we were booked up to go on a holiday together shortly after that, when Ray received news from his doctor that a routine blood test had come back showing an anomaly. After that... well things went downhill really quickly."

Matt put his hand to his face, pinching the top of his nose with his thumb and forefinger and scooping away the steadily forming tears before continuing.

"He'd been waiting in hospital for a few days when they finally put him in for emergency surgery, but by then it was too late. That was just short of four years ago, almost to the day"

Shanna reached for Matt's hand, patting it delicately as they sobbed together.

"It was the worst, most depressing period of my life," Shanna choked through her tightening throat. "Matt was key to me getting through it."

"I don't think either of us would have gotten past it without the support of the other" Matt agreed.

"And at that age," Connor added, "most people would be planning for the future; kids and stuff. Still; I suppose that's a blessing of sorts! I can't imagine having to cope with a kid through that sort of trauma!"

"I lost our child, Connor."

Shanna looked up to the few sparse clouds above her, shaking her head and expelling emotional, exasperated breaths as she tried to accept Connor's consistent lack of empathy. Cooling tears ran down over her temples, changing their course around the curves of her ears before mingling in her hair.

"I was four months pregnant with Ray's child when he died. I thought I was coping but I lost my father too, a week later. The stress was... well... it doesn't take a genius to understand how seriously it affected me."

"Shit; that's tragic. And Kelly? How is it that you came to brighten these two's world?" Connor queried, tact deserting him once again, albeit by a change of subject not wholly unwelcomed by the others.

"Matt and I have been together for three years; married for the last two" Kelly explained. "I never knew Ray. I just came to know Shanna after meeting Matt. They'd obviously remained close after their loss, and I just kinda… slotted in!"

"Totally understandable. I'm sure you've been very supportive."

Connor smiled consolingly at the forlorn pair, all the while listening to the nagging voice in his head. It told him that it had grown tired of their sad faces and whiny tone. There were only so many fond memories he could listen to without becoming numb to them.

"What do you say we change the subject?" he asked cheerily. "I get the feeling I really did manage to bring the mood down in the end!"

"Sounds like a good idea" Kelly winked to him in happy agreement.

"You have a lovely house by the way", Connor complimented. "I was commending Matt when I first arrived. You've both obviously put a lot of work into it."

"Thank you!" Kelly blurted graciously. "I don't mean to sound big-headed, but that was mostly me. Matt doesn't have as keen an eye for interior decoration as I do. I could give you the full tour, if you'd like?"

"I *would* like that", he answered. "Matt? Shanna? Do you guys want to come along?"

"You two go ahead", Matt responded, his voice still crackled with emotion. He looked up briefly, to the clusters of guests dotted around the garden. "Anyway; it looks like everyone could use a top-up, and both Shanna and I could use the distraction. Kelly's more than capable of showing you the sights. We'll see you once you're done."

"Sure thing!" Connor smiled. Kelly smiled back.

Chapter Thirteen

Kelly swept past Matt and Shanna, trailing her arm behind her to lead Connor across the patio and into the house. As they made their way through the lounge towards the kitchen, Kelly proudly explained the inspiration behind the various pieces of artwork adorning the walls. Every ornament; scattered over the various tabled surfaces along the way; seemed to carried a story, which she wasted no time in enthusiastically sharing with her indifferent guest. Once inside the kitchen she began pointing out the many gadgets and fixtures, highlighting the most expensive of the kitchen equipment, her bright teeth gleaming as her outstretched hand swept across each showpiece like a model hamming it up as though touring '*prize corner*' on a TV game-show. Connor showed little interest, occasionally asking questions of Kelly as she performed her overly animated circuit, but refusing to make a concerted effort in building extended conversation over any one thing in particular.

"That's it... we're pretty much done for down here", she announced after giving him the merest glimpse into the utility room.

Kelly fought hard to conceal her growing excitement, while considering how she might push Connor's mind in the same direction of her own.

"Why don't we uh... make our way upstairs?"

"Seeing as this is '*the full tour*', then it *would* make sense." Connor stated ironically.

His unbridled sarcasm stung Kelly a little, immediately turning her thoughts to Shanna's previous derogatory opinion of his character. Nevertheless, she couldn't stop the butterflies within her stomach from bursting to life at his brash, arrogant tone.

"Lead on", he instructed her with authority, a wry smile escaping from the corner of his mouth. Kelly obliged.

Reaching the top of the stairs, she gingerly stepped across the landing and pushed open the door directly ahead of them.

"Here's the bathroom; in case you...you know...need it at any point."

Connor moved alongside her, close enough that Kelly could smell the faint cologne lingering at his neckline. Her eyes closed momentarily as she inhaled the sweet aroma. Reopening her eyes, she found Connor with his head turned, smiling down at her.

"Very nice… as bathrooms go."

Feeling embarrassed, Kelly turned and hurried past him, stopping at the next door on the landing and pushing it ajar. A brightly-lit room containing merely a double bed, wardrobe, and chest of drawers opened up in front of them.

"This is...umm...the guest bedroom" she mumbled quickly.

"Is it available in case I'm ever too drunk to drive home?" Connor asked, widening his eyes suggestively.

Kelly turned to face him. She searched her brain desperately for words, before realising that she had been looking intensely into his eyes without saying anything for an uncomfortable amount of time.

Connor adjusted his tie somewhat roguishly, clasping its immaculately turned knot between his thumb and forefinger to work it from side to side, until it was loose enough to make his unbuttoned shirt collar spring apart by three clear inches. Kelly's cheeks flourished richly. Her pale skin, even with the makeup she had applied earlier that day, was unable to hide her heightening arousal as it surged through her. The muscles in her fingers clenched uncontrollably; she could feel their burning ambition to reach out; to touch. Fighting hard against her impulsion, successfully enough to finally turn away once more from Connor and lead him to the next room, she felt she might go insane.

There was no doubt in her mind; Connor truly represented Curtis Sharp by another name. His demeanour was as magnetic as his counterparts; his suit, and the tailored way it fit over his muscular figure; divine. Kelly's attraction was like nothing she had experienced before, strengthened by the addition of a physical being whom she could now see and, if only she dared, touch; trumping even that of her literary Master's long-held adoration.

Reaching the door to the master bedroom she exhaled heavily, placed her clammy palm against the panel, and pushed. The room was easily as bright as the guest room, but significantly more cluttered with everyday furniture, and with the familiar smell of being well lived-in lingering in the air. The vast array of clothes Kelly had discarded when choosing her outfit earlier in the day were scattered randomly across the room; some laying in unloved heaps on the wooden floor, others haphazardly crumpled over the bed, and on the chaise lounge standing picturesquely under the sun-adorned window.

Kelly was steadfastly facing into the room, embarrassed and anxiously avoiding to make eye contact again. Just one more accidental gaze over him; another glimpse at his stature and masculine elegance; she knew could so easily break down her defences. Her hands were visibly shaking at her sides as she spoke.

"And this is our… our…"

"Bedroom" Connor completed for her.

"Yes. Sorry; I'm struggling with my words a little. I think I may have had one too many in the sun."

"You've no need to apologise for that." Connor laughed lightly; compassionately.

"Thank you."

"If anything, it's the state of this room that's worthy of an apology."

Kelly baulked and turned to Connor at hearing the suggestion, immediately forgetting her self-imposed pact.

"I'm sorry?" she asked, as though having misheard.

"It's actually *'pardon me'*. And I know you heard me correctly. I'm right in assuming you're responsible for this mess, correct?"

"Err… Yes?"

"Clean it."

Kelly stood dumbfounded, her mouth wide open.

"Clean it; Now," Connor reiterated in a sterner tone. "Do you understand?"

Kelly's throat felt desert dry; her heart was pounding against her ribs, as the blood circulating around her head pumped solidly between her ears like the motion of a tide. She felt an odd tickling sensation as she blinked repeatedly, and realised that her eyes had inadvertently welled up in their corners; not through sadness, but from the sense of deep fulfilment at Connor's uncompromising commands.

"Yes. I understand" she nodded, immediately setting about making the room tidy.

Connor stood to the side of the room, watching Kelly from the wall opposite the bed, his arms tightly folded across his chest. Occasionally she would steal a look at him, curious to see if his stern expression might waiver. At some deep level it pleased her to see his refusal to relent; instead he gestured with a nod of his head and a sarcastic look in his eyes each time, as if to tell her *'carry on… you're not finished yet'*.

"You know," he began, "I find it incredibly sad when a woman, such as you, isn't handled in the right way. Matt shouldn't be letting this kind of behaviour go… unpunished."

Kelly surprised herself with her own rapid forthrightness.

"So… what would you suggest if you were him?" she asked.

"I'd say that's none of your business; wouldn't you?"

Kelly timidly ducked her head in submission. Connor watched as she cowered, and smiled.

"Until such a time as I decide you have the right to know, at least."

Kelly instinctively bit her bottom lip. Staring down at the floor, she was desperately screaming at Connor in her mind, begging him to take her; to use her body to demonstrate his darkest intentions. None of her urgency mattered though, she thought. She knew she daren't speak for fear of talking out of turn. All of a sudden, for Kelly, the guilty panic of disappointing was painfully real; a jagged knife of responsibility twisting deep in her gut. Dutifully ignoring her internal conflict, she focussed on the instructed task, collecting up her twisted garbs from their improper resting places before arranging each of them on the bed in a neat, folded pile. A red silken dressing gown, the last item to be gathered up and laid carefully on the large mound, slipped from the bedsheets and back onto the floor causing Kelly to casually swear without thinking.

"Fuck it!"

"Watch your mouth" Connor reprimanded her calmly, but firmly.

Kelly's head span to him, her pulse quickening again as she realised she had once again upset him.

"I'm really…really sorry." She squatted down to sweep up the fallen fabric within her shaking hand.

Connor advanced through the room and lowered his hand towards her, beckoning with his fingers for Kelly to take hold of it. Nervously she accepted and, as she was raised from her crouched position, Connor took a further step forward. At that moment she felt the length of their bodies' touch, her nose coming to rest against the uppermost buttons on his shirt, just below its tantalising opening at the very top of his chest. Once again she lost herself in his heady fragrance, closing her eyes to immerse herself in its apricot-like scent, and quivering at the temptation she felt overwhelming her self-control.

"Matt doesn't strike me as the strong type." Connor questioned in a now more intimate, huskier tone. Kelly raised her eyes, widened innocently as though a deer captivated by bright oncoming danger, and shook her head.

"I have to say, I find it incredibly strange that you're married to him."

"Why do you say that?" Kelly whimpered in monotone; fully caught under his spell

"I can easily read women, Kelly, and deep behind those beautiful blue eyes, you're screaming to be controlled. You have a desperation… a strikingly *obvious* desperation… to be owned. That's how it's known in my world, but I think you already knew that, didn't you?"

"Your world?"

"Don't play naïve, Kelly. You know exactly what I mean."

"Ok. But how can you be sure I'm so desp-"

"Don't question me young lady, and never dare doubt my intuition. I see the look in your eyes. There's a pain behind them that you can't hide from me. I also saw the books at the foot of the stairs; all yours, I would imagine. And I know what's inside of them. All of those dark, intimate fantasies described in lustful, decadent language which, I'm more than confident, fester irresistibly in the deepest recesses of your imagination. And now your heart's against mine, and I can feel its speed… its intensity… It's reacting because it knows its desires; that it's two inches away from the answer to fulfilling them. You can't hide what's natural from me."

He paused, looking piercingly into Kelly's transfixed eyes.

"Still think I'm mistaken?"

Kelly took a sharp intake of air as she suddenly remembered to breathe.

"No; you're exactly right", Kelly uttered without needing to think. She was truly lost in him.

"Good girl. There are two things in this world I can't abide from my submissive, and the worst of them is dishonesty."

"You just said… *'my submissive'*? Does that mean that I'm-?"

"It has no reason to mean anything to you; for the time being." Connor interjected sternly, increasing Kelly's heightened anticipation all the more.

"Will you tell me the other thing you can't abide?"

"Disobedience."

"Believe me, I would never dis-"

Connor raised his finger, fading Kelly's words into silence. Coolly he fixed his tie, drawing his collar closed behind it.

"It's about time we went back downstairs, don't you think?" he asked, in the form of a demand more than a question. Conscientious to not challenge, Kelly followed him along the landing towards the stairs. He stopped at the top step, his back kept towards her. "Matt was right about one thing, mind you" he spoke over his shoulder.

"What's that?" Kelly asked.

"You certainly do seem *'more than capable'*.

Chapter Fourteen

The barbecue had gained a party atmosphere, with loud music streaming into the garden from window-placed speakers. A few of the guests remained sat, eating their extra helpings of food, while the majority mingled, dancing together in small groups and revelling in the sunshine.

Connor sat on a plastic chair halfway between the patio table and the start of the lush green lawn; uninterested in the raucous fun happening before him. With his whiskey glass suspended lazily between his fingertips, he puffed out his cheeks routinely in boredom, until a figure approached and cast him in shadow.

"Hi! I'm Marie", the woman smiled.

"Connor", he replied nonchalantly; reaching forward half-heartedly to shake her outstretched hand.

"We never had the chance to be formerly introduced when you arrived. Welcome to Matt's renowned barbecue experience!"

"Thanks."

"So... How did you come to know Matt and Kelly?"

"I work with Matt."

"Oh, cool! I work not far from the factory myself!"

"Uh-huh."

"I'm always available for lunch someday, if you're free!" Marie laughed.

Connor smiled weakly, looking her up and down. She was of an average age when compared to the rest of the party; somewhere between her mid to late-thirties; and with a pleasant, youthful face. Not unappealing by his standards. Her plunging vest-top provided him ample view of what nestled beneath it but he felt dissatisfied by their heavily sagging flesh; shapeless and rippling with her excitable movements; and forming a flat shelf of seemingly conjoined breast across the top of her broad chest when she stood still. The tell-tale stretch of her bra straps led him to believe they were fighting hard to defy the pull of gravity. Lower down, he could see her well rounded hips jutting out below a pair of love-handles making his, already uneasy, stomach turn. He gripped tighter at his whiskey, throwing it to the back of his throat and gulping down the remaining double.

Marie stood patiently, smiling at him. Eager to keep the conversation moving, she widened her eyes seductively and outstretched her hand.

"Now that you're finished with your drink, come and dance with me?"

"Sorry, Marie; I don't dance."

"Oh, C'mon... Everyone should have a good dance once in a while! I can promise you, these hips will make it worthwhile!"

Connor laughed, feeling the potent alcohol knock his head sideways, and making him instantly want to pour himself another. *Just get rid of the girl first*, his conscience told him.

"I'm sorry; I'm a little bit drunk and I probably didn't make myself clear. You see; it's not that I don't dance; I do dance, occasionally... but never with fat girls. I have my image to think about."

Marie stepped back, visibly upset. Connor reached back to the table, took the whiskey bottle in hand, and bit the rubber stopper from its spout.

"I think *'lunch someday'* is probably a bad idea too," he spoke with the stopper held between his teeth, "unless it's a salad?"

"You rude, chauvinistic bastard!" Marie shrieked at

him.

Matt; dancing nervously at the far end of the garden with a group containing Kelly, Shanna, and a few other couples; heard Marie's raised voice over the loud music. As he turned to investigate, he watched Marie, in an obvious state of distress, storm past Connor and into the house. Through the door he saw her dart to her left, headed for the stairs, towards the private confines of the bathroom. He had turned and begun walking up the lawn when Kelly rushed up to join him at his side.

"What's the problem?" she asked.

"I don't know what's happened, but I thought I heard Marie shouting."

The pair approached Connor just as he was rising from his plastic seat and swallowing the contents of his glass.

"Is everything okay, Connor?" Matt enquired.

"Yeah, it's fine."

"Why don't you come over and join us? You seemed a bit lost sat up here all on your own.

"It's fine, Matt. I was actually just thinking it was about time I made a move anyway. I've got a few things to get done this evening."

"Oh, okay; if you're sure you have to. Do you want to take some of these leftovers home with you?"

Connor glanced slyly over to Kelly, then back to Matt.

"Don't tempt me."

"Well, I hope you've enjoyed today? You're welcome to come along to the next one, although it might easily be a nine or ten month wait! I'll make sure you get an invite."

"It's been great, Matt; thanks."

"Let me see you out", Matt offered, extending a guiding arm towards the patio doors.

"I can do that, sweetheart", Kelly interjected; stepping in front of Matt and taking Connor by the elbow. "It looks like Shanna's missing your bad dancing over there."

"Okay baby. Well; safe journey home, Connor. Thanks again for coming."

"Thanks again for the invite."

Kelly led Connor around the table and across the patio, pulling the doors shimmering purple voile aside and holding it there for Connor to step in behind her. At that moment Marie emerged at the bottom of the stairs, her face flushed, dabbing underneath her eyes with a balled up wad of tissue. She slid between the pair, exiting through the door just as Connor was about to place his foot onto its sill.

"Rude!" he muttered, catching the intense glare Marie shot in his direction from over his shoulder.

"I shouldn't worry about her", Kelly reassured. "Marie can be *so* over-dramatic it's ridiculous. It's no wonder she's still single!"

"What gives you the impression I'm worried?" Connor said coldly.

Behind the obscuring deflection of the patio doors shiny organza curtain, the empty lounge felt cool and welcoming. Connor pulled the material closed behind him as he stepped in behind Kelly, keenly examining the subtle rotations of her drunken hips as she twisted cautiously around the room's intrusive furniture. He followed her route, listening to her mutter the obligatory niceties of a host as she walked ahead.

"Thank you so much for coming, Connor. It's been lovely finally meeting you, after hearing so much from Matt over the past few weeks."

"Same for me too", Connor replied, his tone dry and emotionless.

Kelly had quickly arrived at the narrowing entrance to the hallway, reaching within two steps of the front door, when she stopped and turned to face him.

"Well; don't be a stranger. Our door's always op-"

Her speech collapsed as she realised Connor's tall frame continued to loom in on her; blacking out the remaining light from behind him and giving her the sensation of shrinking as he grew perilously closer with no apparent signs of stopping. He reached the spot immediately next to where Kelly feebly stood; his body little more than an inch from hers, with his rich alcohol fuelled breath wafting down onto her face as he looked over her in commanding silence. Mingling with the satisfyingly sweet aftershave still emanating from his neck, the heady mix of aromas made Kelly's head spin. She allowed herself a generous moment; closing her eyes to become absorbed in it; devouring heavily on the dizzying odour as her imagination went into overdrive.

"Kelly", Connor called out gruffly, ripping her from the fantasy unfolding in her mind.

With her heart thumping excitedly against her ribs, she opened her eyes to find Connor staring back intensely into them. She had just enough time to release the pent up breath she had been holding since his approach, when Connor stepped forward and used his weight to turn her sideways. Taking a step backwards to prevent herself from losing balance, she felt his left hand rise up to her neck, wrapping its thick fingers tightly around and squeezing. He pushed her forcefully backwards. Her shoulders hit the side-wall first, followed by the nape of her neck as she tilted her head forward to avoid making full contact on the brickwork with her skull. His strong grip held her there, his breath swarming over her once more as he leaned in and put his mouth beside her right ear.

"Stop fantasising when the reality is right in front of you."

"I'm... I'm sorry. Please... please loosen your grip a little... my legs are going weak."

"No. That's not the real reason they're growing weak and you know it. I'm tired of watching you lie to yourself, Kelly. It's time you see yourself for who you really are."

"Who am I?" Kelly probed desperately.

Connor placed the widely spread fingertips of his right hand against her heaving breast.

"From the force of those heartbeats I'd say you're being exactly who you want to be, right now. Everything else; this dull existence you're living day in and day out, the mind-numbing relationship you hide your darkest desires behind; those are your lies. And I don't appreciate liars."

"Free me from them; please! I'll do anything you ask of me."

"What makes you think I came here to be your saviour?"

"Well; not to sound out of turn, but it's *my* throat you have in your hand; no-one else's. You seem incredibly keen to instruct me on where I'm failing."

Connor eased his grip a little, stepping back from her, and could not resist allowing a smirk to form at the corners of his mouth.

"Clever girl."

"I'm begging you; stop me from going so wrong. Make me right, by whatever means it takes for me to see *your* truth."

Connor let out a heavy breath and let his body tip forward again, resting his forehead firmly against Kelly's.

They both turned their eyes towards the patio door as a sound and the suggestion of movement came from their periphery. Kelly released a tense breath as a silhouette moved around the patio table, stopping there to scoop up food from its surface.

"You have to be prepared to give up everything for me", Connor stated bluntly.

"I will; I promise I will!"

"I don't just mean this... this life. I mean everything. Your attitude. Your *obvious* need for control. That may well be how you manage your relationship with Matt, but it is simply not acceptable behaviour for a sub; especially mine."

"I understand."

"Do you? Or are you simply thinking you do from what you've read in those books? What we enter into will be a true awakening, Kelly. You'll experience things; possibly much darker than you have *ever* considered. People are often easy to say they have an open mind, but that's bullshit. Most of them wouldn't be able to handle any more than a hard fuck. I need someone who is truly unbreakable; mentally and physically; and who is willing to submit to me testing those limitations; whenever, and in whatever way I see fit."

"I submit to you; here and now. Just... give me the chance to show that I'm worthy to serve you."

Connor took another step back, fixing his intense stare over Kelly's desperate, doe-eyed expression. As she pleaded to him silently he took a steadying breath, then pushed harder against her throat. He lowered his right hand from her breast down to her inner thighs, shoving it flatly through the split material of her sarong and then upwards, until it touched against the damp gusset of her bikini bottoms. She jumped at first, settling back immediately to grind against his firm fingers as a surge of euphoria flowed from her heart down into the pit of her stomach. She felt butterflies like she had never felt before. Her head and legs went light simultaneously.

"I have to go", Connor stated meanly.

Kelly felt every tantalised muscle in her body slump in depression. She wanted to cry.

"If I keep you here much longer they're going to wonder what we're doing", Connor urged.

"I understand."

"You understand... what?"

Kelly's heart began to once again race at the thought of confirming their union with the word she had dreamt of using for so long.

"I understand... Master."

"That's better. You're to take my number from Matt's phone and text me so that I have yours too."

"I will, Master."

Connor withdrew his wet hand from between Kelly's legs and placed it in front of her lips. Leaning forward obediently, she let them into her mouth, sucking them clean. Connor then calmly reached for the front door, opened it, and stepped out onto the porch.

"I'll see you soon, young lady. Then you can start to truly learn what it means to be a submissive."

I can't wait, Master. I won't fail you."

Connor backed away silently. He turned to cross the street, headed towards the car park.

Kelly raised a futile hand as she watched him leave; her body experiencing a strange sensation, as though it were collapsing into itself. Unenthusiastically pushing the door shut, she buckled against the wall, overwhelmed.

Chapter Fifteen

Kelly awoke to the sound of birds chirping melodically outside the bedroom window. The bed beside her was cool and empty, with Matt having left much earlier to begin his working week. She blinked the hazy film from her eyes, peering across to the digital clock. It was eleven forty-three and her head, firmly sunken into the dent of the soft pillow, grew a sudden, intense pain which enveloped her skull and pulsated down into the nape of her neck. The cruel reminder of the previous days excessive drinking; it sent her head into a spin, while a sickening lump rose menacingly from her stomach up into the back of her throat.

As if to combat her growing fragility with self-preservation, Kelly's muscles refused to permit her body to rise up from the bed. *Far too risky*, a caring voice between her ears warned. Providing a further layer of distraction, her brain began replaying images of the previous day to the backs of her eyes, cycling rapidly through each and every one of the time-stopping moments that Connor's gaze had connected with hers from across the garden. Her mind hovered longingly over those moments where he had enraptured her; the way he had initially spoken and controlled her during the tour, their potent embrace against the hallway wall, rounded off by the breath-taking reminiscence of the warming feeling when his skin had finally moved against hers. By the time Kelly realised that she had been staring blankly at the ceiling for eight straight minutes, it was clear the distraction had worked. The awakening that Connor had brought her had returned in full effect. She felt blissfully imprinted by his dominance.

Holding the rest of her body rigid for fear of once again upsetting her tender head, Kelly reached out her arm to the bedside table, hooking at her mobile phone with its outstretched fingers before letting her arm drop back down lazily onto the pillow beside her. The impact of its relatively soft landing was enough to make her eyes flash with stars, but the dizzying sensation subsided quickly. She opened the phones gallery in search of the most recently taken photograph.

The photo had been snapped stealthily at two o'clock that morning as Matt, notorious for his light sleeping, had lay subtly snoring beside her. Getting out of bed had not been an option; Kelly knew from past experience that he would have immediately sensed it and stirred.

It had taken her a great deal of time, spent slowly and delicately inching herself over him, in order to slide his mobile phone silently from his bedside table. Once that particular feat had been accomplished she became aware that she could not risk illuminating the room for a significant amount of time without similarly disturbing him. Manually copying Connor's number into her phone was certainly not going to be an option. The quickest, and safest way, she realised, would be to take it as a photo. One quick flash and Kelly felt confident that she could then easily collapse back into an apparent sleeping posture, should the burst of light disturb Matt from his delicate slumber.

Her arms were draped over the edge of the bed, as near to the ground as she could reach so as to ensure the bright white flare ignited outside of eye line. The duvet was held high, propped up by her knees to provide further obstruction. It took a mere few seconds to open Matt's contacts list in search of Connor's details and then, with one final glance over her shoulder and a hurried tap on her screen, the task was completed. To her relief the spark of light only reached a third of the way up the wall opposite her before it dissipated; aided largely by the crumpled mess of her clothes, covering the floors surface and dulling the lightning effect.

Who says carelessness is a bad thing? She joked silently to herself, smirking. *If they weren't there, the flash would have bounced up and lit up half the room*!

It was clear to her that her thoughts might be considered as outspoken by Connor, compelling her to imagine his reaction if she were to justify herself to him in such a way. A defiance ran through her as she pondered their confrontation of minds. She was not used to being browbeaten by another's opinion; far from it. Matt had always cowered in the face of her hostility, and she liked that. As though to reaffirm her own strength of character, she pictured herself raising two fingers to Connor, waving them audaciously to his face.

As if suddenly taking stock of her indiscretion and realising she had gone a step too far, she recoiled in horror at the undeserved liberty she had taken. *If Connor is to be your dominant then there can be no more of that behaviour*, the voice in her head reprimanded sternly. It was pure carelessness on her part; a sense of guilt and self-loathing arising within her because of it.

Breathing deeply in an attempt to regain a sense of inner peace, she tried in earnest to relax into the bed again, cautiously placing her phone back onto the dock beside her in silence. Laying there in the deadness of the room, staring contently into the pitch black swarm around her, it was only then that she realised her nights tasks were not yet complete; that Matt's mobile phone still remained in her other hand.

Though frustrated by her own short-mindedness, it had not taken Kelly very long to repeat her covert process, replacing Matt's phone into its previous position before sliding back to her side of the mattress leaving him relatively undisturbed. She had fallen asleep quickly after that; eager to welcome in the new day and, more excitingly, new beginnings. Now though, alone in bed with the daylight swarming into the room as she revisited her covert operations, she was struck by the realisation of how foolish she had really been. It was obvious to her that she had still been incredibly drunk at the time, and probably far less coordinated than she should have allowed herself to be. *Either you can class yourself as having been very lucky*, the voice inside her head remarked, *or Matt must have been considerably drunker than you'd given him credit for.*

Kelly opted for luck. *For a start, Matt's rarely deserved credit for anything!* she thought. Besides; she was kicking herself for not taking the easiest option - simply copying Connor's details during any of the numerous times that Matt had left his phone unattended the evening before. She deemed her lack of attention stupid; and reckless; drunk both on the whiskey and the thrill of being caught. She had left everything down to luck, so now it seemed only right that she acknowledge its assistance.

Shuffling zombie-like from the kitchen in her slippers, a steaming coffee in hand, Kelly reached the sofa and placed the mug down onto the table. Her arms fell to her sides, where she used their limited strength to lower her aching body down. She was out of breath already, her head swaying but controlled, her peripherally blurred eyes slowly regaining focus as she slid her phone from the table and swiped it open.

Connor's details had been saved as a new contact. Kelly accessed it before selecting the 'Compose Message' option. She let out a heavy breath as the blank text message screen opened, pondering how she might start their conversation. Having previously felt well versed in the ways of submission, it was only now that she realised the limitations of her knowledge; derived solely from her books; scripted by someone else for her own easy consumption. Now, with the responsibility in her own hands, she could not help feeling utterly clueless. Her weakened fingers began to quiver, hovering over the phones keypad indecisively. After taking what felt like forever, and unable to think past the disappointingly lazy choice of simply writing *'Hello Master'*, Kelly typed the words and pressed 'Send'. Her eyes remained fixated on the small, unchanging screen; anxiously waiting as she picked up her mug and sat back into the sofa.

Matt joined Connor at the canteen table, flustered. It was twelve fifteen and he had been waiting since noon to be served. Connor had almost finished his lasagne by the time Matt sat down opposite him, tinging him with frustration. He had been watching Matt's out of character annoyance from across the room and was not feeling eager to hang around for a conversation.

"Hey Connor," Matt greeted him glumly.

"Hi."

"Jesus they took forever to serve today. Anyway, how was yesterday? I know how hard it can be when you meet lots of new people all at once. I hope you didn't feel like we swamped you?"

"The barbecue was fine, Matt, it didn't faze me. And the food was top notch."

"Well that's a relief, buddy. Looking back on it I realised you were sat a lot at the patio table, away from the rest of us. I don't like to think it was the case, but it concerned me that you might have felt a little bit uncomfortable."

"Like I said; don't worry. It was a good day; gave me a chance to understand a bit more about Shanna and the reason why she's so standoffish with me. It's no wonder she's still a little fucked up, you know? After everything she's been through. It was good to finally meet your other half too, after hearing so much about her. You fell on your feet there, pal! She's a looker, I'll give you that!"

"Thanks. I'm sure Kelly would love the compliment!"

Connor's phone, laid on the table next to his plate, vibrated and lit up with a notification of a new text message. Matt glanced down briefly, reading the upside-down words 'Unknown Number'. Connor cautiously grabbed the handset, holding it vertically in front of his face so as to completely obscure the screen from Matt, before opening the notification.

Hello Master; he read, and smiled.

Matt was looking towards Connor, a pain of concern creeping over his face. "Speak of the Devil, as it happens!"

Connor, nervously switching his gaze between his phone's display and Matt, gulped discretely before coughing to clear his throat.

"What do you mean, Matt?"

"I wanted to speak with you about Kelly, if you're okay with that?"

"What about her?"

"Well, now that you've been introduced; learnt the '*lay of the land*', as it were; I was hoping you might be able to help me, you know, with a bit of advice. I know you're a man of the world, and I can tell that you understand women much better than I do. Kelly was my first - and still is my only - serious relationship, so I get a little stumped when things aren't working out so well between us."

"Things aren't good at the moment? You two seemed okay yesterday."

Connor shared the most believable expression of care that he could muster, while his thumbs tapped furiously on his phones vertically held keypad.

"You didn't hear the handful of sniping quips she delivered when we were all sitting around eating?"

"Sure, I heard her give an opinion on a few things," Connor paused, tapping the send button and watching the small envelope icon ascending, before it disappeared from the top of the screen, "and I must admit she comes across as a little abrasive in the way she states her case, but that's just something you either let women get away with or train out of them. I can't say I thought anything of it at the time. I just assumed you were happy with her strength of character."

"Hang on... You think it can be trained out of them?" Matt asked, bemused. Connor laughed back at him heartily.

"You bet your fuckin' life it can! Don't get me wrong, a bit of character is a good thing. You don't want a fuckin' robot in the sack. So that's where you let them be themselves... unless you're unlucky enough to find they're naturally dull in that area, in which case you have to show them how it's done there too. But in public?"

Connor paused. He watched Matt's eyes as they fixed attentively back on him, appearing to hang on his next words, exactly as he had hoped.

"Well; in public you don't let them say anything to disparage you. You nip that shit in the bud as soon as you catch 'em trying. And if you're wise to it being in a woman's nature, as I am, then you spend a bit of time making sure they know what you find unacceptable well before they get the chance. Then you make it damn clear they know what to expect if they ever dared ignore the warning. Job done!"

Kelly leaned forward with excitement as her phones dulled display, balanced carefully on her right thigh, lit up brightly. It had remained unlocked due to her frequent checking, open on the message she had sent Connor. Now, underneath her brief initiatory greeting, his reply had appeared.
Hello Kelly. I was disappointed not to receive your contact much earlier today, but nevertheless I'm pleased to hear from you now. This will, however, be the last time I call you by your name. We each have titles befitting our status and yours will be in keeping with that. Is that understood?
Yes, I understand, Sir, she typed. *Forgive me, but I'm unsure how all of this is supposed to begin. I need your instruction.*

Matt's eyebrows were raised high as he digested Connor's seemingly incomprehensible chauvinism.

"Do you find women usually agree to fall into line with that? I mean; it's not like I have a great deal of experience to fall back on when it comes to the fairer sex but, from the little I do know, I can't imagine a huge percentage would accept that. It seems quite... extreme!"

"Every woman, without exception, wants it to be like that, Matt. They want a man who takes control. Sets the rules. Sure, some of them like to put on a mask and act offended, but they're fooling themselves as well as you. No woman has, or will ever, make me look a fool. They behave as I expect them to, without question. Sounds harsh, I'm sure, to a... well, I'm not meaning to sound rude but, to an overly compassionate guy like you, but that's how a man has to treat his woman if he wants her respect. If you're serious about wanting Kelly to be more respectful, then you *have* to start putting your foot down and telling her what's acceptable. Show her you have boundaries."

"I know for a fact Kelly isn't the type to accept that, though, and I honestly don't think it's a mask, it's just 'her'. I'm struggling, to be honest, more than I ever thought I would. Our marriage never used to be so... so hard to keep in a straight line. She's forthright, but lately it's gotten a whole lot worse. She used to be so happy, with everything we had, and everything we did. Now it seems like it's never enough, I'm always wrong, and she's too headstrong to ever back down, even when she knows I'm right. Plus I'm shit with arguments, which doesn't help!"

Connor's phone buzzed in his hand again. He looked to it, quickly scanned the text and smiled to himself, then turned back to Matt's sorrowful expression.

"Well I'm sorry if that's the case. I don't know her well enough to judge, Matt, but I've said all I can really say. Listen though, if you want some time out, why don't we hit a bar one evening? Make a night of it? She'd let you off the leash for one night, wouldn't she? She might even appreciate it."

"I should warn you; I'm not much of a night owl; but yeah, that does sound appealing. When are you thinking?"

"I dunno; it's just an idea for now. Sometime in the next couple of weeks, maybe? A Friday or Saturday preferably. I'll check my diary and give you a few options."

"That sounds good to me, thanks!" Matt grinned, excited at the prospect. "Hopefully Kelly won't have a problem with me going. I don't think we've spent an evening apart since we were married!"

"Then it's possible that's half the problem! But you've got to remember, she has no choice in the matter, Matt. You tell her you're having an evening out; she accepts it. That's how it works, and you make sure she fuckin' knows it! Anyway, sorry to leave you in the lurch but you'll have to excuse me," Connor rose up from the table, "I have a few extra jobs to get done this afternoon, so I'm gonna shorten my lunch and get started on them. I can't stand late finishes if they can be avoided, especially on Mondays."

He patted Matt encouragingly on the shoulder as he passed him, heading for the canteens arched exit.

Chapter Sixteen

Kelly wondered whether she would hear from Connor again that afternoon. It had been less than ten minutes since sending her last message but her wounding preoccupation felt as though it was burning a hole in her chest. Unsure of what to do with herself, she sat impatiently, playfully flipping her phone between her hands.

Her heart jumped into her throat at the sight of a bright light against her palm.

I couldn't speak very freely, young lady. Your meek other half was sharing his troubles with me over lunch. I'm back at my desk and free now.

My poor Master. I'm sorry you had to suffer that fool. What's his problem this time?

Nothing you need to concern yourself about. Your attention needs to be set aside for what comes next.

And what will that be, Sire?

Don't ever call me Sire again. I'm a dominant, not a knight of the round table. I need your email address; I have rules to send to you. Without awareness of the rules you will be useless to me.

Give me two minutes, I'll send it to you.

Within a few minutes of sending her details across to Connor, Kelly received the shrill '*ding*' of a new email being delivered to her laptop. Hesitating to open it, she wrote quickly to inform Connor it had arrived. His response was short, and to the point.

Open the email now. You have ten minutes to read the instructions and confirm your acceptance of them.

Kelly clicked on the email. A pop-up window

appeared in the middle of the screen, with a neat column of bullet points running down its left side, each detailing an expectation of the submissive.

- *Above all else, the Master's word is final.*
- *Challenging of His decisions will not be tolerated. Respectful questions may be asked, but it forever remains His right to refuse any such consideration.*
- *The submissive will remember that her purpose is to serve, dutifully and obediently at all times.*
- *The submissive will maintain good manners when in His company, refrain from swearing, and refer to Him by adequate titles so as to recognise His status.*
- *Questions asked by the submissive will be determined as either incidental or inquisitive at the time of asking. Incidental will be answered by Him. Inquisitive may be answered, to a limit of three per day. A Master wishes, by his own nature, to be complex and mysterious, and the submissive will respect that.*
- *Any sexual act may be requested of the submissive, at any time. The submissive will submit to any and all gratification demands placed upon her by Him.*
- *A safe word will be chosen by the submissive, for use only in times of extreme circumstance. Any misuse of the safe word will incur suitable punishment, determinable at the discretion of the Master.*
- *It should not be assumed by the submissive that any or all harmful acts enacted upon her by Him constitute punishment.*
- *Where punishment is to occur, an entry will be made in the Master's Pain Journal, and the submissive will be informed as to the reason or reasons for such punishment, accepting this accordingly as the will of her Master.*
- *The submissive will have no other Master during His ownership of her. His ownership will only cease to be when He confirms it is so, either from his own decision, or by that of the submissive, the latter only given following His consideration of the request and acceptance.*

Kelly read the rules thoroughly; three times over. In her head they made sense. Everything that she had come to expect from each of Curtis Sharp's newly inducted subs was detailed in some way, yet her heart fluttered overwhelmingly at the prospect of giving her full commitment, as the fear of reality overtook her baser desires.

Though fearful of pushing Connor's limit so soon, she could not help but wonder how flexible he might be. She checked her mobile phone, noticing she had just over a minute remaining to confirm her acceptance, and hastily replied to his text.

Forgive my curiosity, Sir, but what would happen if I were to suggest I couldn't commit to one or more of the rules?

Connor's reply came through less than twenty seconds later.

Then I'd suggest that it's better if we don't see each other again, and then we'd part company amicably. Are there things you cannot agree to? You only have thirty seconds to be sure.

Kelly's mind raced. The immediacy was causing her to question what she knew she had wanted for so long. She pinched her eyes shut in deep thought. Brief flashes in the darkness behind them showed Connor taking hold of her spontaneously; manfully. She had only to feel that warming sensation again at the thought of his touch, and the decision was made. Blinking her strained eyes open she thumbed her answer into the keypad and hit send.

She watched the small clock in the top corner of the phone; holding her breath while biting her lower lip. For a heart-stopping thirty seconds she wondered if she had been too late, questioning herself. *Could you have missed it? Surely not. Not even by a second, I'm sure of it.* Then, as if having wished hard enough for a reply to appear, it did.

There's a good girl! Your acceptance is gladly received. From this moment, I am your Master xx

An unburdening ball of air huffed from Kelly's body. Overcome by the sense of relief and intense satisfaction she slumped backwards into the smooth, cold leather, clutching a cushion to her chest and smiling uncontrollably. After a couple of minutes forgetting herself, her phone once more lit up.

Are you happy, young lady? Connor enquired. Kelly hastily responded.

I'm overjoyed Master! I can't stop smiling! I've waited for you for so long.

Opportunities will be rare to find, for now. You have to appreciate that from the outset. I won't stand for frustration when we both know the situation is complicated.

I understand perfectly, don't worry. Our time together won't be used for anything other than my obedience and servitude to your desires.

Good girl.

Master, may I ask you a question? I realise I am limited to three, but I do have one I'd like to ask.

You may ask.

Thank you Sir. You obviously have experience in being a dominant, and I wondered about your previous submissive. Who was she?

She was a woman very much the same as you. Married, no children, with a husband who failed to provide the satisfaction of control she needed.

What happened at the end between you?

It's in no way complicated. I determined that she had come to the end of her service, hence our union was terminated.

Oh, okay. How did she take the news when you told her?

She was hurt, obviously. Very hurt.

Do you still speak?

Three questions, young lady. Never forget your limits. I won't appreciate reminding you every time.

I'm sorry, Master. Forgive me.

It's the very beginning, so I will look past it on this occasion. In fact, I have a gift I wish to give you.

Really, Master? Thank you! What is it you wish to give me?

I assume you're aware of Pagetino's, on Durrell Plaza?

Of course, Sir! I've never been there though, it's so expensive!

I'd like to treat you to a meal, with everything paid.

You're spoiling me, Sir! Really; you would do that for me?

This is my offer to you; however there is a caveat.

What, Sir?

I will not be accompanying you, for reasons I am not prepared to explain.

You want me to go by myself?

I want you to go with your husband.

Is this some sort of test, Master? I would never choose to go with Matt over you.

It is a test, of sorts, however not in the way you believe. All I require is a yes or a no.

Then it's a yes, I'd love to go! It's a shame about my company being less than ideal, but purely for the experience, I accept. Thank you Master.

You're welcome my pet. I will make the arrangements and inform you of the details in the next couple of days.

I can't wait! God, I love you as if I have my whole

life, my generous Master.

One last thing. Terms of endearment can become very tiresome I find. There's only so many times I'm willing to rotate sickly sweet names before I lose interest. I therefore have decided upon a name for you. One which you will come to be known by from now on.

What have you decided my name will be, my owner?

Your name is Blondie.

Blondie. I like it! You chose it because of my hair?

No. I just like eighties music. Plus, whenever I use it, you will be reminded that you have a heart of glass, and that I can break it very easily if I choose to.

Chapter Seventeen

The grand dining hall at Pagetino's was bustling. Every one of its tables was full, while its walkways teemed with impeccably turned out serving staff busily putting smiles on the faces of their high-paying clientele. The vaulted rectangular space was made gloriously bright by its panoramic windows; lightly coloured, almost transparent drapes; and even more so by the exuberant laughter-filled chatter bouncing from its walls.

Matt leaned casually back into the soft padding of his restaurant chair, gazing across the exquisitely decorated table, towards Kelly. Besotted, his eyes poured over her statuesque poise as she delicately sipped from her flute of champagne, absorbed in his fascination of her beauty. Her white silk summer dress; soon to be rendered unseasonable by the now fading weather; emphasised her sumptuous figure beneath it effortlessly. Its material clung tightly to her shoulders and torso, the material across her chest separated in the centre by a vertical split starting widest at its neckline and plunging deeply enough for the inner curves of her well rounded breasts to nestle loosely in permanent view. Matt's eyes were repeatedly drawn to this by the smallest of Kelly's occasional movements. A simple shift in her seat would create a brief flash of an inch or more of unblemished, porcelain flesh, drawing in his eyes and heightening his pulse, before the soft skin would retreat as she flexed again in her seat. He found himself breathing heavier with every such reveal. Kelly had noticed his reaction too, allowing herself to play along with the tease, while working hard not disclose any discernible promise from behind her emotionless eyes.

"A woman as beautiful as you suits a place like this so well" Matt complimented, swelling with pride. "I can't believe you were lucky enough to win a meal here too! Would you look at the people around us?"

Kelly placed her glass down onto the table and turned her head as Matt gestured to his right.

"He's blatantly a politician, and his wife has been handing out business cards left and right. Someone dropped one earlier and I caught a glimpse before they picked it back up; it said she was some sort of lawyer. And up there," he turned his head to his left, "by the far wall, there's a couple of guys who I'm sure I've seen from TV. I just can't think for the life of me what show it was."

Kelly turned nonchalantly to the far wall. She too recognised the pair of square-jawed handsome men, although their on-screen personas temporarily alluded her too.

"Give me a minute," she asked, "I'll figure them out."

A waiter arrived at Kelly's side with a white towel draped over his right forearm and two large bowls of steaming broth covering the length of it. The first he took from its expert placement at the inner bend of his elbow, placing it down onto the table in front of Kelly.

"For Signora" he spoke, in a rich northern Italian accent. Kelly felt her cheeks flush warmly at its seductive tone. He then took the second bowl from his open palm and laid it down before Matt.

"Ee for Signore."

"Thank you" they both replied. Matt looking down into the steaming bowl with a hungered excitement, Kelly looking up into the eyes of the waiter with her own appetite. The waiter's eyes caught Kelly's, then dropped lower as the split in her dress widened and the swell of her breasts pushed against its flimsy opening. He blushed, stumbling a moment, before remembering his lines.

"You are a-welcome. Please; Enjoy your-a starters."

"Mmmm…" Matt's eyes lifted to the ceiling as he tasted his first spoonful of the rich broth. "That is so good! And look!" he exclaimed, scooping deeply at the base of the bowl, "It's got little stars of pasta at the bottom!" Kelly snorted heartily, allowing herself a wry smile. She swallowed her mouthful of soup and scowled at him sarcastically.

"Jesus, Matt. Why do you have to be such a tourist about everything? It's brodo; it's like… the basis for most Italian cuisine; Dumb-arse."

"Well how was I supposed to know that?" Matt laughed, light-heartedly.

"Of course not; silly me." Kelly sneered at him over her second spoonful. "If it isn't raw meat burning rapidly over a hot fire you wouldn't have a clue what it is, would you?"

Kelly watched Matt, visibly shrinking into his seat, turn his attention to eating his remaining broth. She felt tinged with disappointed, but pleased with herself nonetheless. It was then, from down by her feet, that she heard two low beeps and, after digging down into her purse, opened her mobile phone to find a new message waiting. For a moment she froze. On the screen she read the notification. *One new message,* and its sender read *Connor*. She rested the phone on top of her right thigh, balancing it carefully, and swiped the screen to life. Swiftly turning the phone onto its 'vibrate' mode, she opened the message.

Good afternoon young lady.

Kelly hastily tapped at the screen as she tried her best to maintain her above-table activities, going so far as to smile at Matt as she temporarily lost her bearings through multitasking. Her heart felt as if it were running laps around her chest, beating so hard that she could feel her upper arms vibrate.

Good afternoon Master.
How is your meal?
It's lovely, thank you Sir.
And your company?
Well he wouldn't be my first choice, Sir, but I have to make sacrifices.
The food is good?
Yes, thank you. And thank you for your generosity. I still don't understand why you offered me this.
It was somewhat of a test. Somewhat for my own pleasure.
Your own? What do you mean, Sir?
Concentrate on eating your broth, young lady. I'll explain in good time.

Kelly squirmed in her seat at the final message. How did Connor know? She had not told him what she was eating? Her eyes dashed around the room, almost expecting to find him hiding in plain view. She caught the eyes of a few overly interested people as she scanned; thinking that perhaps Connor had a scout relaying information to him. Most of them, aside from one well suited older gentleman who blatantly showed her his instant attraction, appeared disturbed by her prolonged gawping. Still confounded; she turned back towards the table and obeyed, picking up her spoon.

"Are you okay?" Matt asked.

Kelly looked up at him, unintentionally smiling again.

"Yeah, I'm fine."

"Listen; I was thinking about a holiday next year. You've always wanted to go to Mauritius, and there's some pretty good deals out there at the moment, so I reckon we could manage it with a bit of budgeting. How about it? We'd need to book it quite soon if you do fancy it."

Kelly's eyes bulged at the suggestion.

"Could we?" she said with heightened breath. "Oh Matt, I'd love that! You know that's always been my dream."

"So I'll find something in the next few days and make a booking?"

"Definitely!"

Matt watched the smile spread wider across Kelly's face, sending a rush of euphoric warmth circulating around his chest. He set down his spoon and reached his hand across the table to hers, taking hold of it and rubbing it with his thumb. "I love you, Kelly" he spoke amorously, "And I love seeing when you're happy."

"I love you too, Matt" Kelly responded, resting her other hand on top of his and pouting a kiss.

Neither of them had noticed that their waiter had returned beside them at the table. At the sound of his polite cough, Kelly instinctively snatched the white napkin from beside her empty bowl and placed it over her thigh, covering the phone and its illuminated display.

"Aww…you are a-such a beautiful a-couple. Was-a da Brodo to your liking?"

"It was delicious; thank you" Matt praised.

The waiter turned to Kelly.

"Ee for a-Signora?" he asked.

"Yes, it was lovely, thank you" she smiled.

"Prego! Now your-a main meal will be coming out a-shortly. Can I interest you in a fresh drink while we prepare for you?"

"I'm fine, thank you" Matt stated, tapping his fingers on the jug in the centre of the table, "I'm happy just with the water."

"Is the bill already paid for?" Kelly enquired.

"Si, that is-correct Signora."

"Well in that case I'll take a red wine. Whichever you'd suggest, so long as it's rich and heavy."

"I shall consult with our-a head barman. He will decide based on your-a main dish. We have two sizes of a-glass, a medium and a large. Which would you prefer Signora?"

"I'd prefer a bottle; thank you." Kelly turned to the waiter, winking brazenly and pointing to the table with her forefinger. "I already have a glass."

"Si Signora, of course. Uno momento." The waiter stressed a smile to Matt as he set off.

Matt's wandering eyes began to discover some of the intricate elements of the building's design for which it had become so well renowned and, ultimately, such an exclusive venue to dine within. Small but extremely well detailed busts overhung its cornicing which, in turn, held immaculately sculpted frilled edging along their entire length, to such a degree that only a skilled craftsman could have achieved it. Even the aesthetic curtaining; hanging from various areas around the vaulted room; was perfectly pressed, pleated expertly, and lent itself to the overall feel of the space as if it had grown there purposefully. To Matt, it felt as if everywhere he looked drew him in to search for more, captivating his vision. Kelly, noticing his distraction, slid the napkin from her thigh. The screen was still illuminated, showing exactly as it had shown before. Tempted to fold its protective cover closed and place it back into her purse, she jumped a little as the screen suddenly grew fractionally brighter and a series of short vibrations drilled down into her tensed thigh. A new message pushed the previous ones further up the screen. Seeing Matt still gazing into the corner of the far wall to his right, she let her eyes drop.

Have you figured it out yet, Blondie?
How did you know what I was eating, Master?
I'll take that as a no, then.
Please, tell me!
Look up from your seat. Can you see the café terrace?

Kelly peered subtly over Matt's shoulder, through the distant wall of glass behind him, out into a wide patio area. Small tables were spread across its surface, with staff wearing barista uniforms busily delivering coffee to those customers who did not appear to mind the chill in the air. Peering a little, Kelly spotted a coffee cup being lifted a few feet away from a window, on a table partially obscured by one of the restaurants internal stone pillars and the swooping arc of its accompanying draped curtain. She watched as a face leant into view from around the side of the opaque material. It was Connor's face. He raised his cup high and, as he did so, a new message arrived at Kelly's thigh.

Cheers.

Connor placed his cup back down onto the table top and leaned back in the chair; the pillar once again obscuring him from view. Kelly watched intently as he disappeared behind it, subconsciously biting her lip.

You've been sat there the whole time? She typed.
I've been watching you, yes.
And is the view to your liking, Master?
I was certainly happy you chose the correct seat when you arrived. I was concerned that I'd spend all of my time facing your pathetic excuse of a husband.
I'm glad I chose well and pleased you, Master.
You seemed overly affectionate towards him just now. What was that in aid of?
I'm sorry, Master. Are you angry with me?

I'll decide when you need to apologise, young lady. And that doesn't answer my question.

Forgive me. Matt said that we might go to Mauritius on holiday next year. It took me by surprise, and it's always been my dream to go there, so I was taken aback somewhat.

Forgiveness is something you have to earn. While I do appreciate your excitement, if you are thinking that you will still be with him next year, then you're weaker than I had initially perceived.

Kelly frowned at Connor's insinuation. Still, a wave of guilt surged through her, making the pit of her stomach turn over nauseatingly at the thought of his disappointment in her.

"Baby, you okay?" Matt asked, turning back to the table and noticing Kelly's furrowing brow.

"Oh. Yeah. I'm fine sweetie."

"You looked concerned?"

"It's just...Sofia text me. She's having a few issues with her fella, Jimmy."

"Sofia and Jimmy?"

"They're a couple I know through Carolyn. You've never met them"

"Oh; Okay. Just, try not to let it spoil your meal, okay honey?"

"It won't, don't worry. Today has been perfect so far" Kelly smiled through her deception, then turned back to her phone and began typing quickly.

I will make it up to you, Master. Please give me the chance. And of course I hope not to still be in this situation next year. He doesn't fulfil me like you do.

She waited for Connor's response. Agonised by each second ticking past, her anxiety grew in intensity, her hearts echo resonating heavier inside her chest with each response-less moment. The minute on her phones digital clock changed, still; nothing. Over Matt's shoulder, Kelly could see Connor's arm extended across the cafe table, his fingertips rapping down onto its glass surface. Feeling desperate, she began to type again.

Master?

No response came.

Please Master, I know I've let you down. I promise, I understand why you're disappointed in me.

This time, after a few seconds, a response came through.

Then you'll appreciate why you'll be punished to the extent I intend. We'll not speak of this any further today. It looks like your main course is on its way. Enjoy.

Thank you Master, Kelly responded quickly, *and I will accept whatever punishment you see fit to administer. Will you stay?*

I will be taking another coffee, yes.

Kelly exhaled the most controlled sigh of relief she could manage, and closed her phones flip-over cover. The waiter arrived to her left at that very moment, laying down two plates in front of the both of them. Matt's dish; a healthy sized medallion of steak; was cooked to perfection and drizzled with a peppercorn sauce so rich in aroma that his mouth watered from the moment it punched its way into his nostrils. Kelly's was a deeper dish, somewhere between a large round plate and a shallow bowl, filled with a steaming mound of sticky risotto. The rich fresh herbs from within its creamy sauce competed for dominance against the strong peppery bite flowing across the table towards it, but inevitably lost the battle. Kelly seemed unimpressed.

Chapter Eighteen

By the time they had both finished their mains courses, Kelly had managed to comment about Matt's meal overpowering hers on four occasions. Setting down their dirty cutlery onto the now empty dishes, Kelly tried to drive her point home with one final dig.

"Well it would have been good, if all I could taste hadn't been your bloody sauce at the back of my throat."

"Now there's a double entendre if ever I heard one!" Matt laughed. A fellow restaurant-goer at a nearby table overheard and laughed too.

"Hilarious." Kelly threw an infuriated glance at the both of them. She felt her phone buzz at her thigh.

"I'm sorry sweetheart! I was only trying to cheer you up. If I'd have known it would've been so strong I wouldn't... but I wasn't to know, was I."

Kelly glanced over the new message.

Be nice to him. That's an order.

"No... No I guess not. At least dessert can't be wrecked." She forced a smile, while typing awkwardly from the corner of her eye.

You want me to be nice to him, Master? He's being a complete jerk.

Yes, and overly nice if need be. He's putting in a great deal of effort to ensure you have a good time. That deserves some recognition, so you'll do as I say, and show him how much you appreciate his efforts.

If that's what you wish, Master, then I will.

That's my good girl. Kelly turned her attention back to Matt, reached her slender fingers across the table, and interlocked them with his.

"I'm sorry, Baby. I know I'm being selfish. It wasn't your fault, and I know that. I'm just in a snappy mood, I don't know why, but you don't deserve to be on the receiving end of it."

Matt reassured her with kind eyes, looking softly into hers and squeezing her fingers tenderly between his.

"It's fine, Beautiful. I thought maybe what was going on with Sofia and Jimmy was playing on your mind. It's never nice to see friends going through a rough patch, let alone feel like you have to be on hand to help."

"I think that may be it. Jimmy's said some awful things to Sofia, and it makes me mad to think that she's going through such a rough time when we're on the other side of town having such a wonderful lunch."

"It sounds terrible," Matt shook his head, concerned. "I hope they're able to get through it in one piece."

"Please, don't worry yourself, Baby. That's the last thing you should be doing. Not whilst we have this." Kelly raised her hands to her sides, bringing Matt's attention back to the grandeur of the dining hall. Her phone vibrated lowly again. She lowered her eyes to read it.

When he gets you home, he can do anything he wants to you. Make sure he knows that.

Kelly reeled back at Connor's command. There was an intense enjoyment in fulfilling his wishes, even if she could see the damaging games it played in Matt's mind. But to go so far as to offer herself to him? To Kelly, this felt like a betrayal of every natural instinct inside of her. The thought of Matt touching her made her feel queasy, made intensely more wounding by the realisation that Connor was the instigator, and that she was duty bound to accept his wish. She knew better than to question him though. The prospect of disappointing him twice made her swallow the lump in her throat and switch to autopilot.

She raised up from the table, placing her hands on it to steady herself as she moved her unsure body closer to Matt. Standing beside him she leaned forward so that her mouth, with her lips licked moist, popped softly into his ear as she spoke. As she did so she maintained a forward gaze, looking out through the large window, into Connor's commanding stare. He urged her without sound or movement. She felt him give her the momentum to move her lips and say the words.

"The only things you need to be thinking about, are the different ways you're going to make me scream your name when we get home. How does *that* sound?"

Matt gulped, turning his head to stare into her eyes with a sense of disbelief. Kelly, as if to solidify her proposition, leaned into Matt and extended her wet tongue, licking the thin residue of peppercorn sauce from his lips.

"Mmmm...You taste delicious. You wanna taste me now?"

"Fuck yes" Matt muttered in an entranced daze.

"Then I'd suggest you eat your dessert quick... and rush this peachy little ass of mine home."

Matt span his head around the room as Kelly resumed her seat, searching for the waiter. Five agonising minutes later, their desserts arrived. Three rapidly passing minutes after that, Matt had fetched Kelly's jacket and was placing it around her shoulders as they walked briskly out of the restaurant.

The drive home seemed to take an age. Matt was growing frustrated at meeting slow traffic, no matter how many ways he tried to alter his route. At times they were completely stopped, allowing him unhelpful opportunities to turn and look at his wife, her dress twisted as she sat angled towards him in her seat. Provocative flesh exposed itself from both the split at her heavy chest and from the high riding hem of her loosely flowing skirt. Kelly herself did not help the situation, opting to tuck her palms into the inside of her closed thighs, slowly stroking them in and out, each time tucking the silken cloth further into the petite v-shaped pocket where her upper thighs met her body. Matt felt sure she must be touching herself, having her hands positioned so high. He could see from her eyes that she was stimulated to a significant degree. He watched again as she moved her hands slowly between their pale skin, the material remaining poked into her crotch, garnering him with the clear view of every delicate contour. Matt jumped at a loud car horn from behind him, realising that he had become thoroughly distracted from the road which was now opening up in front of them.

As Matt attempted to focus back onto getting them home, Kelly took the opportunity to unfold her phone's flip-cover and checked for updates. There was nothing. No follow up from Connor since he had given his last command. *'Surely he couldn't have wanted this'* she asked herself. *'Would he really test me in this way? To see if I would go so far as to do the one thing he knew I would want the least? I guess it could be the ultimate test; although I can't imagine it's too pleasant for him to know is happening. Fuck, I'm confused!'*

The friction high up between Kelly's thighs began to overcome her thoughts of Connor and his odd decision making. She felt rushed with a sudden wave of warmth through her lower body and soon realised that the desire to perform as Connor expected came with much less discomfort than she had originally feared. For the first time in months, she found herself seriously anticipating Matt's sexual contact. She knew she would imagine it to be Connor's, but the simple prospect of something inside of her, right now when she needed it most - where she needed it most - was consuming her every thought. Unguarded, she released a pleasured exhale as her hands slid deeper towards her seat, her little fingers on each hand brushing over the sensitive folds of her outer labia. Matt, only half-focussed on his driving, heard the whimper clearly and surged with urgency, pushing enthusiastically on the accelerator pedal as he moved into the now free-flowing fast-lane.

As the car turned its last corner, and the stimulated couples house loomed into view at the end of the street, Kelly's mobile phone beeped. It had been so long since Connor's last contact that Kelly had almost believed he had left her free to craft the rest of the day herself. The prospect of a new message, signalling his apparent continuance, sent a bolt of electricity through her body. Matt steered the car onto the gravel driveway as Kelly, anxiously biting her lip, swiped the screen alive. Connor's message hit her full-on, simultaneously confusing her brain, heart, and every sensory anticipation that her body had developed throughout the drive home. Growing frustrated she read it a second time, in the hope that her initial view of it had somehow been mistaken.

He gets nothing from you. I don't care how you excuse yourself to him, but he doesn't so much as touch you. Do you understand?

Kelly's heart sank, deeper than she had ever felt before. There had been no initial mistake; she had read the message correctly. For the very first time Kelly felt the full realisation of the hardship being a submissive would demand of her, and it hurt.

As Matt jogged around the car towards its passenger side, Kelly; her head working in defiance of her heart;

began strategically swallowing large gulps of air. Managing seven or eight by the time Matt had levered the handle open, she took a delicate hold of his outstretched hand and allowed him to guide her from the vehicle. As she straightened herself in front of him she suddenly lurched her head downwards to face his feet and pushed the excess air from her lungs with a solid heave of her diaphragm. A warm rippling belch erupted against Matt's shirt as she tried to raise her head, feigning dizziness, and her hand came to rest fraily on his shoulder.

"Are you feeling okay sweetheart?" Matt asked. Kelly remained silent, simply nodding her head slowly in response while pushing her upper body forward in shallow jerky movements as if retching on the inside. "Come on; let's get you in the house" Matt instructed, wrapping his arm supportively around her back.

Once past the front door; standing just inside the narrow hallway, Matt paused to lean Kelly against the wall. He looked over her as she tried her best to emanate malady, puffing her cheeks while reaching deeply to raise any additional air from her lungs.

"I'm okay… I'm okay" she spoke after Matt's investigative palm began pressing flatly against her forehead. She knew she could not fake a temperature. She pushed him away by his arm and sucked in a healthy draught of air, pushing her body firmly back against the wall. Matt stepped back tentatively, leaving his arms hanging in mid-air in case Kelly might tip forward.

"What happened, Baby? You seemed fine until we got back?"

"Urgh," Kelly expelled, "I think maybe I drank my wine a bit too quick. Either that or your damn pepper sauce turned my stomach more than I thought. *Fuck* I feel queasy!"

"Ah, shit! I'm really sorry if it was that, Kel, although it wouldn't surprise me if it were the wine. You did get through it pretty quickly. How are you feeling now?"

"You know that bit in ALIEN, where that horrible little fucker bursts out of what's-his-face's chest?"

"John Hurt" Matt informed her.

"Whatever. That's pretty much how I'm feeling."

"Well you're a bit steadier now than you were when you were outside. Hopefully it'll pass as quickly as it came. Anyway…maybe it's a sign that we're better off spending the rest of the day in each other's arms, huh?" He smiled deviously into her eyes, hoping to ease her suffering through distraction. Kelly watched his growing expression keenly. She knew in her heart she wanted him, but in her mind she felt bound to search for a way out, no matter how it might frustrate her own desires. Contorting her face to show utter disinterest, she resigned to end the exchange quickly in the most effective way she knew how.

"Thank you so much for the fuckin' care and consideration."

The words tore aggressively from her lips, smattered with distaste. Matt reeled back, instinctively raising his palms in calming defence, but Kelly knew well enough to expect the reaction. Matt spluttered the start of an apology but was immediately spoken over.

"Whatever; I don't want to hear it. I'm going to bed, *Matthew*. Maybe you can keep your fucking selfishness under control long enough to let me sleep this off. "

Matt recoiled from her, placing his hand to his forehead and looking woefully ashamed.

"I'm sorry sweetheart; really! Look, let's just-"

"Enjoy your afternoon, Matt. I might come back down tonight, but at this rate don't be surprised if I don't."

With that, and leaving Matt visibly broken and confused, Kelly made her way through the lounge and up the staircase to the bedroom.

Matt unhooked his shoes by their heels and placed them next to the wall. Letting out a deep sigh, he shuffled into the kitchen and flicked the kettle on. As its element slowly began to heat, filling the room with the graduating sound of its water bubbling inside, Matt placed his hands flat onto the kitchen counter and sank into himself.

Kelly stripped naked and then slid her body under the thick duvet. The comforting feel of a cool, empty bed could always make her forget her sorrows, but this time it would not come so instantaneously. The thought of calling down invitingly through the house; for Matt to join her, lay with her and touch her wanton body in the ways she knew they both ached for; was circling her mind like a lustful whirlwind. She felt shackled by unseen and, for the first time, unwelcome restraints; tormented by the harsh position she knew she must maintain or else risk disobeying Connor, destroying his trust and, more than likely, losing him. Resolutely she persevered, pushing all of her desperate thoughts aside. She scooped up her phone from the bedside table and sent notification of her obedience.

I did as requested, Master. I'm in bed, alone as you asked.

A swift response followed.

I asked no request, young lady. I will only ever give you commands. Your subservience will certainly not go unrewarded, however you're telling me something I already know.

You do? How, Master?

Because I'm watching your morose sap through your kitchen window. His misery is delicious.
What's he doing?
Does it matter to you?
No, Master.
He's sat nursing a coffee and staring out of the patio door. It's pathetic.

Kelly climbed out of bed and walked across to the window. She could easily see the road outside and, with an assisting stretch of her toes, she could also see the furthest couple of feet of the pathway in front of the house, but Connor was too near its front to be visible.

Where are you Master? I want to see you.

A second later and Connor had stepped back, enough for him to see Kelly's craned head and neck peering down at him. A smile, resembling relief, was stretched across her face. He took a look at the house one more time, ensuring he was far enough to the side of the kitchen window so as not to be seen, and began typing a new message.

Is it me, or is that perfect little whore in the window stripped bare?

He watched Kelly's silent chuckle before she nodded her affirmative response.

Prove it. Connor sent, looking Kelly sternly in her eyes.

Kelly looked cautiously down the street. She had noticed a slight movement further up its road, her heart beginning to thump raucously in her chest as she watched a neighbour's car come to a stop on their driveway opposite, and its occupants exit towards their house. Stalling for time, she raised her forefinger to Connor so as to signify him to give her a minute, and dashed back from the window. She opened the wardrobe door closest to her and slid the belt from the waist of her red silk dressing gown, looping one end of it around her neck in a simple slip-knot and then returning with slow trepidation to the window. Seeing the street now empty except for Connor, stood impatiently tapping his foot against the tarmac beneath it, she lifted herself onto her tiptoes and pressed her shapely breasts against the glass pane. Looking down onto Connor's rapidly thrilling gaze, she wrapped the loose end of the belt three times over in her grip and pulled, yanking her head upwards like a dog caught by its master's choke-chain. After a few seconds of not unpleasant discomfort she released the upward tension, her head returning to Connor on the street below, to the sight of him covertly stroking himself through his smartly pressed trousers. Moving fractionally away from the window, Kelly cupped her left breast in her palm and began to tease its nipple between her thumb and forefinger, alternating between rubbing and pinching at it. Her open mouth moved in unison with the differing sensations it brought. In her other hand she held her phone high in the air, using her thumb to type out a message.

How do I look, Master? Do you approve?

Oh I approve, my Princess. You have the most amazing breasts. I can't wait to finally sink my teeth into your soft flesh and taste it.

Just tell me when, Sir. I'm at your complete disposal.

That you most certainly are, young lady. And trust me; it won't be a long wait before I have you demonstrate it.

Connor walked across the pathway past the house, crossed the road towards the bay of parking spaces, and climbed into his car. Kelly bit her lip as she watched him pull away, buzzing from the realisation that Connor had completely distracted her from the satisfaction she had felt robbed of not ten minutes earlier. She walked slowly back to the bed, deep in an emotional trance. Her chest fizzled as though a sparkler had been lit inside of its walls, as the feeling of his power over her consumed her every thought. Falling back onto the bed, she shuffled her lithe body under the duvet, then slid her hands over her stomach, past her waist, towards her inner thighs.

Chapter Nineteen

The deep bass of house music vibrated through Matt's feet well before he and Connor had stepped through Pure Bar's entrance. Each of them pushing on a door to gain entry, Matt was hit full-on by the music's heavy wave; its deliriously jagged drum beats thumping him in the chest while the contrasting layers of thoughtful melody invaded his sensitivity; each playing their part in heightening his senses. He had never claimed to be a fan of the genre but, on this occasion, he felt moved to recognise its appeal.

The novelty of a rare night out, wife-less and in the company of such a gregarious and strong-willed character as Connor, made Matt feel both uneasy and extremely excited in an almost childlike way. The bar seemed to buzz with an excitement matching his own, the choice of music filling him with a second heartbeat; faster and more intense than his own. He felt instantly drawn in to the atmosphere; feeling his pulse quicken; and, for the first time in a long time, he found himself moistening his lips in anticipation of an alcoholic drink.

"It's like being born again!" Matt shouted to Connor, stood to his left-hand side, sharing the inane grin plastered across his face.

"Huh?"

"The quiet from outside and then coming into this... It's like you'd imagine being born must have felt like. You know; in the womb the sounds are all mute and distorted, and then a push or two later and all the noises of the world suddenly hits your ears!"

"Uh... yeah! I guess so! You don't get let out like

this very often, do you?"

"*HAHAHA*! *No!* Is it that obvious?"

"Let's get a drink while the bar's not too busy. By my reckoning mate, you've got at least a decade of catching up to do!"

"Why the hell not?" Matt stated emphatically, almost hopping into a stride as Connor encouragingly patted him on the back and outstretched his arm, offering him the duty of leading on.

An hour into the night and Matt had just finished his second pint of beer. Already his head was woozy as he geared up for the bourbon chaser that Connor had insisted would follow each – what he had referred to as 'sensible' – drink.

"C'mon Son; Get it down you!" Connor encouraged him, "Valuable drinking times a-wasting'."

Matt tipped his head back and let the sour liquid pour itself down his throat, coughing hollowly as his head came back to rest. Two minutes later, a new round of drinks were delivered to their table, this time with an additional shot of Sambuca for each of them. Connor smiled at Matt with a devious look in his eyes. He was serious about getting Matt wrecked, and Matt was starting to lose the control to either think rationally or argue back.

The late night air was crisp and shocking to Matt's skin as he and Connor exited the bar. It was just before midnight, and the street would have been silent if not for the descending trickle of music behind them, growing quieter as the double doors swung slowly closed. Matt felt the fresh, icy air fill his lungs, followed by an intense surge of blood to his already disorientated brain, making him tilt as he took his first few steps out onto the pavement. Connor reached out, pulling Matt straight with a guiding hand on his shoulder.

"Feeling alright, buddy?"

"Yeah... I, err... Yeah, I'm ok. I'm ok."

"You're looking a bit green there, fella!"

"The air just hit me, that's all. Seriously, I'm good. *Jesus*, I'd forgotten that feeling!"

"Well, get your head in shape; the cars just round here."

Connor gestured to his right, towards the distant shape of his Audi; its shiny bodywork glowing through the misty haze, illuminated by the dim streetlight above it. Each of them nodding in turn to the stern faced bouncer, wide-built and stood firmly cross-armed to the left of the doors, they began their slow, measured walk.

As they came within a few metres of the car, Matt and Connor split off from each other.

"Are you sure you should drive, Connor?" Matt called across the bonnet. "I know you're more used to handling a drink, but-"

Matt's comment was halted by the realisation that he and Connor were no longer alone. A male figure emerged from behind the rear of the car, coming alongside Matt on its passenger side. Clad in heavy combat trousers and a black hooded sweater, he approached Matt with aggressive intent, stopping abruptly as he reached within a step of him. Matt could see an impressive, bright orange tattoo curling around the left side of his neck. It showed a carp swimming through a sea of cherry blossom.

"Can I help-" Matt started.

"Shut the fuck up and give me your wallet" the aggressor snarled. A small knife twirled in his grip, held just above his trouser pocket, as if to subtly emphasize his demand. The dim streetlight's beam above them glowed against its blade as he rapidly turned it, summoning

Matt's attention. Panic stricken, he turned to face Connor.

Seeing Matt's face drain to white, Connor leant forward to rest his arms on the roof of the car, and spoke firmly.

"Listen, fella; it's late, we've been out all evening, and our money's spent. How about giving us a break and leaving my friend alone?"

"Brave... but so full of bullshit" a second unknown male's voice drifted out from the shadow-cloaked alleyway a few metres to Connor's right. "Don't you just love it, Jay, when they think they've got the balls to argue?"

The man stepped forward from the shadows. Older, taller, and much heavier set than the first mugger, the man truly terrified Matt. He loomed onto the pavement beside Connor, dwarfing him by at least eight inches, impressive given Connor's already sturdy stature. A shovel of a hand flew towards Connor, taking hold of his tie and lifting him off his feet, to where his face was within a couple of inches from the man's chin. Flecks of spit flew from his mouth over Connor as he spoke.

"Fuck's like you always have money. Doesn't matter how much you piss against the wall in a night, it don't stop you counting the remaining wads when you're in the middle of the street. Walkin' around like your shit don't stink; and thinkin' we're too dumb to see through your bullshit! Well you're wrong on both counts, *fucko*. Now be a good sport and hand the cunt over, or *my* friend here's gonna fuck *your* friend there with his knife while I watch."

Connor looked at Matt with anguish. He slipped his hand into his suit jacket, withdrew his slim brown leather wallet, and half-heartedly relinquished it.

"Good lad." The man smiled, dropping Connor to his feet and tapping him on the shoulder with the corner of his wallet. "I'd call that a choice well made!"

He flipped the wallet open, levered through its leather folds, and slid three notes out from the largest of them whilst tutting at Connor.

"You see what I mean, you misjudging fuck? I ain't stupid! Sixty fuckin' quid you had tucked away in there and you thought you could lie to my face. And to top it off…" he leant forward, sniffing exaggeratedly over Connor, "Your shit does stink! You reek of it. Or maybe that's just your sense of self- importance?"

"Well done you" Connor spoke sarcastically. He adjusted his stance, squaring up to the man's chest, tilting his head back steeply to fix an aggressive eye-to-eye stare. Matt, still held captive within stabbing distance by his own threat, saw the gear change in Connor and felt impressed at his friend's fortitude.

"You've got what you wanted, now you can let us go" Connor proceeded.

"How the *fuck* do you know what I want, huh?!"

The man stepped intimidatingly into Connor, forcing him backwards with his broad body.

"My friend here asked for the money first. I just helped him get what he wanted. Who's to say I wasn't actually looking forward to seeing one of you assholes get knife-fucked?"

"You wouldn't?" Connor snorted anxiously.

"Jay?" the man called across the car without taking his eyes from Connor's.

"Uh-huh?" Matt's knife wielding captor acknowledged.

"Give it to him; nice and slow."

Connor reeled back, measured an arms distance, and swung his fist toward the instigator. The extra height needed was deceptive, his punch flying harmlessly under the man's chin as he ducked back slightly, sending

Connor spinning to his left. The man followed his stumbling arc, his smiling eyes catching Jay's concerned stare from behind the car, to which he laughed heartily. Both of his palms suddenly shot forward, thudding into Connor at his shoulders, pushing him to the floor with ease. Matt nervously lifted himself onto the tips of his toes, hoping to see over the car, but Connor was too low to the ground. He thought he could hear a scuffling, presuming Connor to be scrambling over the unforgiving pavement to find his feet. He watched aghast as the man leant over, dropping to his knees where Matt had seen Connor fall, and began to pound downwards with his fists.

The quiet street was suddenly filled with the dull echoes of Connor's pain, their clarity becoming more stunted with each of the man's oversized fists, mixed almost rhythmically with the stomach churning thuds of bruising bodily impact.

Matt turned to run but was caught mid-stride by the hand of Jay, gripping him roughly by the back of his shirt. As he spun his body round to face Jay he immaturely raised his fist, unsure of how he might use it effectively. This was a first for Matt. His experience of fights could be counted on one hand, with his natural reaction having always been rather to take flight than stand and defend himself. His loose fist swung through the air, his eyes pinched tightly shut through naivety, widely missing his target. As his eyes reopened, he had just enough time to see Jay's head accelerating towards his, the dizzying crack of bone on bone vibrating through his skull as Jay's solid forehead came down hard onto the vulnerable area between Matt's eyes and the top of his nose. Stars exploded behind his eyelids as he stumbled backwards into the road and fell to the ground. Forcing himself to open one weeping eye, he saw Jay tuck the knife in his pocket, and advance. To his side Matt could see the other man; the stuff of his nightmares; walking around the car to join Jay. Matt planted his soles to the road, lifted his body with his palms splayed out to his sides, and scuttled away from them in reverse; hoping to negotiate a well-timed turn, lift and sprint in one quick movement. He knew it would be his last opportunity to avoid a beating. If he failed, what would happen next would be at the complete mercy of Jay and his unnamed goliath.

As Matt made his turn, he heard the four approaching feet behind him react; their quickening pace seeming to reverberate up through the tarmac and into his fingers. He put every ounce of energy into a solid push, leap-frogging his body into the air with enough momentum for his feet to find ground perfectly under his body. They had moved just quickly enough to perform one long stride when Matt felt the body-shaking impact of a shoulder blade as it connected with his lower back. His hips were thrust violently forward, his legs thrown up into the air behind him.

As his arc through the misty street came to an end, with his head slamming into the roads jagged surface, he remained conscious long enough to watch a mouthful of his own blood drain out and under his cheek before the lights went out completely.

Kelly propped herself forward on the sofa and glanced to the wall-clock. *Twelve forty-five AM.* She had not expected Matt to stay out so late with Connor, being such a wallflower as he was. In her mind she had pictured him sitting nervously amongst Connor's crowd, silent and attentive, just too shy to interact; ending his night embarrassingly early somewhere along the line, once everyone's drunken volume grew louder around him and the boisterous guys-out-on-the-town behaviour began. Something about that made her smile. His discomfort, she thought. Reliably pathetic.

Still, time was now getting on and, considering the bars were typically shut by midnight, she could not help feeling curious about his non-appearance. It was not concern, she argued with herself. Concern was too emotionally attaching. Curiosity felt more easily justified. She relaxed back into the soft comfort of the sofa, resuming her fingers tender, circular stroking of her erect nipple through her silk camisole as she returned to reading.

The page was turned and had just fallen against its predecessor when a knock echoed through the lounge from the front door.

Kelly sat upright, momentarily confused. Feeling rudely inconvenienced, she moodily shuffled her feet into her slippers, threw her book across the coffee table in annoyance, and marched to the door. With each step accompanied by its own curse word; Kelly grumbled loudly until she reached the front door; unleashing the most aggressive of her outrage directly through the door panel as if to pre-warn Matt, on the other side, of how well he should expect to be received.

"Couldn't you have used your fucking key, you dumb shit?" she shouted. "I could've been in bed for all you know."

Kelly snatched at the lock lever, flicking it downwards with a loud clunk, before grabbing the door handle and yanking it towards her. Her initial grimace immediately turned to open-mouthed shock as she clutched her chest. She felt her knees wobble, coherent words unable to form fully in her mouth. Yet, despite being so outwardly dumbfounded, her mind was a whirr of questions, most notably…where was Matt.

"Hello, young lady" Connor spoke calmly.

Kelly stumbled back a step, mesmerized. Her heart was pounding under her quivering palm, the diamond wedding ring on her finger growing increasingly heavier and tightening.

"It's… it's good to see you… Master", Kelly slowly stammered through her shock.

"May I come in?"

"Will you stay?"

"Ask me nicely."

"Please Master. Stay with me, if you can. My body aches to feel your control over it, and I will do anything you command in return. I've never given in so completely to the will of another, but I *will* do, wholeheartedly, tonight. If you'll stay?"

Connor looked impressed. Kelly felt impressed with herself too, given her initial attack of anxiety. The desperate words of Isla, the submissive from the first Curtis Sharp novel, had come back to her so easily; a character that she had played countless times in her mind.

Connor smiled wryly back at her. He recognised the familiar words too, but did not let on.

"Good girl. Yes. I'll stay."

He reached forward through the doorway, his sleek black suit-jacket hooked under its collar by his upturned forefinger.

"Hang my jacket," he commanded, "and don't let me find it creased later or you'll be collared; do you understand?"

Kelly shuddered at the thought. Not in fear, nor in displeasure. She shuddered in deep anticipation, even knowing that she would have to disobey her master in order to receive his punishment. This, she could see, was to be her hardest challenge. The urge to give him his every desire without question was strong, but nowhere near the desire that she felt at the thought of his skin lashing violently against hers. To achieve this, to have him reach deep down into his primal base, she would have to push his leniency to its breaking point.

Carefully she replaced Connor's forefinger with her own, navigating the jacket onto the nearest of the coat hooks. Today, she thought, was not to be that day.

Turning back, she found Connor had silently stepped into the doorway, his body now inches from hers. He lifted his right hand to Kelly's cheek, his fingers snaking under her left ear, and their soft tips caressing the small hairs near the back of her neck. A shiver ran down Kelly's spine and she inhaled dramatically. Connor's other hand curled around her petite waist, spreading its web of fingers over the small of her back, drawing her disorientated body into his. Still cradling the side of her head, he moved his right thumb to apply pressure under her chin, tilting Kelly's head upwards as he moved closer to lay a soft and lingering, almost romantic kiss onto the soft skin at the hollow of her neck. There; at that moment; he could feel that her whole body was given in to him, and he liked it.

Taking her head by her hair, he pulled it towards him so she came to be looking down at his chest, and kissed her on the forehead. Then, raising her gaze to his again, he smiled.

The look in Kelly's eyes as he stared into them told of unspoken bliss; a dream realised. She was now his, and he knew it.

"This is where your submission begins," he said intensely, "now fetch us both a whiskey; and make them large ones. We're in for a long night."

Chapter Twenty

Connor remained at the door while Kelly shakily poured their drinks at the kitchen counter. She found it odd that he did not make his way past the kitchen doorway and into the lounge; or even join her in the kitchen itself; but she held her tongue in case his inaction had been meant for a reason. The inner workings of a dominant's mind had always fascinated her, no matter how mysterious their actions may have seemed. To Kelly, the act of complete acceptance was one of the most compelling elements to being a submissive. It allowed for spontaneity and a tantalising amount of danger; from what limited experience she had gleaned from in her books, at least. *This time it will be for real*, she told herself, taking an extra shot for Dutch courage directly from the whiskey bottle.

Connor was stood exactly where Kelly had left him when she returned to serve him with his generously filled glass. Newly appeared within the scene though, sitting up at his feet, was a black rucksack which she could not recall having seen previously.

"Sir?" she enquired, gesturing down to it, "What is it?"

"That, my girl, is what I'll bring with me whenever the magic happens. You'll get to know it well, don't worry."

"Sounds intriguing!" Kelly's eyes widened as they clinked their crystal together in celebration. They each took a sip.

"You could call it my toolkit, of sorts. A submissive

can't be commanded without the right equipment, after all. Punishment may often require more than just a firm hand across the backside, which must be considered in advance. There are numerous tools that a dominant should keep to hand. I keep mine in here."

"I understand, Master."

"No; you really don't," he stated, almost condescending, "but you will very soon. Drink."

Kelly obeyed. They each took a further sip. After swallowing the burning liquid with a tight gulp, Connor crouched and placed his glass down onto the floor next to the skirting board. Taking hold of the two prominent zips resting together at the top of the rucksack, he drew them apart and then reached in. Kelly watched him delve with anticipation, until Connor withdrew his hand, this time holding an item within its grasp. At first it was a handle, thin and leather-bound. As it continued to slowly emerge from the open crevice; seeming to be intentionally prolonged by Connor; it grew longer, and much wider. Covered with small metal studs across its flat surface, Kelly had realised it was a spanking paddle just as the rounded top edge of it was brought out into the open. She felt her already quivering legs grow weaker at the sight of it and looked to Connor with concern.

"Turn around", he ordered her before she could question the purpose of its removal.

He rose to his feet and stepped forward aggressively, taking the hair at the back of her head as she turned away from him. She had just enough time to reach into the kitchen doorway and slide her glass onto the corner of the worktop before he pushed her against the wall, his body pressed against hers from the backs of her feet to shoulders. His heavy breathing blew against the lobe of her right ear and, when he finally spoke, he sounded unfamiliar; as though having become a different person.

Kelly trembled as he rasped angrily.

"You knew to expect this, young lady. I warned you that every indiscretion carries a penalty. In my world no punishable act goes unanswered." Grabbing awkwardly at her pyjama shorts, he yanked the silken material down past her buttocks, exposing them to the cold leather paddle cradled further back in his grip.

Kelly struggled to speak. Empty air expelled from her mouth in rapid, shallow bursts, hitting the wall in front of her and warming her face. She had propped her knees forward against the wall below her, the only means of staying upright when all her legs wanted to do were to buckle and send her to the floor. Her forehead fell forward against it too, in a fear-filled acceptance of what was to come. She could see the paddle in her imagination, being toyed from side to side in his hand, waiting to strike.

"Are you ready?" Connor asked, clearly unforgiving and with a tone expectant of an affirmative answer from her.

"Uh... huh..." Kelly muttered between stilted breaths.

"Tell me."

"Ready... Sir... Ready."

"How many do you think you deserve?" he enquired, prolonging her tension.

"Sir... I... err... I don't know... Two?"

"That would be incredibly lenient of me, wouldn't it? I could take into consideration your amateur status, but even then I would be letting you off lightly with only two; don't you think?"

"I can't say... Master. It's... It's your... your right to decide."

"That is *very* true; so very true indeed, my girl. I think, all things considered, you should receive… five. That seems fair to me."

Kelly looked back over her shoulder, her face almost touching Connor's. Her eyes were like open, bottomless wells, their eyelids stretched wide in obvious terror.

"Five, Sir?" she trembled.

"Yes. That's my decision."

Kelly turned forward again, slumping her head against the wall and submitting to his judgement.

"Okay", she whimpered emotionally.

"Okay, what?"

"Okay, Sir... I accept."

"Much better."

Connor took a large stride back, allowing Kelly's crushed upper body to ease away from the wall. Taking a firm grip of her waist in his free hand, he pulled at her to take a step backwards, before guiding her to bend forward at her hips. Planting both palms firmly against the wall beside her resting head, she tipped her weight into the surface of the wall. Connor, unhappy with the close position of her legs, manoeuvred his foot between them at the ankles and applied pressure, urging Kelly to separate them. Then, placing a hand on her lower back to indicate that she stop moving, he raised the paddle high in the air.

"Just to be clear, I never do things unevenly. When I said five, that means five on each side", he informed her at the last second, instantaneously landing the first of the painful strikes down onto her right buttock before she could dare to protest. The loud contact stung both Kelly's backside and ears, sending her yelping against the wall in pain, scratching at its paintwork and clawing at the floor with her curling toes.

"How did that feel, Princess?" Connor asked, stroking the reddening patch of flesh.

"It hurt more than I was expecting, Master", Kelly replied, panting heavily. "But I und-"

A second blow was struck without warning, this time

across her left cheek. It was lighter than the first, but enough to make Kelly cry out again, in shock more than from the pain. Connor moved his other hand up her back, placing it between her shoulder blades to hold her bucking body firmly in place.

"That's two…"

"Master; I don't think I can take another-"

"Three!"

Connor shouted loudly as the paddle found its mark against the cherry-red square of skin. Kelly's legs slumped, dropping her slightly.

"Don't stop me now, young lady," he continued, "this is where it gets oh so much better for you."

"Sir?"

"Those sexy patches of throbbing flesh are gonna be all but numb in about a minutes time. Then you'll see how pleasurable a good spanking can really be. Now if I can just…"

The fourth spank was to be his hardest yet, hard enough even to make himself wince as he landed it with unrestrained vigour. Kelly's entire rump jolted forward with the impact, its softer areas rippling like waves towards her hips. Connor drew closer behind her, his excited breaths flowing into the depths of her ear.

"It seemed a shame to not get one more juicy one in before it gets too pleasurable for you", he said huskily. "A punishment can only be satisfying for as long as the sensitivity lasts. Then there's no point continuing. Have you learnt your lesson, young lady?"

"Yes, Master", Kelly replied, biting her lower lip as his voice reverberated around her skull.

"I very much hope so."

He took her by the arm, spinning her around to face him. Taking her cheek in his hand once more, he stroked her face lovingly.

"Now get upstairs", he ordered her calmly.

"Please may I ask one question, Master? Just one, I promise."

"You may."

"How is... *this*... possible? You're confident we won't be caught, and without question I'm yours to take if that's the case, but I'd like to be sure myself."

"We won't be caught, I can guarantee that. Matt is... well; let's just say he won't be in a state to come home until sometime tomorrow."

"Where is he?"

"That's a second question."

"I know, Sir it's just not clear what you mean by-"

Connor folded his shirt's wrist back and glanced at his watch.

"Right about now Matt will be checking in for the night at St Miriam's. And trust me, Princess; once they've given him some attention, he's going to need some serious bed rest. We have from now until whenever you receive a call. As we don't know when that will be, I suggest you don't waste any further time."

Kelly stood in shock for a few seconds. Her head became swarmed by graphic images, each depicting a possibility of what could have happened earlier that night. Matt was a born peacekeeper; she knew that. She could see the fear that he would have experienced under any level of threat within her mind's eye, and felt somewhat taken aback by its chilling effect as she momentarily found herself living within his skin. Slowly focussing back into Connor's stern eyes though, she suddenly became aware of a growing sense of apathy. At that moment she lost all feeling, with the thought of Matt fading painlessly into a cold detached compartment of her soul, its door locked securely behind him. Connor's lips were now all she could see, and she desperately wanted them against hers. With a sudden loss of restraint she leant forward and took them passionately, pressing her body against Connor's with abandon until he would tell her to stop. She was surprised to find he allowed it for longer than she anticipated. By the time he finally did separate from her, she was already removing her pyjama top. Connor grabbed her by her closest wrist.

"Did I tell you I wanted that yet?"

"No... But I could tell you-"

Connor raised the paddle to his waist, first ensuring the movement caught her eye, and then began to land sinister taps onto his opposite, outstretched palm.

"You could tell *what* about me, exactly; young lady?" he asked angrily between two deafening slaps.

Kelly paused, thinking. The determined voice in her head screamed for her to take control of the situation. She looked up to Connor, and then down to the repetitive sway of his paddle-hand. A lump raised in her throat as the numbness in her backside began to subside, retreating to unmask the true throbbing pain that lay beneath the skin. Cowardice soon became the overbearing voice between her ears.

"Nothing, Master; I'm sorry."

Connor snatched forward and gripped his wide fingers around her throat, lifting her up onto her toes and squeezing.

"A good sub follows instructions," he growled breathily down onto her face, "and it's disappointing me that you don't appear to be paying any attention to mine so far."

"I'm sorry," Kelly stifled, begging him through watering eyes, "I promise; I'll do better."

"What exactly do I have to do to you, to make you understand your fucking place?"

"I'll behave, Sir. Pleeeease!" she implored him,

clawing at his hand half-heartedly. At that same time, inside her chest, her heart was a contradiction. It beat mercilessly against her rib-cage, burning with the waves of adrenaline that coursed relentlessly around it as she struggled to contain her intense thrill.

Connor's grip loosened causing Kelly to slump back down in front of him. Outstretching his arm, he pointed towards the staircase and barked at her.

"Get your fucking arse up there and behave."

Chapter Twenty-One

The ambulance screeched to a halt outside the paramedic's entrance to St Miriam's Hospital. Inside, strapped to a gurney and unconscious, Matt lay stripped to his waist with his top half covered in blood. The driver hastily climbed out from its cab and rushed to the back entrance, swung the doors open and reached for the gurneys metal frame, unclipping its wheel-lock and dragging it towards him. The frames underbelly fell out to support it as the paramedic and his colleague steered it free and onto the pathway, headed for the entrance. They were joined by two female emergency nurses sprinting out through the hospitals automatic doors to assist in their patient's delivery.

"What's his stats?" the first to reach them asked.

"Male; estimated mid-thirties. Found laid in the road, looks like severe head trauma and probable dislocated shoulder. Bruising around the waist is consistent with collision; unable to rule out spinal injury so far. Seriously; if he hadn't been found in the street I would have sworn he'd been in a car accident. BP eighty-two over fifty."

"Shit; really? Even for a slender guy like him, that's low."

"I took a second reading just to be sure, but that's what it is. Breathing has remained shallow. Unresponsive to stimuli."

The small group cleared their way down the entrances long thin corridor, turning left at its far end, through a pair of translucent plastic doors and into an expansive emergency ward. Matt's gurney was spun into place between two others, where the group were joined by two doctors. Each looking over Matt's battered body from opposite sides, they pushed and teased at his body in order to make their assessments. The informed nurse stepped forward, leant over the foot of the bed, and relayed the paramedic's information to them, which they listened to intently. The doctor to the right of the gurney turned his head as he heard Matt's blood pressure rate, his eyebrow raised in concern.

"Get this man on an I.V." he prompted. "Any worse and he'll go hypotensive, so best we tackle that first. Greg?"

The talkative paramedic leaned his head in closer. "Yep, Doc?"

"Greg, you and your boy have done well to keep this fellow stable. Get his legs up; find some pillows. Then you can sign off and be on your way, there a good chap. I've got a bit of work to do with this guy's face in the meantime."

"Do you think you can sort it, Doc? He's banged up pretty good. I thought for a while his jaw might have been broken."

"Greg, my boy; don't worry. By the time I'm finished with him, even his own mother won't recognise him!"

"I'm pretty sure you know that's not what I meant."

"No? You mean you actually want me to keep this poor sod looking like he always did?"

"Is that not usually the plan?" Greg chuckled.

"I dunno; I've always liked the idea of throwing in a touch of *cosmetic* into the old reconstructive surgery. For all we know this chap might have been wanting to change his life for the last decade, and there's you telling him he can't? Jesus; Greg. You can be such a spoilsport sometimes!"

Connor fixed the second of Kelly's ankles to the metal bed frame with a tight knot, tugging on it to assure himself of its sturdiness. Behind her head, one arm lay similarly tied, the other draped casually across her stomach. Connor had made her remove her pyjama shorts, but her top remained. He leaned further over her to hook his fingers under its material, stretching it up and over the two curvaceous mounds, exposing her how *he* wanted.

"That's better", he said, stepping back to admire his work; stroking and tweaking at the zip of his black trousers. Kelly watched him closely, craning her neck forward to see. She was desperate to ask him to remove them, but every way possible to make her request played out unsuccessfully in her mind, so she resorted to keeping her mouth shut and simply smiling through the urge.

Connor reached beside Kelly's feet to his rucksack. Behind the lowest zip on its front, within the smallest pocket, his fingers wormed their way around until he withdrew a small plastic tube. Kelly's strained peering made focussing over the distance patchy at best. It was only when Connor approached at her side, perching himself near her waist on the bed, that she could see the tube more clearly, and its white, powdery contents.

"Hold still", Connor ordered.

He carefully twisted the small plastic screwcap from the vessel, held it over Kelly's left breast, and then tapped at its rim to sprinkle a thick line of the cocaine across her blushing areola. Turning the cap firmly back in place, he lay the tube on the bedside cabinet and lowered his head, choosing to start his approach from Kelly's midriff. He trailing his thick, saliva soaked tongue across her sensitive skin, his face coming into view after five seconds or so of its teasing, hovering with his eyes just above the curve of her rounded flesh. With an animalistic pounce, he raised himself up in the air and came back down with inconsiderate force, making sure to land the centre of his face over the white line landing-strip of his own making. Kelly flinched downwards against the mattress as she felt the crushing pain of her muscles and mammary gland being pressed so hard inwardly that she thought her ribs might break. If not for her lung forcibly emptying and the sudden rush of air expelling from her mouth, she would have screamed. Connor obliviously continued to grind his face into her skin. His hungry nostrils vacuumed her pinkest flesh clear, whereupon he switched to encasing her nipple within his open mouth and sucking hard on it, making *'pock'* sounds each time he broke his suctioned seal. Kelly was dismayed, unsure of what part of this process she was supposed to be enjoying. *Or maybe that's the point*, she told herself. *Maybe it's not about you; and you're selfish to think it should be.*

Returning to his upright seated position, Connor reached for the tube again, this time tapping a neat line out across the length of his index finger. He kept hold of the tube within his opposite hand; cautious of fumbling the lid back on with the limited use of the other; and extended his white coated finger towards Kelly, hovering it under her nose, gesturing for her to take it.

"This one's for you", he encouraged her

"I've never taken drugs, Master. It's one thing I've never thought of trying."

"Well then that's something we'll have to change, isn't it!"

"It's just… I'm in no rush to try them either, Master."

"You can't say that when you don't realise how it'll enhance your sensations. Cocaine has an effect like you wouldn't believe; seriously."

"That may be so, Sir, but I-"

Kelly neck was forced back once more, her head pinned down onto her pillow before she realised Connor had even moved. He climbed over her restrained body, dropping his knees to her sides and placing his weight on her upper stomach, shifting his mass to dig himself into her torso as deeply as possible. Kelly's discomfort was written across her face in a grimace.

"I suggest; if you'd like me to make you more comfortable again; you'll do as I say, young lady."

Connor held his finger under Kelly's nose, sliding it from left to right and back again, waiting for her next obligatory draw of breath. When she crudely sucked a mouthful in through a crack in the corner of her mouth it enraged him, slamming his other hand down over her mouth to restrict it. For a while Kelly continued to struggle, writhing against the bed and moving her head as much as she could from side to side. Submission was one thing, but the enforced consumption of drugs was another entirely, one which she staunchly felt that Connor had no right to impose on her. As the absence of fresh air in her lungs became apparent, however, her demeanour inevitably changed. Her body eased into the bedcovers and her eyes became glazed, in an almost accepting way. She looked up at Connor, imploring him to release her, but after another five seconds of his ignorance she relented, drawing a desperate breath of air in through her flared nostrils. The line of powder trailed away from Connor's finger; each flake breaking from the rest as it was swept up by the inward tide of air. As the initial effects took hold; numbness in her teeth and throat; a warmth building in her lungs accompanied by a sparkling surge of adrenaline; she stared into Connor's eyes self-righteously. A final controlled act to show him that he had not truly won the battle.

Connor looked back at her indifferently. He could not care less about her lacklustre defiance. All he could think about was how Kelly's state would alter over the forthcoming few minutes; for the better. Then they would have their fun.

Chapter Twenty-Two

Kelly lay bathed in blissful euphoria, her muscles relaxed to the extent that they made her feel as though she were cheating gravity. Her reactions were sluggish; each turn of her head, or restrained movement of her limbs, weightless and in noticeably slower motion. The raw pain in the skin beneath her had long since been subdued by the cocaine invading her nervous system; cheating it of its natural ability to feel.

Before her, keeping a close eye on her changing condition, stood Connor. During his brief wait he had used the time to remove his small array of equipment from the rucksack, lining the items at her feet in size order - smallest to largest – and had begun considering their usage for when he felt the time was right. Kelly; low down on the mattress; rolled her disorientated head to its side, allowing her to see the ordered sequence through her misty right eye.

"What do you have there, Master?" she slurred, grinning absurdly.

"Do you know something? You have the oddest reaction to cocaine, Blondie. Everyone I've ever met who takes it goes hyper to the point of annoyance. But you, it seems, go the opposite way which… in itself… is kind of annoying to me too."

"Ooops! Well maybe that's because it's my first time and I wasn't expecting it." Kelly eked out as much sarcasm as her slowly processing brain would allow.

"Hmm; perhaps, but that doesn't mean you have the right to speak so disrespectfully. To answer your question… what I have here are the tools of my dominance. My armoury so to speak; to facilitate my delivery of either pleasure or pain, whichever I deem most befitting to your behaviour."

Kelly extended her toe, pointing it towards the item at the larger end of the row.

"And that? What the fuck is that?" she asked.

All she could make out was a gnarled lump of black rubber, its length too hard to gauge from her low viewpoint, but clear to her that its weight was considerable as it lay there depressing the mattress near her feet.

Connor picked up the paddle from the beds surface, raising it to his side.

"I won't warn you again, young lady. Watch your language. Do you understand?"

Kelly's head lost its woozy sensation in an instant, as if rediscovering the situation that she was in. She had clearly overstepped the mark, and she began to tremble at the thought of a second series of beatings.

"I'm sorry, Sir; very sorry. I lost myself for a moment" she spoke honestly.

"This item... will go back in the bag for now. There's a time and a place for its use, and that time will not be tonight. It's for when I feel at my most... unforgiving."

Connor scooped the large rubber lump from its indent, briefly raising it high enough for Kelly to see it more clearly. She baulked as she realised it was a dildo of some sort; as thick as a wine bottle but with the added threat of large studs dotted around its entire length and circumference, each about the size of a small marble. Its grip was unconventional, extending from its back end like the handle of a machete, Kelly imagined. It looked impossibly fierce to be a sex toy, shooting a wave of fear through her even as Connor raised his rucksack to the bed and slid it back inside.

"Take your free hand and show me how you pleasure yourself", Connor instructed as he placed the bag back down at his feet with a heavy thud.

Kelly obeyed, shakily lowering her hand between her thighs. Connor stepped back, propping his body against the far wall to watch. Within moments Kelly could feel the familiar warming surge forming in the pit of her stomach, drifting rapidly down towards her feet. The first of the fireworks were being lit, preparing to launch and shoot through her body in delightful, explosive bursts. Her eyes remained fixed in Connor's direction as she readied herself, lowering them further down his body to where his hand moved rhythmically against the material of his trousers. Her bottom lip curled inwards, held pinched under her teeth, so hard that she felt the soft fleshy pillow might puncture if she bit down any harder.

Connor was moving more now, unbuttoning his white shirt and letting it fall from the backs of his shoulders. In the dim light Kelly could see each muscle in his torso becoming visible, toned to perfection and smooth underneath his taut skin. She felt near; so near she thought she might not last long; but knowing that she had to for her own sanity's sake. She needed to see him in his entirety.

His leather belt was loosened now, the trousers' buttons worked free from their eyelets, as he spread the two sides of the waist area apart to reveal tight black boxer shorts. Kelly pulled her wickedly dancing fingers free, to be set to work against her small sensitive button for the final stretch towards reaching her climax. Her near-soaked fingertip encircled it, hardening it even more, as a slow trickle of sticky nectar ran down her finger like a constant aide to its rotating journey.

Connor's trousers fell to the floor before her. He approached the bed as her speed increased; her heart pounding in her chest; intermittent breaths becoming shallow and wheezy. A short moan escaped her lips as Connor reached for both sides of his waistband and hooked them away from his body. The front lowered teasingly at first; their intense suggestion leading Kelly to feel a burst inside her so strong that she could not stem the tide any further. She let out a throaty groan as the muscles in her legs and buttocks tightened, shaking violently underneath her, all the while maintaining a quivering gaze over Connor; though her mind urged for her to close her eyes and revel in the pure sensation.

Connor slid the boxer shorts down the front of his thighs, allowing then to drop to his ankles, and took a step forward out of them. As his naked pelvis became clearer to Kelly's still slightly blurred vision, she was hit by a sudden loss in momentum within her. At first she did not believe her eyes, leaning forward as much as her neck would allow to look over him again. She had not been mistaken; she discovered. Still; the preconception that she had lived by for so long, having been so different from the now *actual* truth, caused her to question her own sight.

Connor was, and had always come across as, supremely confident. And yet, looking at him now; naked and standing proud with his erection poked forward in front of her, Kelly felt a shattering pang of utter disappointment. She judged him to be three inches long at best, and thin; much thinner than she had ever encountered; even when flaccid. Around it grew the only part of his body left unshaven. With his seemingly arrogant posturing; hands firmly gripping his waist and thrusting the area self-assuredly towards her; she assumed he must have been proud of his thick mane of brown wiry pubic hair, regardless that it rose up so abundantly that it obscured two thirds of his diminutive member's length from view.

Having selected a black handled whip from his toolkit, Connor pushed the rest of the items to one side and clambered onto the bed at Kelly's feet. He flicked his wrist, sending the leather coil out to his side, its multiple talons unravelling as they fell through the air. He shuffled his weight to find comfort on his knees, as he swung the length through the air by its thickly bound grip, pulling it down sharply to land simultaneous strikes across Kelly's tender thighs. She winced at first, but felt a small sense of relief as the electric sensation slowly gained momentum within her once again. To quicken its progress further, she closed her eyes to Connor, preferring to imagine him as she had long since anticipated him to be. A guiding steer from Connors rough hand pulled her over, onto her side; twisting her arms above her until she found herself laid on her front, with her arms crossed awkwardly over each other. Although mildly greater in discomfort, she felt safer then, to open her eyes and enjoy the sadistic experience her Master wished to bestow upon her. A further series of lashes landed against the already inflamed patches of buttock skin, igniting them with a ruthless efficiency, sending her heartbeat racing once more.

'*More*' - her inner voice begged him – '*Give me more*!'

To her dismay Connor's attacks abruptly ceased after just two more strikes. Unable to turn her head far enough around to see why, she sunk her head into the pillow and waited, fighting to control her growing impatience. She could feel him repositioning behind her; his weight moving up the bed as his knees brushed against the inside of her legs, separating them. Suddenly, two firm hands landed against her buttocks. He was forcing them wide, stretching the delicate skin at their centre, when Kelly felt him slide himself forward as closely as he could get between them.

His penetration was despairingly shallow, but she felt it. He ground enthusiastically down onto her in his eagerness to reach deeper, a task that Kelly; trying hard not to think about his meagre size; found laughable to envisage. His thrusts were excessively powerful, jutting Kelly's hips hard into the mattress, relentless yet unfulfilling. Kelly lay still, unsure what she should do in order to improve her state of dissatisfaction. In a moment of clarity, between two of Connor's heavily impacting thrusts, she reached back with her free hand to touch his franticly lunging hips. Craning her head around as far as it allowed, she looked pleadingly into his eyes, urging him to bring more additional force.

"Spank me, Master. Hit me again with your whip. Hurt me, please!"

Connor looked up from his thrusts; excited by her imploring request, yet oblivious to the reason for its necessity. The first beads of sweat were seeping profusely from his forehead and chest, his breath now raucous and gravelly as if obstructed. He reached to his side, grabbing the whip and raising it into the air again.

Leaning forward awkwardly in order to remain tucked inside of her, Connor's splayed hand pressed painfully onto the small of Kelly's back, steadying himself before swinging his other arm vigorously. He brought the whip down with a loud *crack* across the midpoint of Kelly's back. She screamed, her body shuddering intensely and lurching forward up the bed. Connor felt himself separate from her, his erection squeezed free as Kelly's vaginal muscles tightened and her weight shifted away from him. Incensed, he threw the whip furiously to the floor, pouncing on her lower body and pinning it down. Reaching up to grab at the wild straggles of hair at the nape of Kelly's neck, he shoved his other hand down to his groin, taking his penis and fumbling it into her again, this time misjudging his position and belligerently entering her anus by mistake. Once inside he shoved hard against her, lurching forward on his knees to ensure that Kelly's body had nowhere to go.

The painful, uncontrolled yanking of her thin wispy hairs gave Kelly some pleasure, but she was shocked to find Connor's rapid abuse of her backside unexpectedly pleased her more than she had ever considered it could. She remembered back to when Matt had first attempted, at her bequest. Back then it had been painful; his significantly larger equipment struggling to squeeze into her until she had finally forced him away from her in angered frustration. Coming back to the moment, however, she allowed Connor to continue unrestrained; his few inches feeling much less threatening; more suited to her tight orifice.

Kelly watched the bedside clock as Connor continued to pound single-mindedly into her rear. After three minutes, she felt his body stiffen against hers; his dead-weight falling over her, pushing the air from her lungs, as he wheezed and grunted against the back of her head. A flood of warmth seeped into her as he ejaculated noisily, before the dying spasms of his softening erection tapped at her inner walls.

Sliding away from her body, Connor fell onto the mattress at Kelly's side, landing with his head on the neighbouring pillow and his face two inches from hers. His eyes reflected his brutal exhaustion. Kelly's showed indifference, as she tried her best to hide her abject disappointment. *Maybe in a few minutes he'll be ready for more*, she desperately justified to herself. Connor ended her hope immediately, leaning forward to unshackle her wrist before placing a half-hearted kiss on her lips.

"Wake me up no later than four-thirty; or earlier if my phone rings."

Kelly glared at him with a look as if to say '*are you serious?*' but her expression was met by Connor's drooping eyelids. In less than a minute the room echoed with his snores. Kelly leant forward, untied her legs from the beds metal frame, and then laid back down onto the bed facing the ceiling. She sighed, depressed, into the darkness. After setting her mobile phones alarm for four-thirty, she drifted into sleep.

By the time her alarm rang out, terrorising her loudly from her deep sleep, Connor had left. Kelly rose from the indented hollow of the mattress and walked slowly down through the house, discovering that his things were gone. A cursory glance out of the kitchen window revealed his car to be missing from the parking bays opposite. Feeling somewhat confused, she climbed back up the stairs and slid back under the covers, unsure of whether it had all been a bad dream. A growing burning sensation deep under the parts of her body that Connor had spanked and whipped told her that it had not been. Still; she wished it had.

Chapter Twenty-Three

Bright white overhead lights blinded Matt even before he could open his eyes. When he eventually did; following a short period of time spent struggling to focus them; he realised he was laid on a metal framed bed within a private hospital room. Sparsely furnished, the room contained the single bed, a small plastic chair on which his clothes from the night before lay folded, and an inactive wall-mounted television, under which sat a second, empty chair.

Though still dazed, he repositioned himself in an attempt to look around. Each slow movement caused him a sharp, intense ache, in places he had never known could. Staring into the chilly silence, indistinct memories of the previous night began to drift into place, as a piercing headache ignited and spread across the entire width of his forehead. He lay his rapidly spinning head back down onto the thin pillows, cradling it in his hands, when he spotted a buzzer attached to a cable beside him on the bed. He pressed on it desperately. A few seconds later he was joined in the room by a red-headed twenty-something nurse, smiling pleasantly at him as she adjusted his bed.

Kelly awoke with a jump to the sound of her phone ringing loudly beside her. She grabbed it, noticing that the caller was unknown, but that it originated from a local number. Taking a moment to compose herself, she swiped to accept the call, and placed the phone to her ear.

"Hello?" she trembled.

"He's just come around, Princess. Not sure of his

condition yet, but I'll be going in to see him soon. I'll let you know."

"Okay, Master. Thank you. I suppose I should get ready anyway. I expect I'll have to go in and visit him."

"Well it would certainly seem suspicious if you didn't. I'll have to stay here anyway; the police have just arrived and they're talking about asking the both of us some questions. If nothing else, at least you'll get to see me."

"And you'll see me" Kelly smiled down the line.

"Yeah;" Connor said coldly, "Just… get yourself ready. I'll call you again soon."

Kelly was left feeling stung by the abrupt click of the call being disconnected.

The friendly nurse helped Matt sit his bruised body back against a stack of fresh, plumper pillows.

"I can give you some morphine for that head if you like?" she asked, observing his pain through the tight squint of his eyes. "I think you deserve it! Plus it won't be long until your body starts to give you some serious grief over the rest of that damage."

"Thank you; I'd appreciate that. The stronger the better."

Matt felt a sickening wave of nausea start at the back of his skull, like icy hands wrapping themselves around the sides of his head, their creeping fingers meeting just above his brow. His skin tightened with the sensation of the ice cold tingling; his face contorted in discomfort.

"Close your eyes, breathe steadily, and concentrate on pushing it away. Give it a few minutes and it will ease" the nurse encouraged. "It's natural to get a bit queasy when your bodies been through the mill to the extent yours has. Once your brain has come to terms with the shock you'll be just fine."

Matt did as he was instructed, rhythmically filling his cheeks with air and then puffing it out as he tucked his shoulders back into the pillows for an increased sense of support.

"I'll leave you in peace for a short while honey; to let your head settle. I won't be long though. When I come back you should be ready enough for the morphine."

The nurse placed a liver shaped cardboard tray beside him on the bed.

"Just in case" she said in a caring tone.

As she left the room Matt, focussing on battling his instinct to vomit, nodded languidly in silent gratitude.

It was no more than a minute later when the door swung open again and a loud voice popped Matt's sedating bubble.

"Hey, Bruiser!" Connor boomed in his usual gregarious fashion.

Matt slowly turned his head to him, looking pale and unamused.

"Jeee-sus, take a look at you!" Connor spluttered. "They really did a number on ya, huh buddy?"

Matt looked Connor up and down, growing puzzled.

"You were... I thought you..." he stammered breathlessly, growing disorientated as the nauseating waves crashed back over him with renewed intensity.

"Looks like I got off lightly! I mean; that big fella took me down first, so I never got to see how badly you got taken attacked. I'm not trying to make it worse or anything, but you look as if they took some serious time and pleasure while doing it."

"Thanks... I guess?"

"Sorry; I know I must sound a little uncouth. How are you feeling?"

"Like two big fucking gorillas took turns feeding me into a road!"

Matt looked over Connor in continued disbelief.

"I can't believe you came away from that without even so much as a bruise on your face! That mountain of a guy had you down on the floor and must've punched you at least a half a dozen times."

"I don't know, maybe it's just that I've just seen my way through a few more fights in my time than you have. But that doesn't make me the lucky one. That just makes me the stupid one! Maybe this time I was just lucky; who knows. I wish I could've stuck up for you a bit longer than they let me; that's all!"

"You shouldn't blame yourself, Connor. It's not your fault."

"I know. I guess it's just natural to feel a little guilty when your friend's laying in a hospital bed all beat up. Just concentrate on getting yourself back on your feet; okay mate?"

"Would you mind getting a hold of Kelly for me?"

"Whatever you need me to do, buddy. Kelly doesn't know yet?"

"I don't think anyone's thought to contact her. My phone's still in my trouser pocket, from what I can tell."

Connor walked closer beside Matt and reached down to the pile of clothes, fishing the mobile phone from the trousers pocket.

"I'll have to take it out with me. Obviously I don't have Kelly's number on my phone, and I can't use a mobile phone inside the hospital anyways."

"Yeah, no problem. Just bring-"

Matt stopped abruptly as the nauseating waves became too much and his chest began to heave. Concentrating, he caught his stomach muscles each time they tensed, somehow retaining the barest of control over them.

"Look, I'm gonna go and make this call. You just

rest up for now. The police are out in the waiting area. They want to have a word, but the nurses have said they can't until you're feeling considerably better. They want to speak to me at the same time too, so I'll be hanging around. I'll see you again in a little while, alright Champ?"

Connor convivially slapped Matt's shoulder, ignorant to the fact that he was barely maintaining his composure. The sudden shove caused a rumbling groan to erupt from Matt's throat as he finally lost his thin grasp on control. The contents of his stomach rose up and shot out from his mouth in an arc, spraying over Connor's legs and down onto his shoes. Connor reeled back in horror, looking down at his soiled clothes, open-mouthed and speechless with disgust.

Looking across to Connor pitifully from his bed, Matt lethargically wiped the corner of his mouth with the arm of his hospital gown.

"Sorry buddy," he began to smirk ironically. "Looks like you didn't get off so lightly after all!"

Kelly approached the hospital entrance to find a dishevelled Connor puffing angrily on his fourth cigarette. He was stood uncomfortably, his body tilted forward slightly, constantly pulling at his wet trouser legs to stop them from resting against his skin. Their material was still visibly sodden, stained a mixture of vibrant green and pinkish-red. His shoes, wiped hastily clean-ish, had dried with thick smears and still contained remnants of the vomit within their stitching. Looking over the sorry sight as she drew closer, Kelly didn't know whether to feel sympathy or laugh out loud. She composed herself as they met, knowing that she could only take one of those options seriously.

"Are you okay, Master?" she asked dutifully, careful

to avoid the ears of the other hospital-door smokers.

"I'm okay. The suit's pretty much ruined, but such is life I guess. It's fuckin' gross being stuck in it though, and the police still haven't spoken to us yet. Matt needs to hurry the fuck up so I can go home and get changed!"

"I'll go straight in and see him. Give him a nudge in the right direction."

"Listen, and listen well. Once we're inside you're not my sub, regardless of how good last night was. You're his wife. You do understand that, don't you?"

Kelly looked at Connor with a tinge of sarcasm, restraining the actual amount of it that she wished she could vent. In her mind she was screaming at him *'Of course I know that! I'm not a fucking idiot! Wait; what? You thought last night was-'*

"I understand, Sir. I won't make any mistakes" she spoke calmly, pushing her internal bemusement to one side.

"Good girl. Now come on..." He threw his cigarette butt into the road and grabbed Kelly by the wrist, half dragging her through the doors. "I'll show you where Mr Fuckin' Feeble is."

"I'm sorry, Officer", said a stern looking middle-aged nurse, firmly blocking the door to Matt's room, "but it's been less than an hour since he came around, and we have had to administer further pain relief for his injuries. Until we're sure that they are working, it would be highly inconsiderate of me to allow you to proceed with your questioning!"

The middle-aged male policeman frowned, shaking his head as he walked back to his female colleague. He joined her in the half-filled waiting area, crossing his arms emphatically as he churlishly slumped down into the plastic seating.

The nurse was just taking a step away from the door when Kelly approached her.

"I'm told my husband is in there" she stated bluntly.

"Mrs Buchanon?"

"Yes, that's correct."

"Hello Mrs Buchanon. I'm Charge Nurse Brenda Ormerod. I'm responsible for the running of this ward. I've been heavily involved since your husband was brought in."

"How is he?"

"Well he's awake, and for the most part he's not showing any signs of what we might term as significant injuries. He did wake up with a lot of pain though, and it may take him a few days to regain his flexibility as the various stages of bruising come out. I'm afraid he's not a pretty sight right at this moment, however a lot of it is purely superficial, and the rest will heal. Considering the horrendous event he's been through, he's come out the other side like a true fighter. Would you like to briefly go in and see him?"

The male officer, listening intently to their distant conversation, eagerly raised up out of his seat. Nurse Ormerod, turning to him with an intense glare, raised her forefinger as if cautioning him not to test her patience. Heeding the mute warning, the officer immediately sat back down, to the irritating sound of his colleague's giggles.

"Yes, please" Kelly confirmed.

Chapter Twenty-Four

Matt looked up as he spotted the door opening to his left and the raucous noise from the waiting area outside flooded in. Standing there rigidly, with a face torn by her clearly mixed emotions, was Kelly. She looked to him with what appeared to be anguish throughout the lower and more upper contours of her face; her mouth wide open in shock, her forehead rippling as she slowly perused the extent of his visible damage. Her eyes betrayed her though; clearly tinged with a glare of criticism, as though disappointed – in *him* – to find him in such a state as he was.

Matt; without having received his anticipated swoop of Kelly's protective arms and long, passionate hug; found himself struggling to determine how exactly to engage with her. It was as though the situation changed nothing. He was back to being unsure of her indecipherable mood.

In reality, Kelly was in a state of shock. A heavy wave of guilt was passing through her at finally witnessing Matt's widespread injuries. Her growing sense of personal responsibility for every one of them gnawed at her; making her stomach turn, and a discomforting shiver run up her spine, where it paused to mingle its knotting fingers into the base of her neck. *You did this* - the lesser heard and more often ignored voice of her conscience accused her.

"Hey Baby", Matt said tentatively.

"Hey."

"I know I look a mess."

"That's an understatement! After Connor told me

you were here I came rushing in, but I had no idea it was so..." she paused.

"It looks worse than it feels, sweetheart; don't worry."

"The nurse out there told me that too, but she said the worst of it's yet to come. Things will get worse before they get better, I'm afraid."

"Well I'm still breathing, that's the main thing."

"Yeah; that's the positive way to look at it, I suppose."

"I'm not so badly hurt that you can't come over here and give me a kiss, you know?"

Kelly treaded slowly over the linoleum-tiled floor, concentrating hard on keeping the guilty sensation; still twisting in the pit of her stomach; from acquiring the freedom to spread further. Her mouth was watering with the potential to vomit as she closed her eyes and placed her lips against Matt's, pressing them together. Not noticing Matt's shift in weight onto his side, she was surprised to feel his arms come around her sides and lock him into her, tightly. Her instinct told her to push him away; the battle of contradictory thoughts in her head sending her into a confused panic. She let him hold her there for twenty seconds or so, and then reached up to brush at his hair with her fingers, hoping to signify her readiness to separate from his embrace. As though seeming to take her hint, Matt loosened his grip and brought himself away from her by a few inches. Kelly was startled by this. His usually needy nature meant that he had never been the one to break a cuddle; a trait which had always grinded on her.

"Are you ok?" Matt asked, looking concerned. "You're looking a bit green around the gills."

"I just... I just don't like hospitals, Matt. They always make me feel queasy."

"Have a seat up here."

Matt shuffled his body across the narrow, single bed, ignoring his wounded body's numerous objections. He patted the now clear area beside him, where Kelly joined him, perched half on and half off the thin mattress.

"I'm sorry for worrying you, sweetheart. I literally woke up here, Connor popped in to see how I was doing not long after that, then I got him to call you. From the way I felt when I woke up it was pretty easy to tell that I wouldn't simply be walking out of here straight away, otherwise I wouldn't have suggested getting you out of bed. Did you sleep okay?"

Kelly stared at him, curiously. "Yes; why?" she asked.

"Connor said that when he managed to get hold of you, you sounded whipped. I thought maybe you'd had one of your bad nights?"

"No..." she paused again, angry with Connor's frivolously dangerous use of language, but with her busy mind refocusing to the memories of their time together; both the good and the bad. Suddenly she remembered her instructions; her real purpose for being there.

"Speaking of Connor... you really did a number on his suit, huh!"

"Yeah, but it wasn't as if I could help it. My head was really messed up earlier, a lot more than it is now. I think the meds the nurse gave me have started to kick in now. I'm still feeling a little woozy though."

"The poor guy's out there with your messed up head all over his trousers. He's having to wait for the police to take a statement from you first before he can give them his and then get home. You could at least let them get that out of the way and give him a chance to get cleaned up."

"I don't mean to sound unfair, honey; I feel sorry for him and all; but there isn't much that's come back to me yet, at least not very clearly."

Kelly grew frustrated. Matt could feel the change in her body as it tensed next to his.

"If you can't remember everything perfectly after this past couple of hours, then who's to say you'll remember any of it today. Or tomorrow for that matter? You'll just have to tell them what you can for now, and they'll tell you if they think they'll need to follow up later down the line, won't they?"

Matt's heart rate quickened. He could feel it in his chest and in the sides of his head as Kelly's insistence pushed him into a corner. From the small glass panel of the door came a series of light knocks. Kelly and Matt both looked over as Charge Nurse Ormerod held the door ajar.

"The police are eager to take a short statement from you, if you're feeling up to it?"

"Yeah, he's fine." Kelly said on behalf of Matt, before he could have a chance to speak.

"Mr Buchanon? Is that okay?" the nurse asked, tilting her head to look directly at him around Kelly's obstructive arm.

Kelly turned back and shot Matt an insistent glare. Leaning down to his ear she whispered sternly.

"I want to go home, Matt. I don't want to be in this fuckin' place a minute more than I have to be."

Matt nodded his forced approval to the nurse, the small movement sending his head into another queasy spin. He felt unready in himself, but he could not deny that he would rather be more comfortable recuperating at home too.

"Okay, but let me know if those meds start to wear off at any point. The police can wait."

"Thank you, nurse!" Kelly said aloud, powdering her words with obvious sarcasm.

The matriarchal fifty-something returned the backwards compliment with a sarcastic smile rich in her own sass, sending a furrowed scowl rapidly across Kelly's face. Switching to show a smile more genuinely kinder, she nodded back to Matt, and then left the room. Through the small glass rectangle Matt watched as she approached the pair of seated officers and instructed them of his willingness to proceed. They had rose from their plastic chairs and were beginning to draw closer, adjusting their cumbersome layers of uniform and removing notepads from their pockets, when Connor stepped into Matt's view and inexplicably stopped the pairs approach.

"All this time you've been waiting there and not one of you considered that you could've been taking my statement!" he confronted them.

The younger of the two, a female officer, started to speak.

"Sir; if you wouldn't mind taking a seat and-"

"Great! More waiting! Trousers and shoes swimming in someone else's puke, and I get to *hang around*. Awesome! Any idea how long I'm gonna have to sit here for?"

"Sir; we have a gentleman in there; an apparent friend of yours, no less; who has sustained serious injuries. Now; to speak frankly, you have no visible injuries, and I'm led to believe that you have not requested any medical attention. I do appreciate that you've been here some time, and your statement *will* be taken as soon as possible but, for the time being, I'm going to have to ask that you stay on the hospital grounds and be patient until we've had a chance to talk to your friend."

Connor slumped down into the nearest seat, shaking his head while exhaling lengthily in disgust.

The two officers entered the room. The first of them; taller and older than his colleague, and carrying an air of seniority; made his introductions while the female; elegantly thin under her bulky uniform and topped by hazel coloured, loosely curled locks as if she had just emerged from a hair salon; closed the door firmly behind them. Though dainty, both Matt and Kelly could tell from her exuding demeanour that she was no pushover.

"Special Constable Malcolm Hogwood, and this is Senior Officer Kirsten Dallery."

"Pleased to meet you;" Matt replied nervously, "I'm Matthew Buchanon, and this is my wife, Kelly.

Hogwood gave a cursory nod of his head to Kelly as he stepped to the side of the room and took the empty plastic chair, which he placed a few feet away from Matt's bed before prompting Dallery to sit on. She did so, folding one leg neatly over the other and resting her hands halfway up her thigh; her notepad held open by her left, and a pencil poised in her right.

"Forgive me for jumping straight in, Mr Buchanon, but I see no sense in wasting any time. You've sustained, after all, what from your appearance would lead us to believe to be, a quite vicious attack. Now; as clearly as possible, I'd like you to talk me through what you remember of the moments before you were assaulted. What was the reason for you being in the Meresden Park area of town?"

"We... Connor and I... had been out for a drink. You see; I don't get out of the house very often, what with work and home life... and Connor suggested it might be a good thing to take a night off. He picked the bar; Pure Bar if I remember right; and we stayed there for the whole evening."

"Uh-huh. And then at the end of the night you left

and went... where?"

"By that time things must have gotten a little bit blurry. I remember coming out through the doors into the street... the fresh air hit be like a tonne of bricks, I can tell you that for sure! Then... there was something about Connor's car. What was it?"

"Take your time Mr Buchanon; think carefully." Dallery spoke calmly, leaning forward to press a supportive hand on Matt's knee. Kelly looked down at the gesture, quietly seething internally.

"I think we were talking about him driving us home."

"And this Connor... how inebriated was he by this point?"

"Oh, I... err... I don't honestly remember, I guess he can't have been too bad, if he was thinking about driving back."

"He'd been drinking steadily with you the whole night?"

"Well I wouldn't consider myself having been drinking steadily, I was pretty drunk from the second pint or so to be quite honest, but Connor's much more of a social drinker than I am. He says he can handle his drink and, well... from what I can remember from the early part of the night, I'd be inclined to believe him. Look... what's this got to do with me being attacked?"

"Just trying to summarise the initial scenario for now." Hogwood replied, "I find it's best to get that out of the way first, then it tends to clear a space for the deeper details to come forward."

"Oh... okay; that makes sense. Right, where was I? Okay; so... out of the bar, walking to Connor's car... there was a guy! That's right, a thin little guy, shrouded in a hoodie. A sinewy little shit, he was, but I do remember his eyes; menacing. He just felt dangerous from the outset. I'm sure I looked at Connor for help; I'm no fighter you see, I never have been. Connor was on the other side of the car. What was he doing? He was... Oh shit!"

"What is it?" Hogwood pressed him.

"The thin guy; he had a knife. It's just come back to me! He got it out of his pocket and was holding it to my stomach."

"And Connor? Can you remember what he was doing?"

"He was... he was looking away. We'd both heard another voice, and then... Oh shit, yeah! This absolutely *enormous* guy comes out of the alleyway next to where the car's parked and goes for Connor. They both disappeared behind the other side of the car, and by the way the guys arm was coming up in the air and back down it seemed as if Connor was getting one hell of a beating. I waited, but Connor didn't come back up. Next thing I know I'm..." Matt paused, placing his fingers to both sides of his temples.

"Go on" both officers said in unison.

"I'm not sure how I got there; everything in between is too hazy; but I was flying across the road. I saw the ground getting closer and then that was it. This morning I wake up here."

"Did you recognise either of the men?"

"No."

"But you saw them clearly enough to be able to give us a description, d'ya think?"

Matt exhaled heavily through his almost closed lips, making them whistle.

"I don't know. The thin guy near me; maybe. But the bigger guy? I just remember his size, and briefly trying to get the hell away from him. The thin guy though... for some reason I think he had a neck tattoo. I can't for the life of me remember what it was though; my memory's not giving it to me clearly enough. I definitely know he had one though. Sizeable too."

"Okay. You can take a breather, Mr Buchanon. We're going to take a step out to review what you've told us but, if you don't mind, we will be back in ten minutes or so with your friend, Connor. There are a few questions we need to ask him too, and he may be able to corroborate and possibly add to some of what you've told us already."

Matt looked to Kelly, her shoulders sinking either side of her head and with a spreading look of disappointment in her eyes. Feeling guilty, he nodded to her calmly and reached down to take her by the hand; patting it.

"Not long now, sweetheart. Then we'll be on our way home."

Chapter Twenty-Five

Connor sat slouched deeply into a plastic chair opposite Dallery, his legs outstretched towards her purposefully in the hope that the pungent, wafting smell from his trousers would overcome her. He did not seem to care that Kelly and Matt, situated on either side of the bed merely three feet away from him, would suffer from the same discomfort.

Hogwood stood behind Dallery's shoulder, causing Connor to tilt his head back in order to meet his eyes as they spoke. His whole demeanour exuded unadulterated apathy.

"From the cut of that suit I wouldn't have taken you for a teenager!" Hogwood laughed.

"Ha… Ha…" Connor smirked back sarcastically. "I hadn't realised you were the 'Fashion Police'. I thought you jokers said you had some questions for me?"

"We do, Mr…" Hogwood let the silence hang in the air for a good ten seconds before Connor found the motivation to respond.

"You can call me Connor; I'm easy."

"We'd like your surname please, Connor."

"Ridley. So; questions?"

"You seem to have a problem with authority Mr Ridley."

Connor caught himself laughing again, this time in irony. He couldn't help throwing a subtle glance towards Kelly, whose own mouth was now curling at the edges. Matt, laid on the far edge of the bed, was left obscured from the pair's magnetism by the rear of her head.

"I'm sorry; you'll have to excuse me. I've been

awake for a hell of a long time, not helped by you mismanaging your time earlier. The lower half of my body is coated in vomit and I'd like to get home, cleaned up, and sleep. Can you blame me for being a little short-tempered?"

Dallery bit instantly back at him.

"Your friend is laying there after receiving a fair amount of damage. Given the circumstances I would rather '*not blame you*' for wanting to invest as much time as necessary for us to pin down whoever might have done this to him, so that we can take them off our streets purely for the safety and concern of others."

Connor raised his hands in mock-defence.

"A fair point. A little over-dramatically put for my liking, but I'm with you. How can I help?"

Hogwood leant forward, placing a hand on Dallery's shoulder to steady her.

"You were with Mr Buchanon at the Pure Bar on Meresden Park, is that correct?"

"Yes. We were considering a night out a week or so back, and I thought it would be the type of place he could settle into, given that he's not much of a drinker. You know; lively atmosphere with good music, not your usual dive filled with ageing alcoholics and seasoned Friday-night fighters."

"Okay. So I understand you stayed there together for the whole evening, and when you left to return to your car is when you were confronted. What do you remember from that point in time?"

"Firstly, we were walking *past* my car. I'd parked it close thinking I might only have a couple and then drive, but by the end of the night I was in a bit more of a state than I thought I would've been. Certainly not sober enough to where I felt safe to attempt it! Matt was insisting I'd be fine though, and he'd just started walking around to the passenger side of the car like he wanted to get in it."

Matt propped his body up awkwardly and peered around Kelly's shoulder. He looked over to Connor in surprise; a mystified expression creeping across his face. Connor briefly caught his eye, and continued.

"Then this guy; quite young, maybe twenty-five or so; comes out of nowhere and stands right in front of Matt. All of a sudden Matt's telling me the lad's got a knife against him, and then I hear this mean sounding voice to my right. And then this fuckin'... seriously; a fuckin' man-mountain; steps out from the alleyway and lumbers over to me. Starts demanding money from me... telling me I'm somehow misjudging him if I think I can get away with bluffing him."

"Can you describe either of the men?"

"Well, the man who was in front of me, aside from being gigantic... No; not really! He was stood in a dark area; the only lights on were looking straight down onto Matt and the other guy. Even when he was stood close up to me his features were hard to make out. Everything about him was dark. He grabbed me so hard by the throat that I couldn't help but wince and, as quick as he had knocked me to the ground, he had gotten back up and had moved around the car after Matt."

"I remember that slightly differently, Connor." Matt challenged. "I'm sure I saw him punching you when you were down and, to me, everything happened a lot slower. I waited to see if you got back up, but you didn't. That had to be at least a minute or more."

"Look at my face, Matt. If that freak of nature *had* hit me, I'm sure I wouldn't still be looking so attractive!"

Dallery let out a reactionary tut at Connor's display of bravado.

"What?" Connor glared across to the young woman.

"Don't tell me I don't look good. Unless you're a dyke; that is. God knows there are more of you coming out of the woodwork every frigging year."

Hogwood stepped forward, placing himself between Connor and Dallery, who he could see was now fuming and considering reaching across to slap him.

"That's enough, Mr Ridley. One more word out of line and you'll be spending the rest of the day sat in a prison cell instead of a hospital, and I can guarantee you that the smell of puke will still be there to keep you company. Give me one more reason… just one more… and I may even consider making it the night too."

Connor shifted uncomfortably in his seat. As much as he thrived on the idea of working the cute young officer up until she snapped, he could not bring himself to accept the thought of being kept so uncomfortably for another twenty-four hours. Judging from the looks on the officers faces as he glared at them each one more time, the threat was very real.

"So, the bigger man knocked you to the ground, then came around the car towards Mr Buchanon. Then what?"

"I don't know."

"What do you mean?"

"I… well, I don't know. I ran; I had no bloody choice!"

"You ran." Dallery repeated in disbelief.

"Like I said; I was hardly in a fit state to jump in the car and drive it away, and there was no way I was gonna get the better of that behemoth as well as his little follower, especially considering if he had a knife like Matt had suggested."

"O-kay… So you… got somewhere safe and called the police? What?"

"I just ran! I looked back briefly and saw Matt running the other way, so I assumed he'd got free."

"He didn't get free, Mr Ridley. That's pretty evident, isn't it?"

"Look, I may have a pretty thick skin and, trust me, I know how to handle myself, but... well I had no chance, and Matt's no fighter! Look at him! I took the only option I considered myself to have, and I had to hope Matt did the same."

"And so you ended up where, exactly?"

"Home. I got home and went back for my car early this morning. Then I tried calling Matt and when there was no answer I feared the worst and came here to look for him."

Dallery wrote her final entry in her notepad before closing it and looking up at Hogwood.

"Wow!" she said sarcastically.

"Wow", Hogwood replied.

"Are we done?" Connor asked abruptly, "Or should we all just sit around for the rest of the day saying *'Wow'* to each other?"

"How tall would you say this guy was; the giant?" Hogwood asked.

"I dunno; maybe a foot or so taller than me. Matt, what would you say?"

Matt looked at Connor with distrust. Significant chunks of his explanation seeming to ring wholly untrue in comparison to Matt's scant memories, but he felt adamant that he remembered particular parts well enough to believe Connor had surely lied about them. He certainly remembered the height of the man though; Connors face having been level with his broad chest when they were facing off. He nodded cautiously in agreement.

"About a foot and a half difference; yeah."

"I think we've got all we can take for now then," Hogwood took the seat from under Dallery as she lifted from it, swinging it around himself to place it back in the position it had originally been against the far wall. "We'll be in touch if we learn anything more, or identify who these two assailants might have been."

"Thank you, Officers."

Matt held a hand forward for them to shake. Hogwood took it, giving it a single tug downwards, eager not to hurt him unnecessarily. Dallery followed suit, giving Matt a humbling smile in recognition of his physical state. He could tell she cared, maybe not for him as such, but for the injustice he had endured.

"It's a shame you couldn't enjoy a pleasant night in town, Mr Buchanon, especially with it being such a rare treat", she told him. "Rest assured we'll do everything we can to ensure that the next time, you will."

"Thank you. Let me know if I can help any further."

Connor was too impatient to wait for the niceties to be completed. He walked briskly out of the room without shaking hands or announcing his departure.

It took the nurses a further hour to put together a prescription of pain-killers and anti-inflammatory medicines for Matt to return home with. Kelly was growing increasingly impatient with their perceived inactivity, snapping routinely at Matt each time she felt the urge, regardless of whether he was lucky enough to find himself lulling into a state of semi-consciousness at the time.

She felt a low buzzing in the right hand pocket of her jeans. Sliding her phone out, she opened its cover and read the message that appeared.

Hello Blondie. How did earlier go? I think I did quite well, considering I was mostly thinking about the whip marks no doubt still visible across your slut backside.

Kelly replied immediately.

Hello Master. I keep thinking about them too… it's hard for me to sit straight, but I love how they're a constant reminder. You did extremely well, I'm proud of you Master.

We have to ease off for a little while, Blondie. Matt will be at home with you for some time to recover, and you must be seen to be the devoted wife, as I'm sure you have already expected. One week, maybe two at a push. Your Master will be thinking about you though, remember that.

Kelly looked disappointedly at the last message. Aside from her initial disappointment of their night together, she admired his confidence with the police, and the prospect of what he might do to her if they were to have a second encounter still appealed to her. She desperately wanted to reply honestly; to scream her disapproval down the connection; but she knew better than to antagonise Connor's easy temper. The still burning score-lines across her tender rump were a sign of pleasurable punishment; a game that she had always wanted to play. He had delivered them as a warning against indiscretion. The thought of how they might feel if they had been delivered in momentary anger made her muscles flinch tightly under her skin.

I wish it didn't have to be that way, Master. But I do understand. I'll let you know immediately once he's not inconveniencing us again. I love you Master.

Master loves you too, Blondie.

Chapter Twenty-Six

Matt had been home and bed-bound for four days. His crumpled body was now more purple than pink, but he was sure he could feel the constant pain easing with each passing day. Still; his energy was sapped with the slightest exertion and, as he limped back to bed from his umpteenth challenging trip to the bathroom, he felt he could sleep the rest of the day away as soon as his head hit the pillow. The deep gnawing of pain as he found his position under the covers once again soon put pay to that notion though and, following a few minutes trying desperately to settle, he found himself reaching for the TV remote control.

Downstairs in the gloomy cocoon of the living room, Kelly's frame lay sprawled across the sofa as she stared out at the blustery garden through rain-spattered patio doors. The weather had evolved into a true stereotype of autumn, covering the ground in piles of mulching leaves and dense pools of rainwater, with more of each falling on an almost constant basis. The sky loomed overhead; stained a menacing, claustrophobic grey; changed only by the night-time when darkness came to shroud it.

Kelly felt oppressed. The house felt as though it enclosed her like a prison cell in the turret of some fairy-tale castle, with Matt envisaged as its unrelenting guard jangling keys just out of her reach, and Connor somewhere on the outside; clad in strong armour and her only means of escape.

The first two days had been hard work for her. Endless trips upstairs to steer the then immobile Matt to the bathroom. Cooking their meals. Answering his requests for drinks. All interruptions which she could well have done without. She craved time for herself. Matt could be so selfish sometimes.

Her phone bleeped, vibrating noisily over the coffee tables hardwood surface. Kelly's heart jumped at the initial thought of Connor making contact. Excitedly she scooped it up, kick-starting its display only to find a text from Matt. Disappointment was soon overtaken by angry frustration.

Hey baby. I was trying to call down but my lungs hurt too much to shout today. Would you mind making me a coffee and bringing up a book? I'm really bored and daytime TV really is shit!

"Oh, for fuck sake!" Kelly fumed; unrestricting her volume for the first time in days in the hope that Matt would hear it.

Five minutes after sending his request, Matt watched as Kelly carelessly shoved the bedroom door aside with her foot and marched into the room. His coffee was placed down onto the bedside table with unguarded haste, knocking the bottom of the mug and spilling a hot ring of swirling coffee over its sides. Matt ducked back as two books were thrust in front of his face; one a historical fantasy which he had bought and read recently, the other an autobiography he had been meaning to read for some time, of an actor he had admired since his teens. Neither seemed appealing though. He looked at Kelly with an inquisitive smile as he summoned the courage to ask the unthinkable.

"What?" Kelly demanded.

"Would you mind if I had a different book? It's just... I've read that one... and I'm not feeling in an autobiographical kind of mood."

"Well what mood *are* you in then?"

"Well I was thinking; since I've got so much time on

my hands, and it would constitute enough reading material that I wouldn't need to disturb you so often; that I could have a go at those Curtis what's-his-face books for a change?"

Kelly's answer was swift and defiant. "Dream on, Matt; they're mine."

"I'm just trying to give you a bit of time off, sweetheart. I can get lost in a book for hours, and there's at least three to get through, isn't there! I can sort my own drinks out, I'll just have water from the bathroom if I get thirsty; I'll reuse the mug. I just... I haven't got anything else that's unread *and* appealing."

"Those books aren't your sort of thing, Matt. They're written for women; men just don't get them."

"I'm dying of boredom here, Kel."

"Well maybe you should have learnt a long time ago how to stand up for yourself, then you wouldn't be in the state you're in."

Matt was left speechless. For a few seconds he stayed silent, subduing the voice in his head as it urged him passionately to call Kelly out on her lack of sensitivity. His more rational, understanding, side argued back that she had never been the sympathetic type; that it was just not in her DNA to be so, but personality being genetic meant that it was not her fault. It was an age old internal battle Matt knew well.

"Give me both those books. I'll read them", he smiled.

Satisfied with herself, Kelly placed the books on the bedside table next to Matt with a wry smile escaping from the corner of her mouth.

"So; you'll be alright if I get out of the house for a while this afternoon then?" she asked so matter-of-factly that it came across as rhetorical.

"Of course; if you need to sweetheart."

"Yes; I need to! You're not the only one feeling trapped between four walls, Matt! I'm not your damn slave, and I need fresh air."

"I never considered you my-"

"It doesn't have to be said, Matt. It's been so easily implied by the countless requests for-"

"Countless is a bit of an over exaggeration sweetheart! And I never expected you to stay indoors just because I'm in bad shape. All you had to do was say earlier and I would have-"

"What? Given your approval? *Allowed* me to go? How awfully generous of you!"

"*I would have been fine with it...* was what I was about to say!"

"Whatever, Matt; I'm telling you now."

"And I'm saying that's fine! Have a nice time, whatever you're planning on doing."

"I'm gonna call in on Carolyn. I might stay late; we need a good catch up. You can sort your own dinner out tonight if I do, right?"

Matt's body pulsed from head to toe with aches at the thought of how much movement it would require to get down the stairs for the first time, let alone cook a meal once he was at the bottom, but his conscience told him not to argue.

"I'll give it a go," he nodded.

"You don't have to worry about me; I'll see if Carolyn cooks something, or else I'll grab something while I'm out."

Kelly strode around the bed, scooping up clothes from the floor on her way. Dumping them on her side of the duvet, she rummaged through the pile and picked out a silky pink blouse along with a pair of cut-off jean shorts. She stripped in front of Matt, slowly peeling away her pyjama set to reveal bare flesh from head to toe, except for a thin pair of red panties. Intrigued, she turned her head to see if he was watching, catching his eye and smiling teasingly back. Gripping the waist of the jean shorts in her fingers, she lowered them to the ground at her feet, making sure to bend from her waist while keeping her legs straight. She parted her legs slightly, peering between them just underneath the thin red gusset, into the hungry eyes watching her every movement from across the mattress. Hooking her feet into the leg holes, she slowly raised her body upright; emphasising the moment where the rear of the jean material slid over her rounded backside, before rubbing her hands smoothly over its curves.

"It's a shame you had to be so *'out of action'*," she turned to Matt and smouldered, "All this time together could have been so much more… fun… if we were both fully functioning."

Matt sighed. His weary body sank into the bed beneath him and gave up. He was physically and now mentally broken.

"You better take a coat if you're wearing that, sweetheart. Even with the curtains drawn I can hear how miserable it is out there."

"*Wow!* Is that *all* you can think of as a response?" Kelly pulled the pink blouse over her head, straightening it around her body, before sliding her hands intentionally over the rounded mounds of her breasts and their visible nipples. "I sometimes wonder if you find me attractive anymore!"

"You know I do!" Matt assured her enthusiastically. "But you're not exactly wrong when you say I'm out of action."

"Well that's very much a *'you'* problem, isn't it? Best you just concentrate on resting up and trying to get some sleep. I'll see you when I get home; just… don't wait up."

Kelly swept past the bed, reaching down to grab a pair of white ballerina-style slip-ons as she headed purposely towards the bedroom door. She was gone in a flash, not leaving Matt enough time to follow her out of the door with his hastily stammered "Okay; love you…"

Chapter Twenty-Seven

On hearing the front door slam, Matt released the chest-emptying sigh he had been holding back since hearing Kelly's quip about him not finding her attractive. In truth, every part of him, aching or not, had wanted to reach across the bed and pull her beside him. Seeing her naked had reminded him of how long it had been since he had last experienced the touch of her bare skin, and the thought hit him poignantly in his heart. He raised his hands to his face as he began to weep, as silently as he could for fear of Kelly hearing him from outside of the house.

It took almost twenty minutes for a sense of self-control to drift over him, whereupon he leant away from his pillow, feeling strangely empowered. His chest hurt from his now upright position, but his mind was whirring with the realisation that he had inadvertently placed himself in a position of freedom. It had been almost two weeks since Matt had last read any of the book he had purchased, interrupted at first by the necessity of barbecue planning, then by ongoing drama from Kelly, and finally by the surprise late night snack of asphalt and tarmac he had received. He sat, overcome with the sense of enablement, coupled with the hope that Kelly would stick to her word and return late. Hastily, he downed his coffee and manoeuvred himself to the edge of the bed.

Ten minutes later and Matt had tenderly descended the stairs, taken the book from its snug slot on the shelf, and position himself on the sofa as comfortably as his body would allow. He had considered taking the book back to bed with him but, with the potential of Kelly's early return home, he knew he would not have been able to replace the book as quickly as necessary. He glanced up at the wall clock. It was one-thirty p.m. Matt determined that he would allow himself five hours. If Kelly returned before that, then he would have a panic on his hands and accept the pains a rush would induce. If not, then he could prepare his dinner with ample time to eat it and return to bed. A quick glance into the outside world; a sight which he had not seen in what felt like a very long time; and he opened the book at its centre, looking for the page number he had memorised all those weeks ago.

At a cash point in Archer's Plaza, Kelly entered her pin number to access her bank account. Feeling a rush had become commonplace for her when performing this secretive routine, and on this occasion it was just as exciting, if not more so. At the very start of Matt's recuperation he had received his salary from the previous month, with Kelly's regular allowance contribution having been immediately transferred into her account like clockwork. She tapped her long fingernails against the machines stainless steel plating until her longest held secret finally appeared brightly on-screen, making her grin and look over her shoulder, as if bragging to the few uninterested passers-by.

Current Balance: Four Thousand, Two Hundred and Twelve pounds, plus change.

She withdrew fifty pounds from the account and removed her card, taking care to set aside the obligatory printed receipt, readying herself to throw it into the nearest rubbish bin as she made her way down the street. Her secret would remain undiscovered; on that she had always remained adamantly cautious.

Sat nursing a cappuccino within the first café she

had come to, Kelly took her phone from her purse and opened Connor's most recent text message. It was from the Saturday morning, when Matt had been delivered to the hospital; a desperately long time ago, she felt. Having started to type, she paused momentarily, and checked the time. Just before a quarter past two. *Connor would be back at his desk by now*, she thought, *getting back into the swing of things for the afternoon. Maybe I'll interrupt him. He might not appreciate that. Oh hell. Should I? Should I leave him be? Fuck it; it's the first time in ages I've gotten out of the house, and I'm sure he'd appreciate the contact. He must've missed me too, surely! Mustn't he?*

"First sign of madness, that is."

An unrecognised male voice drifted across from an adjacent table. Kelly looked up, somewhat disgruntled at her thoughts being interrupted.

"I'm sorry?" she said coldly to the man in the smart black suit staring back at her.

"Talking to yourself. First sign of madness; so they say."

"Suuuure... I didn't realise I was speaking out loud, but thanks for the tip", she said bluntly, looking back down at her phone, eager to get back to her decision making.

"You weren't really speaking at full volume. I could just hear you mumbling away to yourself. You... you don't remember me, do you?"

Kelly looked up again, exhaling a short burst of frustrated breath through her nose to signify her loss of patience, as she scanned the man's features in more depth. At first she saw nothing from memory but, as the man readjusted his waxed brown hair into a slightly more curved style at its front - pompadour style - and smiled, she suddenly came to know him. No name, but from the depths of her memory banks his face was successfully retrieved.

"You were talking to me over the railings at La Tartaruga Scattare, when I was there with a friend a month back."

"Actually it's nearer two, but I'll forgive you since you remembered our chat", the man laughed.

Kelly paused; unclear of what to say in response. Sensing the growing discomfort, the man leant forward across the table with his hand outstretched. "I'm Calder."

"Kelly", she responded, shaking his hand loosely.

Calder slid a business card across the table to her. Kelly left it where it stopped.

"I was kinda hoping I might bump into you again at some point. Looks like today's our lucky day!"

"*Your.*"

"Excuse me?" Calder asked politely.

"You said it's *our* lucky day. I was clarifying that what you should have said was that it was *your* lucky day, meaning your own luck, not mine, just in case you getting that confused too."

"I just thought, ya know… you're here on your own, so am I… you'd made an impression on me, and I hoped I had on you… so, after seeing you sat there, like it was some kind of fate, I thought now was the opportune time for us to get to know each other a lot better."

"I'm taken; sorry."

"I saw your wedding ring; I'm not daft," Calder said jovially, "But that doesn't mean we can't shoot the breeze with each other, does it?"

Kelly glimpsed down with distaste at the diamond on her hand, glistening brilliantly from the overhead lights. Looking back up into Calder's hope-filled eyes she could not help feeling that she might have taken him up on his offer on any other given day, but all she could really see in him was Connor, sat at his desk, anticipating a delivery of her words. A second frustrated breath was forced through her nostrils.

"Calder; *Sweetheart*… I've never believed in fate, and I don't class this chance meeting as '*lucky*'. I class this as two people who once bumped into each other and shared a simple '*Hi*', being followed up by you acting like a creep and not taking a clearly straightforward 'No' for an answer. Now; my best friend's husband is a policeman and I'm sure that, with a little persuasion, I could have him drive over here and have you arrested for pestering me. Is that clear enough a reason for you to leave me in peace?"

"Pestering? That's a bit harsh, don't you think?"

"Let's just call it stalking then. My friend saw you two months back, she'd remember you, and I can guarantee she'd back me up."

"Wow! Really?" Calder looked at Kelly, horrified. "You're a real class act."

"Oh, Calder," Kelly sniggered, "You don't know the half of it."

Calder gathered his things from the table, lifted his coat from the chair seat next to him, and made for the door.

"Un-fucking-believable", he muttered, looking back over his shoulder at Kelly. She was smiling inanely at him, waving her hand from side to side. Noticing his growing frown, she turned her hand around in the air, then lowered every finger except the middle digit, emphasising its purpose by thrusting it emphatically towards him.

Pleased by her success and the now resumed peace and quiet, Kelly slouched back into her chair and lifted her phone before her eyes. The text message was still half-drafted, and she pondered on how to complete it. She began typing again, entering what came first to her mind, and hit 'Send'.

Chapter Twenty-Eight

Connor was swivelling on his office chair, staring blankly at the computer monitor in front of him. The overly complicated spreadsheet that he had been tasked with analysing had remained unaltered for at least a half an hour before he had left for lunch and, now that he had returned, he found little motivation to resume working on it.

He raised his eyes, letting them wander the office space around him, allowing them to rest at length on his female colleagues as they busily typed at their desks. He was one of only two men in the department, a ratio which filled him with supreme confidence and allowed his arrogant charm to thrive. In his mind he began to rate them individually on his own scales of desirability. This was measured, essentially, by collective scores related to breast size, breast shape, thinness of frame, tightness of backside, and how much of a smile they were willing to share with him. The limited criteria made his selection process easy, to some extent.

There were those who made no secret in finding him too arrogant. *Those bitches can be discounted*, he told himself, *that's their loss!* There were also those who were not slim; whose clothes betrayed them by outlining the extra weight they held around their hips and stomachs. *If you'd take some fucking pride in yourself maybe you could've had a chance*, his inner voice ridiculed them. Once these groups were filtered out, it left Connor six ladies still under consideration. He looked over each of them a second time, burning his gaze into them from a distance in the hope they might feel his interrogative stare and turn. Then he might see their smiles and be guided to make his next culling.

Focussing on one of them as she stepped away from the printer at the side of the office, he followed her slender body intensely, all the way back to her chair. He saw she was youthful, with an attractive mess of curly brown hair falling onto her shoulders, and a chest full of potential. He was feeling somewhat enticed until he noticed, as she resumed her seat, that her seemingly trim backside spread to her flanks as she lowered herself. This, he thought, could not be forgiven. *You need to tighten that shit up. Get your fat arse on a treadmill*, the opinionated voice screamed at her from the soundproofed walls of his mind. Needless to say, she was now out of the running.

Connor was placing every ounce of his concentration on the remaining five's potential when he became aware of their common interest; shocked to find they had all turned to look in his direction at the same time. The sight overwhelmed his charm limitations – he knew he could deal with one at a time, but not all together – and he was in serious danger of looking like a creep. Self-consciously, he recoiled back into his chair, averting his eyes back over his monitor. It was then that he heard the cause for their collective attention, having seemingly been too preoccupied to notice earlier. Just above his right hip, melodically humming from the pocket of his waistcoat, his mobile phone lit up and sang out. He removed it; acknowledging the disturbance it had caused to the group of spectators by briefly mouthing '*Sorry*'; then swiped it alive, silencing its repetitive jingle, and read the message.

I've missed you Master. I have the afternoon free so I wanted to tell you how much you've been on my mind these past few days. I'm incomplete without you.

Connor replied immediately.

It's good to hear from you Blondie. Master has missed you too. I thought I made it clear that you must focus on your duties as a wife until it is safe for us to connect again?

It's okay for us to talk at the moment, Sir. I'm not at home. I'm at a café right now, to allow us to talk. Is that okay?

Is the victim back to full fitness yet?

He's doing a lot better, but not 100% yet. Good enough to take care of himself for the afternoon though.

That's not what I commanded of you originally, is it? What you're doing is reckless and could lead to suspicion. Would you like us to be caught just as we're getting started?

I didn't intend to act recklessly, Master. I just needed to speak with you. I feel destroyed inside without your command. I crave your touch, your influence, both in body and mind.

As your Master it's great to know you feel so strongly, but we have to be sensible. I shouldn't have to reiterate that you're creating unwelcome risk, even if you feel you're simply escaping the house for an afternoon. Finish your coffee and go straight home.

I asked for the afternoon and he said he would be fine for the rest of the day, Master. Please let me make the most of it. I'd like to see you after work, if that's possible?

I'm afraid that simply is not an option, my pet.

We can be discreet?

I'm now placing an entry into the Pain Journal, young lady. For disobeying two commands and continuing your selfish demand which I have stated that I cannot meet.

No; please Master! I'm sorry for pushing you, I

didn't mean to.

It's too late for your apology. I've had to warn you too many times and I find your behaviour grossly unacceptable. If you won't pay attention or heed my will then you will accept the repercussions. Am I making that clear enough for you to understand?

There was a pause of a minute between texts. Kelly sat staring out of the café window, bunching and squeezing her fist, furious with herself while also frustrated at Connor's refusal to take the opportunity that she had engineered. Inside she fumed at him, but felt simultaneously overridden by excitement at the power he wielded so ruthlessly. Torn in two, she dutifully responded.

I understand, Master. I will accept the punishment willingly for my disobedience. Forgive me.

It's in the Journal, so now we move on, until we are together again. When Matt has returned to work we will find our next moment, and only then. Do you know when he is expected back?

He isn't too happy about being stuck indoors. I think he'll try to get back either next week or the week after at the very latest.

The Thursday of the following week is the 24th, yes?

Kelly checked the calendar on her mobile phone to be sure.

You're correct, Sir.

Then we will aim for then, if all goes to plan with his anticipated return to work. Does that sound fair?

That sounds perfect! You'll take the day off work to be with me?

I will, young lady. So long as it remains feasible. Now do as I say, and take your delectable backside home.

Okay, I promise I will. I'm sorry for not listening before, Sir. I just find myself getting impatient when it comes to you, but then you always manage to show me the level-headed approach. I can't wait for our next encounter, Master. Thank you.

Patience is a virtue, Blondie, and one that I expect at all times. Never fail me on that again. We'll speak soon.

I love you, Master.

Behave yourself. Master loves you too.

Kelly laid her phone to rest on the table's surface, picked up her coffee mug to swirl it around a few times, and then downed the remaining froth in a single gulp. Losing herself in thought; staring out of the window into the street again; she was startled by the café waitress's arrival at her side.

"Can I get you another?"

Kelly took a moment to consider Connor's instruction. She knew it would be foolish to disobey him again, and that she should act on his command. She looked up to the waitress; petite and elfish, with a modernistic crop of brown hair, dramatically swept to the side. She was hanging patiently on Kelly's response.

"Yeah, go on then", she said cheerily, handing her the empty mug back.

As the waitress disappeared behind the counter, Kelly took her phone back in her hand and searched for Carolyn's number. She opened a new message and began to type.

Hiya! I'm just in town having a coffee and was thinking about popping in. Are you free this afternoon?

Matt had been absorbed in the book for more than four hours. Time had escaped him, coming as a shock when he finally thought to look up to the wall clock and saw how late it had become. It was a quarter to six.

"How did that happen!" he asked aloud to himself.

He let his finger flick through the corners of the

books remaining pages, counting what he had left to read before it would be finished. It was less than twenty. The task of preparing dinner could wait.

From his right side, Matt's phone illuminated, ringing out loudly and buzzing with continuous vibration. Intrigued; he ignored the complaining tug in his ribs and leant over to investigate. It was an incoming call, from Connor. He swiped to accept the call and lifted it to his ear.

"Hello Connor", he answered.

"Hey there, buddy!" Connor chirped. "How you doing? Feeling any better yet?"

"I'm doing okay, thanks. First day back on my feet today, and it was hard work. It's been good to see a little more of the house than just the bedroom though!"

"I bet it was! Good man! So what are you up to?"

"Just sat chilling on the sofa right now. I'll sort some dinner out in a little while. What about you? What are you doing?"

"Me? Oh I just... well; shit day at work... you know! Just got home and thinking of cracking open a beer or two."

"Really? What's up at work?"

"Nothing you need to worry yourself about mate. Office politics; you know. Went down into the factory earlier though, the place looks like carnage! They'll be welcoming you back with open arms when the time comes, I can tell you that!"

"Well hopefully it won't be too long. Seriously; I've been dying of boredom here."

"How can you die of boredom with a cracker like Kelly in the house?" Connor laughed, probing.

"I couldn't even if I wanted to, buddy. I'm in no capable state, and Kelly's feeling like she's been run ragged these last few days. I've tried to keep my pestering to a minimum, but sometimes it's had to be necessary, unfortunately."

"Well what did she expect? Get *her* on the dinner tonight, mate. You sound knackered!"

"She's sorting her own dinner tonight. She's been out visiting a friend for the day, and she was saying something about either eating with her or grabbing a takeaway on the way home later this evening."

"Oh; I see. Well that's… inconsiderate."

"I can't say she doesn't deserve a bit of time out of the house, to be fair."

"Yeah… maybe that's true. Listen buddy, I'm gonna shoot. Got a few things to do before I can relax for the night."

"No worries. And listen, thanks for checking in, Connor; I appreciate it."

The call abruptly disconnected; its hollow silence ringing in Matt's ear.

Chapter Twenty-Nine

Matt awoke to his alarm like clockwork, despite having lived for two full weeks without it early morning call. Having always been a light sleeper, he had never begrudged his morning routine but, on this occasion, he felt substantially more cheerful than usual as he rolled over to tap it silent.

Within twenty minutes he was up, washed and dressed; eager to start his first day back at work. He leant over Kelly's rigid body, parting her hair and kissing her softly on the cheek. Then he made his way downstairs, slid his feet into the familiar sturdy feel of his work boots, and walked out the front door into the biting autumn wind.

Over the past week and a half Matt had found pockets of time to continue his quest to finish the series of books. He was now all three books down, with the fourth having been available in stores for the past couple of weeks. Kelly had been waiting on her obligatory copy from Matt but, with his recuperation to contend with, she had been left disappointed. Something in his mind; a touch of competitive spite, he wondered guiltily; told him to stop at the supermarket on his way to the factory, to collect his own copy from the book aisle and see how far he could get through it before Kelly thought of requesting he buy a copy for her. Behind the wheel, as he made his way onto the dual carriageway which would inevitably lead him to the supermarket he had in mind, he cautiously chuckled to himself at the once ridiculous notion of reading the whole thing before Kelly did.

Pulling into a parking space outside the locked factory doors, Matt was stunned to see a flow of his colleagues trailing towards his car from all sides. He tucked the white plastic bag containing his new purchase into his workbag and swung his door open to a hail of cheers and applause. He rose from the car, blushing uncontrollably; and was immediately swarmed by the well-wishers, led by his young apprentice.

"It's really good to see you're okay, boss", Danny said, smiling and throwing his arms around him.

"Thank you Danny; I really appreciate that."

"We all heard what happened. Your pretty friend from the directors offices came down and filled us all in. It sounded like you must've went through hell there for a while!"

"Well, Danny; I'd never suggest eating the road as being a good idea. It doesn't taste too great, I can tell you that".

Matt's manager, a broad, round-bellied man named Trevor, was the next to approach him, taking his hand firmly within his own and shaking it enthusiastically while gripping Matt's shoulder.

"You can play it down all you like, Matt," Trevor started, "but we're all friends here, and we've all been sending good thoughts and wishing you a speedy recovery. It's good to see you so easy on your feet again and ready to come back. We've arranged a little welcome-back treat for you inside; when you're ready."

Matt had been working for a few hours when he was interrupted by a loud cough from the entranceway of the department. Appreciating the chance to stop momentarily, he set down his tools and looked to the grinning face poking its way through the thick opaque vinyl curtains. Smiling inanely at him, Danny gave a knowing wink then reached out to either side, pushing on the overlapped flaps to clear a gap. There, stood waiting behind him, were the group of Matt's colleagues from earlier that morning, joined by a few extra latecomers.

The first thing brought through the gap was the largest cake Matt had ever seen in person, decorated with piped icing around its whole circumference and topped with sugar shapes and candles in a variety of guises. As it drew closer Matt was able to read the message scrawled colourfully across its centre.

'*Matt; from all of us, to the bravest of us all*'.

Matt was floored, stood with his mouth wide open in shock.

"You deserve this, Matt", Trevor stated kindly, stepping out from behind the cake carriers. "You do so much over the years, to help and teach us, and we've truly missed you while you've been away. We also had a little whip around the factory, and the offices, and arranged a little collection for you."

He handed Matt a large white envelope, crudely sealed, but thick and heavy at its base with notes and the jangling of coins.

"Oh, no; you really shouldn't have!" Matt modestly complained.

"Yes; we bloody well should have!" Danny urged, "Now stop being humble and accept it!"

"Thank you... all... so much; that's really kind of you."

Matt's lip had begun to twitch with rising emotion. The cake was set down onto a clear area of the neighbouring workbench, and a knife offered handle-first towards him.

"It's only fair that you do the honours", a familiar voice rang out.

Looking around the side of the group, Matt saw

Shanna; her head cutely tilted, a beaming smile spread across her face. She raised the tips of her fingers, pressed them against her pursed lips, and blew a kiss out from them as they fell forward towards him. Matt's heart warmed. He beckoned for her to come forward, taking her in his arms as she reached him, where they gave each other a heartfelt embrace.

"I'm so glad you're okay," she whispered into his ear, "You really had me worried for a while."

"I'm fine Shanna; thank you. You should've come around and visited. I wouldn't have minded the company."

"I wanted to, but I spoke with Kelly a couple of times for updates and she warned me off. She'd said at the time that you were still in a bad way and needed time to heal."

"Oh; sorry honey, I didn't know. Kelly never mention you'd spoken."

"Well… you're back now and healthy again, that's the most important thing."

Beside them, the small crowd began to whistle and chant.

"Cake! Cake! Cake!"

Matt, feeling rushed, threw them all a questioning eyebrow. Someone in the midst of the impatient group shouted out.

"Stop your flirting you two, and get on with the cake cutting!"

Feeling embarrassed, Matt drew slowly away from Shanna; smiling awkwardly to her as he reached for the knife's handle hovering in mid-air beside him. Shanna smiled back, unashamed.

From his office window, overlooking the factory floor, Connor stood watching as Matt plunged the knife deeply into his cake. He could hear the roaring cheer of celebration, making him shake his head and grimace.

"Anyone would think it's a fucking children's tea party." He muttered to himself.

Reaching into his pocket for his phone, he removed it, swiped it to life, and began typing out a message.

Good morning Blondie. I see Mr Can't-Take-A-Punch has returned today as expected. They're holding a party for him right now, it's all very sweet...

Kelly awoke to her phones shrill beep as it received the message. She opened it, tutting distastefully as she sleepily read over the text, and then replied.

Good morning Sir. That does sound very cute! Bless their juvenile hearts.

Now that he's no longer a hindrance we can begin to plan, my pet. I can't now make the 24th as it's a bit too soon. I suggest we consider the 1st instead. It's the next day that I can realistically be free.

If that's what you wish, then I can work to that, Master.

Good girl. It makes me very happy to see you're learning. I'll send your instruction's shortly. There are things you will need to prepare in advance, but mostly they are rules for your adherence on the day. Make sure you read them, understand them, and follow each instruction to the letter.

It was not long after everyone had finished eating their cake that the familiar klaxon sounded to signify the start of the lunch hour. The group dispersed, leaving Matt on his own in the workshop. He walked across the room to his locker, unzipped his workbag, and removed his new book from its white plastic wrapping. Perching on the edge of his workbench, he folded the first few pages aside, eager to begin its first chapter.

Kelly felt eager too; out of bed and quickly dressed in anticipation of the impending email. Connor's texts had sparked her into an uncharacteristic vibrancy.

She glided down the staircase as though she were high on drugs, her dizzy mind fixated on what was to come the following week. Stopping halfway down, she looked out over the lounge, considering how much attention she should give it before his visit. *Master must notice your efforts*, her subservient ego warned her.

As she walked through the kitchen to start the kettle she could see, through the open utility-room door, two large stacks of dirty clothes. To their right were three more piles, washed and neatly folded by Matt during the last week of his time spent convalescing at home. Kelly looked to them angrily.

"You could've taken them upstairs, couldn't you; you lazy bastard", she ranted. "Could've at least put another load on before you left for work too; but no, that would've been too thoughtful! Always gotta be left down to me, doesn't it. Selfish prick."

She pulled the door closed, blocking the unwanted chore from sight.

Taking her freshly brewed coffee to the sofa, Kelly sat down in front of her laptop and opened its lid, just as its bottom corner flashed with an email notification. She leant forward and clicked on it keenly, watching as a window opened in the centre of the screen, before reading Connor's instructions aloud to herself.

Chapter Thirty

Matt felt; as he had similarly while reading the previous instalments; utterly consumed by the latest book. He was into the last ten minutes of his break, and was coming to the end of the fourth chapter, when he became aware of a soft voice drifting across the workshop. He looked up and over his shoulder towards a giggling Shanna, stood at the far end of the room, just inside the entrance.

"Must be a good book!"

"Yeah; it's pretty good as it goes."

"I'm sure it is! I had to call your name four times!"

"Really? Shit! Sorry Shan; I didn't mean to be rude."

"That's okay mate; I'm an avid reader too, you know that. Sometimes what happens in a book can be far more interesting than what's going on in real life. Anyways; I just wanted to check in; see how you were doing? Are you coping okay with being back?"

"I gotta say, I wasn't expecting it to be as much of a struggle as it is. I'm just out of practice I guess. You wouldn't believe how heavy everyday things become once you haven't had to lift them for a couple of weeks!"

"Well you just take it steady, and ask for help if you feel like you're pushing yourself too hard. The guys here really were concerned for you while you weren't around, and I know they'll do what they can to support you. Don't be stubborn and overlook them; okay?"

"I won't. Danny's been offering every five minutes, and I've appreciated him lending a hand when he has. I was so frustrated at being stuck at home; I'm not gonna risk sending myself back there!"

"I should hope not! Listen; about that night… You were out with Connor when you were attacked, weren't you?"

"Yeah."

"Well I'm not being funny but, from the few details that I've been told, some things about that night just don't seem to add up to me."

"To be honest, Shan, I'm not entirely sure they do to me either. According to Connor's version of events, a lot of how I remember things happening is simply wrong. We shared information when the police interviewed us the next day, and I couldn't get my head around half the things he told them. They were a complete contradiction to what I'd experienced."

"You didn't challenge him on them?"

"Don't get me wrong; I wanted to, and I even tried at one point! I didn't really have a leg to stand on though; I was the one with a concussion and head injuries. Which is *another* thing I don't get. I saw Connor get pushed to the ground behind his car and pounded on like beef. I couldn't see it, but I can literally still hear the thumps he took. *He* shows up the next morning with *nothing!* Absolutely no damage on himself whatsoever. Of course, he then tells me that part of my recollection is bullshit; never actually happened!"

"That's odd. I mean; I've got nothing solid to really work on, but he didn't show up for work until the Wednesday, and his excuse as far as I understood it was that he needed time to recover. Obviously he explained you'd taken a much worse beating, but I'm sure he said he had his own healing to do too."

"Well according to his statement, and from what I saw of him the next morning, he had nothing to heal from! My opinion of him has seriously changed since then, Shan. I know he was sweet on you, and I know you weren't interested at the time, but just be careful around him. Something's not right; I can feel it."

"It'll be a cold day in hell before I get tangled up with that creep, Matt. I've been trying to tell you what I think of him for ages; I'm just glad to know you're seeing him for how I do now. It's a damn shame it had to go so far though. I've spent the last couple of weeks wishing I'd tried harder to explain.

"It's not your fault if I wasn't prepared to listen at the time, Shan."

"How was Kelly while you were recuperating? Did she look after you well?"

"She did; bless her."

Shanna's jaw fell in genuine surprise, which she tried her best to minimise. Matt continued.

"I think it took a lot out of her though. After a few days it all got a bit too claustrophobic for her and she needed fresh air, so at that point I just let her do her own thing while I did my best to sort myself out. To be honest I was getting fed up of eating takeaway and having no clean clothes anyway. I quite enjoyed getting stuck into a few chores during the second week!"

As Matt explained, Shanna's expression had slowly changed from disbelief, through pleasant surprise, and had finally settled on disappointment. Realising that it was not the time to be confrontational, she kept her thoughts inside. Deep within her though, she felt sorrow; painfully sad – and guilty that she had not been there to help him when he had so obviously needed some.

The silence in the air between them suddenly became all too apparent, making Shanna uncomfortable.

"So is that the most recent book?" she asked in desperation.

Matt cocked his head to one side, smirking.

"I thought you said you weren't a fan?"

"Oh, trust me, I'm not," she replied forthrightly, "but I've heard enough about the series from Kelly to know that *'The Sharp Tongue'* isn't a title she's mentioned before. Have you read all the others?"

"I worked my way through all of them over the last week and a half! Kelly spent quite a lot of the time around her friend Carolyn's in the end, so I had plenty of reading time to myself."

"She'd kick your arse if she ever found out; you know that..."

"She doesn't know, Shan. I made sure to cover my tracks well" Matt winked at her. "I couldn't stop myself from buying the new one on the way here this morning. I'll have to buy Kelly a separate copy though; she'll be able to tell this one's been read if I tried giving it to her. The spine's already starting to crease, and I'm only a few chapters in!"

"What do you see in them, Matt? Kelly's literally told me every bit of detail but she still can't sell their appeal to me."

"It wasn't as if I was expecting myself to like them. Kelly made me feel like I was being held back from something significant, but once the characters developed in my mind it was like I had a constant need to know more. It's like any other book really, I guess. Curtis Sharp has a certain charm – written more for the ladies, obviously – but I get the attraction they must feel towards him. He's a very strong character. He just seems to absorb these women into his world and then, once they're a part of it, that's when it becomes dramatic. He's got more history than you first think. The women aren't neglected either though. They each have their own story to tell, and sometimes they can be far more dramatic than Curtis's."

"I have to say; you explain it a lot better than Kelly

ever has. I don't think she's ever once taken me through a storyline without throwing in what Curtis ends up doing sexually to his subs. That's what turns me off about it. I mean; the idea of what he does doesn't freak me out as such. It's more that I see how worked up Kelly gets when she's talking about it and that's... well it's just weird to witness, if you know what I mean?"

"It's disturbs you because it's a friend talking so... explicitly?"

"Well... yeah; to some extent; but it's not just the description. It's the look in her eyes, as though in her mind she's participating in the acts at the same time as telling me them."

"I get it. I'm not so blatant, but I have to say I've been thinking a little more open-mindedly since I worked my way through the other books."

"Thinking about what?"

"I dunno; it probably sounds stupid, but I've kind of become absorbed in the whole thing myself; not that I want to make you feel any weirder!"

"You couldn't make me feel weird, Matt", Shanna smiled.

"Well I was thinking – since I've still got some leave to take, and how I can relate now with what Kelly's been into all this time – that I could take a day off soon and surprise her."

"Matt, honestly; if you're going to say what I think you're going to say; I don't think it's a good idea."

"No?"

"Oh God, Matt; I really don't want to get into this right now. Just... just don't make any rash decisions, okay? Take some time to think rationally about it."

"You think I'm jumping into the whole sub-dom thing too quickly?"

"I think you're getting wrapped up in it without

seeing the bigger picture, and it's not something Kelly would necessarily want."

"But I know she fantasises about that sort of thing. Like you said, she obviously plays around with the thoughts of it in her mind?"

Shanna glimpsed at her wristwatch.

"Shit! I'm gonna have to go; my break's already finished and the board are expecting me. I get what you're saying but just...don't rush it. Please, Matt?"

"Okay Shan. Go on, you should get going."

"Yeah, I should. We'll pick this up another time, okay?"

"Got it." Matt nodded.

Shanna turned on her heels and jogged out of the room. Matt, watching her leave, thoughtfully considered her opinion. Shanna had always shown an aptitude; a natural instinct for rationalising things; even during those times when Matt had seen her to be at her most fragile. Normally he would never deny her ability to see situations as they truly were and, for that very reason, he trusted her advice implicitly. Even so, he could not help feeling his own desire arguing against his better judgement on this occasion. The thought of tearing himself away from his idea; though having only been momentarily considered up to that point; immersed him in disappointment, making him yearn to defy Shanna's plea all the more.

Following Shanna's departure Matt had managed to read a sneaky fifth chapter, although it had meant continuing to read for ten minutes after the post-lunch shift had started; the first occasion Matt could think of where he had cheated his employers out of his services. He was placing the book back into his locker while simultaneously scanning the wall calendar to his left, when Trevor entered the workshop smiling, still deep under the spell of gratitude at having his most experienced staff member back in the fold. He ignored Matt's obvious late return to work.

"How you doing, buddy?" he asked, moving in close to place a hand on the side of Matt's arm.

"I'm fine, thanks Trev. The breaks for cake and then lunch came just at the right time. I was feeling a little overstretched, but I'm much more refreshed now."

"Do you think you can manage a full day? It's totally fine with me if you wanna be put onto gradual return hours? All you have to do is say."

"No; that's not necessary. I do appreciate it though. From looking at the planner it seems as though the workload's just as heavy as it ever was. I'd rather be here to help."

"Good man. I'll ask a favour though; for the first few days I want you taking it slowly. Okay?"

"My body won't let me rush even if I wanted to!" Matt smiled. "Hey Trev, tell me something."

"What's that?"

"You've got the Wagner order needed for Wednesday next week, but after that there's no details. Got anything in the pipeline?"

"Nothing yet. Word from up top is that it'll be a quiet end to the week, so we'll just be making stock units. Why's that?"

"I was considering taking a day off, that's all."

"Put the request in through the system, mate; I'm happy to approve it if you want it. You got plans?"

Matt thought quietly for a moment. Shanna's concerned words whispered from one side of his head to the other as he fought the urge to make straight for the nearest computer to enter the booking request.

"I... ", he paused, attempting to silence his internal

conflict.

"Hey fella; if it's for personal reasons just tell me it's none of my business!"

"It's not that," Matt blurted, anxious not to appear rude. "It's my other half. She was good to me while I was out of action so I wanted to treat her to say thanks. I thought a surprise day off; letting her do the things she likes; would make up for it, that's all."

"So that's the secret to marital bliss? Wish I'd learnt to think like that before Mrs K had buggered off! There's no better reason I can see for a day off, Matt. Get it booked now, before anyone else does. You deserve it more than they do!"

Matt felt as though he had put himself on the spot. While he had not said anything untruthful when he had told Shanna that he had been considering it, the very notion was still in its infancy; none of his plans were set in stone. Now he faced a dilemma. His head steadfastly told him to heed Shanna, while his racing heart told him to take the day, but both of their subtle voices were influenced upon hearing Trevor's intimation that someone else in the team might beat him to taking the same day off. In a split second the decision was taken.

It has to be, or else how long will I be waiting for another opportunity – he questioned himself.

Sheepishly he made his way out through the workshop doorway, towards the slumbering computer workstation. Steadying himself, he entered the '*Staff Annual Leave*' section and requested a new booking. A calendar appeared in the centre of the screen showing the current month, and the dates still free to take. He clicked on the forward arrow to move it to the start of the next month, then selected his preferred day. Thursday next week.

Thursday the first.

A D Hook

Chapter Thirty-One

Matt laid the softest of kisses on Kelly's puffed cheek, pulled the wayward duvet over her exposed torso, and made his way out of the house as though it were any other normal working day.

It was Thursday, 6:30am, and the weather outside was miserable. *'Autumn's well and truly engrained now'*, he thought to himself, as he leant out of the doorway and watched the misty blanket of dense rain falling noisily over the street. A strong wind whipped through the cul-de-sac, stirring the fallen leaves from the ground and spinning them into a violent whirlwind, careening them against the row of garages to his left where their curled, withering edges scratched and scuffed at the metal doors.

Matt pulled the front door closed behind him and made his way swiftly across the street to where his car was parked. Hoisting the collar of his coat up high, he held its two corners tightly around his neck with one hand, his other pressing at the boot release switch on his key fob as he drew nearer. Reaching the back of the car, he quickly ducked into the slowly opening space, shielding himself from the relentless downpour under its angular lid. He peered inside the shadowy hollow and could see the edge of his rucksack, the majority of it hidden from view behind the heavy steel box that he used to keep his car maintenance tools within. Matt had been careful to place the rucksack precisely there, conscious that; at any point during the week that he had been planning the course of this day's events; Kelly may have wanted to use the more spaciously booted car of their two. Fortunately that scenario had not arisen, but Matt did not question himself for being so cautious. He wanted today to go exactly as planned, and his planning had been meticulous.

An excitement coursed through him, its intense adrenaline surge warming every part of his body except for his feet. His feet were so cold he felt as though his socks were lined with ice, a chill so intense no amount of heart-pumping anticipation could disguise, but worth ignoring for a few more seconds as his mind raced through the itinerary of everything soon to unfold. He rolled his shirts sleeve back in defiance of the elements, and glanced at his rain speckled wristwatch.

Three hours.

Matt stood there, almost frozen in his deep, anticipating thought. Three hours until he could return as an entirely different persona, to share the most thrilling of fantasies with Kelly.

Snapping out of his daydream, he clicked the boot lid shut and made for the driver's door. As he slid into the cold leather seat he reached across to the glove-box, rummaged through its contents to remove *The Sharp Tongue* from its hiding place, and checked the amount he had yet to read. Three hours was a lot of time to kill. It was just under a fifth of the book; maybe nine or ten chapters, he estimated.

The roadside diner's carpark echoed with a sense of eerie desolation. Matt glanced over to the illuminated dashboard clock; it read *6:47 a.m.* As he steered the nose of the car into a parking space opposite the buildings front entrance; facing away from it; he watched as a series of other vehicles slowly made their way along the distant road towards its entry. From the approaching drivers faces, each of them bleary-eyed and devoid of any noticeable enthusiasm, he assumed them to be staff arriving to start their shifts.

He remained in his car as the zombie-like workforce continued to trickle in, some by car, but the majority; largely made up of moody-faced teens; shuffling lazily past on foot. As the restaurant windows gradually flickered into artificially bright life in his rear-view mirror, Matt laid his seat back by a few inches, reached for the book from the passenger seat, and made himself more comfortable. Twisting slightly so as to rest his right shoulder against the driver's door, he tucked the elbow of his left arm between his side and the leather backing of his seat; pinning the book in mid-air; and began to read.

The new chapter opened at an emotionally heavy scene. Curtis Sharp had uncovered a usurper in his midst; a man he had once known as a friend only now revealing himself to be have been a dominant all along; had made attempts to court his submissive of six months, Leah. It had angered him but, in a rare move highly uncharacteristic of the consummate Master, he was showing unexpected restraint. More shocking to Matt than that though, Curtis was, for the first time, becoming emotional. Matt felt somewhat taken aback by the impassioned dialogue that accompanied the tense storyline. How Curtis spoke with Leah, his usually blunt and intense use of language subsiding into a now poetic monologue on his deep hurt and the very real fear of losing her, made Matt feel as though a window had formed into the man's soul. A soul so well hidden since the very beginning. There was a surprising beauty in the words which touched Matt's heart and which, for the first time, tempted him to believe there was a delicacy to Curtis underneath his preposterously manly persona. Matt read through the entire chapter with his mouth agape. His ears muted the sounds of the outside world as his eyes moved slowly between each line, the tension building in time with his own quickening pulse. He could actually feel his breathing grow dizzyingly shallow as he neared the chapters end paragraphs, consciously choosing to ignore his bodies warning calls through sheer determination and, as Leah finally took Curtis's hand in hers and softly stroked his palm; telling him ardently that she would never leave his side for another's; Matt's body was rewarded with an almighty inhale of air. He stared up from the book; his eyes transfixed through the windscreen into the blurred distance; and wept.

Kelly steadily awoke to a melodic chiming from her mobile phone. For a few seconds she watched it in a sleepy daze as it grew louder and vibrated across the nightstand. It took some time for her brain to engage; for the realisation to form that the noise was not simply from a call which she could choose to ignore, but from an alarm that she herself had intentionally set and one that, if she continued to push away as an annoyance would; aside from scupper her chance to fulfil her fantasies a step further; lead to a rightfully unhappy master.

Through an escalating series of disgruntled huffs, Kelly forced her unenthusiastic body across the bed towards the phone, where she slid her deft forefinger across its touchscreen to silence the shrill ringing. Under her fingertip she felt a low vibration; a pulse that she instinctively recognised to be a sign from her phones haptic sensors, informing her of a missed text message or phone call. She scooped the handset from the table-top with a curious interest and swiped again, unlocking its bright display. A grey notification bar spread across its waist that read *'One New Message - Connor'*. Kelly eagerly pressed down on the *'Open Message'* option, smiling as it unfolded before her eyes and they took in his enthralling words.

Good morning my pet. I hope you're awake and making ready for my visit. You have your instructions. Make sure they're followed. ETA 9:30am.

Kelly sat herself up on the bed, her back tightly pressed against the headboard, with her legs entwining each other as the beginnings of a fire ignited between her inner thighs. She bit her lip and, for a few seconds, forgot to breathe.

Exhaling deeply out of eventual necessity, her mind suddenly began to race.

'*The instructions. What were they? Have I covered them all? Left anything out? Oh shit, what if I've missed something?*'

Kelly jumped from the bed, dashing recklessly out through the bedroom doorway and down the staircase. She grabbed her laptop from the coffee table and threw herself back-first onto the couch. Opening the lid she waited anxiously, tapping her fingers nervously on its metal casing as the ageing system booted up. When it finally had, she swept her finger across the mousepad frantically to open her email application. The inbox filled the screen instantly. Kelly looked for the folder named 'Phishing', a self-made repository created for the purpose of throwing Matt off of the scent; should he ever get wind of anything suspicious and go investigating.

Connor's most recent email topped the list, which she duly opened, before scanning the message for his list of demands. They were, to her exultant relief, exactly as she had remembered. Unlock the front door five minutes prior to his arrival, make sure that there was a hot cup of coffee waiting for him by the kettle, ensure a freshly frozen tray of ice in the freezer, and position herself spread across the bed, naked and uncovered, shackled to the bed at both feet and with at least one of her wrists handcuffed, the four limbs spread to each corner. Finally, upon hearing any sign of his arrival, she would slide a blindfold into place and wait.

Kelly let out a deep, calming sigh and sank back into the leather seat. Feeling the thumping beat steadying within her chest she looked to the bottom corner of the laptop, to its digital clock. It showed *08:36 a.m.*

"Plenty of time for a coffee first", she rewarded herself proudly.

Matt sat beside the widest window in the corner of the now heated restaurant, its far end; the space just in front of the serving counters; now lively with a constant stream of fresh-faced customers. With his back tucked tightly into the space where the glass met the wall, he had neglected his, now cold, plate of fried breakfast, continuing instead to read chapter after chapter of his book without thinking to consider the time.

As he made his way halfway through his fourth chapter of the morning, Matt noticed a man drawing closer from over the top of the book. Fractionally raising his gaze, he watched as the man continued to approach, coming to a stop directly in front of him, the tops of his thighs touching at the edge of the table.

The stranger stood roughly six feet tall, with greying hair finished into a stylish cut. From first appearances, Matt estimated him to be in his late forties; perhaps even early fifties; although his clothes led Matt to believe that this man had not seen the best of years. His jeans were scruffy; ill-fitting, and dirtied with stains. The thickly knitted argyle sweater hanging above them was no better; possibly marginally worse; with gaping holes in its once cream-coloured wool. In fact, after scanning over the overall sight before him, Matt considered the man's smart hair to look strangely out of place.

The man loomed in towards him, picking at his yellow teeth with a dirty, overly long thumbnail, noisily sucking it clean whenever it appeared to reveal a reward for its efforts. Matt calmly lowered his book to the table.

"Can I help you?" he asked, somewhat nervously.

"I know you, son." The man grinned toothily.

"I'm not sure I know you. Have we met before?"

"Son, I know you! I'm telling you!"

Matt looked at the man in utter confusion.

"You're that guy!" The man pronounced enthusiastically.

"I'm that guy, am I?" Matt laughed, assuming that a request for spare change might shortly be forthcoming.

"Yeah man; that's what I've been trying to tell you! You're that guy who's fooled himself into thinking he's got what it takes to be the kind of bad boy his wife needs!"

The man lowered his eyes to the table, to the closed book in front of Matt's now anxiously twitching fingers.

"Catching up on a few last minute tips before you get your sorry arse home and pretend to fuck that slut like she's nothing, are ya?"

Chapter Thirty-Two

"Excuse me?" Matt looked at the man, horrified.

"Oh come on, son. It ain't like we haven't all been there before. Sure, you spent your formative years being told to respect the girls. Don't ever hurt 'em. All that shit. We all did! Only to find out when you hit your thirties that you've spent the whole time training yourself to be exactly what they don't fuckin' want! Well, some of 'em at least. Then that's the next damn challenge, right? Working out which of them *want* to be treated like a bitch. Sure, they can hide the imagery under a fancy suit and tie like the fucking bullshit in them books, but the truth still remains the same. They want treating badly, made to feel like worthless shit. Don't ask me why, they just do. Makes no fuckin' sense if you ask me. But then I did just say don't ask me, didn't I!"

"How do you know so much about me?"

"None of your fuckin' business, son. We each made our own mistakes and we live with 'em. Don't mean you get to know my life story though. I will tell you what *is* your business, mind. You ain't got it in ya. Do you get me? Am I talking clearly enough?"

"You're talking perfectly; I'm not an idiot. Are you suggesting I don't have what it takes to fulfil my wife's fantasy?"

"I'm not saying you're lacking what your wife needs. What I'm sayin' is she don't want it; at least not from you. Understand that?"

"With all due respect, *stranger*, I don't think you know what the fuck you're talking about. You think you know me? My wife? You think you know what she needs better than I do?"

"I know what they all need, son; the ones with *that* look in their eye, and she's no different. I can see it a mile off! You should look at her a bit closer once in a while. You'd see the same signs I do, creeping out through the cracks. A good hard slap across that slut's cheek and I bet her whole damn mask would crumble away, but it ain't you she wants slapping by."

Matt sat forward, his body physically shaking, and pointed directly to the man.

"You have no right to talk about my wife like that, but I'm gonna offer you the chance to walk the fuck away before I-"

"Wha' you gonna do, huh?"

The man backed away a couple of steps and threw his arms out in disappointment.

"I'm trying to help you! For Christ's sakes Matt, take a step back and assess the situation!"

It was the first time Matt had heard the stranger use his name. He was taken aback, trapped into a stunned silence; entirely lost on how to respond.

"I'm telling you; trying to be someone you're not will only hurt you more in the long-run. You only get one chance to be the hero; if indeed the chance ever comes; but you gotta pay attention for when that opportunity truly presents itself. Otherwise you're just gonna fuck it up like the rest of us losers."

Matt glared back at the man.

"I'm no fucking loser. And anyway; who said anything about being a hero?"

"Well then you've got two choices, son. You either take on board what I've told you, forget what you think was gonna happen today, and keep that little lady sweet on the *you* she knows *you* to be; or you pick up that knife, cut my lyin' fuckin' throat out, and shut me up for good."

"What kni-?"

Matt paused in astonishment as he followed the strangers extended finger down to the table and saw a thick black handle protruding from the bottom of the closed book. As he slowly pulled it apart a shining silver blade revealed itself, as tall as the paper was long and with its sharp edge tucked deeply into the spine within the pages he was yet to finish. It was a hunting knife, the type used by hunters for gutting fresh kills, with a five inch blade and a perfect row of ferocious looking razor sharp teeth cut into its back edge. Matt took its neatly finished, sculpted wooden handle in his palm and pulled it free of its paper sheath, brandishing it at the man.

"Did you put this here?"

"I dunno what you mean, son."

"Stop calling me son; I don't know you."

"Now listen, Matt…"

"Did you… put this fucking knife… in my book?"

The man looked hesitantly at Matt, their eyes locking deeply as if they shared the same consciousness.

"It was always there, Matt. You're so closed in by your little life that you never notice what's in front of you. It's painful to witness."

Matt looked over the knife's smooth blade.

"I can think of something much more painful", he said suggestively.

The man placed his forearms on the table and lowered his upper body until it was horizontal. Tilting his head upwards to look into Matt's increasing anger filled eyes, he moved his right arm from underneath himself, poking with a long, dirt-filled fingernail into a soft patch of skin just off-centre below his throat, and offered.

"Right there, son; then snatch it to the right. That's where it goes to make my lights go out, and for yours come back on. Assuming you've got the balls, that is"

Matt looked around the restaurant. Even after all of the man's loud, wild gesturing, the other customers seemed oblivious to their escalating quarrel. Not one of them were looking over in their direction. Matt did not know why, but he was suddenly fuelled by an immense urge to end their dialogue; no matter the consequence. Rationalism deserted him as he instinctively moved forward in his seat, driving the knife up meaningfully into the man's gullet, right next to where his scrawny finger still pointed. Warm blood gushed out from the ragged wound and down onto the top of Matt's gripping fingers, running around the ball of his fist down onto the table top in a pool of thickening splashes. He looked up to the strangers now flickering eyes, rolled so far back into his head that only the merest of his irises bottom edges could be seen under his eyelids, dancing from side to side in violent spasms. Matt let go of the handle in shock, scuttling back into the protection of the space where the glass met the wall, and began hyperventilating. He was finding it increasingly hard to breathe, but that did not stop his panicked mind from screaming repeatedly at him *'WHAT THE FUCK JUST HAPPENED?'*

The man's entire body was twitching, still hunched over the table with his quivering legs barely supporting him. He opened his mouth and Matt heard the faintest of words escape. He leaned in to listen closer, and the man repeated his gravelly sentence.

"I said... I knew you didn't have the balls to finish the job..."

Matt collapsed back, his mouth wide open in shock, his head hurting from the relentless pace of blood surging through his temples. He watched dumbfounded as the man took the handle of the knife in his own hands and ferociously yanked it sideways, opening his throat like a flesh-filled envelope. A torrent of darker blood rained down on the table, splashing the open books pages and landing dots of crimson over Matt's trousers. Matt screamed, crawling back tightly into the limited safety of his corner but, looking into the distant melee of customers, found no-one even seemed to hear him. The man coughed loudly, drawing Matt's horrified gaze back onto him.

"You pussy!" he gurgled sarcastically, then placed his hands on opposite sides of the wide tear in his neck pulling them apart.

Matt thought he saw a brief flash of yellow from within the gaping hole, and threw himself back against the window as a roar of flames shot out from it and consumed the man's head, followed by two loud pops ringing out as his eyes exploded into vivid blue flames. Matt could feel the intense heat rush against his face, forcing him to cower into a protective ball, while keeping one frantic eye on the man from over his guarding forearm. None of this made sense to him. *'This can't be happening! And why is no-one reacting?'* he asked himself. He grimaced, watching as the fire took hold; confused to see the man's skin flake off like burnt paper and float to the ground around his weakening feet. Morbidly, Matt began to ponder the biological science, questioning to himself why fat would not simply melt; leaving a gross pool of the guy's wet skin on the floor. Regardless of his confusion, though; that was not what was happening.

The fragments of paper-skin were piling up around the floor by the time the man's hand weakened and the knife became so loose it fell. Matt watched it as though the descent was in slow-motion, first dislodging from its place between his twitching fingers, then bouncing loosely between each of them individually before its short fall to the floor. It had rotated a couple of times as it neared the ground, its pin-sharp point just piercing the restaurants laminate flooring when a… '*BEEP! BEEP! BEEP! BEEP!*' rang out.

Without warning Matt's telephone alarm rang out loudly, snapping him awake and jerking the open book from his grasp and across the table's surface. It fell to the floor on the other side with a loud thud. He anxiously looked around, his heart thumping in his chest. There was no man. No pool of blood, nor flakes of skin. A few heads were turned but, aside from a couple of grumpy expressions borne seemingly from sleepy workmen having been similarly disturbed, there was pure disinterest on the faces he saw. Still, he felt deeply embarrassed. Snatching his rucksack from the seat beside him, Matt hurriedly moved from the table and made his way through the nearest door, leading to the bathrooms. It was nine o'clock. He had thirty minutes to get changed, prepared, and then home.

Kelly nursed her near-empty coffee cup on her knees. Sat forward on the couch, she stared catatonically towards the wall in front of her, smiling. The wall had ceased to be for some time. It was now a white canvas, onto which she projected her deepest anticipations, playing out her vision of the day ahead before it had actually unfolded. In truth, she was aware this was yet to be determined, having submitted to this being at Connor's complete discretion, with her role willingly limited to simply accepting his choices. This was the way of the submissive; ever eager to please their dominant; and she wanted for nothing more.

Two subtle chimes drifted out from the kitchen doorway. It was a sound which, on any other day, Kelly would ignore hourly, but which on this occasion jolted through her like a slap to her face. She had thirty more minutes to wait, she thought; although waiting was not an option. She had thirty minutes to prepare. Preparation, as she had come to understand through Connor's repeated urging, was key.

She sprang up from her seat and made her way up the stairs, a last minute clean of the bedroom in mind. This was not a required element on Connor's list. Kelly wanted to do it, thinking it might displease him if he were to see the room's common disorder, no matter how minimal a mess it may have seemed to her. She scrolled through his list one last time in her head. All of Connor's requirements were to be done relatively last minute anyway. She looked guiltily into the bedroom through the open doorway as an appalled voice within her muttered the word *'Filthy!*

Kelly set to work.

The bathroom cubicle was cramped but; as Matt laughed heartily to himself in an effort to not lose his cool; they were never meant to be used as changing rooms. His black trousers had not caused him any particular distress, but then that process had not been governed by the restriction of width which was now causing him a large degree of difficulty as he fought to slide his arms angularly into his shirt sleeves.

'*Either this cubicle is incredibly narrow*', he asked himself as his funny-bone hit the partition wall for the fifth jarring time, '*or I'm actually a much broader guy than I give myself credit for!*'

A deep, disgruntled voice drifted over the top of the partition as he shuffled within the tight space.

"What the hell are you doing in there?"

Matt felt a wave of awkwardness crash over him.

"Sorry" he spoke towards the flimsy wall. "I didn't

mean to disturb you".

The neighbouring occupant made a loud huff, and Matt listened as the sounds of a belt rattling and clothes rustling filled the small room. The next thing Matt heard, the toilet was being flushed; the squeaky cubicle door simultaneously yanked open as his gruff neighbour exited towards the sink basins. Water spat forcefully into the porcelain basin for what, to Matt, seemed to be around a full minute. He was frozen where he stood, his open and twisted shirt held halfway up his back, with its collar rested tightly at the mid-point of his spine. The tap finally stopped, after which the wall-mounted hand-dryer blew loudly for roughly the same amount of time. When he finally heard the sound of the bathroom door being opened, shuffled through and then closed, Matt let out his long-held breath. His nerves were already heightened enough without the unnecessary fear of making enemies of strangers.

With a renewed sense of urgency, Matt worked the shirt up his back and over his shoulders, hastily buttoning its front before anyone else might come to occupy the bathroom space. Unhooking the suit jacket from the simple brass hook on the cubicle door, he stepped out into the bathroom and used its more reasonable width to swing the final piece of his dominant uniform around himself. He watched his reflection within the broad mirrors above the basins; pressing the few creases in his shirt carefully flat; and smiled. There was something uncomfortably rigid about wearing a full suit, he felt; but he could not deny the sense of power he also claimed from it.

After running his hands under a flowing tap, and then sweeping them through his cropped hair, he looked at himself again and felt satisfied. A quick glance down to his watch told him the time had come.

9:15 am.

Matt grabbed his rucksack; stuffed haphazardly with his original clothes and book; and fished for his car keys from within its zippered front pocket. He was ready.

Chapter Thirty-Three

By the time she had cleaned the bedroom to the extent she felt necessary, Kelly had formed a sweat. She stretched the hem of her pyjama top up to wiped away the glossy sheen from her forehead before glancing across the room to the alarm clocks yellow illuminated display. It read *9:20 am*.

Having descended the stairs, she headed for the front door. Reaching it, she levered its latch downwards and pushed the deadlock button into place, fixing its mechanism into its unlocked position. Kelly then walked into the kitchen and flicked the kettle switch. By the time it had reached its boil, a mug for Connor had been prepared, filled with coffee granules and milk. She filled it with the hot water, making sure to stir the mixture thoroughly, anxious to ensure no gritty brown granules remained floating on its surface. *Everything should be perfect for Master*, she told herself as she wiped the rim of the mug with the corner of a dish cloth and positioned it thoughtfully on the counter. There she left it; steaming profusely and filling the space with its richly nutty aroma; and returned to the bedroom.

Gathering up the restraints from where she had previously placed them in the centre of the bed, she began attaching the two makeshift silk anklets. One was made from the simple silk belt belonging to her kimono styled dressing gown; the other, a long since used tie from Matt's small collection. Long enough ago used that its disappearance should not become immediately apparent, should it become collateral damage in Connor's games and need to be disposed of.

She fixed both lengths with tight knots to the furthest opposed vertical bars at the foot end of the bed, before looping the opposite end of each length and tying them into slipknots, forming loose sleeves ready to slide her ankles into. Pulling open her bedside draw, she removed her black silk blindfold from its furthest depths, fixed it by its elasticated strap around the circumference of her skull, and propped its eye-patch panel high up her forehead ready for last minute manoeuvring into position. As a surprise addition; unrequested by Connor; she removed a black and red leather ball-gag, tying in around her neck loosely. Next she removed two pairs of newly purchased handcuffs from a small green bag and opened their boxes, slid the heavy ringed shackles from their trays, and looped one of each of their wrist openings around the bars at the head end of the bed. She squeezed their coiled, ratcheted arms firmly into place with a series of slow, satisfying crunches and let them hang there, smiling excitedly to herself. Stepping back to look over the bed; assessing her preparation for a generous moment; Kelly felt ready. Nervous, but ready.

The handcuff boxes were placed hastily back into the small bag and thrown dramatically from the bed, sending it skidding loudly across the floor where it hit the plinth at the base of the sturdy walnut tallboy and came to rest. Kelly quickly stripped herself naked, placed herself on the edge of the duvet, and sidled across the bed until her backside sat centred within it. Leaning forward, she took the silk belts loosely knotted end and placed it around her slender left ankle, fixing it tightly in place with a sharp jerk on the slipknot. The tie was then used to replicate the process for her opposite ankle. Its tethering felt noticeably weaker than the other but; Kelly hoped; would be tight enough to maintain its hold and not loosen from movement. She was struck by the fear of causing Connor any cause for disappointment in her.

The head end of the beds frame was made up of a series of vertical, black, cylindrical metal bars; similar to those at the foot of the bed but considerably thicker, each welded to the underside of a width-long, two inch wide metal plate. Onto this plates flat surface Kelly carefully placed her mobile phone, before leaning back against the short stack of pillows and extending her left arm. She fixed the available ring of the handcuffs by its first ratchet around her wrist. She was wary to leave this intentionally loose, enough so as to enable her whole forearm to pass through its hole. Shifting her weight onto her side, she then placed the right sided cuff around her other wrist and squeezed it tightly closed, enough so that she could feel the cold steel pressing lightly into her radial artery.

Manoeuvring herself flat again, she pushed her now vertical left wrist against one of the metal bars behind her, feeling the metal reverberate with rapid clicks, until it too was tightened against both sides of her thin skin and the fragile veins beneath it.

After checking it was possible to reach her mobile on its thin shelf above her head, she relaxed into the soft Egyptian cotton of the duvet cover and turned her head to glance again at the alarm clock. It now read *9:29 am*.

'*Well*', she thought, letting out a huge sigh of trepidation. '*There's no going back now, even if I wanted to!*

Connor draped his arm lazily out of the car window, feeling the wind brushing through his open fingers as he pushed hard onto the accelerator. He was running slightly late, based on his own timings, but he knew that by taking the Curlingbrook underpass he would claw back some of the time. He passed by each of the other possible turnings; every one of them capable of leading him to the Buchanon residence, but less desirable, less straight routes; and carried on following the signposts for the more direct option of the tunnel.

As he neared the slow cars ahead of him, he thought briefly of overtaking, but was halted by the sight of a trail of cars approaching from the opposite direction. At the head of the approaching convoy sat a beastly looking white articulated lorry, pumping out clouds of smoke from its exhaust and filling the entire width of its lane. Connor applied his brakes sharply, narrowly avoiding a collision with the rear bumper of the people carrier in front of him; slowing rapidly to a frustratingly slow pace. Two young children; Connor estimated them to be perhaps four or five years old; peered over their headrests and stared blankly at him through the rear windscreen. A boy and a girl, their heads were hung either side of the more distant rear-view mirror reflecting the angry face of their mother. Her eyes showed the type of protective anger only a parent could muster, while mouthing her significant distaste at Connor clearly. He stared back callously into the reflection of the woman's eyes. Raising his middle finger first to her, he then thrust it one by one towards each of the children, watching with a wry smile across his face as they reeled back in shock. Intimidated, they span around in their seats to face forward. Their mother shook her head in disbelief.

Connor sat stuck to the back of the trail of cars, gradually picked up speed over the next half-mile, allowing his temper to ease a little as his foot teased at the accelerator pedal. In his rear view mirror he could see that the earlier slowdown had caused traffic to back up, causing a significant tailback stretching further than his mirror could show. The underpass was nearing though, and he felt content with the sight of the easing traffic ahead as he watched from over his snarling bonnet.

The Curlingbrook underpass was not a typical tunnel built to simply avoid an overhead road or train-track. It had been engineered to take those commuters not wishing to enter the sprawling network of streets which made up the smaller neighbouring suburbs. This meant that, even on its best days, the route remained consistently busy all the way through from dawn until dusk. Its two lanes curved to the right a little more than a hundred yards into the tunnels mouth, appearing pitch black to the naked eye when approaching, whatever the time of day. Dim orange lights; capped with dirtied transparent glass covers and fitted to its curved walls; illuminated from the bend onwards giving the roof above the disappearing road ahead a distant, ominous glow.

Connor fixed his eyes to the road markings just ahead of his wheels, following them confidently as he maintained his speed through the dimly lit entrance. As he began to navigate the turn something bright made his gaze deviate upwards. It was oncoming headlights, high-beamed and flashing frantically. Connor watched intently as the car with the warning lights raced towards them, hugging itself tightly against the tunnels curved wall. Suddenly the people carrier's brake-lights lit up in front of him, the woman's wheels squealing against the road as her car lurched forward on its suspension and came to an abrupt stop. Connor reacted quickly, slamming his foot down onto his own brake, his front grill stopping just a few millimetres from the people carrier's red rear-bumper. His eyes anxiously flicked between the now slowing trail of cars in his rear-view, and the approaching line of cars ahead, led by the car with the flashing lights. The car directly in front of the people carrier was continuing through the tunnel, but it was apparent to Connor that something was wrong with its driver. The side of its chassis was weaving perilously over the centre-line, encroaching into the oncoming traffic by at least twelve inches by the time the car with the flashing lights collided with it. Metal crashed loudly into metal. Plastic and fibreglass bodywork splintered into thousands of pieces, flying out in all directions, hitting the other cars and bouncing off of the tunnels walls and ceiling. The impact caused the oncoming cars nearside corner to buckle inwards, stopping it momentarily until momentum caused it to spin sideways, sending it into a roll through the tunnel and past Connor's window. A trail of debris followed behind it, while sheets of sparks flew out under the line of stationary cars and up the curved tunnel walls. The car ahead of the people carrier; similarly brought to a sudden stop; jumped off of its rear wheels and began to flip over itself, until its boot met the unforgiving stone roof and sent its back end forcefully back to the ground. Its rear axle shattered on impact. Connor watched the bend of the tunnel ahead as the battered chassis limped uncontrollably into the orange gloom, its wheel arches scuffing on the tops of its tyres.

The tunnel echoed with the sounds of emergency brakes, grinding metal, and a cacophony of shouts and screams erupting through open car windows. Then, as if a dimmer switch had been slowly turned, each source of noise faded and the tunnel descended into unnatural silence.

Chapter Thirty-Four

Kelly couldn't stop herself from watching the bedside clock. It was *9:32*, and she was growing increasingly nervous. To the right of her head her mobile phone bleeped twice, followed by the soft hum of vibration against its metal shelf.

Craning her restricted right arm, she took the phone from its perch and swiped the screen alive. It was a text, from Connor. Her heart began to pump faster as she pressed to access the message, only to read its contents and slump further into the bed.

I'm going to be delayed, my pet. Accident in the underpass and I'm caught in it. Hopefully won't be too long. I'll text when I'm on the move and you'll prepare for my arrival then.

"It's a bit fuckin' late for that!" she snapped loudly into the empty room.

Bending her wrist to place the phone back onto its shelf, it slipped from her pinched grasp and hit the metal ledge, spinning precariously for a moment before coming to rest. Half of its casing lay over the metal ledge, its other half hovering over the thin gap between the bed and the wall. Kelly shuffled her weight carefully to her left, hoping to allow her right arm more extension but, as she slid her body into position the movement made the beds frame lean away from the wall enough for the gap to widen, and for the phone to fall down through it. Directly below her head, Kelly heard the phone first connect with the wooden floor and then skid out further underneath her body, stopping somewhere around the centre point of the bed.

"*FUCK IT!*" she screamed out in temper.

It was a couple of minutes later, as her tensed body was beginning to ease, that she heard the familiar squeak of the front door being pushed inwards from its tight wooden frame.

Matt stood staring through the partial crack of the open doorway, perplexed. He didn't remember leaving the front door on its latch and yet, from tentatively peering inside, he could see no sign of Kelly having gotten out of bed yet. The curtains remained drawn; the interior of the house shrouded in darkness and silence. He raised a heavy foot over the threshold and stepped in; slowly and with caution. Something which he felt unable to rationalise felt worryingly wrong with the situation.

Carefully pushing the door back towards its frame he stopped short of closing it entirely, aware that the action would cause a repeat of the tightening squeal; a further tell-tale warning of its movement. If someone was in the house, he feared, they would immediately be made aware of his presence - unless they already were.

A smell hit his nostrils as he slowly palmed the door away from him. Sniffing the air to be sure, he was puzzled to arrive at the same conclusion he had initially thought it to be. Fresh coffee. Glancing over his shoulder into the dim house again, he sensed no change to its unoccupied stillness. It was only as he pressed forward with soft steps through the entrance hall that he noticed the smell grew more intense, leading him to turn his head to his right towards the open kitchen doorway. There, on the counter, sat a coffee mug, the air above it still swirling with wisps of steam. None of this made sense. Matt's imagination raced with possibilities. *Had Kelly made a coffee and then for some reason gone back to bed without taking it? Perhaps she had taken a bath and planned to drink it afterwards?*

He listened intently for a moment, thinking he might hear the sounds of water flowing, but found nothing in the distance for his ears to grasp hold of. The eerie silence made a cold shiver run up his spine.

Each of his steps were placed with attentive care against the laminate floor as he moved through the rest of the house, stealthily manoeuvring his body between the narrow pathways separating the lounge furniture's angular edges. Stopping at the base of the staircase, Matt turned his ear to the landing above him and paused, listening again. Pure silence seemed impossible to achieve at first, as he became acutely aware of the blood pressure behind his ears surging in direct rhythm with his thumping heartbeat; like the sound of the ocean when heard through a conch shell, but played at four times its normal speed. He exhaled heavily, concentrating on his natural ability for self-calming, and noticed the almost instant decrease of the swaying tide between his ears. After a few seconds of composure, and feeling the ambient silence surrounding him once again, he returned his attention back to the top of the stairs. Nervously, he placed his quivering foot on the first of its flight.

Sat anxiously waiting on the bed, afraid to move a single muscle or to speak out, Kelly's mind was consumed with the premise that Connor had cruelly tricked her; a little white lie of deceit in order to subtly manipulate her mood into one more conducive to their relationship. Perhaps he had purposely wanted her to become riled up prior to his arrival, she thought; to make her feistier and more deserving of the treatment that he wanted to bestow upon her body. Maybe that would somehow serve as justification for his actions - assuming that he felt some psychological need for justification in the first place. Or maybe she was simply overanalysing his state of mind.

Kelly reprimanded herself guiltily about the depth of her consideration; entering the psyche of her master so intrusively without his knowledge or permission. She knew that she had no right to do so. She knew that he would exact punishment if he knew. An electric-like thrill ran up through her thighs, into the pit of her butterfly-filled stomach as she imagined the anger in his face, and the forceful ways he might reprimand her if he knew. So enraptured was she by these blissful thoughts, she began to consider telling him; curiously eager to see his reaction or, better still, to feel them acted out upon her. But that would have to wait; as agonisingly as the concept of patience ate into her soul. Master was taking his time; presumably having found, and now drinking the coffee that she had so dutifully prepared. Suddenly remembering the blindfold hitched tightly across her forehead, she bent her arm towards her head to slide the thick leather band down with two fingers; her anxiety growing feverishly higher as the room was shuttered from view and the immediate blackness took her sight.

Outside the deafening silence of the bedroom Kelly heard the merest of sounds, pulling her attention sharply away from her thoughts. It was soft, like a gentle brushing against material, perhaps; or of bare feet being swept over deep-pile carpet. Whatever the cause might be, Kelly was sure that she could hear its volume steadily increasing. It was drawing nearer. Slowly and silently she outstretched her naked body over the bed, moving into the most alluring position her mind could picture and the restraints would allow. Staring into the black abyss she strained at her hearing; exhilarated; listening for any tell-tale movement of the bedroom door.

Chapter Thirty-Five

Matt stood frozen in the bedroom doorway, his body collapsing against its wooden frame as his heart sank towards his stomach. Before his eyes, the scene they relayed to him was pure nonsense, a jumble of visual information which his brain found unable to comprehend with any reasonable logic as it rushed to take it all in. His heart, however, found the sickening scene to be crystal clear.

Kelly was laid awkwardly; her head and shoulders were raised from the pillows, held in mid-air by the tensed, straining muscles in her stomach. Though bound within the grip of abject darkness, she was becoming acutely aware of subtle changes in the bedrooms ambience; the increased circulation of air which brushed more consistently across her naked body as it flowed freely through the wider opened doorway, and a deadening of the familiar whistle of silence she had become accustomed to hearing when so often alone in the room; both of which signified a new presence to the blind captive. As the agonising seconds ticked by and the deafening silence scorched her racing imagination, Kelly began to feel hurt both by her own impatience and by Connor's apparent teasing. Struggling to handle the sense of isolation consuming her, she stretched her mouth around the restrictive plastic ball and called out, timidly.

"Master; Are you there?"

The silence continued at first. Pinching her eyes shut and with her ears straining to isolate the numb sound around her, Kelly heard the faintest shuffle, like the scuff of material as it moved against a surface. It had been caused by Matt, open mouthed in horror at hearing Kelly's incriminating query, pushing his body forward from the doorframe. He contemplated taking a further step across the room but snatched himself back at the last moment, unsure of what his next move would be. His heart sank further as Kelly called out again.

"Master?"

"Yes", Matt spoke, deepening his voice in the hope that Kelly would not find its tone suspect. He questioned his actions immediately, unsure why he had responded, but was met with a surge of his own curiosity.

Kelly seemed visibly relieved. Matt watched as her body relaxed back down onto the bed and expelled a deep, satisfied breath. He tentatively stepped forward, stopping at the corner of the bed. Trembling, he reached forward to lay a nervous hand on her ankle, stroking her noticeably charged skin as his fingers slid upwards, over the smooth curve of her calf. His other hand reached up to pop the ball gag free. Kelly let out a pleasured whimper as the tips of his rising fingers reached the back of her knee, her muscles twitching above their soft, tickling touch.

"My God your fingers feel so good, Sir!" she praised ecstatically.

Matt paused there for a moment, concentrating on easing his runaway heartbeat to compose himself. His urge was to continue; to explore the body he had, for so long, been denied. He would have, had his conscience not stepped in and spoken to him so adamantly. It extolled to him the virtues of honesty, pleading with him that he was too good a person and not to disregard his habitually noble standards.

Kelly's eyes, having grown accustomed to their black veil, blinked excessively as the blindfold was slid away from them and the rooms light flooded into her retinas. Her heartbeat surged as she awaited their clarity; to welcome her Master and begin their day. As the bright haze grew clearer, and her eyes found the outline of her vision-giver, she noticed the curiously narrow width between his shoulders. The colours of his suit came through next, exciting her all the more, but confusing as the contour of his jaw gradually revealed itself to be less chiselled than she had remembered. The ball of mist in the centre of her vision broke away and there, looking down at her in a state of utter heartbreak, she saw Matt.

"SHIT!" she screamed out.

"Oddly enough, I was thinking the exact same thing!"

"What the fuck are you doing here?"

"I took the day off thinking I'd surprise you. Not to this extent, but it seems as though I achieved my goal, doesn't it?"

"Well don't just fucking stand there; get me out of these!" she urged him, gesturing to her handcuffs.

"Why don't you start by explaining to me why you're like this in the first place?"

"Matt; get a grip! Do what I damn well asked and un-"

"No, Kelly." Growing agitated, Matt raised his voice. "You owe me an explanation, don't you think? I mean... there's obviously something going on."

"Oh; piece it together yourself, you fucking idiot."

"I'm pretty sure I already have, but I'm giving you the opportunity to put it into your own words."

"There's really no need, Matt; I'm sure you've got it all figured out just fine."

"So you're having an affair."

"Well, bravo to you, Sherlock. If my hands were free I'd clap."

"For at least a year you've been distant to me. I haven't been able to touch you without feeling your body cringe away from me. How long has... whatever this is... been going on?"

"Nowhere near that long!" Kelly chuckled sarcastically. "But you're very astute; I really cannot stand it when you touch me."

"Odd that you should say that though, isn't it? When, right before I removed your blindfold, you were loving the feel of my hand rising up your leg."

"Yeah, well... that's different."

"Silly me... of course it would be; that makes total sense! Tell me, Kelly; how long?"

"Little more than a month."

Kelly had no reason to lie; Matt knew that. The truth could not remain hidden now; further subterfuge made little sense. Thinking about the timings; how Kelly's affair must have started shortly before his assault; Matt's eyes grew wider as the pieces fell into place.

"Dawned on you, has it?" Kelly mocked.

"You... and... Connor?"

"Jeez Mr Clever; you're on a roll!"

"Holy SHIT!" Matt reeled back in anguish, clasping a hand to his mouth as his jaw dropped.

"So now you know. The truth's out, Matt; deal with it how you will, but you can start by getting a grip of yourself and letting me out of these", Kelly demanded again.

Matt heard little of Kelly's cold instruction. His head was a mess of emotions, barraging his usual ability to handle their attacks by combining forces in a full assault. His only reaction; the one release his overwhelmed feelings could channel; was a throaty, rage-laden scream at the top of his lungs. His hands rose up in the air beside him, their fists tightly clenched, threatening the ceiling as he roared his frustration towards it.

"Let's not get theatrical about it, Matt", Kelly stated. "You must've known this was coming at some point."

"I should, should I!" he blasted back uncontrollably.

Kelly looked at him in silence, rotating her stretched shoulders forward enough to shrug.

"I'll tell you what I thought was coming. I thought I was coming home to spend the day with my wife, in our bed preferably, making up for all the lost time since we were last intimate, by experiencing something new that we both could enjoy."

Suddenly the suit made sense to Kelly. Her face stretched into a wry smile.

"Is that what the suit's for? Mr Feeble was gonna come home all dominant, to take me by the hair and put me under his control, is that it?"

"That's beside the point now, isn't it? Yes... I had plans to give it a try, but it looks as though I was beaten to the punch."

"Trust me, Matt; you weren't beaten to anything. You weren't even in the fight."

"It was something we could have shared, Kelly; a new experience to get things back to being exciting between us, like they used to be."

"I don't want to share that experience with you, Matt! Jesus Christ... why do you think I looked elsewhere? You're not that guy!"

"And Connor is!"

"Yes! I know that's probably hard for you to stomach, but I can't help it if it's true! You're too weak a man, Matt. Connor's got charisma, the type of guy who can believably act dominant. With you it's totally different. I can't take you seriously at the best of times!"

"And yet, he's not your husband."

"Are you?" Kelly asked sarcastically. "Tell me... when was the last time we felt like a true couple? Whatever we had at the start disappeared a long time ago, Matt; and you're to blame for that!"

"I'm to blame? None of that might be your fault too?"

"You've spent the last two years caring more about work than about me! That fucking place sees more of you than I do each week, and I've grown tired of being neglected."

"I haven't neglected you, Kelly" Matt pleaded, "Every hour of overtime that I've put into work was to spend on you; for treats, nights out, money you needed... whatever you wanted. And then, whenever I took the initiative to be romantic or... or amorous, you rejected me."

"Do you really expect me to feel sexy, or desirable, when you're constantly treating me like an afterthought? That's not how a marriage works! You have to put in some effort if you want the rewards, you selfish prick!"

Matt faltered. The impact of Kelly's persistent attacking had built up to the point where he was unable to think clearly. He was lost for words, staring over her seething expression and beginning to hate himself for her feeling so negatively, when a strengthening voice sheared through the self-deprecating tornado in his mind.

'You're not the man she's making you out to be', it reassured him mutinously, its disgust of Kelly's insinuations obvious from its tone.

A previously unfelt level of anger stirred deep within Matt's core. He felt instantly empowered by it; every muscle in his upper body thickening; tensed and urging him to unleash. He knew that he could not allow it to overwhelm him, though an urge to surrender to their relentless pleading was building steadily inside.

"I... I have to... "

"I... I... I..." Kelly sneered. "Spit it out!"

"I have to go... downstairs... just for a moment."

"Matt, I'm not kidding around. Let me the fuck loose."

Matt knew that if he were to take a step closer, his strained command over the persistent anger inside of him would likely break. He shook his head sorrowfully, walking briskly out through the bedroom door to Kelly's livid screams of displeasure.

Chapter Thirty-Six

He could not recall descending the stairs. When his brain finally kicked back into gear he found he was standing by the patio door, staring out into the garden and breathing excessively against the thick glass pane. He could still hear Kelly's angry protests as he struggled to pull himself together, desperate to feel any less on the brink of madness. He rested his head on the door, closing his eyes and concentrating to slow his erratic breaths. As the controlled intake of oxygen began flowing into his lungs he could feel the taut sinews easing throughout his chest and arms. A wash of euphoria came over him as he realised he had taken back control, although joined by a sharp intense pain, stabbing into his head beside his right temple, which he pushed away as best as he could. Kelly had gone quiet above him. Now, feeling a sense of space returning inside his head, he began summarising the mornings depressing events. His thoughts were drawn back to the disturbing dream he had lived much earlier, of the man who seemingly knew his life so intimately, and who had warned him so accurately. Matt shook his head in denial as the strangers face floated eerily behind his eyes, his ears replaying the man's distressing warning he now felt so foolish to have ignored. Without realising it, his hands were curling inwards again, bunching up into quivering fists. The scene upstairs now moved like a panorama through his mind. Kelly's naked, exposed body; her limbs shackled in preparation of Connor's arrival; rage began to fill the vacant space within Matt's head again. Trying to regain control once more, and as he wiped away fast flowing streams of tears from his cheeks, a distant voice rudely broke him from focus.

"*HEY! MATT!* I'm tired of this shit. Dry your eyes; grow some balls, and get me the *FUCK OFF OF THIS BED*! Then we can talk."

A black mist swarmed over Matt's vision, accompanied by shrill whistling in his ears as blood surged into his head. The sharp pain grew rapidly outwards from his temple, enveloping his forehead and seeping around to the other ear. A loud bang came from in front of him and, glancing to its source, he was shocked to find his fist against the glass, its knuckles burning from their forceful impact. He glanced over his shoulder and up the staircase, the mist forcing his view into a thin tunnel of light, with the bedroom door fixed at its end.

Before Matt knew it he was striding up the stairs, three at a time, with fierce intent. It was as though he could see from above himself, the actions of his body somehow disconnected from receiving his synapses true instructions. He arrived at the entrance to the bedroom, his chest heaving in and out, where he watched helplessly as his foot rose up and jabbed forward, sending the door spinning inwards on its hinges before crashing into the wall with a horrendously loud smash. From behind it he heard the fracturing sounds of the door handles impact; its components breaking free from its fixings and hitting the floor with an echoing clatter of metal.

Kelly's stiff body jumped up from the surface of the bed in visible panic. She watched breathlessly as Matt entered the room, his face flustered in red; palpable anger emanating from him like an aura.

"I've never wanted anything from you; just your love", he fumed, "so why is it so impossible for you to do the same and accept me for me? I'm still the same man you married! I haven't changed! You've changed; or at least your expectations have; but that's not my damn fault."

"Matt; let me go, then we can talk this all through."

"Oh no! No fucking way! I want straight answers, not some politicians' avoidance. Tell it to me straight, and then you get your freedom."

"What, Matt? What the fuck do you expect me to say?"

"I want to know how it's so wrong for me to be empathetic; to act selflessly. I've put you first the whole time we've been together, but you've taken all I've given, refused me at every turn, and then shared your lust with essentially a fucking stranger without a single care for my feelings. Now I want to know why that is? What is it I've done to you that's so wrong it deserves that treatment?"

Kelly sighed.

"Matt; it's not that I don't love you."

"Then what the hell is it?"

"It's just... It's like I'm unfulfilled by having just you. You're generous. You give; and give more without any expectations, but that's not what I need."

"You need a Curtis Sharp; is that what you mean?"

"Listen, I don't expect you to unders-"

"I understand perfectly, Kelly. I may be a quiet guy; unassuming for the most part, and that's just in my nature. I'm no idiot though. I pay attention to the world around me. I've read your books; I know what you think you need to be complete."

Kelly's eyes lit up with instant fury.

"You've read my Curtis Sharp's? You fucking arsehole; they were mine! It's the one thing I asked you not to do!"

"*I'm* sorry, baby. I must have got confused, what with the long list of things you were constantly expecting me *to* do! Still; the damage is done. There's no going back now."

"Oh, how very witty of you! So, what? You think you know the ins and outs of my mind now? It's not in your character to be dominant, Matt; don't kid yourself."

"I think you should be more concerned about not kidding yourself. If there's something missing within our relationship then I'll make damn sure you're not gonna find it until you make the grown up decision and leave me."

Kelly shook her head vigorously. "I don't want to leave you, Matt."

"Too beneficial; is that it?"

"You're my safety net, Matt. I don't want to give that up. I want you here... at night... with me."

"So you can sit at the opposite end of the room and constantly snipe at me? That's awfully generous of you. Can't Connor offer you that? No; I suppose he'd be keen to train that sort of shit out of you."

"Connor's not caring; at least not in the ways you are. You're loving and considerate; much more than he can be. It's not in his nature."

"It must be really hard for you; determining which of your options to take based on so many opposing factors."

"Please Matt; don't be like that. I'm telling you I want to stay with you."

"Sure. Unhappy and unfulfilled, but with a safety net; as if that's going to stop you fooling around behind my back."

"You asked me to give it to you straight, Matt."

"Tell me how you and Connor started this... betrayal. When was the first time?"

"Matt, please! I don't want to get into that."

"It's not your choice, Kelly. I deserve to know, and I will before I even consider unlocking those cuffs."

Kelly looked hard at Matt, the sinking feeling in her

stomach reflected sickeningly through her growing frown. Her arms, stretched out above her, were growing paralysed. Her wrists chaffed uncomfortably in their unforgiving metal traps. The sense of depression at the thought of being held there for another minute made her crack.

"The night you two went to the bar. Connor showed up on the doorstep really late."

Matt reeled back in shock as another piece of the puzzle fell into place.

"And you didn't think to ask why I wasn't with him?"

"Oh no, I did ask; I did! He said something about you... not being in a position to disturb us."

"And you just accepted that? Jesus, Kelly. That's cold."

"It's whatever, Matt. He stayed the night and left before sunrise. The next thing I knew he was calling me from the hospital to tell me you were there. That was the first I knew; honest!"

Matt felt the leather belt around his waist sliding through his belt-loops. He looked down to see his own right hand, tugging on the belts now separated buckle, slowly dragging its thick length free. Kelly saw its movement too, turning defiant at the threat of aggression, and threatening back.

"Do not even fuckin' think about using that on me."

"I... I don't know why I was, I... I didn't even realise I was doing it", Matt looked up to her, mystified.

"It doesn't impress me, Matt. I'm serious when I say that it's not what I want from you."

"I assume you wanted it from Connor though? How long did it take... that night... for Connor to give you the same?"

"Matt, please!"

"You let him, didn't you? You let him strike your body – my wife's body – just like in those damn books; didn't you?"

Matt's arm shot through the air, bringing the loose belt end down onto the beds metal frame near Kelly's feet. The room echoed with its impact, a heavy thud which startled the both of them with its ferocity. Kelly took a moment to compose; sneering sarcastically into Matt's overwhelmed eyes.

"Feel better for that, do you? Did it make you feel like a big strong boy; taking back control?"

Matt stood mute; his lips quivering frantically with the silent words they begged to utter. His eyes were glazed over a stony grey, staring back at Kelly as though she were not there, seeing through her to the wall behind or maybe further; Kelly could not tell. His brow was curled, its broad ripples of skin bunched tightly together, furrowing down into a deep 'V' between his eyes. His hand felt the warmed leather bound tightly around it again and, before realising his own actions, he had stepped forward and raised it high in the air once more. He brought it down again with unconscionable force.

Kelly's howled into the air, her inner thigh stinging unbearably, recoiling in pain as the pointed leather tip found its mark. Enraged, she looked first at the angry welt forming under her skin, then back up to Matt.

"What the fuck, Matt?"

He made no hint that he had heard her outburst. His expression remained the same; trapped deep in thought; devoid of any other discernible emotion.

Kelly pulled fearfully at her restraints; pleading with the knotted links at her feet to relent, or for a weak weld behind her head to give way; until a second lashing struck her other thigh and sent her body thrashing back down to the mattress with a scream.

"How does that feel?" Matt finally spoke; little more than a whisper.

His voice was distant; monotone. Kelly stared back at him; speechless. The sight of Matt so possessed; the feel of his scathing attacks on her skin; no words could summarise the confusion she felt so inexplicably surrounded by.

"How does that feel?" Matt echoed, this time a little louder.

Kelly; with a forthright voice in her head reminding her not to back down, opened her mouth to protest.

"How do you think it fuckin'-"

Matt brought a third slap of the makeshift whip down across her already tender thigh, silencing Kelly as her anger took over and she bit her tongue through sheer defiance.

How does that feel?" Matt's voice began to escalate, from raised to shouting as he began whipping it across her each time. "HOW DOES THAT FEEL? *HOW DOES THAT FEEL?*"

"Matt; you're scaring me!"

"*DOES THAT FEEL GOOD...? YOU SELFISH, CHEATING WHORE!*"

"Matt! Please!" Kelly begged, masking her still furious attitude behind emphatic pleading, in the hope that his conscience would hear it.

"Why, Kelly!" Matt ceased his downward strikes, seeming to finally find himself through the haze; his eyes becoming sharper. "Because you think you don't deserve it? Explain it to me because I'm confused. How is it that your actions are unworthy of consequence? This is the fucking consequence, you self-centred bitch!"

"Don't you ever call me that... *HOW FUCKIN' DARE YOU!* I'm no bitch, Matt; I'm your wife!"

"If you acted like it I might agree; but this? You're

massively contradicting yourself; don't you think?"

"Take some fucking responsibility, Matt! This is because of you, regardless of whether you have the balls to admit it or not."

"Say that to me one more time." Matt placed his hands on the metal bed-frame, turning it in his grip; challenging her.

"Read my lips, you self-righteous twat. It's... Your... Fault."

Matt charged ferociously around the side of the bed, throwing his arm towards her as he came along side Kelly, locking his fingers tightly around her throat.

"One more time?" he challenged her; the corners of his mouth starting to foam with rabid anger.

Kelly looked up to him helplessly as she felt his firm grip squeezing tighter. Her eyes bulged; their intense glare digging into him like knives, frantically urging upon him a sense of incrimination. Defiant to the end; the repeated words escaped her lips in short, stunted bursts; unable to flow cohesively through one breath.

"It's... Your... Fault..., You... Pa-the-tic... Cunt."
Matt's palm was raised high to his side as the devil in his conscience compelled him to turn it into a fist and shut Kelly up for good. Holding it there, desperate for his principles to win the opinionated struggle, he heard Kelly deliver one last insult.

"Do... It..."You... Pussy."

The strike came down quickly; stinging broadly across her cheek with a loud crack, its sound sent echoing around the bedrooms walls.

As Matt stepped back in horror of his own ferocity, and the vicious sound dissipated, a second sound came to the fore. A car engine, deep and throaty, rumbling from the far end of the street and drawing nearer. Both Matt and Kelly looked to the small curtain-shrouded window as the gravel drive beneath it crunched with heavy disturbance. A squeak of brakes later and the crunching motion of the small stones ceased; replaced by the low murmur of the cars idling.

Chapter Thirty-Seven

Connor sat absorbed in his driving seat, passionately revving the engine of his Audi as it cooled from its journey. Each tease of the accelerator rumbled the chassis beneath him, his face stretched broadly with the pleasure that the visceral power sent through him. A further couple of short bursts and then he relented, turning the key and shuddering the car to silence. He straightened his tie before checking his hair in the rear view mirror. With distaste he scowled at the few stray wisps hovering just above his ears. They had somehow avoided the hair wax he had applied in good measure, sticking out on his periphery, springy with dehydrated, greying fatigue.

"Fuck it!" he muttered.

Licking the length of his extended fingers, he swept them, saliva coated, over the errant patches to bring them back into formation. They fell into line and Connor, after feeling the need to adjust his tie one final time, stepped confidently out of the car and began to whistle.

He reached into the open boot, drawing out the black rucksack which he threw over his shoulder while simultaneously slammed the boot shut again, and strode confidently towards the house; abruptly ceasing his whistling upon arriving at the door. Finding it to be tightly closed against its frame, Connor slid his finger under the steel letterbox flap and levered it up. He hunched down, peering through the narrow slot into the oppressive darkness of the lounge. Considering the internal gloom strange, he paused to take a second glance, but quickly arrived at a suitably just conclusion to appease the festering concern in his mind.

"Obviously the little whore wants it everywhere, so long as the neighbours don't catch get an eyeful!" he encouraged himself.

Glimpsing down the street at the parallel rows of car-less driveways, Conor could not help but question whether a witness was even a possibility, given the time of day.

Still mildly cautious, he pressed his fingers firmly against the silver plate below the keyhole, and the door fell inwards. With a devilish grin forming, he looked through the open doorway towards the now faintly lit lounge.

"That's my girl" he whispered into the open space, hopping up the step and into the narrow hallway.

He carefully pushed the door closed behind him, silently disengaging the deadlock. He was eager to keep his arrival a secret, revealing himself only as he stepped through the bedroom door or; more preferably; by the placing his hands on Kelly's taut, electrified skin – although he knew this was only possible so long as she had worn her blindfold as he had instructed - and assuming each of his further steps through the house would fall without any sound.

The cold coffee on the kitchen worktop concerned him. He touched at its side and felt no heat, at first incensed by Kelly's apparent lack of timely preparation, but quickly resolving that she may had of committed herself too early; not knowing that that had been the case. He anticipated the scene awaiting him at the top of the stairs; how she would be presented. He could almost picture her in his mind; helplessly waiting for him there with her self-administered shackles in place. Ready to have her body be devoured and abused. Gratified by his dominant strengths.

As he reached the foot of the stairs he peered around

the bannister, stroking the length of his growing erection through his sleek black trousers in anticipation. With an unintentionally heavy breath of determination he stared himself into character, and began his stealthy ascendance of the flight.

The bedroom door was pushed closed, so far as to leave only the merest sliver to squint through. Connor carefully placed the rucksack down at the side of the door and peered forward. The curtains were drawn, but enough daylight filtered through them for him to see Kelly stretched over the bed, the dim light reflecting from the metal restraints at either side of her head. As he gazed in, breathing heavily against the door panel, Kelly turned her head as if noticing the shadow of his movement behind it. Realising the lack of a blindfold, Connor felt an intense rage building inside of him, disgusted at the realisation that his full intentions could not now be achieved. He pushed the door inwards with angered intent and strode into the room, questioning her failure with his arms outstretched at his sides.

"Connor!" Kelly exclaimed.

He failed to notice the tone in her voice, deafened by his own disappointment, and pointing his index finger at her harshly.

"How dare you fail me at the first hurdle? You had a simple list of commands! That's far from the best start for a submissive to-"

"You need to listen to me, Connor", Kelly interrupted, "You need to leave, right now!"

"Excuse me?!"

"It's Matt!" she cried out.

"What about the little prick?"

"He's-"

"He's stood behind you", Matt spoke angrily from

the open doorway. Connor span around to him in stunned disbelief.

"No fuckin' way!" he spluttered.

"Oh, very much *'fuckin' way'*, Connor. Surprised to see me? Did you think I'd be at work today? Leaving you free to come here and fuck my wife?"

Connor made a step towards Matt. He flashed his intent by means of an aggressive, hardened stare, the oncoming threat transmitted clearly and making Matt visibly tense.

"Get out of my way, Matt, or you're a fucking dead man" he challenged sincerely; so aggressively that Matt considered him to look rabid.

In response Matt moved to his left, leaving the doorway clear, an offer Connor took immediate benefit of. He dashed past Matt and out of the room within the blink of an eye, and was taking three steps of the stairs at a time when he heard Matt jest sarcastically to Kelly, loud enough to be sure Connor would overhear.

"Say goodbye to your Master, sweetheart. Shame he couldn't stay as long as intended."

"Oh; go fuck yourself, Matt", Connor could not stop himself from spinning around at the bottom of the stairs and retorting. "It seems that's all you're good for; otherwise your slut of a wife wouldn't have come running in my direction with her pussy gushing in the first place!"

"Is that right?"

"Yeah; it is! Or maybe you're just too much of a useless cunt to notice."

"Oh dear. Well, either way, that is a shame. Anyway, you better be going. I'm sure you have another submissive somewhere, waiting desperately for your next punishment…or whatever it is they *think* you do."

"I could quite easily knock you the fuck out right now, Matt. Don't tempt me."

"You're not my Master, Connor. I could barely even call you a friend; even before today! Why don't you just get the fuck out of my house?"

"Gladly."

Connor was halfway through the lounge when he heard Matt continue.

"By the way, *Master*; nice rucksack! Shame it somehow ended up in my house. See ya!"

"*FUCK!*" Connor berated himself, his shoulders hunched as he stopped in his tracks. "Matt?"

"Yes, *Sir*?" he asked sarcastically.

"I'm gonna need that rucksack back. You can either drop it down here, or I can come back up and get it, but I won't be leaving here without it."

"Shame," Matt called down, "but since it's not mine or my wife's, I'm concerned that it's in my home. It could have anything in it, couldn't it? Dangerous weapons…homemade bomb equipment; maybe even just a poorly wired vibrator! I'm sure they can be dangerous too! You never know how well those things are made. I just wouldn't feel comfortable without disposing of its contents responsibly."

"Seriously, Matt. I'm asking nicely. Don't push me."

"Ok; alright. How about I drop it at your house later today once I'm confident it doesn't contain anything which might cause anyone injury? I'd offer to do it sooner, but I'm afraid I'll be busy for the next few hours sorting out my marriage! I'm sure you understand?"

"What marriage?" Kelly muttered from behind him, just above her breath.

Matt turned to her, his face expressing his sincere distaste.

"Last chance, you sad little prick. You either bring me my bag right now, or I'm gonna come upstairs, and I promise you I will end your miserable fucking life in the process, do you understand?"

"Wow! You sound like a man on the edge, Connor! Out of interest, have you ever tried counselling? I'd love your opinion on how effective it is, just in case my wife and I decide to give it a go in the not so distant future."

"That's it; you're a *fuckin'* dead man" Connor growled, sprinting through the room. He grabbed at the bannister to guide himself around the lower corner of the staircase, then pulled hard on it to propel himself upwards.

Matt had let things go too far. He knew it, and suddenly he realised he was trembling so violently that simple coordination had deserted him. He had just enough time to step shakily backwards into the bedroom doorway before Connor's wide grip took him by throat. Forced further into the room and turned, Matt found himself pinned against the wall opposite the bed; his feet up on tiptoes, his head bent forward from the pressure of Connors crushing palm as it sank effectively into his windpipe. Through watery eyes he could make out Kelly over Connor's right shoulder, arms awkwardly outstretched as she leant forward from the pillows, gazing upon the violent scene with a sickening smile. As his vision went blurry, her row of white teeth was the brightest thing to remain semi-visible. He began to cough uncontrollably, his phlegm rattling through the squeezed hole of his throat.

"Stop!" he garbled desperately. "Connor, don't!"

Connor scoured the floor around their feet. Behind the closest pile of clean laundry, stacked against the wall, he noticed a rubberised handle zipped into a black leather casing. Reaching down, he pulled it free. The casing was branded with a logo and the words *'Ten-Pro'*, which Connor read sadistically aloud, followed by the strapline which proceeded it. '*The heaviest hitters in Tennis'*. He scoffed at Matt, placed the side of the racquet to his temple and began tapping it repeatedly against the side of his head.

"Somewhat ironic, isn't it?"

"It doesn't have to be" Matt mouthed, almost silently.

"Whose is this then?" He glanced between the two of them, spinning the racquet by its grip.

"Mine, Master", Kelly answered.

Matt felt a true tear roll over his eyelashes and down his cheek; much warmer than the water which had previously leaked from his strained eyes.

Connor fixed his furious gaze on Kelly, and a deviant grin snaked across his face.

"Well, well; looks like this is fate then, doesn't it!" He turned back to Matt, resuming his tap-tap-tap of the racquet. "I'd say I'm about to fulfil one of your wife's fantasies! I mean… I can't imagine the amount of times she must have dreamt of smashing your whiny fucking face in with something. Am I right, young lady?"

"Do it, Master" Kelly whispered, hoping for Connor to be the only one to hear.

Matt turned his restricted head from side to side as best he could, urging Connor to relent through emotive eyes.

"Please" he begged, little more than a whisper.

The lights abruptly went out as the heavy metal edge smashed against Matt's skull. He did not feel his descent to the floor, nor the impact of his body bouncing against its unrelenting surface but, when he came back to consciousness, he swore the echo of the racquet was still reverberating through his head.

"*ARRGGHHH!*" he cried, cringing from the fast consuming pain of the attack. He placed his hands to his temples, cradling his head whilst the swirling throb surged around the inside of it. He curled protectively into himself as a sharp kick connected with his lower back, hurting his kidney but offering little distraction from the pain in his head. Kelly's distant voice sounded fuzzy through the whistling in his ears.

"Get me out of these damn cuffs for Christ's sake. I've had enough of being stuck here."

"I'm afraid you're going to have to exercise some patience, Blondie" Connor quipped.

"Seriously?"

"Yes; *unquestionably*." He glared at her. "I came here for a reason today and, as yet, I haven't been satisfied. Now, you're going to stay exactly where you are while I finish my task at hand, and then I'll turn my attention to you. If you choose to do the right thing; keep your slut mouth shut and behave like a good sub, then perhaps I'll see fit to go easy on your punishment. But seriously, Kelly… *FUCK* with me…and I don't think much to your chances. Do you understand?"

"Yes; I understand" Kelly conceded shakily, her heart visibly pumping in her tightening chest.

Connor charged towards her, taking her lower jaw in his hand and raising her face to his as he hovered commandingly over her.

"Yes, what?" He demanded, feeling Kelly's quivering increase.

"Yes, *Master*. I understand."

"That's much better." He smiled sinisterly, slapping Kelly's left cheek firmly with his free hand, before pushing sharply away from her. "Now… be a good girl and leave the men to do their thing."

"What will you do to him… Sir?" Kelly asked hesitantly.

"Is there a reason why you should care?" Connor

glared at her.

"Well, aside from a beating, there's not much more you can do, surely?"

"Princess..." he paused, absorbed in the deep stare between them, "I gave him a warning which he failed to heed. I'm only just getting started."

Chapter Thirty-Eight

Matt was jabbed cruelly in the spine by the unforgiving toe of Connors black leather shoe. He groaned, rolling to his front and finding himself breathing in the fine dust from the laminate floor.

"Come on, you gobby fuck" Connor shouted down to him. "Get on your feet and try again."

Coughing, Matt placed his palms flat at either side of his body and pushing upwards, attempting to rise from the floor. His weak arms trembled from the strain and, after a few seconds, he knew he would have to turn over in order to take a more successful approach. Tucking his right arm into his side, he rolled to his shoulder and then onto his back, finally coming to rest with his upper body propped in the air by his elbows. His eyes had dried and, seeing Connor approaching, he knew he did not have enough time to evade his next attack. It came in the shape of a fist, pounding down onto the bridge of Matt's nose; the intense pain spreading from his eyebrows through to his skull as he was knocked to the floor and the back of his head collided with the hard floor beneath him. A second punch connected with the right side of his jaw, knocking his head violently to the side as he lay prone and incapacitated; but this time Matt felt it was not so heavily delivered. Something inside propelled him to find his feet much quicker and; within a few seconds; he found himself stood once again at eye level with his attacker. Connor seethed at this, gripping Matt by the throat again while aggressively pointing his finger an inch away from his eyes.

"What you gonna do? *Huh?* You fuckin' pussy?"

"I'd like you to leave, Connor." Matt said bravely, his voice quivering.

"I don't give a shit what you want!" Connor replied instinctively, pushing Matt back against the wall. "You brought this upon yourself. You think you can just order me out; like it's that easy?"

Matt puffed out his chest in defiance, his voice deepening.

"Take your fucking rucksack... and leave. Last chance."

Connor laughed hard in Matt's face, stepping back from him just enough to cause Matt the nervous assumption that a further attack was on its way.

"Is that so?" he threatened, jabbing his pointed index finger hard into the soft flesh under Matt's shoulder-blade. "Let me in on the big secret, Matt. You tell me exactly what it is you'll do if I say no."

He hacked back in his throat, then spat a thick globule of mucus over Matt's cheek. Smiling at its well-aimed delivery, he slapped across the plump skin where it had landed with the back of his hand. Matt felt daubs of the fractured phlegm land across his face. He felt instantly sick, grimacing at the sensation. His insides turned upside down; an intense queasiness surged upwards from the pit of his stomach to his held throat, where it shrunk the skin on the back of his neck and caused him to shudder. Connor watched on satisfied as Matt stammered for words.

"You got nothing to say, you hopeless bitch? You know what; I'm sorely tempted to put you in the corner and show you how a woman like that..." he gestured toward Kelly, "...needs to be treated."

"Fuck you Connor" Matt mustered angrily through his teeth, twisting his neck determinedly to free it from Connor's clutch. He raised his hands to Connor's shoulders and shoved him, toppling him backwards into the horizontal metal bedframe. Kelly watched in surprise as Connor bounced back from it and slumped to his knees, holding his lower back as his body crumpled and fell from view. She looked up to Matt; open-mouthed in shock, and secretly impressed.

It took around ten seconds for Connor's hand to take hold of the vertical metal bar at the base of the bed, and another ten for him to shakily resurface. He placed his palm to support his back as he slowly straightened it, cursing profusely through his pained, jerky movements. Kelly winced as she heard its audible crack when he was back to his feet and fully extended.

Connor was breathing heavily in and out. Matt could see a red flush in his face and was not surprised to find a look of pure rage behind Connor's eyes as they were finally raised to meet his.

"You *prick!*" Connor said angrily. "You're fuckin' dead!"

"You keep saying that, Connor, but I'm yet to see you really try. I don't honestly think that's what you want. Do yourself a favour; take your stuff and just go! This has gone too far already; it doesn't need to go any further."

Connor swept his ragged hair from his face, straightened his collar and rolled his stiff shoulders to settle his dishevelled shirt around them.

"That's it, is it? One cheap shot on me and you think you're a fuckin' hero? Have you *ever* had a serious fight in your life, Matt? Do you *not know* how this shit works? One of us isn't gonna get back up, *that's* how this ends. *That's* how a fight ends."

He slipped his hands into his trouser pockets, seeming to twist its material to turn them straight, but

Matt noticed the addition of a key neatly tucked between Connor's fingers as he removed them. He watched the room's weak light glide faintly over its silver ridges as the tiny dagger was jabbed towards his face.

Matt stepped to the side and swung his arms out wildly in defence, parrying Connor's lunging arm to the left, sending the key flying out of his grip and across the room. Connor froze in stunned amazement as Matt's bunched fist moved rapidly towards his face. He was locked in the moment, a look across his face as if to suggest he had never anticipated the possibility of Matt attaining the upper hand. His confused expression remained there even as Matt's thin, stud-like knuckles broke through the skin on the bridge of his nose, sending him reeling; white stars in his eyes; into the centre of the room to the left of the bed. His legs teetered on his ankles, yet somehow he retained a loose balance; eventually finding himself stumbling forward again towards Matt and towards a second, surprisingly solid, punch to his solar plexus. Connor grabbed at Matt's shirt in dizzy desperation, taking hold and pinning himself against his body. As he wheezed into Matt's chest he raised a hand, raking its fingernails across Matt's eyes.

Matt tried in vain to move his head away but the wall behind trapped him. Temporarily blinded by stars, he attempted to lean his weight into Connor and push him away, but Connor's broad, impressive size worked against him. Suddenly he felt fingers back near his eyes again, clawing at them wildly, uncoordinatedly gouging into their sockets. Matt curled his right arm up between their bodies and; looking through the protectively thin slits of his guarded eyes; raised his palm, connecting resoundingly with the underside of Connor's jaw with a loud smash of teeth. Connor howled out in savage pain, clutching at his face as the sound of them breaking on each other echoed through the room. Stumbling back in a daze, he left Matt just enough space to raise his leg and kick out; the unbroken heel of his new black shoe finding the spongey fluid-filled area just above Connor's right knee. The joint folded dramatically inwards on itself, accompanied by a loud snap, causing Connor to scream high-pitched and lash out in automatic defence. As he lurched closer Matt laid a final blow across Connor's left temple causing his toppling body to spin to its right and, as he dropped through the air and fell forward, his face hit the wardrobe doors mid-centre; the rounded metal doorknob punching its way deeply into his left eye-socket. Blood sprayed forward against the wooden panel in sporadic gushes and, as Connor's legs buckled and his knees hit the floor, his body – unable to fall gracefully due to the penetrating handle - twisted and slumped against the solid frontage. A thick pool of blood; some having run down the wardrobes panelling, and the rest steadily trickling from his chin; gathered around Connor's knees. The room fell eerily silent.

"Con... Connor?" Matt called out.

Nervously, he moved to the middle of the room, stooping to peer from the side at Connor's face. From the narrow angle Matt could see little more than the undamaged side, but Connor's expression made it clear to him. Open mouthed and holding a permanently fixed stare towards the wooden panel ahead of his good eye, Connor leaked a trail of saliva down his chin. There was no movement in his throat; no blink from his eyes. Matt, resting his fists on the floor to steady himself, exhaled heavily and called out to him again.

"Connor...can you hear me?"

There was no response. Matt turned to look at Kelly; her entire face painted with an expression of deep shock mirroring his own. His hands began to tremble as a cold sweat chilled his forehead; the pit of his stomach bubbling with anxiety.

"You've fucking killed him!" Kelly exclaimed.

Chapter Thirty-Nine

"You don't know that, Kelly!" Matt snapped; delirious. "He could just be unconscious!"

"Are you fucking crazy, Matt? Are you missing all of that blood? Or are you simply choosing to not see it?"

Matt turned back to Connor's slumped figure. He certainly *had* seen the blood, but had deluded himself into believing it was not as bad as he had first determined it to be. Depressed; Kelly's passionate affirmation contradicted his hope.

"*FUCK!*" he scolded himself, punching at his knees and cursing to the ceiling.

Desperately, he leant forward to lay his hand on Connor's shoulder, urging a response; any response.

"Connor? Wake up!" he shoved him by the arm. There was nothing but silence.

"You fucking wish, Matt. He's dead; look at him!" Kelly screamed. "How the fuck do you expect to explain that away? Besides the need to already explain this!"

She held her cuffed arms in the air, her wrists raw from the unforgiving metal grips.

"Jesus Christ, I don't know whether to hate you or fuck you!"

"Excuse me?!" Matt spluttered, turning to her with a look of confusion.

"That was, without a doubt, the manliest thing I've ever seen you do. Hell! It's the manliest thing I've ever seen *anyone* do! It's not every day you watch a murder committed for love. I think I get all of those documentaries now; the ones about murderous couples who get off on it. Like; it's fuckin' horrible, but...

arousing! You know?"

"No, Kelly; I don't! You can't be serious? This has... what? Turned you on?"

Matt put his hands to his head, threading his fingers through his hair and pulling tightly on the clumps in frustration.

"You don't feel it?"

"Feel *what*, Kelly?"

"Intense... like an energy? Lust? I don't know! The raw fucking desire to take my body and... and fuckin' break it! I'm asking you Matt; no... I'm begging you. I need it! Oh God I need you inside me like never before, please!"

Matt, rising to his feet, stared across to her dumbfounded.

"There's something very... very wrong with you, Kelly. I've just-" His stomach growled so angrily he felt urged to place a hand to steady it, his other raised to cup his mouth as a foul tasting belch rose up from his throat. He shuddered from his core with nausea, then paused for a moment to compose himself.

"I can't say it. I feel fucking sick just thinking about it."

"There's no fucking winning with you, is there!" Kelly snapped impatiently.

"I'm sorry... winning?"

"What has all of this been about, Matt? You show up here unexpectedly in your shiny new suit and your fake persona, wanting to play the dominant. And then, when things finally get interesting and you get me worked up enough to actually want it... then you can't handle it! I honestly don't know what the fuckin' point was!"

"This is *not* what I intended, Kelly! Jesus Christ, get a grip. A man's dead!"

"Well funnily enough I've lost my buzz now

anyway. Do you know; I can't decide what's worse? The fact he's dead, or that he had to die at the hands of the biggest pussy in existence!"

Matt stood, speechless.

"You can take these bastard things off now. You've done more than enough damage for one day."

"I... I..."

"Oh for fuck sake, Matt. Quit stuttering and just do it."

"I can't."

"What do you mean you can't?" Kelly stared at him intensely. His body remained rooted to the spot, seemingly unable to comprehend his next move. "Find the fucking keys and unlock them!"

"I'm sorry; I won't. Not yet."

"You damn well will or so help me God, Matt, when I do get free there'll be two dead bodies lying in this room! Now take some fucking control of yourself."

"I am, Kelly. That's exactly what I'm doing."

"I don't think you have a clue what you're doing, you retard."

"Don't *fucking* call me that!" Matt exploded.

"Would you rather I called you a murderer?"

"I'd rather you called me your husband, treated me like one, and showed some fucking compassion for what's just happened."

"Well I'd rather you hadn't come home when you did, but hey-ho, it just goes to show we can't always get everything we want."

Matt, clenching his fists into balls, raised his eyes to the ceiling again and screamed.

"*FUCK!*"

"Uh-oh! *Misss*-ter Cool is *looo*-sing it" Kelly sang mockingly.

Matt sank an unsteady hand into his trouser pocket

to retrieve his mobile phone. He pressed the button at its side, launching its screen into vivid life, and then blankly stared at it, unsure of what to do next. His head began to pulse feverishly, each fuzzy throb of rushing of blood causing his ears to hum and his eyes to lose focus. Trying to think rationally, he could feel his heart escaping him, fluttering wildly and immersing him in further, deeper panic. His body swayed from side to side as his energy waned and he felt the colour draining from his cheeks.

Subconsciously he swiped at the touchscreen with his thumb. Though paralysed with confusion, at his core he knew that he needed help; Kelly could simply not be freed without the aid of a rational voice in his corner. A mutual ally to talk Kelly down from performing the extreme retributions Matt's racing imagination bombarded him with. *'Would anyone rationalise this if they saw it? Could they?'*

None of this had been intentional, he told himself repeatedly, but the obvious indignation behind Kelly's eyes made it explicitly clear to him that he was the enemy. They bore into him from across the room like a pair of red torch beams, glowing menacingly with her venomous desire. He knew that, at the very least, she would call the police. But at her very worst? Could she go so far? Would it be possible she could feel so wounded that he might suffer the fate she threatened by her gaze so passionately?

He catatonically watched her writhing hands; somehow mesmerised by them. Despite the visibly sore, cracked skin on her wrists, Kelly was rotating them; rubbing them around the inner rims of the handcuffs, grinding her weakening flesh against their blunt steel edges. A thin, almost artistic line of red trailed around her right forearm as she twisted it, resembling the delicacy of a cherry blossom tattoo, Matt thought. In his coma like state he reminded himself how he had always loved their elegant imagery. The sight of the line growing thicker; now running in a heavier stream down from her forearm to her elbow; prompted him urgently out of his daze and, as he watched Kelly's sick smile grow across her face, his awareness reengaged and he realised her intention.

"Kelly; *NO!*" he urged, concerned.

She shook her head, disregarding his plea.

"If *you* won't get me out of this, then I will!"

"For fuck sake, Kelly, *stop!*"

He rushed towards the bed, diving over her body to grab at her hands. As he did so, and as Kelly turned her body sharply away from him, she felt her right leg unexpectedly follow her across the bed. Peering curiously around Matt's shoulder as he fought to control her gyrating arms, she watched as the loop of her ankle restraint slid free from the bedframe; Matt's silk tie having worked its way loose from her intense jerk. Relieved, she exhaled in disbelief; a short laugh escaping her before conscientiously silencing herself. Matt; hearing her odd response and wondering why she had inexplicably ceased her struggling; pulled away from her, at which point they both realised that Matt's mobile phone now lay nestled between Kelly's breasts, its screen active, and a call in motion.

Before Matt could grab it Kelly twisted to her body to the left; the phone snatched away from his frantic grasp. As it landed on the bed to her side, the ringing stopped, and a faint, tinny voice echoed out from its speaker.

"Hello?"

"*SHANNA?*" Kelly cried out. "Oh God Shanna, help me! Come as quick as you can, it's Matt-"

The phone went dead as Matt slammed his palm down onto its screen and scooped it from the mattress. He climbed away from Kelly and had just put his feet to the floor when he stopped to look at her, hearing her begin to cackle uncontrollably.

"HA!-Ha Ha-Ha-Ha-Ha! Now you're fuckin' screwed, and it'll serve you right, you sad little fuck. I gave you the chance to make this right, but you chose not to take it. Just wait. Just wait!"

"Shanna's a good friend, Kelly. Hopefully she'll understand. She can help make this right."

"Understand? You're delusional! I mean; that was obvious to me already, what with your desperate, wannabe dominant routine, but do you honestly think she'll take one look at me... or Connor... and think you're anything other than a fucking psychopath? Fuck, Matt! And you've got the nerve to say there's something wrong with me!"

"If she gives me the chance to explain, then-"

Kelly interrupted. "Maybe you can explain something to me, Matt."

"What?"

"What's the quickest way to lose teeth?"

Matt turned his head to her, puzzled.

Kelly hiked her free leg back, her knee tucked tightly into her lower body, before launching her heel outwards as she thrust her body high off of the bed and drove the hard rounded bone with full force into the lower half of Matt's face.

Chapter Forty

Shanna pulled her car to a stop alongside Kelly's red Prius. Looking up at the facade of the house, she noticed it remained shut off to the world, with each set of its curtains drawn.

Stepping out of the car and moving closer, she saw what appeared to be a pair of anxious eyes, peering out at her from between the curtains of the upper right bedroom window. She inhaled sharply; her heart leaping up to lodge firmly in her throat.

As she reached the front door; she paused. She placed her palms on its glossy mahogany panelling and leant inwards, pressing her ear to the thinnest part of the wood, squinting to listen. Through it she could hear the faintest of conversation; a deep, masculine voice responded to by a second, lighter tone.

"Oh thank God", she muttered to herself; her tension momentarily easing.

She turned the handle and pushed, but the door refused to open. It stopped her mentally for a few seconds, allowing her to question whether she was doing the right thing. Glimpsing down the length of the street, all she saw were empty driveways, the army of workers having long since departed for their morning commute. Off white clouds were gathering overhead and the faintest signs of rain were starting to fall. Light speckles landed delicately on the shoulders of her cream leather jacket as Shanna debated whether entering was sensible, unsure of what lay behind the door. After thirty seconds of watching the raindrops grow in size, she resolved to her intrigue; too strong to ignore. She felt compelled to investigate Kelly's cryptic message.

Under the middle of three rocks bordering the thin stonewalled front garden, Shanna found the plastic hatch. Prying it open, the emergency key; of which she had been told of numerously in case of emergency, but had never seen; beamed brightly at her with the reflected aura of the mid-morning light. She slid it into the lock with trepidation, slowly turning until she felt the grinding engagement within its mechanism. With a controlled twist she levered the key around further, feeling the door lurch inwards as it sprang loose from its catch, with just the tiniest scraping of metal upon metal.

Peering through the slowly increasing gap, all was in darkness. Every window was closed. Every curtain drawn in front of them. The subtle glow from their slender cracks gave each piece of lounge furniture an ethereal glow at their edges. The distant conversation was now fractionally louder, but with its tone still overwhelmed by a lack of clarity in the words spoken. Shanna was careful to draw the door closed while paying permanent attention over her shoulder. She managed to turn the latch and walk it closed, lifting its weight to place it back within the doorframe without making a sound. Navigating her well-known path through the living room, she reached the foot of the stairs in a matter of seconds. She stopped there; and listened again. This time she could not hear voices; only an atmospheric silence which made her heartbeat sound cavernous. Cautiously she took a breath, opened her mouth for what felt like a silent eternity, and called up loudly to the floor above.

"Kelly?"

Matt was slumped down with his back against the wall, directly in front of Kelly, with his thumb and index finger pinching the top of his nose. Feeling mentally exhausted, and struggling to think straight, an intense headache pulsed heavily behind his forehead. His bottom lip was split widely through its middle; rich red blood and saliva oozing out from the wound, over his chin and down onto his chest, where it lay; soaking into his fresh white shirt.

Across the room, Kelly lay visibly agitated. Her chest rose and fell rapidly, raising high before sinking deeply, but her eyes remained fixed across the room as if waiting for Matt to react. She had stayed that way for the last ten minutes, throughout which time he had showed no sign of interest.

"Say something!" she demanded, having fought against her impatience for long enough. "Hit me! Make me feel the pain you're feeling. *UGHH! Fucking do… SOMETHING!*"

"No", Matt replied under his breath.

"So that's it, is it? It's taken a long time to get here, but you've finally realised what a fucking mess you've made of this. Well praise be for that little revelation!"

"You can't stop yourself for one minute, can you?" Matt sighed. "Not one tiny part of you can be brave enough to just listen. Not one! Do you not feel in anyway sorry about this? About Connor? About how finding out would've made me feel?"

"I'm gonna put this in the simplest way for you to understand, okay?" Kelly surged.

"Please", Matt begged, his voice breaking with emotion.

"Put it this way, Matt. If I ever truly loved you, I'd never have married you."

Matt lowered his hand to his mouth, staring at the floor in disbelief. Kelly's words cut through his heart like a chainsaw, draining the blood from his face and making his stomach churn; so much so that he leant to his side for fear of vomiting. He dropped his hand to the floor to steady himself.

"I *know* the type of person I am, Matt; I've known for a long time. But that doesn't mean I didn't want a *normal* life. It's what makes *exciting* life exciting! Don't you understand that? If we settled for just a normal life, and ignored the other chances of excitement around us, we'd go fucking insane!"

"No, Kelly; that's just you. I'd have gotten along perfectly satisfied with just you and a normal life"

"I married you... because we got along. You're like my camouflage against the outside world; to let them see what they deem as acceptable; and you came with a great pack of benefits. Money, this house, the cars. Plus it's not like you didn't benefit from me too! I was in my late twenties, youthful, attractive and... well, let's be honest... you couldn't have got much better, being the way you are. Don't get me wrong; you certainly made me the woman I am today, but not the woman I've always been; and, trust me, that woman can take everything you've thrown at me over this morning and more, if it's coming!"

"None of this was about the books..." Matt said morosely. "It was just about being the way you say you are? That's bullshit Kelly; I've known plenty of people who had a wild time in their teens, even twenties, but even they learnt they had to settle down in the end. Have you never once felt any honour in just being with someone who's devoted to you?"

"Firstly, you're wrong. *This... Connor...* what was *intended* to happen when he showed up today... *that* was about the books. Connor had everything I needed to fulfil the fantasy as I saw it in my head. Quite simple really. But secondly; let's not be mistaken, Matt. Devotion doesn't mean shit to me. It's the road to guaranteed boredom. The way I see it, these are just the sad circumstances in which you ended up finding out. If it wasn't now it would've been later, and the circumstances would've probably been just as terrible for you to bare"

Matt's tears dropped to the floor as he shook his head, smiling in sad disbelief. Kelly kept her eyes fixed on him. She was smiling too.

She began muttering about being *'sorry, not sorry'* and *'unable to change'* but all Matt could hear were her previous words bouncing around inside his head like a pinball. Suddenly something stuck; a few of her words dropped into place and made Matt's heart sink even lower. His mouth dried up, the pinching sensation snapping him back to consciousness. Kelly was still nonchalantly justifying herself, seemingly nowhere near finishing her point, when Matt sternly butt in.

"Other chances? Are you saying there were previous times I didn't walk in on?"

Kelly looked across to him guiltily.

"Tell me!"

Kelly hung her head and slowly shook it. She exhaled heavily through her nose, tilted her head to her right, and looked to him sarcastically.

"What do you want me to say, Matt?"

"Nothing. That expression's the only answer I needed. I don't want to hear any more."

"Good, because I'm done talking; although I will say one more thing. I really like your lip. It suits you, in a strange way. Kinda makes me sad that I haven't kick you in the face more often!"

"*Kelly?*" Shanna's voice from the staircase took both of them by surprise.

Chapter Forty-One

Matt jumped up as he heard the echoing voice enter the room. Physically shaken; he paced the floor, staring at Kelly wide-eyed and with his eyebrows raised sharply, showing the pain of his anxiety. Kelly stared straight back at him with the faintest of smirks poking out from the corners of her mouth, delivering a silent answer to his unspoken question.

Matt's hands fell to the nearest laundry pile, where he quickly found a dirty bedsheet. He picked it up, letting its folds fall free, and threw it delicately over Connor's awkwardly postured body. Drawing in a deep breath through his nose, he then huffed out an even louder sigh. He did not know what would happen next. He felt clueless as to what he should do. All that his head could tell him was to fear each and every scenario now doing circuits at lightning speed inside of its walls.

Apprehensively, he sneaked from the bedroom, out onto the landing. The split second he saw Shanna's outline at the foot of the stairs, he imagined himself ducking backwards, somehow managing to evade her sight within the safety of the dim corridor. Jolting back to reality, he cursed his recent inability to think straight, finding he was still exactly where he stood, with Shanna now looking directly at him through the gloomy haze.

"Matt?" she called up to him.

He moved to the landing and groped for the light switch, flicking it into life. The bulbs along the hallway seemed exceptionally bright after spending so long without natural light. His eyes instantly stung, their pupils retreating.

"Hey Shanna", he replied, quietly.

"Is Kelly here? She called me. She... Well, she sounded in trouble!"

"Kelly's here Shanna. She's in our bedroom", Matts voice started to crack, "She... She did something terrible, and my heart feels... oh God... it feels so broken... and now I've... *I've hurt her*".

"What have you done to hurt her, Matt?" Shanna urged. "How badly is she hurt?"

"It's pretty bad Shanna. She's on the bed. I think she'll need a hospital, but I... Oh *fuck*, I've done so much! I don't know what to do!"

"Come upstairs Shanna", Kelly called out loudly from behind him.

Shanna looked at Matt, half with an expression of relief, but half in desperation of wanting to take immediate flight up the stairs.

"Would that be OK, Matt?" she asked, almost pleading.

Matt let out a heavy, involuntary sigh; knowing full well that his time had run out. Knowing that he would now have to face the consequences of all that he had done. Yet, somehow, it came as something of a relief to him. He nodded his agreement.

Shanna ran speedily up the flight, brushing past him on the landing so closely that she could, for the first time, see the deep division in his lip and the impressive blood trail from his chin to his sternum. She gasped.

"Oh Matt....What happened?"

"I wasn't paying attention and she kicked me. Don't worry about it, you just go and see Kelly. I'll be fine".

Shanna took another close look at the lip and grimaced. She looked up into Matt's eyes and, with a sad glint behind her own, smiled a smile of caring consolation. She cradled his cheek momentarily in her fingers, then made her way along the corridor.

Slipping through the bedroom doorway, Shanna came upon a scene that left her dumbfounded. Before her eyes lay Kelly, naked on the bed, her body marked with bruises of every imaginable shade. Red lipstick streaked messily across her cheeks, with mascara trails running down from underneath each eye. Three of her limbs were tied to their corresponding corners of the bed, leaving Kelly fully exposed. Shanna, trying to take it all in, found it hard to find words to say.

Matt dashed in through the bedroom door to grab another bedsheet from the laundry pile, hastily launching it into the air and letting it fall over Kelly's beaten body.

"Such a gentleman", Kelly sneered at him.

Slumping back down against the wall, Matt resumed his previous position with his nose pinched; attempting to regain control of his, once again thumping, headache.

"So; Hi Shanna!" Kelly quipped, ironically. "How's your day been? As you can tell… and all thanks to dickless over there… mines been *ahh-mazing!*"

"What the hell's happened here?" Shanna asked, bewildered. "I could almost hear your shaking over the phone, and now… this? *What the fuck!"*

"Well Shanna," Kelly huffed, "I guess I got caught out! My afternoon tryst with Connor got rudely interrupted, after which-"

"Wait; what? Connor? You and Connor have been-"

"*AFTER WHICH…* my wonderful husband over there proceeded to show me just how much of a fucking man he is!"

Kelly turned her head away from Matt, speaking directly to Shanna in an almost whisper.

"It took him fucking long enough. And, between you and me, he didn't exactly excel!"

She winked slyly before turning back and speaking at normal volume.

"And now I'm a beaten and bloody mess. At least I'm not Connor though, huh Matt?"

"Where's Connor?" Shanna urged.

"Oh, Connor? Oh, well he's under the fucking sheet over there!" Kelly laughed. "Matt? MATT! Why don't you show Shanna your handiwork?"

"Why is he under the sheet?" Shanna asked nervously.

"My man Matt over there beat him up so bad that he killed him!" Kelly replied, almost proudly. "Seriously; smashed his fuckin' face apart, all because he loves m-"

"That's *NOT* how it happened, Kelly", Matt screamed; startling Shanna and causing his brow to pulse in increased agony.

Kelly beckoned with a jerk of her head; aiming to catch Shanna's attention. Once she had it she spoke, raising a vertical index finger as close as she could to her lips.

"Shhh. The Beast wants to speak. Let's hear what he has to say."

Shanna could not help but feel uncomfortable at hearing Kelly's mean, sarcastic tone. Unable to smile, she found herself instead staring at Kelly with concern.

"I'm sorry Shanna," Matt started, looking up at her and shaking his head, "I never intended things to go the way they did, or for you to be brought into this. I can understand that this shocks you, and I really wish you hadn't had to see it. I… just… I just snapped; I guess. What happened to Connor, I… I don't know. It happened really fast and I think he, like… tripped somehow. He hit his face on the handle of the wardrobe, and then he… he just kinda slumped there. He went down so hard on it; right on his eye socket. Long story short; he's dead… but

I hadn't meant to kill him; I was just defending myself! He was talking about killing *me!* You *HAVE* to believe me!"

"That's a likely story, *Connor Killer!*" Kelly jibed.

Shanna looked with uncontrollable disdain at Kelly. Softly stepping across the room, she bent down onto her knees, and placed her left hand on Matts shoulder.

"Matt; tell me what happened. From the start", she asked calmly.

Matt let out a long heavy sigh.

"I just wanted to surprise Kelly. I pretended to leave for work this morning, sat in a café for an hour or two, and then I snuck back. I know you'd said before about thinking it was a bad idea, but I'd booked the day off because I wanted to help her live out that fantasy… you know… like the books. I wanted to fulfil it for her, you know? To be her Curtis; to show her what it would really feel like."

"Jesus, Matt; I tried to warn you off for a reason. I knew it wouldn't end well if you did. So, what happened when you came home?"

"Well; I found the door was on the latch, and I hadn't left it like that! Kelly was nowhere to be seen, so I made my way upstairs and that's when I found her strapped down on the bed, exactly as she is now.

"Not quite *exactly*, Matt. I had a few less bruises back then, if you remember?"

Shanna ignored her.

"Did you find Connor here?" she delved deeper.

"No; no, he arrived maybe an hour later," Matt answered, looking over Shanna's shoulder towards Kelly. "But I still can't get over my darling wife being here, ready and waiting for him to arrive."

His expression grew fierce as he recollected the morning's discovery, bright red fires sparking into life behind his eyes, but retaining a delicate voice clearly struggling to control its emotions.

"Oh... fucking do something!" Kelly intimidated, noticing the change in him. "Or won't you, now that Shanna's here? *HUH?? FOR FUCK SAKE MATT!* I've spent the whole fucking morning tied to the bed, for this? So you can turn into an even bigger pussy when we have company?"

"Right, Kelly", Shanna said authoritatively. "Your turn. Why don't you tell me what happened from there".

"Huh?" Kelly responded insolently, struck by Shanna's aggressive tone.

"Matt came home and found you like this... but why were you in this position when Connor wasn't actually here?

"Connor was supposed to be! I didn't plan on being stuck to the bed on my own, obviously! I'd tied myself up, then Connor text to say he was stuck in fuckin' traffic and was gonna be late, so all the planning turned to shit. Tiny-bollocks over there ended up coming back home, refused to set me free, and there was nothing I could do."

"You did that to yourself?" Shanna gestured to her shackled limbs, puzzled.

"Isn't that what I just said? Connor wanted it that way. He'd given me instructions and I followed them".

Shanna stood open-mouthed in shock at the blunt, matter-of-fact way Kelly spoke. It took a few moments, and a couple of pained looks towards Matt, before her composure returned.

"So Matt found you here, handcuffed and waiting for Connor, and you just expected him to let you go like nothing had happened?" Shanna's tone rang out, tinged of disgust.

"That was three fucking hours ago Shanna! And yes; I've been here ever since then. Now is it too much to ask for one of you to unlock these *fuckin'* cuffs and untie me?"

Shanna stared at Kelly in bewilderment, sensing the clear rage building within her friend, but overcome with her own sense of unease about fulfilling the demand. It did not come instinctively for her to reach forward and help, and she suddenly realised that ever since she had first walked in the room she had not thought once to aide Kelly in any way.

With a growing conscience, she placed her hands at Kelly's foot and began pulling on the one remaining looped silk knot. It was halfway to becoming free before she realised Matt was on the move, rising up to his feet and standing beside her within a second.

"She's not going anywhere yet, Shanna" he pleaded adamantly, his voice tremoring.

"How long can you keep Kelly like this, Matt? Seriously; C'mon!"

Matt turned his head slowly from side to side, pleading eye to eye with her. He had no need to speak; she could see the true fear that lay behind them.

Shanna pulled the silk shackle tight again and spoke calmly, taking delicate hold of his clenched hands.

"I understand Matt; I really do. Things went extremely far, and you're scared to face what you've done. You're scared for anyone else to see what you've done. I get that, but now you're only left with two options sweetie and, unless you're really thinking of killing her too, that leaves just one. That's to free her now, rather than later when the consequences could be much worse. You know that, right?"

Matt took a deep breath in.

"Yeah", he conceded lethargically.

Shanna drew Matt into her, wrapping her arms around him, her right arm around his back and the left trailing up his spine. She softly reassured him; promising him that everything was going to be ok, as the tips of her fingers softly stroked the hairs at the nape of his neck. Matt buried his face deep into her shoulder and wept.

"Touching!" Kelly growled. "Now… Am I right in thinking I can get free now?"

"Matt?" Shanna asked, her voice now extremely light, almost hesitant.

"Yes?"

"This is a really fucked up time to tell you this, but there's something I've always wanted you to know."

Matt raised his head from her leather coat and took a step back. He looked her in the eyes, puzzled. Kelly looked up too, both puzzled and irritated.

"What is it, Shanna?"

"You remember back when Ray died?" Shanna asked.

"Of course."

"You were the best help I could've hoped for back then. You gave me so much support at what was the darkest time I've ever experienced. And you showed just how much you truly cared for Ray as a friend"

"We were best friends" Matt said lowly, looking down at his feet and reflecting. "I miss him every day".

"And even though we didn't really know each other that well, you passed that care and love onto me, to help me get me through it. I always appreciated that."

"It was a gloomy period for both of us Shanna; we both felt the same loss."

"Well, from that came something I wasn't expecting. You two… Ray and you… were like twins. I still can't understand how two completely unrelated guys could be the exact same person underneath their skin. It was like… like everything I *loved* about Ray, I saw in you too. I… I still do, Matt. I always have."

The room fell silent.

Chapter Forty-Two

"ARE YOU FUCKING KIDDING ME, SHANNA? SERIOUSLY?" Kelly screamed furiously.

Shanna spun around to face her with a bitter scowl; presenting, for the first time, her honest, long-since-felt level of scorn. Her mouth was pursed, with her tongue pushed heavily against the backs of her teeth, and her eyebrows lurched sharply downwards.

"You never once listened to anything I told you, did you?" Shanna snapped. "All those times you thought you should bare your dirty fucking soul to me and I warned you not to. *I FUCKING WARNED YOU!* But *no*; you didn't want to hear it – you just talked over me until I gave up, and then carried on telling me all that selfish crap anyway. All that talk about wanting more than Matt could give; slagging him off unnecessarily. Well, now you're paying the price Kelly. You're such a spoiled, selfish, stupid little cunt and now you can't handle paying the price. I'm sorry Matt;" she turned to face him again, flustered and with wet wells forming at the inner corners of each eye, "I didn't think I'd be saying this now; in fact, I never thought that I would *ever* risk taking the chance, but now I can't help but want you to know. *I love you*. To the point that I don't think I could be the same person without you in my life. And this?" She gestured to the carnage throughout the bedroom, "This has been a long time coming, all thanks to that... that *bitch!* You didn't deserve any of this, and you shouldn't feel ashamed for what's happened".

"I shouldn't?"

Matt's sullen shoulders began to rise; a glimmer of

increasing hope emerging behind his eyes. Shanna cocked her head to its left, widening her kind eyes, then reached out to take Matt's left cheek in her palm once again.

"No!" she urged, "You really shouldn't! All of this occurred because of how *she* chose to treat you. That pain you feel. Each of those marks you've made on her. Connor. *Jesus Christ*, he was an arrogant dick, but he didn't deserve to die. That's on *her* conscience. She played you for a fool, Matt; and you're no fool. It was cruel and unfair, and I've sat by watching her do that for far… *far* too long."

"*You fucking bitch!*" Kelly raged, thrusting herself towards Shanna as best she could; her hands clawing forward, scratching at the clear air between her fingertips and Shanna's face.

"Tell me one thing Kelly." Shanna asked defiantly.

"*What?*"

"When you first got the inclination that you might want to delve into the world of Curtis *fucking* Sharp; to actually experience your fantasies for real; did you even suggest it to Matt?"

"No… and before you-"

"Did you ever consider that he might actually want to be the one to fulfil it for you; either out of his sincere love for you, or from his incessant and, quite frankly, *unnecessary* need to make you happy?"

"I've explained this to Matt already Shanna; I don't have to justify myself to you! You're supposed to be my fucking friend! If anyone should be made to feel ashamed, it's you! Now take me out of these fucking shackles, Shanna!"

"Tell me how she explained it, Matt?"

"She basically described me as some sort of safety blanket. Said I helped her hide her real self from the world and gave her a 'normal' life, but that she'd always felt prone to cheat, and that basically I was never a good enough cause to change that. She was just attracted to me because of my benefits."

"What did she mean - '*her real self'?*" Shanna asked, puzzled.

"To be honest, I'm still not overly sure. I don't mean to sound crass; and I'm sorry if you think this is a bit harsh, Kelly; but I think she was admitting to being… well; a bit of a slut?"

Shanna frowned as Kelly nonchalantly raised her shoulders as if to say *'what's wrong with that?'*

"*Jesus Christ, Matt!* You really did pick a winner with this one!" She almost chuckled from her discomfort.

"Yeah, yeah; I'm a fucking whore; and you're both assholes" Kelly ranted. "But, despite wanting to tell you to go fuck yourself, Shanna; I think its best that you know Matt's 'benefits' never really stretched to this bedroom; if you catch my drift."

She extended the little finger on her left hand and wiggled it in the air, looking unashamedly content with herself and giggling. Shanna leant over the end of the bed, confronting her with eye contact as her hands wrung its thin metal shelf like a wet towel. The muscles in her arms made the bed vibrate, quivering under her temper.

"I've got a very different bedroom, Kelly" she stated defiantly. "Mine has a significantly brighter atmosphere; and is much more grown up inside. Matt might prefer it; what with it containing a functional vagina!"

"Yeah, well… it's like I said; Go fuck yourself, and your fuckin' bedroom."

"I think we need to talk, Matt; just the two of us. Would you mind that?" Shanna asked over her shoulder.

Matt began wringing his hands together; overcome by a nauseating wave of anxiety. He breathed in heavily through his nose before exhaling slowly out from his mouth, trying to catch a hold of his spiralling balance. In his mind, everything was conspiring against him. *What might happen if I do? Would Shanna reveal herself to be Kelly's saviour? Can I trust her enough to be sure this wouldn't somehow all turn out to be a trick?* She seemed so genuine, he thought; and he could not help but think back on all the times he too had felt strongly for her. She had summed up his often felt feelings so accurately as her own. All except for the guilt. The guilt he had felt at those weak times, for Kelly, as well as for Shanna; but worst of all, for his best friend. *Poor sweet Ray. He would have been shocked by all of this. Who knows; maybe he would be content in some way to know that his heartbroken wife, after going through so much loss, could find a way to love again with a man he knew as a brother.*

With that thought Matt felt a peculiar swell of pride; the heavy pumping in his chest working to subside the sickening spinning in his head.

"Okay" he spoke clearly, determined to try.

"Throw a shirt on, Honey. We'll go and talk in my car."

Matt set to looking through a toppled pile of clean laundry, grabbing at the first item of his clothes he saw; a blue and white striped polo shirt. It was in the process of being slipped over his head when he heard Kelly voice her disgust.

"I can't believe you, Shanna. More than I can't believe him for doing all he's done to me! And after the last few hours, that's an impressive feat, I have to admit! You're really gonna make me wait here while you have a nice little chat? Have you not seen my fuckin' wrists?"

"We won't be long, Kelly. You're just going to have to be patient for a little while longer. I mean… I say *patient*… but I haven't really seen you show *any* patience up until now. You really do have so much to learn about how relationships work."

"So what? I should just bow down and thank him? For showing me the errors of my ways?" Kelly scoffed stubbornly "I'm sure he'd like that, but it's not going to happen."

Matt had replaced his black leather shoes with comfortable sneakers and was stood with his back to the wall, waiting.

"Have a nice chat guys!" Kelly mocked "Don't keep me in suspense!"

"We won't. Just give me time to work it through with him", Shanna requested. Kelly shot back at her with a sarcastic glare.

"Shanna... take a look at me! I've got all the time in the world and no choice in the matter! Just do me a favour, and free me the fuck off of this bed when you come back; there's a good best friend."

Chapter Forty-Three

Kelly watched the clock on the wall as its hands crept at an agonisingly slow pace through each minute. Its monotonous ticking became louder as her impatience grew; distant and yet somehow echoing within the depths of her ears. It had been fourteen minutes and she was mentally aching from the unending countdown to freedom. Momentarily she slipped into a daydream state, her mind fantasising about the things she would do after regaining her liberty. A very long, and very hot bath. A pizza loaded with double toppings for lunch. *'Who gives a fuck about cholesterol?'* her mind coerced. And best of all, the forceful desire in delivering the mother of all beatings to Matt and Shanna; assuming she could stop herself from going much, much further, that was.

Snapping out of her daydream Kelly found she had inadvertently clenched her fists, so hard that she could feel the blood pumping through the tight curl of her fingers. Loosening their iron grasp, she flexed them and let out a sharp exclamation, as what felt like electric shocks bolted from her wrists into her forearms. Examining the pulsing muscles dancing just below her skin, her gaze drifted past her left forearm, where it fell upon a green bag on the floor beneath the tallboy. It was crumpled up, laid against the plinth where she had previously thrown it, in what seemed an eternity ago. It was then that she suddenly recalled what lay inside the bag, visibly pressing at the weak, thin plastic with its pointed corners. The handcuff packaging.

Shuffling as best she could to the side of the bed, Kelly pulled on her one remaining ankle restraint with every ounce of her strength. The semi fastened knot holding her left leg in place unravelled surprisingly easily, its loose end arcing through the air and whipping her painfully across the torso. Grimacing, she raised both knees up to her stomach to stretch their rigid joints, feeling the muscles in her locked calves, thighs and shins burn in unison as they gradually stretched out.

The lower two-thirds of Kelly's body were now mobile, a fact which gave her cause to pause; a brief moment granted to exhale a heavy breath of relief.

Returning her attention to the small bag, she swung her left leg heavily to the floor; its prolonged immobility having exhausted the muscles more than she expected they would have been. The outside of her foot lay flat on the polished wooden flooring, inching slowly towards the bag until she felt the slightest glance of the plastic brush against her skin. She outstretched her toes over it and brought them down, flattening the closest lip of the bag to the floor, before edging her foot carefully back towards her. Frustrated, she watched as the plastic stuck to the floors surface, pinging out from under her toes as they glided ineffectively over it; but, as its material slowly unfolded in an attempt to regain its natural shape, a narrow glimpse of its handle popped into Kelly's view. She beamed ecstatically, directing her big toe towards the loop before hooking the bag into the air with a confident upward snatch. *'Now; how am I going to get it into my hands?'* she asked herself.

She tried in vain to lift it to her shackled grasp; her awkward, alien-like leg proving too weak and uncoordinated to twist in the direction it required. Irritated by her continued lack of flexibility, she lay her leg at an angle off of the bed; her foot, with the bag entwined between her toes, resting on its edge; with her knee hanging out over the floor. She took a deep breath and a precious moment to find clarity. Sure; Shanna and Matt would return and release her soon; but Kelly neither wanted to wait for that nor, much worse, feel the indignation of their power over her for doing so. Feeling the particular irony within the situation, she almost laughed at herself.

'After all of this shit...' she thought, *'and I don't even like the feeling of actually being controlled!'*

Then came an idea. A solution.

Kelly slid the bag to the end of the bed, bringing both feet together around it. She deftly levered its handles apart with her big toes, wiggling them into the wide opening and pinching the opposing sides of the small plastic handcuff case within it. As she lifted her knees above her hips she saw the case emerge and, as it swivelled between her toes as if teasing to fall through them, she heard a small rattling sound. Leaning forward; her heart skipped a beat. There; little more than a metre away, nestled in the corner of the clear box, lay a small metal key.

Next came the lift. It took every morsel of determination to widen her knees to either side of her body, dipping her head low into the pillows and her feet overhead. The backs of her thighs shook violently from the muscular strain, so much so that she paused for a second to ensure the grip on the collapsing plastic was still holding tight between her toes. Almost without realising the speed of her success, she looked up to find that the key; peeking out at her from the base of the box; was now hovering directly above her eyes. She squealed with delight, hastily twisting her hips to the left in order to line the box up above her hand, and then, as she gently eased her toes apart, she watched it slip free, falling onto her open palm. For one gut-wrenching second, it bounced; tumbling away towards her wrist, but not far enough to prevent Kelly instinctively clamping it between her thumb and forefinger with a focussed grab. Manoeuvring her fingers to its end, she managed to sink her thumb into the closed fold and pry it loose. Cautious not to let the box open too quickly, she slid her thumb to meet the key as it slid towards it and, as she methodically rubbed her forefinger backwards and forwards against the outer plastic while edging her thumb out from the box, the key emerged and was secured within their pinch. Kelly flicked her wrist out, returning the now empty box across the floor towards the plinth of the tallboy. *'Now comes the really tricky part'*, she cursed to herself.

The lock of the handcuff sat high and snug against Kelly's radial artery, held close by the natural angle of her horizontal position. She sat herself up and shuffled backwards; her spine almost touching the headboard to create a more accessible angle to the keyhole; but she found that twisting her pinched fingers downwards and towards her wrist while maintaining a secure grip on the key was impossible. She would have to lighten her grip to allow it, and her fingers, more flexibility. As she set about sliding the key to within the barest limits of her fingers control, she heard a noise. It was the heavy squeak of the front door.

Shanna made her way up the stairs and entered the bedroom. Crossing the floor, she placed her arms around Connor's limp body and lifted him, half dragging him towards the door. Stepping out onto the landing, she leant into the bedroom doorway and smiled at Kelly.

"I'll be with you again in just a second", she chirped, her tone noticeably more vibrant than when she and Matt had left the bedroom.

Kelly glimpsed at the clock and calculated that they had made her wait twenty-two minutes in total. *'What the fuck did you two need twenty-two minutes to talk about?'* she ranted silently.

Shanna struggled slowly backwards into the bathroom, dragging Connor's lifeless feet over the laminate flooring, before turning him and pushing his body towards the bath. His back hit the wall; sitting him upright inside the tub with his legs dangling over its side. She closed the door behind her.

As Kelly waited, she found it impossible not to listen to the noises coming from the far room, guided by a curious compulsion. Shanna was urinating, the sound of the water being disturbed in the toilet bowl was evidence enough. After a few seconds the noise ceased; followed the clunk and rattle of the cistern as the toilet was flushed. The pipes whistled in the wall as the sink taps ran; and then, silence. It was the silence that seemed louder to Kelly than anything else. An agonising numbness in her ears which, mixed with her growing curiosity, was driving her mad; especially when, after a further three full minutes without a sound, Shanna had not re-emerged from the bathroom.

"What the fuck are you doing in there?" Kelly called out angrily.

"Almost done" Shanna replied.

Ten seconds later the bathroom door squeaked open. Shanna walked into the bedroom and made her way to the right-hand side of the bed next to Kelly, taking subtle note of her liberated ankles as she passed them. She pulled the stool from the dressing table, positioned it two feet away from the side of the bed, and placed her legs on either side of its cream leather upholstered top before squatting down to sit.

"Sorry, Kel. It's a bit disconcerting trying to take a piss when there's *your* dead master staring at you through his one good eye! I couldn't help but feel fascinated by him though; as tragic as the situation may be. I'm here now though, and I think it's for the best that we clear the air between us. Matt's going to stay in the car a little while longer so we can talk; okay?"

"Talk about what Shanna?!" Kelly blasted, "I've been waiting here half an hour to have these fuckin' handcuffs taken off while you've been having a powwow with *my* husband in your car and then making me listen to you emptying your bladder! I don't owe you clear air. Suffice it to say; I don't owe you *jack shit!*"

"Ok, Kelly. Hold on." Shanna leant forward and reached her arms over Kelly's head.

"Oh thank God!" Kelly praised as she felt Shanna touch at the cuff on her left wrist. Before she had realised though, Shanna had moved her hands back and taken a hold of the rear strap of the ball gag still looped around Kelly's neck. Sliding her slender fingers quickly around the inside of its material until they met on opposite sides of the leather ball, Shanna took hold of it and yanked it upwards; letting her fingers flick loose and sending the hard rubber ball flying backwards towards Kelly's face. It connected powerfully with her top lip, punching into it and making her yelp in pain. Shanna smothered the ball with her palm and pushed it firmly into place.

"*Wha' va Fug?*" Kelly garbled through the obstruction.

"I'm sorry Kelly," Shanna spoke plainly, "I didn't want to have to do that to you. Lord knows you must be tired; you've already been through so much. But now that Matt and I have had a good talk, there are some things I need you to understand, and that means you have to listen. Seeing as you can't be respectful and keep your mouth shut, and since we're running short on time, then that means I have to *make* you listen. Do you understand?"

Kelly glared at her with a newfound depth of hatred. She forced her right hand high in the air and turned it, extending her middle finger defiantly.

"Protest noted; but I'll take that as your way of saying yes", Shanna quipped. "Now; for what it's worth, Matt wants you to know he's sorry; and he truly regrets everything that's happened between you over the past few hours. I'm sure it's well apparent to you by now, but you owe all of this to your own actions. You've shamed yourself, Kelly; and in doing so, you've broken that poor man. He did nothing but give you love and devotion, along with everything you ever needed or wanted, and the best you could do in return was betray him for the prospect of a cheap thrill. He could have easily been the one to fulfil your fantasy, but you ignored the possibility of him in favour of Connor; and why? Because Connor looks better in a suit? Because he had a nice haircut, pecs and a six-pack? You're a vain bitch Kelly, pure and simple, and every bruise on your nasty little body is a testament to that. Maybe I'm being harsh; maybe not… My point being; you deserve everything he's done to you, and a whole lot more that he hasn't but that he should've."

Kelly's expression switched dramatically from anger to naive puzzlement. Shanna was unimpressed.

"Don't act dumb, Kelly. You've made it no secret between us, and I'm just glad Matt's had the chance to see it now. When I said I loved Matt earlier, I meant it. I told him again just now, in the car. Tell me honestly, Kelly; did you feel betrayed when I did that?"

Kelly nodded, looking at Shanna and, for the first time, a solitary tear began to form in the corner of each now sad, glistening eye.

"It hurts to be betrayed; doesn't it?"
Kelly nodded.

"And yet you somehow can't make the distinction between the hurt you feel, and the betrayal you've engineered? Can't you see how truly damaging your actions have been, compared to a simple piece of honesty from me to him? You broke his fucking heart, Kelly. Do you see that now?"

"Mm-hmm" Kelly nodded remorsefully as her slow tears trickled over the mounds of her cheeks.

"Don't get me wrong, Kelly. It's nice to see that you actually have feelings somewhere underneath. But are you weeping for the right reasons? It's important for me to know."

With her body convulsing with the motion of each sob, Kelly raised her left eyebrow and tilted her head to the side; giving Shanna a questioning look.

"Are you on the verge of all-out crying because you regret any of the pain you've put him through? Or are you just sad simply because I'm going to take away the source of your protection in the real world? Your safety net; the shroud you've hidden behind for normalities sake. The cash cow you've lived off intentionally ever since you met him? I'll be honest; he told me everything you'd said to him before I came back into the house, Kelly. Not just today, but other occasions too. It was heart-breaking to listen to."

Kelly took in Shanna's words, gulping painfully around the hard rubber ball. She tried her best to control her emotions, to show compassion and level-headed understanding but; when Shanna spoke of greed and the selfish theft of Matt's good nature; the depth of hurt she felt took her by surprise. Shanna's suggestion that Matt was no longer hers, though, tipped her resolve over the edge, sending a realising pain through her; cutting her deeper than she could hide. In herself she knew the loss of Matt was what she feared the most. The contrasted reactions on display could not have been any clearer to Shanna; and as the fluid tears began streaking down Kelly's cheeks, staining their clear path to the underside of her chin, Shanna nodded to her silently in disappointment.

"That's incredibly sad, Kel. But at least, with your mouth shut, you had no choice but to answer my question honestly, right?"

Kelly's face was fraught with guilt.

"The first time you show any sense of remorse is when you realise you're losing your easy life. After today, how are you gonna cope? Starting from scratch is no easy thing; I should know. But that's unfair on me really; I didn't engineer that fate. I was robbed of an amazing man well before his time; you've done everything to rob yourself, and you were too blind to even see you were doing it."

Kelly continued to sob; each pained exhalation muffled by the hard rubber blockage filling her wide stretched mouth. Saliva had begun to trickle from the underside of the ball, running in a slick stream over the middle of her chin and down her neck. The lower half of her face was starting to look a mess.

"Do you want forgiveness, Kelly? Or compassion; perhaps?" Shanna asked.

Kelly stared at her, unsure of how to react. She could feel herself shrinking, the bed starting to consume her as she silently wished she could simply disappear into it. The handcuff key was locked in her left fist. Shanna hadn't noticed Kelly's closed hand yet, and Kelly knew that she would have to wait for a lengthy opportunity to use it while Shanna was not looking; unless she was actually going to free her at the end of this as promised.

Shanna suddenly leant forward and, with the tip of her forefinger, hooked the ball from Kelly's mouth, taking her by surprise. Kelly stretched her aching jaw for a few seconds, feeling her facial muscles burn as they began to relax back to their normal positions. Sullenly, she looked Shanna in the eyes, a fire of defiance reignited in the knowledge that she had lost. '*If this is how it was to be,*' she told herself, '*then I won't go down quietly.*'

Chapter Forty-Four

"You're enjoying this a touch too much Shanna; it's really quite sick. And no; I don't want either your forgiveness *or* compassion. You've said more than enough for me to know that you don't think I deserve any."

"Wrong, Kelly," Shanna sat back and shook her head, "You've *done* more than enough to know you don't deserve it. But very well deflected all the same. Either way; it's a good thing you don't expect either, because Matt doesn't forgive you and I sure as hell have no compassion for you."

"Let me go, Shanna." Kelly pleaded. "You've made your point, and I get it. Take Matt. Go and be happy together. It's not like I can take any of this back."

"It's not as simple as that, honey." Shanna said dryly, looking at Kelly almost apologetically. Kelly felt tension sink its tightening claws into her body instantly.

"What do you mean?" she asked, her voice starting to tremble.

"You're a mess, Kelly" Shanna replied. "The moment you're seen looking like... that..." she paused, "Well; questions are going to be asked, aren't they! Not to mention Connor of course! Matt and I spoke about everything that's happened and we think we've come up with a way to explain it, but you're gonna have to agree to play ball if it's gonna work."

"What do you mean? You're saying Matt takes no blame for this?" she gestured down to her body. "For murdering Connor? Jesus Christ, Shan; for someone who raves on about morals, that's a pretty astounding secret you're suggesting we all keep!"

"Matt doesn't deserve any more punishment, Kelly. And it's unfair to call it murder, don't you think?"

Kelly was taken aback, astounded and with a wounded expression painted across her face. She began to laugh cynically.

"He pounded Connor's eyeball into his fucking head, Shanna! He's lying in the bathroom dead because of it! How is that not murder?"

"There was no intent from what I can understand. Connor had his chance to make amends, but he chose to attack Matt. As far as I see it, it was self-defence; and Connor did the major damage to himself by falling against the wardrobe handle."

"So what bullshit are you two suggesting we spin?"

"It's really quite simple. Matt and you had argued after he'd found out you were cheating on him with Connor, so he'd stayed with me last night. Connor met up with you here for sex today. He turned into a psychopath, tied you to the bed, and hurt you. You managed to call me, both Matt and I rushed over as quickly as we could, and then Matt had to fight Connor off of you. We saved your life but, in the struggle, Connor fell; exactly as it actually happened. It's obvious they'll find Matt's fingerprints in here, since it's been his bedroom for nearly ten years, so there can't be any suspicion if they do go so far as to search for fingerprints. All of the things Matt used on you can be wiped clean, and we transfer Connor's prints onto them afterwards. Frankly, it's a fool proof plan. Matt agrees. So all that's left is you. We need to know you'll follow our lead, Kelly."

"So, what? You call the police, direct them to me up here all tied up, and then hope that your story washes with them?"

"I don't need to hope, Kelly; it will. There'll be no evidence left to say otherwise, even if you were to open your spiteful fuckin' mouth and betray Matt yet again. Make no mistake, you'll do this, for your own sake. All you have to do is tell the police exactly what I've just told you, and if we're all on the same page, then this whole situation goes away without any of us getting into further… inconvenience."

"Inconvenience!" Kelly snorted. "And Matt? What does Matt say will happen between the two of us, after this is all covered up?"

"Matt's coming home with me. He'll give you enough time to find somewhere else, and to move your things. He's offered to help you with a deposit if it makes things quicker, although personally I disagree wholeheartedly with him giving you anything! But if that's what he decides, and you take him up on the offer, I won't stand in his way."

Kelly's face cracked as she dramatically broke down, crying uncontrollably.

"It's over, Kelly. It's best you make peace with that sooner rather than later. Don't worry though; I'm sure there's another unsuspecting pot of money just waiting for a girl like you to take care of." Shanna sneered, feeling somewhat cruel, but ultimately justified.

"Can you really be that heartless?" Kelly choked through her tears.

"If I was," she paused, biting her tongue, "then that would make two of us, wouldn't it."

Kelly let out a lung emptying sigh, a signal Shanna

took to be resignation of the fact that the good life Kelly had known for so long had now come to its end. A few seconds of uncomfortable silence followed. Kelly swallowed what felt; and that sounded to Shanna; like a brick in her throat, coughing past it painfully before agreeing solemnly.

"Okay. I'll go along with it."

"Good girl."

Shanna could not help but sound condescending, though smiling sincerely at Kelly all the while. Kelly did not recognise her honesty however; preferring to concentrate on the patronising tone while seething silently behind her docile façade.

"I've got to go and clean everything; then I'll call the police. If they say I can free you when I speak to them, then I will, but I have a feeling they'll want to inspect the scene as it currently looks."

"It's okay; I understand", Kelly nodded.

Shanna lifted herself from the stool and made her way across to the bedroom door, collecting the spanking paddle and the belt that Matt had previously used to whip Kelly. She had stepped half out of the doorway when she paused, turning back into the room and towards the bed.

"I hope you realise I'm doing this for you too, Kelly." she said.

"How do you mean?"

"I mean, I'm giving you the chance to right your wrongs. Think of this as an atonement. I know that Matt went extremely far, but you gave him good cause. Doing this will prove that you can be a much better person than you've led us to believe up until now."

"Just go and do what you need to, Shanna", Kelly spat despondently, trying her best not to feel belittled by the comment.

Unable to feel anything but fury towards Shanna; she

watched her leave the room, pulling the door near-closed behind her and disappearing down the corridor, Uncoiling her fist, she took another look at the small metal key wedged tightly between the bunched pillows of skin within her palm, and quickly summarised the two options left available to her. Toe the line; as much as she might have despised the idea of submitting to their controlling demand; or use the key; but then what? Run? Attack them? Hurt them in the ways she had been fantasising? Get to a phone and contact the police with the true account of events?

She knew it was exactly like Shanna had said; all of the evidence would be gone within a few minutes; and, with all credit to her, Shanna's fabricated version of events would be pretty convincing to anyone looking at the scene after the fact. She questioned herself; was it really worth the fight to tell the truth? Or did Shanna's well-crafted deceit hide a level of common sense that she couldn't ignore?

"I have to say; after all the negative things I said about him, he was a good looking guy, Kel!" Shanna's voice trailed out between the rooms.

Kelly; after being so absorbed in her contemplation; fell back into reality and frowned. To her mind, Shanna knew full well that she was goading her; with every sly comment feeding her appetite with new a reason to use the key.

'And it would be so easy' she thought. *'Free myself, then take one of those old metal coat hangers from the wardrobe, unwind it, and drive it straight through that blonde bitch's pretty fucking face. I'll be intrigued to see how much the spineless cunt fancies her after that!'*

Realising her returning anger, Kelly's loose grip on rational thought was lost again. The key; burrowing into the centre of her hand with the increasing pressure of her clutching fist, a persistent reminder of an opportunity expiring by the second. She was consumed by the prospect; growing more and more infuriated by her own frustrating indecisiveness.

Shanna leant over the bathtub surveying Connor's broken eye socket. Its edges had swollen thickly; a sticky mixture of blood and clear fluids leaking from its deep black abyss, tricking slowly down into the crater of his dented cheekbone. She looked distastefully over it for a few seconds, grimacing, before turning her head to look around the bathroom's interior.

Rising to her feet, she took two slip-on flannels from the towel rack, turned the hot tap on, and held one of them under the stream of warm water. Sliding her hand into the second flannel; she gripped her fingers around the flat surfaces of the heavy paddle, meticulously scrubbing at its handle to remove Matt's fingerprints. Placing it down onto a towel to dry, she then reached for the belt to repeat the process.

Once both of the items firm leather had run almost dry, she took a clean towel and picked them up again, mopping away the streaks and few drops of water remained; careful not to let her skin touch against their surfaces. Removing an armful of dirty clothes from the laundry basket, she threw both the wet flannel and damp towel in, then placed the pile back on top of them. With the dry flannel slid back onto her hand, she proceeded to grip the belt strap in the mitt and moved across to Connor.

Interlocking her fingers between those of his right hand, she raised the pairing into the air; and, with the mitt flatly outstretched, lowered his hand back down onto the belts length. She cautiously wiggled her fingers free, bringing them directly over his so as to guide them into a firm grip. They curled inwards, fixing against either side of the belts inch wide sides, where she pressed on his knuckles to imprint on the malleable hide. She counted to five before easing her pressure, sliding the belt through his pinching grip, and placing it back onto the towel. The same procedure completed on the handle of the spanking paddle; she then placed the pair of items together in the centre of a new towel, folding it over and bundling it under her arm, and headed out of the bathroom into the corridor.

She was making her way between the rooms when she heard sounds echo out from the bedroom; an odd jingling over what sounded like clicks; strangely out of place and immediately put Shanna on edge. Tentatively, and with the bundled towel moved to hug tightly against her chest, she stepped up to the door and leant to her side; just enough to peek with one eye through the small gap.

Chapter Forty-Five

Kelly paused, staring at her sore right arm as it lay flat on the bed beside her, desperately urging its blood flow to return. For now, she had just enough strength to turn it over on the bed, following the persistent line of inflamed red skin around the circumference of her wrist with her eyes as she did so. The handcuff key was still gripped between her lame fingers when Shanna burst into the room; elbow first, flying through the air towards her. In one simultaneous move Shanna threw the bundle onto the bed at Kelly's feet, threw the small plastic bag to the floor, and dived heavily on top of her; knocking the wind out of her chest and making the key fly out from between her fingers. It hit noisily against the wall next to the tallboy and rebounded, skidding across the floor and under the bed. Kelly heard the distinct metallic tinkling as it came to a spinning stop below her, and sank inside.

She did not feel Shanna's grip around her forearm; just the jarring twist of her shoulder as her arm was being lifted back towards the headboard. Expending what little muscle she still had in her arm to fight against its replacement made little difference. She watched helplessly as the metal was passed around her wrist once more, listening as the mechanism clicked agonisingly through each ratchet.

"*NOOOOO!*" she wailed, "*PLEASE SHANNA; I'M SORRY!*"

Shanna looked back at her, incensed. Pure fury burnt like fires behind her eyes and, for the first time since they had met, Kelly felt truly scared of her.

"Is that how much you can be trusted, is it? *IS IT?*"

she screamed. "I told you I wouldn't be long; that I had things to do... to clear this whole *fuckin'* mess up. A mess *you* fuckin' started! Then, and *only* then... if I'm told its okay... I'd take away the cuffs. What is so *fuckin'* hard to understand about that?"

"I'm sorry!" Kelly sobbed. "I... I wasn't thinking! It was a stupid thing to do, and I won't try anything again, I promise!"

Shanna bunched her right hand into a fist at her side, and brought it pummelling sideways into Kelly's cheek, making it crack loudly and causing Kelly to yelp.

"Seriously; it's no wonder Matt wanted to beat the shit out of you!" Shanna said in amazement. "Connor too, for that matter! Is it so difficult for you to just do as you're asked, just once?"

"It won't happen again", Kelly gulped uncomfortably, flexing her lower jaw. "I swear."

Shanna raised herself off the bed and stood next to Kelly's prone body, massaging the sides of her head with her fingertips.

"You better hope it doesn't", she warned. "Now... there's something I have to do, and you're going to have to trust me."

Kelly looked up at her nervously. "What is it?" she trembled.

"I've transferred Connor's prints on these," she said, unfolding the towel and gesturing towards the belt and paddle, "but in order to do that I had to clean them first. Which means they may no longer have traces of you on them. I can't be sure."

"Oh", Kelly muttered, soberly.

"So I'm gonna need to... use them."

"You can't be serious? You expect me to let you-"

"Trust me; I'm not thrilled at the prospect either, but it's necessary unfortunately. It won't be sufficient just to make the place match with the story. The DNA evidence has to back it up too."

"That's just sick! You're gonna pay for this, Shanna; one way or another."

"Careful now, Kelly. That almost sounded like a threat!"

"Oh it was; trust me!"

"Well; that is *very* concerning. How exactly is it that you think I'm going to pay?"

"Once everyone finds out what a turncoat, malicious bitch you are. My friends… Matt's friends… They're all gonna know what you did. Then you're deader than dead; along with that pathetic weasel hiding in your car."

"Is that so?"

"Don't even think you can trivialise it, Shan. They're gonna want your blood for this, so fuckin' badly, and I'm not gonna say a word to stop 'em."

"You know, Kelly; it's really rather hilarious when you harp on in that winey, cocksure voice of yours. Do you think all of those so-called friends will be as supportive of you once they know the full story? You think they'll see you as the only one to have been betrayed?"

"So Matt's friends might not be so supportive of me; who the fuck cares! Mine though? Mine are gonna want to rip your spiteful little head from your shoulders and deliver it to Matt in a box. You don't know them, Shanna. You have no idea."

Shanna removed her mobile phone from her purse, opened its Facebook application, and began searching through its menu.

"Let's test that theory, Kel. You can prove me wrong, and then I'll know *exactly* how much I've fucked up, and you can be freed immediately. Sound appealing?"

"How about you take these cuffs off me now so I can

demonstrate how bad you've fucked up?"

"No, Kel. Actually I have a very different idea. I think maybe it's time I let you in on a little 'inside joke'."

"What the fuck are you talking about Shanna? Just let me go."

"Facebook is a wonderful thing, isn't it?"

"What?"

"So many people to talk to! So many groups for you to join if, say, you have a particular special interest. I dare say you've joined a few of those in the past, haven't you? Some fangirl page or other; more than likely related to those *oh so exciting* books of yours? Or maybe to talk to dominant guys who you so desperately hope one day might want to leave you looking like... well; like you do right now!"

"What's your point?"

"My *point*, Kelly, is that people are naturally drawn to many different talking points, on a multitude of subjects. But, for the most part... it's mainly just bitchy gossip! Like this, for example."

Shanna opened a themed page which lay stored in her Facebook menu under the subheading 'Liked Pages'; then, extending her arm towards Kelly, allowed her to read its contents. The upper screen displayed what appeared to be a recent, close-up image of Kelly as its profile photo; looking hugely aggravated and sticking her fingers up towards the back of what appeared to be Matt's head. From items in the photo's background she realised it to have been taken in her own back garden. She judged from the neckline and colour of her blouse that it had been taken fairly recently; from a barbecue earlier in the year. The page was boldly entitled *'Our Dear Friend, Queen Bitch'*.

"What the hell is this?" Kelly raged, pulling vigorously at her restraints. Her right hand grasped unsuccessfully at the three inch gap between her fingers and the floating handset.

"This… is insanely popular; that's what it is! It's what you might call a… 'anti-fan page'. Basically it gets updated every time you show someone your selfish, malicious, ridiculous, drama queen side. That's actually more often than you'd think! It's been going for a good year-and-a-bit now; ever since you so openly started treating Matt with contempt. And boy, does it get heavy traffic! For someone so vain and self-centred, it's almost a shame you never got to know about it until now! We had to block you from it, of course; once we saw how popular it was becoming. Friends were telling friends. Then *their* families and friends somehow got in on the joke. It blossomed pretty quickly, from just a handful of us at first, into the almost a thousand followers that it has today! There's people in Australia watching your antics! You're a local celebrity! You must be so proud."

"You're fuckin' kidding me? You dare to consider yourself a better person than me, and all the while you've been making social media pages about me; spreading malicious rumours and gossip behind my back? That's low, Shanna. Seriously fuckin' low. And then you're stupid enough to question why I feel so sure about the state my friends are gonna leave you in!"

"Oh yeah! I get so distracted sometimes; I'm sorry. Allow me to get back to my original point. *Your friends.* Give me a name, Kelly. I'll see if I can find the last thing they posted on the page."

"Get real, Shanna. Like my friends are gonna have-"

"Oh but I think you'll be surprised, Kel! Go on… just one name. Give it your best shot."

"Carolyn Dene" Kelly gave hesitantly.

"Woah; spooky! I'd call that a jackpot!"

"Fuck y-."

"Carolyn Maria Dene... Created the page in September last year it says here."

Shanna watched as Kelly surged with anger, a look on her face suggesting that she refused to believe a word of what she was being told.

"Oh I'm sorry, Kel. Did you assume *I* created this page? I never meant to suggest that at all, and I'm really sorry if you got that impression! From what I understand, Carolyn started it around the same time you arranged for your close little circle of girlie chums to come over one evening and enjoy a few drinks. Rumour has it you then proceeded to make your much-liked husband cook, clean, and serve the whole night whilst you openly belittled him in front of your guests. Really very unimpressive in the eyes of your friends. I mean; obviously I wasn't one of the ones there to witness it, but I can clearly remember some of their comments from when I first joined the page, which wasn't long after that. *Incredibly* derogatory towards you at the time, they were. Although; having known you on a more personal level for some time now, I can honestly say, I understand their sentiments entirely. Here you go; take a look!"

The phone was thrust back into Kelly's view, an early status from Carolyn being pointed to by Shanna's guiding index finger. It read:

'*Some of you might wonder why I set this page up. Others will instantly understand exactly why I did! There's been so many times we've seen Kelly at her overly dramatic worst. Embarrassing and offensive, even at the best of times. We wondered whether she'd settle down after marriage; looks like we were wrong to hope! She's my friend and, for my sins, I love her. But I could've pulled her greasy blonde extensions out and clubbed her round the head over the way she talked to her lovely fella last night. I make no bones, she deserves this. Anyone who can keep the secret is welcome to share their stories and experiences. C.'*

Chapter Forty-Six

Kelly looked up to the far wall; ashen faced and stony silent. She had no words to say. Inside she felt broken by betrayal. She remembered well the night in question, and she knew from Shanna's description of it that there were no lies to defend herself against. Everything stated had been true and, with that being so, there was now no reason to suggest her friends would indeed support or protect her. Carolyn had been her best friend since school, and remained her closest confidante. All hope was gone if she had lost her allegiance. Once again, Kelly found herself sinking heavily into the mattress; desperate to be swallowed up by the bed and to vanish from view.

"So you're gonna toe the line now, right Kelly?"

"You're siding with a murderer Shan. What the fuck are you thinking?" she implored.

"Matt didn't deserve to be put in this situation Kelly. I haven't sided with him because he unintentionally took a life whilst having to save his own. I side with him because he's always been an outstanding human being, and because the most important person to him has *blatantly* abused his good nature for her own gain. Questioning my intentions does nothing but show how ignorant and scared you are. Now; can I count on you to toe the *fucking* line or should I just go ahead and update this page with everything you've been up to today? If so; hold still for the photos."

Shanna's thumb hung poised in the air over her phone. Kelly held her eyes shut, fresh thin tears streaking down from their outer corners. After a few moments battling her urge to resist, she finally threw her hands open in dramatic dismay.

"Okay, fine!" she grunted belligerently. "But you can take this as a generously friendly warning Shanna. If your cock and bull story doesn't wash with the cops, or if they end up piecing the truth together, then I'm not living the lie any longer than I have to."

"That's not going to be a concern, Kel. I've already told you; I've got this covered."

Shanna took hold of the towel and wrapped a patch of its material around her palm, before reaching down for the buckled end of the belt. She raised its length high in the air, pinching its metal clasp between three fingers, and looked uncompromisingly into Kelly's anxiety stricken eyes.

"Are you ready?"

"That's a ridiculous question, don't you think? Just get it over with… and be sensible."

The long leather strap whistled as it flicked through the air, landing across both of Kelly's thighs with reverberating crackles of sound. Kelly howled out more in shock than of pain; the sensation being far less intense than she had felt previously. Shanna's grip did not allow a great deal of control over the strength behind the strike, feeling more club-fingered than accurate. Kelly found herself somewhat disappointed; lacking the sense of fulfilment which she opted to keep to herself. A second whipping strike came down, this time around Kelly's waist, making her lurch upwards as her abdominal muscles took the firm leathers stinging impact. Far more tenderer there; the whipping sound echoed through the room and filled Kelly's ears with a satisfaction matched by the warming sensation cultivating between her hips.

"Okay, that's all we're gonna need with that", Shanna said, replacing the warmed length carefully at the base of the bed, unaware of the abject disappointment seeping from Kelly's every pore.

Second came the paddle.

"Okay; the last couple are on their way and then we're done!" Shanna encouraged.

"Get the hell on with it. I haven't got all day."

From the way the solid plaque hit Kelly's rounded hip, and the sound of its contact mixed with Kelly's subsequent scream, Shanna wondered what protective benefit the leather casing actually provided from the hard piece of board just beneath its surface. *'It must be purely decorative; meaningful to the sentimentality of a sadomasochist'*; she thought; as the board was dragged away to reveal a well-defined square welt growing viciously under the skin. The flesh was thickening by the second; a raised patch quickly developing and turning reddish-pink. The sight made Shanna reel back with a hand to her mouth. She felt both physically and mentally sick. Kelly, stretching out before her with her body tensed and quivering, bit hard into her lower lip as she let the intense pain subside into gratified delirium.

Shanna stood speechless for a moment, watching Kelly's body writhe while listening to her subtle, muffled moans. Snapping out of her dumbstruck state, she abruptly snapped at Kelly in anger, fuelled by the shock of what she had witnessed.

"Shut up! Just... Shut up!" She held her hands to her ears as Kelly, red-faced and panting, turned her head to hers. A muffled apology bled through the thickness of her palms as she watched Kelly slowly and sincerely mouth the words. Eventually lowering her hands, Shanna looked at her, simultaneously furious and horrified.

"You actually... enjoyed that?" she accused.

"I didn't think it would become so obvious; I'm sorry. I tried to be quiet!"

"There was nothing subtle about that, Kelly. It was... weird!"

Shanna's hands dropped to the horizontal bedframe as her eyes lowered to the floor in embarrassed aversion. Kelly, with a growing sense that something was not right, lifted herself as best she could to look down her body. Parting her thighs, she instantly located the source of Shanna's discomfort. A wet patch lay soaking into the bedding below her, spreading steadily wider as it seeped further into the mattress's material.

"I... I don't know what you want me to say, Shanna. I'm sorry an' all, but... well, it's not like you didn't already know I liked that sort of thing. It's kinda dumb to do it to me in the first place, but incredibly short-sighted to expect no reaction at all!"

"Do the circumstances not make it any different? Or were you simply shutting your eyes and imagining someone else was doing it to you?"

"Would it confuse that tiny, close-minded brain of yours if I said that the circumstances don't matter *shit* to me? That it has no bearing what so ever on who delivers a spanking, and that I just happen to love the feel? Forgive me, Shanna; and I've in no way ever considered you in a sexual context... but you could do that to me all fuckin' day if you liked and I wouldn't complain! I like the way it feels, whether it's coming from the hands of a big meaty Dom... or even just from little old you."

"Just as long as it's not Matt though."

"That's... that's not my point. You're twisting my words now."

"Fuck you, Kelly. You've twisted them enough already; to the extent where you can't hear their hypocrisy anymore. Or maybe that's just you all over. You choose not to hear it."

"Are you gonna finish up or what?"

"Are you gonna grow up and see this for what it is? It's as much about saving your arse as it is for Matt's. You understand that, right? It's not about you laying back and getting kicks from it."

"Yeah, yeah; I know. I'll shut up and keep still."

"Good; you'd better!"

"Won't seem too out of the ordinary anyway!" Kelly scoffed loudly, "It's not as if Matt ever had me making any noise in this bed!"

Without warning, Shanna suddenly lunged forward, taking hold of Kelly's throat in her fingers and squeezing into it. She felt the windpipe crush beneath them as Kelly, gasping for precious air, looked up into Shanna's storm clouded eyes in absolute fear.

"I'm sorry!" she rasped.

"I could abandon my plan, you know? I could take a walk downstairs and take the biggest fucking knife I can find in that bastard showroom kitchen of yours, come back up here and bury it in your thick, arrogant *fuckin'* face. Sure, it'll mean adapting the story slightly, but the cops would still buy it. The only difference will be that I won't have to live with the dissatisfaction of you breathing clean air meant for decent caring people. How does that fuckin' sound?"

Kelly's eyes were narrowing, her hands flapping in panic as she felt the light leaving her eyes. She implored Shanna with pure expression, begging the good will out of her. Just as she thought it was no good, and that Shanna would end her right there and then, Shanna released her grip and a bullet of air shot into Kelly's empty lungs. She collapsed flat; huffing strenuously.

"Go ahead; you make your nasty jokes. But trust me, Kelly; I've got options and you don't. I suggest you remember that."

Kelly nodded, her throat too tight to allow a verbal

response.

"Shit; what about the ball gag? Where did that come from?"

"Mine." Kelly screeched quietly, pointing a finger down to herself.

"Pleasant. Well at least we can explain that one away. Besides; it would be fair for the police to appreciate we might have moved it out of your mouth at some point anyway, even if it hadn't have been yours. I think we're done here."

Kelly breathed a sigh of relief.

"I can get loose now?" she asked; quietly, but with determinable, uncharacteristic politeness.

"Not yet; sorry Kel. Gotta call the police first. Evidence in a crime scene and all that. It's better that they free you once they've arrived and have done what they need to."

"You know; I never thought of you as this much of a schemer, Shan. I've misjudged you."

"You've misjudged everyone; but that's what happens when you think only of yourself. You take your eye off the ball and miss the signs all around you. And I've not always been a schemer, Kel; but I'll sure as hell fight the corner of someone who deserves a fighting chance."

Shanna spent a few minutes pumping herself up, pacing around the house with her thumb poised over the screen of her phone. When she felt her level of nerves reach breaking point, she dialled the emergency services. She knew how vital the panic in her voice needed to be.

When she had finally relayed the news of her discovery to the concerned dispatcher and ended the call, she breathed a hefty sigh of relief, and made her way down the stairs to the front door. Matt was beckoned to come back in from the car and then, having reconvened together in the bedroom with Kelly, Shanna explained how the police were en route.

"What do we do now?" Matt asked.

"Everything is arranged. Kelly knows the score, don't you Kel?"

"Yep."

"So we wait. And when they arrive, we go through it just as we discussed in the car; no changes. Okay?" Shanna reiterated.

"Okay", Matt confirmed, visibly anxious. He threw a tense look towards Kelly. Odd for him to see, she smiled back at him, nodding her head slowly in affirming collusion.

Chapter Forty-Seven

Shanna fixed her face to a frown, and answered the knock at the front door.

Stood before her was a tall, gruff looking man; dressed in a smart black suit and sporting a well-groomed hairstyle; his greying unkempt straggly beard seeming out of place among the rest of his neat features. Tiptoeing over each of his shoulders, Shanna could see the man was accompanied by two uniformed police officers.

"I'm Detective Inspector Caverhill," he stated, flicking his black leather wallet open to flash his identification, "and these are Officers Campbell and Small. I understand you called regarding a situation you have inside?"

"Yes, Detective Inspector; thank you for coming so quickly. It's our friend, she's upstairs."

Shanna had just finished her sentence when she heard sirens in the distance, and the trio watched as an ambulance sped around the far corner and up the road towards them. DI Caverhill stepped out to hail them as they slowed to a stop. The paramedic in the driver's seat wound down his window and greeted him.

"I need to assess the crime scene first, so I'll have to ask you to wait here until I say otherwise. If there's any need for immediate medical intervention I'll call for you, understand?"

"Understood", the paramedic responded, winding his window back and relaxing into his seat.

"Campbell; you take the front door. Small; you're with me."

"Yes Sir", the officers confirmed in unison.

"Take me to the victim please, Miss", DI Caverhill requested, fishing through the pockets of his suit jacket and bringing out two sets of blue latex gloves, one of which he passed to Officer Small. Shanna nodded and began guiding him inside the house, Officer Small following closely behind them, closing the door against Officer Campbell's back.

"I'm Shanna," she introduced, "Kelly's upstairs, in the bedroom with Matt, her husband. I have to warn you, it's quite a scene, Detective Inspector. Even so; I wasn't expecting someone so senior to come?"

"There's a reason for that Miss," Caverhill replied abruptly "You could call it a professional hunch, but we'll soon know if my attendance was necessary."

Shanna swallowed a lump; anxious to what that might mean. She tried her best to stop her limbs from shaking as she started the climb up the staircase, but it was hard to control her impulses. Reaching the top step she let out a sigh and pointed to the semi open doorway, three doors along the narrow landing. "Kelly's in there," she informed him, "and Connor's in the bathroom, through there." She pointed to the closed bathroom door directly in front of them. "He's dead."

DI Caverhill took the lead, striding towards the bedroom door, easing it cautiously ajar with the tips of his fingers. As the panorama of the room drew into view he initially saw Kelly, laid on the bed with both hands raised up by her shackles, the fresh white bed sheet once again spread across her body to secure her modesty. He noticed the wardrobe door, the visible damage to its panelling, and the streak of rich crimson which had run from its impacted round wooden knob down to the floor. As he turned his head to the left, following the furthest edge of the slowly moving door as he pushed against it, he noticed various toppled piles of clothes, some strewn across the floor, others arced precariously over the bedroom furniture. He stopped pushing at the loud thud of the door handle hitting the wall and there he caught sight of Matt, a broken shape cowering with his back against the wall, his head in his hands with only his closest eye visible between his widely spread, bloodstained fingers.

"Young lady?" he called over to Kelly. She looked up at him with exhaustion. "Are you OK?"

Kelly nodded, the motion of her head much slower than a nod would normally inspire.

"Sir?" he looked at Matt; anticipating him to move his hands away from his face, but it didn't happen. "Sir?" he tried again, "I'm Detective Inspector Caverhill. Are you OK?"

"Hmm?" Matt tilted his head, springing his fingers apart to see more clearly through comatose eyes. "Oh, thank god! Can you help my wife, please?" He moved his hands away from his face, gesturing with them outstretched as if imploring the man's attention back towards Kelly.

"I will Sir, but I understand there's a gentleman dead in your bathroom. I need to inspect him first and understand the full circumstances before I can assist your wife; do you understand?"

Kelly groaned in fatigued disappointment.

"Yes; yes we understand… just… please be quick as you can", Matt pleaded.

"I'll be as quick as possible", Caverhill reiterated with authority, before turning in the doorway and exiting the room.

With his back now turned, Kelly looked up and threw a pained glance towards Matt, causing him to level his palms in the air at his sides as if to say *'what was I supposed to do?'* Kelly frowned at him in response; very clearly mouthing the words *'You're gonna burn in hell for this'.*

In the corridor, Shanna stood with Officer Small; her arms tightly folded across her chest and feeling helpless. Caverhill took her by the elbow, lowering his head slightly to meet her eyes.

"I'm going to need to see the situation in the bathroom."

Shanna nodded her agreement, stepping aside to allow him past her, followed by Small. Caverhill leant his ear to the bathroom door momentarily, listening, then placed his fingers against its panelling and turned to his junior.

"Officer Small; if you wouldn't mind?"

Small moved between Caverhill and the door, pushing down on its intricately twisted metal handle. As the door crept inwards, Caverhill lifted himself on tiptoes to peer over the Officers broad shoulders. Placing his hand up onto the highest point of the doorframe, he leant forward as far as he could, and Shanna heard him mouth the words.

"I *fuckin'* knew it!"

"What do you mean?" Shanna asked instantly, surging with panic. "What… Is there something you think you already knew?"

Caverhill pushed past Small and stepped towards the bathtub. He lowered himself to Connors level, reached forward and holding his palm out flat, just in front of the side of Connor's face where the impact had destroyed its structure. Obscuring the damage; he was left with a fairly clean representation of the dead man's face, which he gazed over as if he were an old friend. After what felt like a silent eternity to Shanna; but in reality was little more than ten seconds; Caverhill rose to his feet, heaving out a relieved breath. Shanna nervously broke the silence.

"What is it, Detective Inspector?" she asked.

"Your friend has been very lucky, Miss." Caverhill said, exultant. "Come with me. There's something I need to explain to all of you."

Shanna and the two policemen entered the bedroom just as Kelly was trading another of her inflammatory glares towards Matt. He had remained on the opposite side of the room, with his head tucked in towards his knees. Kelly instinctively looked away as the group approached the bed; fixing her face from anger to naivety in preparation for their anticipated onslaught of questions. By the time she had turned to face them, she found it odd that Caverhill was instructing Shanna to perch on the end of the bed, and that he himself was pacing the room in front of the crouching Matt. He seemed as though full of bluster, a kettle seconds from reaching boiling point, and eager to unleash.

'Perhaps he knows?' she thought. *'Maybe he's seen through all their bullshit and he's about to call those two backstabbing fuckers out on it! God I'd fucking love it! I mean; really! How the fuck did they think they could get away with-'*

Her rioting imagination fell instantly silent upon hearing Caverhill gravelly cough. He was clearing his throat, and beginning to speak.

"A little over a year ago, the wife of a university lecturer was murdered at her home not far from here. I investigated it with a colleague whom, we subsequently found out, had been having an affair with the woman for the few weeks leading up to her death. We'd discovered traces of his DNA at the scene, which should have been impossible since we'd both been suited and gloved when we'd first attended. When we looked deeper into the circumstances surrounding the murder, we discovered there were further unsolved cases from the twelve months prior which bared distinct similarities to those of the lecturer's wife, including the pattern of her injuries and ultimately the final method of her execution. My partner was a distinguished, medalled officer; but underwent investigation as per protocol. The DNA linked him to the scene, but uncovering the affair meant that we couldn't emphatically prove that he was her killer. Thanks to our counterpart's poor processing of the previous crimes, we also had nothing to link him to the murders, so he was never charged. He was, however, suspended from his job and ended up accepting a professional discharge due to the affair. My colleagues name was Conrad Johnson and… without a doubt in my mind… he *is* the dead man lying in your bathtub."

Chapter Forty-Eight

Lost for words; the trio sat staring at each other in amazed silence. Each of them shared the same dumbfounded expression, their faces contorted with shock and abject horror.

"You mean, Connor is your ex-partner?" Matt asked, regaining the use of his voice; sure that he had misheard somehow.

"Correct, Sir. *Connor* would appear to be a pseudonym he adopted, but it's him all the same; and, if he had intended to carry out the kinds of torture the other victims endured prior to their deaths, and you two hadn't arrived when you did... then this pretty young thing would be heading in very much the same direction."

He turned to Kelly, resting his hands on the metal bedframe and leaning towards her.

"You're incredibly lucky to be alive, Miss. You owe these good people an impossible debt of gratitude."

Kelly gawped back at Caverhill, overwhelmed; with her lower jaw hanging down in uncontrolled bewilderment. Her head rocked slowly back and forth; not through any intentional movement, but by the tremendous pulsing of her blood pressure now jolting through her body. Her ears were whistling with its sound as she felt herself edge towards fainting.

"I can imagine you're in shock, honey. You've been through an ordeal, that's for sure. But trust me; there could have been many more ways this ended, and they could've been a whole lot more unpleasant... and more than likely final... than this." Caverhill looked around the room. "Do any of you know where the handcuff keys are?"

Shanna lied, expertly.

"Kelly told us Connor had thrown them somewhere, but we honestly didn't have time to look yet"

Kelly didn't react. Still reeling; she stared silently into Caverhill's eyes, lost in a catatonic stupor.

"Small?"

"Yes, Sir" he replied.

"Check under the bed. I'm going to try to see under these clothes. Try not to disturb things too much though. This is a crucial crime-scene; it is *imperative* that we keep its integrity if I'm gonna be able, once and for all, to nail that son of a bitch for all he's done."

Small lowered himself to his knees at the foot of the bed, craning his neck to peer into its subterranean gloom.

"Hold up a second, Sir. I think I see something shiny halfway under here. It definitely does look like a key."

Small moved swiftly around the base of the bed, flattening himself against the floor and outstretching his arm. For a few seconds he swept it across the wide space aimlessly, before a fleeting touch of something brushed under his fingertips. He began to feel around the area with a focussed caution.

"Have you got it?" Caverhill urged.

"I felt it, Sir. I'll have it with one more try."

He reached out again, this time dropping his fingers directly on top of the key, and then carefully dragged it towards his body. As soon as Caverhill caught sight of the glistening silver between Small's fingers he lunged down to retrieve it. He lifted it into the air and smiled broadly as if displaying the greatest of successes. "Good work, Officer" he grinned.

It was at that moment, with Caverhill crouched down at Matt's level, that the ageing officer's face suddenly grew a seed of familiarity to him. Leaning forward to study his features more intensely, Matt formed a picture in his memory.

"I've seen you before, I think." He blurted.

"You have?"

"It was at my workplace. I saw you in our car park, arguing with Connor about something. I mean; this is going back easily a month or so ago; but it *was you*; wasn't it?"

"You've got an excellent memory, Mr Buchanon! I tried my best to keep a close eye on Conrad since his discharge; I was sure from the start that he wasn't as squeaky clean as he would adamantly insist. I followed him to the factory that one day; staked him out for the whole damn morning; but he got wind of me being there and... well; you must have seen how he lost his temper."

"You know; I forgot how curious that was at the time. He was so cagey about what had happened when I asked him, but I just forgot about it over time! It makes so much sense now! *Jesus!*"

Unlocking the nearest of the handcuffs, Caverhill raced to catch Kelly's falling arm. He could feel its veins and muscles pumping under the skin as the blood immediately surged through them after being starved for so long. The impact of its deadweight hitting his grasp snapped Kelly out of her trance; the return to reality, and the sight of her arm now free and laid at her side, hitting her like a freight train and making her collapse in a convulsive fit of tears.

Caverhill walked to the other side of the bed and perched on its edge. He took the second pair of handcuff in his hand, eased the key into place, and turned it. Her other arm sprang free and dropped, this time caught in mid-air and held. Placing his other hand on top of her palm, he stroked it soothingly to calm her.

"Now, Kelly; I'd like you to tell me, in your own words, how the events of today played out. Can you do that?"

Kelly started at the very beginning. The books and how they led to her fascination with playing the part of the submissive. The promise of realising her fantasies after having met Connor, and their subsequent arrangements. Matt and Shanna were growing nervous, exchanging anxious glances as Kelly neared the point of explaining the morning's events. From that point onwards though, she followed Shanna's concocted testimony to the letter. By the end of her explanation both Caverhill and Small were left dumbfounded and it took some time, the entirety of which Kelly spent staring into Caverhill's widened brown eyes, before he could give her a measured response.

"Well, Kelly! All I can say is, you've had luck on your side from the word go! Matt and Shanna intervening here is the sole reason you're still breathing." Caverhill leant in towards Kelly. "Personally... and, as a married man myself, I hope you can understand where I'm coming from... but, after everything you've just told me, it's a good thing you're not *my* wife." He leant in even closer, lowering his voice so as to be heard solely by her, "Because, if you were... I'd have been sorely tempted to do this to you myself!"

Caverhill looked around the room, curiously.

"Kelly?" he asked, "You mentioned Connor brought a bag with him each time. You said he called it his toolkit?"

Matt stood up and walked to the door, leaning out to grab the black rucksack by its top loop.

"That's this, Detective Inspector", he informed him.

"Interesting. None of you have been inside of it since he brought it here?"

The group replied together negatively.

He took the rucksack and placed it at the foot of the bed, opening its zip carefully with his gloved fingers. As it sprang apart, he recoiled.

"Fuck me!" he cried, placing his hand into the opening and withdrawing the enormous dildo Kelly had seen previously. Turning it around in his hands, he felt the imbalance within its length, a bottom heavy pull which led him to adjust his grip and pull at the lower half. A few tugs and wiggle later; the rear end of the plastic mass separated.

"Oh, holy shit", he cried again as a smile crept across his face, and he brandished a full size hunting knife from a concealed slot within it.

"You've gotta be shitting me!" Shanna gasped.

"And there's the murder weapon..." Caverhill beamed, overjoyed. "Conrad; I fuckin' got you now!"

"That's the murder weapon? A knife inside a dildo? What the hell did the sick bastard do to those women?"

Caverhill turned to Shanna, twirling the knife by its rounded handle between his fingers.

"Anus to sternum, in one cut."

Encouraged by the find, Caverhill turned to Matt.

"Now I appreciate you weren't aware of an awful lot of this before today, Matt, but you're the first person I've been able to speak with who has formed any type of friendship with Conrad. Neither of the previous victims husbands had any prior knowledge of him, so that makes you practically gold dust to me, if that doesn't sound too crass. Is there anything else of note you can tell me, from what you knew of him?"

Matt thought for a moment.

"Well; other than what I knew of him from work, which you've just told me was essentially fabricated anyway; no I guess. No... wait! There was this one night we spent drinking in town, at... umm... *Pure*. It's a bar, do you know it?"

"Sure; it's a tacky little place up in Meresden Park, I know it well. Go on."

"I don't drink often, and I'd quickly gotten into a bit of a mess, but I had enough sense about me to get it back under control by the end of the night. Anyway, as we were leaving, these two guys jumped us. I thought it was random, you know. Opportunistic thieves, homeless maybe. I thought one of them had beat the shit out of Connor, on the other side of the car, and it wasn't long before I got put in hospital for the night. But Connor seemed to be fine when we saw him the next morning. Do you think that has anything to do with it?"

"You may be onto something there, Matt."

"Yeah? You think?"

"Each of the husbands I spoke to, while they had no knowledge of Conrad when we showed them his photo, had been assaulted within the fortnight before their wives were murdered. We made enquiries, but they didn't see enough of the attackers to identify them, although they could confirm that they were jumped by three men, and that one, if it helps, was particularly large. Now, it's safe to assume that if there were three, then one could feasibly have been Connor on those occasions. I don't suppose you saw the two who attacked you that night, did you?"

"Clear as day!"

"Could you describe them to me, if I got you in later today, to compile a photo-fit?"

"Yeah, I'd be glad to."

"Good man."

"I'd consider it a duty, if I can help. They were mean sons of bitches, and I hate to think they could do the same to someone else. I mean, the shorter guy with the tattoo wasn't too sharp without the other, but fuck me, the other made up for him! He was scarily big!"

"You said the shorter one had a tattoo, Matt? What tattoo?" Caverhill's eyebrow rose.

"It was curled around his neck from the back of his shoulder. It was dark by that time, but I remember seeing it quite clearly. It was vibrant orange and white; a carp in a sea of cherry blossom. Quite artistic really; considering the sinewy piece of shit the lad actually was. I remember thinking it was a pretty decen-"

"Small!" Caverhill shouted, interrupting Matt mid-praise.

"Yes Sir?"

"I need you to do something, and I need you to not question it; do you understand?"

Small looked at his commanding officer, confused.

"If you give me a command, Sir, I'll follow it. No questions."

"Go downstairs to the front door, and place Officer Campbell under immediate arrest."

Officer Small paused. Caverhill looked at him and reiterated their agreement.

"No questions, Small."

"Understood; Sir."

Caverhill turned to Matt, gesturing with a pointed finger towards the bedroom window.

"Take a look outside, Matt. Tell me if you can be sure the officer in the street is the same man you were attacked by."

Matt sprinted across the room, stood upon the chaise lounge, and looked steeply down through the glass pane. He could see the back of Campbell, stood a couple of metres out from the doorway, talking to one of his neighbours. Small emerged into view and began walking towards Campbell, his heavy-booted steps on the pavement making Campbell aware, causing him to turn and face him.

The tattoo jumped out at Matt as if he were just a few inches from it, taken back to the night of the attack; and, as Small made his arrest, Campbell looked up to the window with an infuriated glare. Matt felt it bore into him, recoiling from the window in shock, his hand covering his mouth.

"Yes?" Caverhill pushed him. Matt nodded silently, his fingers quivering over his face.

"Jesus", Caverhill sighed, sitting himself down onto the bottom corner of the bed and running his hands over through his hair. "I always knew Conrad must have had some help; the slimy little prick. I could tell he was in it up to his fucking eyeballs and yet he always came out the other end looking like a god-damn saint. If Campbell's been covering for him all this time then he'll pay for it, you can bank on that."

"What about the other guy?" Matt asked.

"Well you'll have to give us your description. That'll give us something to work on; provided I don't beat the answer out of Campbell first. I hope to God it's not another member of the force, or else our department are gonna be under investigation by the superintendent 'til hell freezes over!"

Chapter Forty-Nine

One Month Later

Matt awoke and looked across to the clock on the bedside table. It read *10:28am*. He smiled to himself, feeling his soul swell. It was the first time since *that* day; in fact since the first few months of his marriage to Kelly; that he felt comfortable enough to lay in bed until such a late hour of the morning. He felt no guilt. He had no reason to get up. It was Saturday, and he was going to make the most of it.

Kelly had moved out within two weeks of being exposed, during which time Matt had not slept well from the shock of everything that had happened; but divorce papers were now filed between their solicitors, accompanied by a police report to back up Matt's side of the story and expedite the process. The investigation had been concluded; Caverhill had called him mid-week to confirm that. Connor had been implicated in not just the two murders prior to the near-attempt on Kelly's life, but for a trio of other killings too, sharing striking similarities to his method of despatch and stretching back for a further eighteen months. Campbell was awaiting trial for his complicity, aiding and abetting, and for multiple counts of grievous bodily harm. It turned out, from what Caverhill could divulge, that the whole merry dance Connor had led them on was a well-rehearsed, well scripted routine. The mystery third man had not yet been identified. Caverhill had not succeeded in getting Campbell to turn him over, even with the tempting offer of a reduced sentence later down the line. Privately he had confided in Matt that, if that were to eventually be the position they went to court with, he would be waiting outside the prison gates on Campbell's release date with a photograph of each of the murdered women and a baseball bat. Matt considered Caverhill to be the type of guy who would not take rejection easily; so much so that he had grown to pity Campbell's stupidity, should he be so foolish enough to keep silent.

Time would tell if the identity of the mountainous assailant would become clear, but Matt's fear of taking trips into the city had begun to ease over the last week or so. Things were starting to get back to normal. *In fact*; Matt thought as he turned in bed and was met by the open, smiling eyes of Shanna staring back at him; things were rapidly becoming better than he could have ever imagined.

For the next two hours, Matt and Shanna made love. They gave their bodies to each other, exploring every inch, relishing every intimate touch. Their caresses were passionate; authentic. They took their time to heighten each other's senses; learning their body's secrets, electrifying their skin, before coming together and becoming one. Shanna at times took the lead. She could tell Matt was easily made shy, anxious at times with the fear of doing something unwanted or by hurting her. She reassured him patiently, taking his hands and showing him what she liked; the sharp pinch of his fingers into the soft flesh of her nipple; a tight grip around the back of her neck as they kissed intensely. Holding herself over him, she draped her torso to his face to place her breast to his mouth, and told him to bite it. Her slow moans soon escalated into screams, and she held his head in place for fear of him stopping as her orgasm built within her. He understood and continued, holding onto her hips and pulling her onto him harder, timing the grind of her hips with his own upward thrusts, until she let her body lose control against him and climaxed, shuddering and whimpering her hot breath down onto his face. Matt watched her expression change, mesmerised by its contortions as Shanna's body weakened and she collapsed down onto him. She kissed at his neck gratefully and stroked his face. Likewise; he softly stroked the dip of her back between her shoulder blades, feeling hot sweat under his fingers, and let her catch her breath. After a few minutes Shanna slid slowly from him, her body falling next to his, and she looked him deeply in the eyes.

"I love you, Matt."

"I love you too, Shanna", Matt replied, smiling at her with a look of adoration.

He took her jaw in his palm and leant forward, placing a soft, sensual kiss to her lips as she lay static, still breathing excessively. Then, as he pulled his hand away, Shanna took it in hers and kissed its fingertips, looking at him devilishly.

"You ok?" he asked.

"I'm perfect" she answered. "Everything's perfect."

Matt watched her slide away from him across the sheet, towards the edge of the bed. She draped her arm to the floor, shuffling something with her fingers for a few seconds before pulling his jeans to the surface. Taking the waistband in one hand, she quickly manoeuvred the black leather belt from the waist loops with her other and showed it to him; discarding the jeans back to the floor.

"What are you up to?" he asked, curiously smirking.

"Watch" she replied suggestively and then, kneeling in front of him on the mattress, draped the mid-point of the belt from the back of her neck, over her shoulders, then brought both sides around to fasten it at her throat with its small steel buckle. She laid the stray leather length on top of her fingers, outstretched her hand to Matt, and offered the strap to him.

"I don't know about you," she stated, "but *I* think this little slut deserves a firm hand..."

* * *

Matt leant back into the leather couch and stared out at the miserable weather. The patio doors were being pelted with some of the thickest raindrops he could ever recall seeing, and the sky had grown progressively darker as the afternoon settled in. To his right, Shanna danced around the kitchen, fixing a mid-afternoon snack for the two of them. To Matt, the dreary weather did not matter. In himself he felt utterly content, smiling appreciatively as Shanna placed a fresh coffee and a well stacked sandwich on the coffee table in front of him. In that moment he realised the room had not been altered since Kelly's departure. Her new flat had been too small to take the majority of the furniture she had previously insisted Matt purchase and only now was he realising that he had complete authority to make the room his own again, let alone the rest of the house. He was considering which of the pieces he might discard, when his eyes fell upon the three-shelved bookcase at the base of the stairs. Its two uppermost shelves still laden with Kelly's favourite books; it suddenly dawned on Matt that he had never finished reading the final instalment of Curtis Sharp, and an awkward pang hit him in his chest. A heartfelt desire to finish what he had started so earnestly pitched battle, against the contradicting opinion in his mind of the damage that the saga had initiated. Inevitably he reached the same conclusion as before; that the damage had been done by Kelly's weakness in the end. Her personality; her naive wanderlust; had led to their violent undoing, not the books. The books had simply given her impulsive nature a catalyst she could have chosen to ignore, but didn't. Before Matt realised his actions, he had risen from the couch and was halfway across the room, hand outstretched in preparation of wrapping his fingers around the book's thick spine. As he picked it from the shelf, Shanna emerged from the kitchen doorway holding her own coffee and sandwich.

"Are you going to finish the book?" she asked.

"Do you know; I never thought of it at all this past month but, now I just have, my intrigue's got the better of me!"

"Good!" Shanna said with exuberance, taking Matt somewhat by surprise.

"You think so?" he asked.

"Yeah, I do. After everything that's gone on; what you've been through; I think it's a great sign that you're emotionally ready to finish it; to draw a line under it and move on. I might even have a read after you're done with it!"

Matt beamed, empowered by Shanna's encouragement, and walked across the room towards her with the book now in his hand. He crushed his face into hers, kissing her passionately. Shanna responded in kind, breathing heavily into him, then took her food and sat in the armchair by the patio door. She reached for the TV remote and turned it on, setting the volume low. Matt returned to the couch, tucked his legs beside him to get comfortable, and then opened the book at his long-since-placed bookmark.

It took just over an hour for Matt to reach the story's finale; ending with a cliff-hanger so devastating that it left him anxiously considering his immense wait for the next instalment. It was just as he was folding the back cover

over that Shanna jumped up in her seat, reaching out and tapping Matt on his foot.

"Hey; look Matt!" she cried out, "The author of those Curtis books is on TV! It looks like they're gonna be making movie adaptations of Curtis Sharp! Did you know the author was a local? I had no idea!"

Matt looked from Shanna over to the far screen. A news reporter was in the author's home town, a suburb less than twenty minutes away. The reporter was stopping people in its main shopping street, asking what they thought of the exciting news. And then, a series of photographs of the author filled the screen.

Matt retreated firmly into the couch's leather backrest, quivering in shock. A cold sweat formed instantly across his forehead, sending him into a shiver. He turned to Shanna; now sitting forward, concerned having noticed his sudden change in condition.

"Matt? What's wrong?" she urged.

Matt found it impossible to find the words. He raised a shaking finger to point across room towards the TV, where she dutifully turned to look. The photograph on screen made her baulk. It was of the author; according to the reporter; stood beside a studio executive, signing the contract for the first movie to be made. He dwarfed the executive by a clear foot and a half in height; his muscular body broader by roughly the same amount.

Shanna turned to Matt again; observing him swallow a hard, visibly painful lump in his throat.

"Jesus, he's a big guy!" she exclaimed. "He's like a fucking man-mountain!"

The End

What You Wish For

What You Wish For

A Note From The Author

I hope you have enjoyed reading this novel as much as I have enjoyed writing it. As an independent author and self-publisher my dream is to share this book as widely as possible with the world and its readers.

Above all else, recommendations and reviews are what will drive most readers towards picking up their next book, so I humbly ask you to leave a review for this novel on my Amazon page.

Your thoughts on my work are appreciated immeasurably, as is your readership, and I hope to have you turning pages again very soon.

Thank You.

A. D. Hook

Want to be kept up to date with my future projects?

Everything you need can be found in one place:

adhookauthor.wixsite.com/hooksbooks

Interested in following my occasional ramblings through social media?

Twitter: @ADHookOfficial

Facebook: www.facebook.com/hooksbooks1981

A D Hook

Printed in Great Britain
by Amazon